INTO

THE

DROWNING

DEEP

By Mira Grant

PARASITOLOGY

Parasite
Symbiont
Chimera

NEWSFLESH

Feed
Deadline
Blackout
Feedback
Rise: A Newsflesh Collection

Apocalypse Scenario #683: The Box (ebook novella)

Into the Drowning Deep

WRITING AS SEANAN MCGUIRE

Rosemary and Rue
A Local Habitation
An Artificial Night
Late Eclipses
One Salt Sea
Ashes of Honor
Chimes at Midnight
The Winter Long
Once Broken Faith
The Brightest Fell

Discount Armageddon
Midnight Blue-Light Special
Half-Off Ragnarok
Pocket Apocalypse
Chaos Choreography
Magic for Nothing

Sparrow Hill Road

Every Heart a Doorway
Down Among the Sticks and Bones

INTO
THE
DROWNING
DEEP

MIRA
GRANT

www.orbitbooks.net

Author photograph by Beckett Gladney
Cover design by Lauren Panepinto
Cover illustration/photo by Arcangel-Images and Shutterstock
Cover copyright © 2017 by Hachette Book Group, Inc.

Orbit
Hachette Book Group
1290 Avenue of the Americas
New York, NY 10104
orbitbooks.net

Simultaneously published in Great Britain and in the U.S. by Orbit in 2017
First Edition: November 2017

Orbit is an imprint of Hachette Book Group.
The Orbit name and logo are trademarks of Little, Brown Book Group Limited.

The publisher is not responsible for websites (or their content) that are not owned by the publisher.

The Hachette Speakers Bureau provides a wide range of authors for speaking events. To find out more, go to www.hachettespeakersbureau.com or call (866) 376-6591.

Library of Congress Cataloging-in-Publication Data

Names: Grant, Mira, author.
Title: Into the drowning deep / Mira Grant.
Description: First edition. | New York : Orbit, 2017.
Identifiers: LCCN 2017020686| ISBN 9780316379403 (hardback) |
    ISBN 9780316379373 (trade paperback) | ISBN 9781478923466 (audiobook
    downloadable) | ISBN 9780316379380 (ebook open)
Subjects: | BISAC: FICTION / Fantasy / Contemporary. | FICTION / Fairy Tales,
    Folk Tales, Legends & Mythology. | FICTION / Science Fiction / Adventure. |
    FICTION / Horror. | GSAFD: Adventure fiction. | Science fiction. | Sea stories.
Classification: LCC PS3607.R36395 I56 2017 | DDC 813/.6—dc23
LC record available at https://lccn.loc.gov/2017020686

ISBNs: 978-0-316-37940-3 (hardcover), 978-0-316-37938-0 (ebook)

Printed in the United States of America

LSC-C

10 9 8 7 6 5 4 3 2 1

For Mike and Marnie.
Stay away from the water.

AUTHOR'S NOTE

American Sign Language, regularly abbreviated as ASL, has its own grammar, which differs from that of either spoken or written English. For ease of reading, all ASL conversation in this book has been rendered as if it were SEE (Signing Exact English). This is an imperfect choice, but was necessary for the sake of textual consistency.

SURFACE

We have no comment on the *Atargatis* incident at this time.

—Matthew Kearney,
Imagine Entertainment legal counsel

Did you really think we were the apex predators of the world?

—Dr. Jillian Toth

Founded by James Golden in 1972, Imagine Entertainment was intended to "restore the fun" to the entertainment industry. Golden—an aspiring media mogul who felt movies and television had become "too serious"—proceeded to make his name producing a string of B-grade horror movies, latter-day grindhouse films, and remarkably ambitious science fiction epics. Called the King of Schlock by his detractors and Monster Midas by his fans, there was no question the name Golden carried substantial weight by 1993, when he announced the establishment of the Imagine Network.

Originally envisioned as a home for Golden's prodigious backlist, many dismissed the Imagine Network as the final vanity project of an aging man, noting that the Sci-Fi Channel, launched the previous year, had a larger and more robust stable of original programs. Still, the Imagine Network endured and, by 2008, was providing a reasonable return on Golden's investment.

The first Imagine "mockumentary" was conceived and scripted by the Imagine Network's then president, Benjamin Yant. *Loch Ness: A Historical Review* brought in high ratings, renewed advertiser interest, and strong DVD sales, sparking a wave of similar programming. *The Search for the Chupacabra* aired in 2009, followed by *Expedition Yeti* in 2010, *The Last Dinosaur* in 2012, and *Unicorn Road* in 2014. It seemed the public's thirst for cryptozoological fiction thinly veiled as fact was insatiable.

Then came 2015. The filming of *Lovely Ladies of the Sea: The True Story of the Mariana Mermaids* should have been routine. Imagine filled a ship with scientists, actors, and camera crews, and sent it out into the Pacific Ocean.

Communications were lost on May 17. The ship was found six weeks later, adrift and abandoned.

No bodies have ever been recovered.

—From *Monster Midas: An Unauthorized Biography of James Golden*, by Alexis Bowman, originally published 2018

People like to pretend that what happened to the *Atargatis* was a normal maritime disaster: the people on board got too wrapped up in filming their little "mockumentary" and forgot to steer the damn thing. They ran afoul of a storm, or pirates, or some other totally mundane threat, and they all died, and it was very sad, but it's no reason to be scared of the ocean, or start wondering what else might be out there. The *Atargatis* was what they call an "isolated incident," the recovered footage was and is a hoax, and there's nothing to worry about.

Those people never explain how the camera crews on the *Atargatis* did their special effects in real time: no amount of prosthetic work in the world could turn a human being into one of the creatures seen swarming the ship during the most violent of the leaked footage.

Those people never explain why, if what happened was weather related, not a single scrap of data supporting that theory has ever been released by either Imagine or the National Weather Service. The loss of the *Atargatis* was a public relations nightmare for the company: if Imagine had a way of reducing their liability, they would certainly have offered it by now.

Those people never explain a lot of things.

The *Atargatis* sailed off the map, into a section of the sea that should have been labeled "Here be monsters." What happened to them there may never be perfectly understood, but this much seems to be clear: the footage was not faked.

Mermaids are real.

—Taken from a forum post made at
CryptidChase.net by user BioNerd,
originally posted March 2020

Monterey, California: June 26, 2015

The sky was a deep and perfect blue, as long as Victoria—Vicky to her parents, Vic to her friends, Tory to herself, when she was thinking about the future, where she'd be a scientist and her sister Anne would be her official biographer, documenting all her amazing discoveries for the world to admire—kept her eyes above the horizon. Any lower and the smoke from the wildfires that had ravaged California all summer would appear, tinting the air a poisonous-looking gray. Skies weren't supposed to look like that. Skies were supposed to be wide and blue and welcoming, like a mirror of the wild and waiting sea.

Tory had been born in the Monterey City Hospital. According to her parents, her first smile had been directed not at her mother, but at the Pacific Ocean. She had learned to swim in safe municipal pools by the age of eighteen months, and been in the ocean—closely supervised—by the time she was three, reveling in the taste of salt water on her lips and the sting of the sea spray in her eyes.

(She'd been grabbed by a riptide when she was seven, yanked away from her parents and pushed twenty yards from shore in the time it took to blink. She didn't remember the incident when she was awake, but it surfaced often in her dreams: the suddenly hostile water reaching up to grab her and drag her down. Most children would have hated the ocean after something like that, letting well-earned fear keep their feet on the shore. Not Tory. The riptide had just been doing what it was made to do; she was the one who'd been in the wrong place. She had to learn to be in a better place when the next riptide came along.)

Her big sister, Anne, had watched Tory's maritime adventures from the safety of the shore, slathered in SPF 120 and clutching her latest stack of gossip magazines. They'd been so different, even then. It would have been easy for them to detest each other, to let the gap in their ages and interests become a chasm. Anne had seven years on her baby sister. She could have walked away. Instead, somehow, they'd come out of their barely shared childhood as the best of friends. They had the same parents; they had the same wheat-blonde hair, although Anne's had started darkening toward brown by the time she turned seventeen, prompting an endless succession of experimental dye jobs and highlighting processes. They both sunburned fast, and freckled even faster. They even had the same eyes, dark blue, like the waters of the Monterey Bay.

That was where the similarities ended. Tory was going to be a marine biologist, was doing a summer internship at the Monterey Bay Aquarium and starting at UC Santa Cruz in the fall on a full scholarship. Anne was a special interest reporter—read "talking head for geek news"—and well on her way to a solid career as a professional media personality.

The last time they'd seen each other in person had been three days prior to the launch of the SS *Atargatis*, a research vessel heading to the Mariana Trench to look for mermaids.

"We're not going to find them," Anne had admitted, sitting on the porch next to Tory and throwing bits of bread to the seagulls thronging the yard. "Mermaids don't exist. Everyone at Imagine knows it. But it's a chance for the scientists they've hired to do real research on someone else's dime, and it's a great opportunity for me personally."

"You really want to be the face of the cryptid mockumentary?" Tory had asked.

Anne had answered with a shrug. "I want to be the face of *something*. This is as good a place to start as any. I just wish you could come with us. We could use some more camera-ready scientists."

"Give me ten years and I'll come on the anniversary tour." Tory had grinned, impish, and leaned over to tug on a lock of her sister's sunset-red hair. It was a dye job, but it was a good one, years and miles and a lot of money away from the Clairol specials Anne used to do in the downstairs bathroom. "I'll make you look old."

"By then, I'll be so established that they'll let me," Anne had said, and they'd laughed, and the rest of the afternoon had passed the way the good ones always did: too fast to be fair.

Anne had promised to send Tory a video every day. She'd kept that promise from the time the ship launched, sending clips of her smiling face under an endless ocean sky, with scientists and crewmen laboring in the background.

The last clip had come on May seventeenth. In it, Anne had looked...harried, unsettled, like she no longer knew quite what to make of things. Tory had watched the short video so many times she could recite it from memory. That didn't stop her from sitting down on the porch—so empty now, without Anne beside her—and pressing "play" again.

Anne's face flickered into life on the screen, hair tousled by the wind, eyes haunted. "Tory," she said, voice tight. "Okay, I...I'm scared. I don't know what it is I saw, and I don't know how it's possible, but it's real, Tory, it's really real. It's really out there. You'll understand when you see the footage. Maybe you can...maybe you can be the one who figures it out. I love you. I love Mom and Dad. I...I hope I'll be home soon." She put her hand over her eyes. She had always done that, ever since she was a little girl, when she didn't want anyone to see her crying.

"Turn off the camera, Kevin," she said, and Tory whispered the words along with her. "I'm done."

The video ended.

Six weeks had passed since that video's arrival. There hadn't been another.

Tory had tried to find out what had happened—what could have upset her sister so much, what could have made her stop sending her videos—but she'd gotten nowhere. Contacting Imagine led to a maze of phone trees and receptionists who became less helpful the moment she told them why she was calling. Every day, she sent another wave of e-mails, looking for information. Every day, she got nothing back.

She was starting to think nothing was all she was ever going to get again.

She was sitting on the porch six weeks and three days later, about to press "play" one more time, when the sound of footsteps caught her attention. She turned. Her mother was in the doorway, white faced and shaking, tears streaking her cheeks.

Tory felt the world turn to ashes around her, like the smoke staining the sky had finally won dominion over all. She staggered to her feet, unable to bear the thought of sitting when she heard the words her mother didn't yet have the breath to say. Her laptop crashed to the steps, unheeded, unimportant. Nothing was important anymore.

Katherine Stewart put her arms around her surviving daughter and held fast, like she was an anchor, like she could somehow, through her sheer unwillingness to let go, keep this child from the sea.

Footage recovered from the *Atargatis* mission, aired for the board of the Imagine Network, July 1, 2015

The camera swings as the cameraman runs. The deck of the *Atargatis* lurches in the frame, slick with a grayish mucosal substance. Splashes of shockingly red blood mark the slime. There has been no time for it to dry. There has been no time for anything. The cameraman is out of breath. He stumbles, dropping to one knee. As he does, the camera tilts downward. For a few brief seconds, we are treated to a glimpse of the creature climbing, hand over hand, up the side of the *Atargatis*:

The face is more simian than human, with a flat "nose" defined by two long slits for nostrils, and a surprisingly sensual mouth brimming with needled teeth. It is a horror of the deep, gray skinned and feminine in the broadest sense of the term, an impression lent by the delicate structure of its bones and the tilt of its wide, liquid eyes. When it blinks, a nictitating membrane precedes the eyelid. It has "hair" of a sort—a writhing mass of glittering, filament-thin strands that cast their bioluminescent light on the hull.

It has no legs. Its lower body is the muscular curl of an eel's tail, tapering to tattered looking but highly functional fins. This is a creature constructed along brutally efficient lines, designed to survive, whatever the cost. Nature abhors a form that cannot be repeated. Perhaps that's why the creature has hands, thumbs moving in opposable counterpoint to its three long, slim fingers. The webbing extends to the second knuckle; the fingers extend past that, with four joints in place of the human two. They must be incredibly flexible, those fingers, no matter how fragile they seem.

The creature hisses, showing bloody teeth. Then, in a perfectly human, perfectly chilling voice, it says, "Come *on*, Kevin, don't you have the shot yet?" It is the voice of Anne Stewart, Imagine Entertainment news personality. Anne herself is nowhere to be seen. But there is so much blood...

The cameraman staggers to his feet and runs. His camera captures everything in fragmentary pieces as he flees, taking snapshots of an apocalypse. There is a man who has been unzipped from crotch to throat, organs falling onto the deck in a heap; three of the creatures are clustered around the resulting mess, their faces buried in the offal, eating. There is a woman whose arms have been ripped from her shoulders, whose eyes stare into nothingness, glazed over and cold; two more of the creatures are dragging her toward the rail. The cameraman runs. There is a splash behind him. The creatures have returned to the sea with their prey.

Some of the faces of the dead are familiar: employees of Imagine, camera operators, makeup technicians, all sent out to sea with the *Atargatis* in order to record a documentary on the reality of mermaids. They weren't supposed to find anything. Mermaids aren't real. Other faces are new to the silent executives who watch the film play back, their mouths set into thin lines and their eyes betraying nothing of their feelings on the matter. A dark-haired woman beats a mermaid with an oar. A man runs for the rail, only to be attacked by three of the creatures, which move surprisingly swiftly out of the water, propelled by their powerful tails.

Around the boat, the sea is getting lighter, like the sun is rising from below. The camera continues to roll. The cameraman continues to run.

A thin-fingered hand slaps across the lens, and the video stops. The screaming takes longer to end, but in time, it does.

Everything ends.

Western Pacific Ocean, east of the Mariana Islands: September 3, 2018

The yacht drifted on the endless blue, flags fluttering from its mast and engine purring like a kitten, the man at the helm making small adjustments to their position as he worked to keep them exactly where they were. On any other vessel, he would have been considered the captain. On any other vessel, he wouldn't have been subject to the whims of a reality television personality and his bevy of hand-selected bikini models, all of whom had been chosen more for their appearance than for their ability to handle being on a yacht in the middle of nowhere. They weren't just miles from shore; they were *days* from shore, so far out that if something went wrong, no one would be in a position to rescue them.

That was what Daniel Butcher had been aiming for. The married star of three reality cooking shows just wanted to "escape" and "unwind," far from the prying eyes of the paparazzi and their long-range telephoto lenses. He had the resources to take his entourage to the ends of the earth, and enough of a passion for fresh-caught seafood that this was his idea of paradise. He had the waves. He had the sun. He had a wide array of beautiful women happy to tell him how smart and handsome and witty he was, without his even needing to prompt them.

"Dinner's at sunset, ladies," Daniel called, checking the lines hanging off the side. This far from the commercial fishing lanes, they should be drifting in fertile waters. He'd even gone to the trouble of buying data on the known dead zones manifesting in the west Pacific, just to be sure he wasn't being steered away from where the fish were. Wouldn't that be a kick in the teeth? Pay tens of thousands of dollars to rent a top-of-the-line yacht, stock it, crew it, sail it away from civilization for three days straight, and wind up someplace where nothing was biting. But no. They'd eat well tonight.

(The actual gutting and cleaning of the fish would be left to his sous-chefs, two of whom had been brought on this voyage for just that reason. Daniel Butcher believed in roughing it, but he was still a star, and stars didn't get fish guts on their hands unless there was a camera rolling to capture the rugged masculinity of the moment.)

The bikini models giggled and preened, their oiled skins shining in the tropical sun. This was the life. This was the way things were *meant* to be: just him, and the sea, and people who actually appreciated his brilliance.

He didn't notice that they stopped preening as soon as he walked past them, or that some of them directed looks of frank disgust at his retreating back. He stopped to check one of the lines. A pretty black-haired girl in a green bikini withdrew a camera the size of a flash drive from under the skimpy fabric covering one breast and snapped a quick series of pictures, making sure her shots included as many of the other women as possible.

The redhead next to her gave her a quizzical look before asking, voice low, "Wife?"

The black-haired girl's fingers tightened on her camera. "Yes."

"Network," said the redhead. "I set my cameras when we came aboard."

"Nice," said the first girl. She tucked the camera back into her bikini before offering her hand. "Elena."

"Suzanne."

"We looking at cancellation, or . . . ?"

"Not yet." Suzanne turned a predatory eye on Daniel, who had stopped again, this time to flirt with two *actual* bikini models. "The network's concerned about reports of debauchery. They wanted someone to come on this trip and see how accurate they were. They hired me."

"How did they know Daniel would pick you?"

"How did his wife know Daniel would pick you?"

"You saw the man behind the wheel when we boarded?" Elena nodded toward the cabin. Sunlight glinted off the windows, making it impossible to see inside. "He's my brother. Technically I'm along because I wanted the ride, not because Daniel wanted access to my sea chest."

"Clever," said Suzanne approvingly. "We're not going to make problems for each other, are we?"

"Why should we?" Elena's smile was quick and predatory, a shark cutting through calm waters. "We're both getting paid. Your pictures don't change mine. And the man's an ass. Let's take him down from every angle at once."

Suzanne laughed. So did Elena. They were still laughing when there was a commotion from the side of the boat, a splash and a scream and the sound of bodies rushing toward the rail. Their heads snapped around, Elena half-rising from her deck chair before she realized what had happened.

Daniel was gone.

"Oh my God," she said, in a tone of fascinated horror. "The narcissistic bastard knocked himself overboard."

"Come on." Suzanne grabbed her hand, dragging her toward the chaos. "I want pictures of this, and all my cameras are *on* the boat."

There was no sign of Daniel when the pair reached the side. The sea was calm, giving no indication that it had just swallowed a man. Bikini models leaned over the rail, shouting and cursing, eyes scanning the horizon. Elena felt her stomach sink. She'd grown up in the Mariana Islands, been born and raised on Guam, and she'd heard stories about this stretch of ocean.

How could I have been fool enough to take this job? she thought, turning to the cabin. *Only fools sail where so many have been lost.* She waved her arms frantically, hoping he would see her even though she couldn't see him. They needed to turn around. They needed to get out of here.

Elena didn't consider herself a superstitious person, but she would have had to be living under a rock not to have heard people whispering about what happened around the Mariana Trench when the sun was bright and the waters were still, when the fish had moved on and the things in the deeps grew hungry. There had been that mess a few years back, with a research vessel and the television network that showed all the *Star Trek* reruns. How she'd laughed at the thought of their being foolish enough to sail there, in the open waters where the bad things were.

She wasn't laughing now.

She wasn't laughing when the screams started behind her, high and shrill and terrified, or when she felt the touch of a hand—oddly long and spindly, covered in a cool, clammy film, like aloe gel was smeared across the skin—on the back of her ankle. Elena stopped waving her arms. She closed her eyes. If she couldn't see it, it wouldn't be real. That was the way the world worked, wasn't it?

Her scream, when it came, was short and sharp and quickly ended. The boat began to move, her brother finally throwing it into gear, but it was too little, too late; his own scream soon joined the fading chorus.

The yacht rented by Daniel Butcher for his private entertainment was found three days later, drifting some eight hundred miles from its chartered destination. No survivors were ever found.

Neither were the bodies.

ZONE ONE: PELAGIC

Imagine a better future. Imagine a better past. Imagine a better version of you.

—Early Imagine Entertainment slogan

Is it really so bad to want to be famous? Isn't that what everybody wants?

—Anne Stewart

In a shocking upset, the Imagine Network, its parent company, Imagine Entertainment, and its CEO, James Golden, have been found not guilty of criminal negligence in the disappearance of the SS *Atargatis*.

"While we remain shocked and saddened by this incident, we are gratified that the court has recognized our lack of culpability," said Mr. Benjamin Yant, president of the Imagine Network. "The loss of the *Atargatis* was an unpredictable tragedy. We are doing everything we can to cooperate with authorities and determine what happened to our people."

John Seghers, father of Jovanie Seghers, captain of the *Atargatis*, had this to say: "Those bastards at Imagine don't care about my daughter. They don't care about anything except their damned ratings. They're still going forward with the documentary. Did you hear that? They're still going forward."

Efforts to block public release of the footage recorded on the *Atargatis* are ongoing, but are not expected to succeed. Interest in the so-called "ghost ship" remains high, and all parties on board had signed releases prior to departure. Imagine has filed several motions to suppress, stating that the footage has no relevance and contains proprietary special effects techniques which have not yet been brought fully to market. "This footage will be taken as a hoax at best, and an insult to the memory of those lost at worst," said Mr. Yant.

—Taken from the "Entertainment News" subforum of WorldReports.com

Do we have any more questions? Yes, you, there in the back.

Come again?

Ah. I see. You want to know what I think about the *Atargatis*. Of course you do. That's all you people want to talk about these days. Yes, I had a berth on that ship, and yes, I turned it down. The contracts they wanted us to sign put too many restrictions on what we could do with our findings. When I make it out to the Mariana Trench, I am going with full ownership of my research.

Do I think they found mermaids?

Yes. Of course I do.

And I think the mermaids ate them all.

—Transcript from the lecture "Mermaids: Myth or Monster," given by Dr. Jillian Toth

CHAPTER 1

Monterey, California: July 28, 2022

The *Monterey Dream* pulled away from the dock at a slow, easy pace, drawing gasps of astonished delight from the tourists crowding her decks. The crowd was good for a morning whale-watching expedition: thirty or so on the bottom level, closer to the water, where they'd be able to look into the churning waves and imagine they could see jellyfish tangled in the snowy foam. There were another fifteen on the upper deck, high rollers who'd been willing to shell out an extra twenty dollars for the privilege of sitting in the sun, with no shade or windbreak, for the duration of the trip. They'd have the best view of any whales that deigned to show themselves.

Half of them would probably also have vicious sunburns, if their snowy complexions and lack of hats and windbreakers were anything to go by. The tour company recommended customers wear adequate protective gear and sunscreen at all times, but a lot of them ignored those instructions; between the lack of shade and the windburn that came with sailing for miles, many of those people would be in a world of hurt by bedtime. Tory often thought, privately, that she could make a killing by smuggling personal-size bottles of Coppertone onto the boat and reselling them to tourists once they were far enough out to realize what they'd done. Not that she'd have time, or be allowed to perform that sort of independent action. The people who ran the tour company knew exactly what they wanted from their employees—how they wanted them to act, dress, smile, stand, even look, although they were more lenient about that during the off-season—and they weren't afraid to enforce those standards with an iron hand. Whale-watching employees who went off script were likely to find themselves in the market for another job.

As one of the company's four marine biologists on retainer, Tory stood at the front of the boat once they were under way, pointing out and identifying marine animals large and small. It was incredible what people—especially tourists—would get worked up over. They were here to see whales, sure, but some of them had traveled from landlocked states, and would happily flip their lids over sea lions, otters, egg jellies, and other creatures native to Monterey Bay.

Tory knew some of the people she worked with looked down on the tourists, calling them "flyovers" and laughing at their amazement. She thought that was uncharitable and, well, *wrong*. She'd lived next to the ocean for her entire life, had learned to walk with salt on her lips and learned to swim before she could read. She loved the Pacific as she loved nothing else in the world, and sometimes she worried she would start taking it for granted, letting familiarity wear away the sharp, startling edges love needed in order to stay bright and strong. The tourists were seeing everything for the first time. Through their eyes, she could do the same. She could be amazed by things that might otherwise become less amazing, and she'd never be jaded, and she'd never forget how much she loved the hammered silver shine of the horizon.

One of the deckhands walked over with her microphone. Tory leaned against the rail, trying to look casual, and not like she was bracing for the coming acceleration. That was another trick to working with tourists: everyone on the crew had to seem so comfortable with life at sea that they could never be knocked off balance, no matter how high the waves got or how much the boat rocked. Anything less could reduce passenger confidence, and when the passengers weren't confident, well...

Tory had been present for one passenger panic attack, a businessman from Ohio who'd been on a long-anticipated vacation with his family and somehow hadn't realized that going on a whale-watching tour would mean sailing for open waters. He'd been fine until he'd seen a crew member stumble. Then he'd started screaming that he couldn't breathe, that the boat was sinking, that they were all going to drown. Panic was contagious on any sort of sailing vessel, especially one packed with people who didn't often leave shore. In the end, they'd been forced to return to the dock, where tour fees had been refunded by a scowling manager. None of the crew for that tour had been paid; since they were technically contractors, rather than hourly employees, they had to go all the way out if they wanted to be compensated for their time and trouble.

Keeping the passengers calm and happy was key if they wanted their paychecks signed. Tory was less worried about that now than she'd been at the start of the summer—the boats would still be going out in a week, but she wouldn't be going out with them. She'd be safe and snug on the UC Santa Cruz campus, peddling knowledge for wide-eyed undergrads, working on her dissertation, and, by God, finishing her degree.

Most of her fellows in the Marine Biology Department thought she was nuts for taking the summer off to spend on whale-watching boats, seeing children's eyes light up when they saw their first real dolphin. Her ex-boyfriend, Jason, had been particularly impassioned in his attempts to convince her that she was throwing her future away.

"I know this is a thing you do, and it was cute when you were a freshman, but you're in grad school now," he'd said. They'd chosen the campus coffee shop as neutral ground, and Tory had regretted it the moment she'd walked in and seen him sitting there with a cardboard box of her things next to his right hand, a wordless accusation of everything she'd done wrong during their tempestuous attempt at a relationship. She couldn't say, even now, that they'd ever been particularly successful. In that moment, looking at the compact reminder that she'd been cut from his life as easily as cutting an abalone from its shell, she'd felt like a failure.

"I have to," had been her reply. "I have a contract, and it's connected to my research. The tour company owners let us take the boats out when nothing's scheduled, as long as we pay for fuel, and I've gotten some great data." What she hadn't been able to say was that the faces of the tourists were also part of her research: the wonder and the horror and the quiet mass delusions that spread through them like ink through water. The official policy of the tour company was that if no one on board saw a whale—not a single sighting—everyone would get a free pass to come back and try again. But that almost never happened. All it took was a murmured suggestion in the right ear and half the boat would swear they'd seen a whale's shadow passing under the boat, too shy to break the surface, but absolutely there, clear as a picture, what a moment, what a *memory.*

All those things played into her research. But Jason had never been able to understand that when they were together, and he certainly wasn't going to make the effort now. "There are research positions open," he'd said. "There are professors in your field looking for interns. This is when you should be planning for your future, not chasing the ghosts of your childhood."

"Thank you for your thoughts," she'd said, and taken her things, and walked away, leaving him behind. It had been too little, too late, but it had felt like a victory, and she'd been trying to cling to it all summer long, as one day melted into the next, as good weather kept the tours running and kept her research boxed away. She could make notes on tourists, draw conclusions from their microcosms of mass hysteria, but she couldn't do deepwater sampling or take the sort of detailed pictures her work required.

The deck bucked and rolled beneath her feet, a sure sign that they were about to start gaining speed. She brought the microphone to her lips and put on her brightest, blithest museum docent voice as she said, "Well, hello, everyone! Welcome to Dream Dives Whale-Watching. You're currently on board the *Monterey Dream...*"

She could recite the specs for this ship in her sleep, having done it dozens if not hundreds of times. She let her mind drift as she scanned the horizon, looking for things to point out to the hungry tourists. They'd take sea lions and gulls as things to ooh and aah over, as long as she identified them in an authoritative voice.

The spiel caught up with her contemplation, and she smoothly shifted gears, saying, "If you look to our left, you'll see a group of sea lions sunning themselves on the rocks at the mouth of our harbor. These majestic, if noisy, neighbors come to Monterey Bay to have their pups and raise them in the relative safety of our waters. They enjoy the sun and fishing, just like we do."

The roar of the engines drowned out most sound, but she heard a few people laughing. One woman in particular brayed like she thought she was in the audience for a live taping of *The Late Show*. Tory smiled to herself. This was going to be a good crowd.

"But you can see sea lions back on the dock, and we have places to go. Brace yourselves, because we're going to get this party started." Tory gripped the rail with one hand as the boat accelerated. "It's mealtime for our visiting whales, and we're heading for a canyon roughly two miles offshore where they tend to congregate. Because of the season, we've got a lot of whales in the area, and we might see anything from orcas to big blues. It'll be a while before we reach their feeding grounds, so relax, enjoy the trip, and watch the waves for little orange blobs. Those are our egg jellies, a favorite food of sea turtles and dolphins, and they'll show through the blue just like the fried eggs that give them their name. Our crew is here if you need anything at all, and I'll check back in with you in a while."

Tory put down the microphone, checking twice to be sure it was off. It was a small thing, but a live mic had gotten several of her coworkers in trouble, and had gotten one of their regular marine biologists fired when he'd been caught broadcasting unpleasant statements about the physical appearances of their passengers. His loss had been her gain; since every trip needed a marine biologist on board, she'd been able to spend a lot more time at sea than she'd been anticipating at the start of the season.

It hadn't been enough. It was never going to be enough. She gripped the rail with both hands, watching the horizon grow bigger and broader as they left the land behind, and wished with all her might for the waters to open wide and give up all their secrets.

They didn't. But then, they never did.

Global climate change had been impacting the world's oceans since the early 1980s, although most people hadn't noticed the transformation until the mid-2010s, when the reduced surface temperatures, increased ferocity of storms, and seemingly endless blooms of toxic algae had become severe enough to make headline news. As the glaciers melted, they dumped their runoff into the deep currents that warmed much of the world. The sudden freshwater influx lowered the ocean's temperature and overall salinity even as temperatures on land continued to climb. Fish were dying. Whales and other large sea mammals were changing their ancient migration patterns, following the food into waters where they had never been seen before. Sharks were doing the same, sending scientists into tizzies and panicking the public.

Monterey had been lucky. It was sheltered from the worst of the weather by its place on the California coast. El Niño winds still blew in warm water and kept the surface temperatures where they needed to be, while natural rock formations blocked toxic algae and the increasingly common jellyfish. As a consequence, more and more whales arrived every year, to the point that scientists were becoming concerned about the ecosystem's ability to sustain them. Eventually there would be another collapse, this one brought on by overfishing by both humans and marine mammals. It was a serious concern, and one Tory was glad she wasn't a part of: whales featured in her research only tangentially. Let other people, smarter people, figure out how to save the whales from this latest man-made catastrophe. She would be hundreds of miles away, sailing in deeper waters.

Not that she didn't love the vast seagoing mammals. It was impossible to look at a pilot whale cutting through the water, or a dolphin leaping out of a wave for the sheer joy of being alive, and not love them. They were majestic wonders of the natural world, and if mankind had any obligation left to the sea that had been its birthplace, it was preserving the ones who'd stayed behind.

The ship rumbled under her feet, the song of the engine traveling through her shoes and into her bones. She could have stayed out here forever, if not for all the things that needed doing back on land. "We have some company out here, folks," she said into the microphone. "If you look to either side, you'll see that we've been joined by a group of bottlenose dolphins. These curious creatures love to follow boats and see where we're going, what we're up to—and, of course, to feast on the fish disturbed by our passing. This is a large family grouping, somewhere between fifty and seventy individuals..."

Dolphins were easy. They were common enough to show up almost without fail when the ships went out, and exciting enough to rouse passengers who might have been starting to feel like the trip had been a waste of time and money. To tourists, wasting time was often the greatest sin; they'd traveled from their homes expecting to return indebted but happy, with phones and digital cameras packed with blurry memories to get them through the lean times ahead. An extra fifty dollars was a more reasonable request than an extra fifty minutes for someone whose itinerary was planned to the second, and a whale-watching expedition was by its very nature a substantial time commitment. Just getting to where the whales were could take up to an hour, and woe betide the boat that turned around without giving its passengers time to see everything they wanted to see.

The dolphins had finished the most dramatic part of their visit, fading into the occasional flash of bright gray against darker blue. Now that they were almost to the whales, Tory kept talking, about migration patterns, likely sightings, anything to keep the tourists looking at the water. Not that most of them were listening to her; she was a service offered because it made the whole production seem more impressive, and less like the rehearsed thing it was. The whales came and went as they liked, sometimes showing themselves and sometimes not, but the boats went out all the same.

The ship rumbled to a stop, still bucking and rolling with the motion of the waves around it. People who never went out to sea didn't realize how much of a difference even a small ripple could make to a maritime vessel's stability. They complained when a whale watch was canceled due to inclement weather. Tory, who had been out in her share of storms—sometimes that was the best time to gather data—always wanted to laugh when she heard some petulant tourist from Idaho or Wyoming complaining about how their day had been ruined, and couldn't they just take the damn boat out anyway? The sort of seasickness that came from riding a small craft into a big storm would ruin their day a lot more conclusively than a little rescheduling. But there was no explaining that to someone who didn't want to hear it.

"All right," she said. "We're going to hold here and see if we— there we go, folks! Those of you on the right-hand side of the boat, if you'll check your two o'clock, you may see the characteristic black-and-white coloration of a pod of orcas coming up to breathe. These majestic creatures can hold their breath for up to twenty minutes, although most will surface every four or five when they feel comfortable. This is a large group, and they've been seen in these waters before, so they're definitely comfortable. The boat doesn't bother them. If anything, we think they find us reassuring, since we're such a common presence. They may swim over to the side to say hello."

No one seemed to be listening. There were more interesting things at hand, like the whales themselves. Tory rolled the microphone in her hand, weighing what she was going to say next.

Oh, go for it, she thought. *What's the worst they can do?*

The worst they could do was tell her boss, who could yell at her for going off script. The worst they could do was leave a bad review for the service. But the best they could do...

The best they could do was listen.

Raising the microphone again, she said, "Sometimes called 'killer whales' by fishermen who wanted an excuse to paint them as vicious monsters, orcas are intelligent enough that some marine biologists argue they should be considered people. They're potentially as smart as you or me—and smarter than some of us. Despite this, marine parks continue to display wild-caught orcas. Orcas are captured as calves, separated from their parents, who will continue to cry for them long after they have been removed from the water. Orca parents have been known to recognize their adult children after twenty years, and are always overjoyed to have them home again, assuming those stolen calves live long enough to be released. Eighty percent of wild-caught orcas will die in captivity, never seeing their families again. If anything is going to drive the orca to live up to the name 'killer whale,' it's the way they've been treated by humanity. Orcas—"

A hand landed on her shoulder as the microphone was plucked from her fingers. She turned to see Leroy, their "first mate," standing behind her and scowling.

"You *know* better," he hissed. "Stay on script for the rest of the damn trip."

"Sorry," she said, and reached for her microphone.

After a brief, wary pause, he gave it to her.

"Sorry about that, folks," she said, turning back to the water. "Now, if you'll look to the left, you'll see the distinctive spout of a gray whale coming up for air—"

She spoke, and the boat rocked, and the sea, deep and dark and endless, spread out all around them, and for a little while, she could pretend she was home.

CHAPTER 2

Monterey, California: July 28, 2022

W hat do you mean, *fired*?"
Jay O'Malley, owner and operator of Dream Dives Whale-Watching, looked impassively at the young marine biologist. "I mean, you're fired," he said. "You're a smart girl, it's a simple phrase, you should be able to get it if you think hard. I believe in you."

Tory sputtered. "But—but—the season isn't over!"

"It is for you," he said. He sighed. "When we let Jon go for calling passengers names, you were fine with it. I didn't find you in here fighting for his job. You took his shifts and you smiled and told me to my face that you'd rein in your tongue, and like a fool, I believed you. I don't like it when people make me feel like a fool, Victoria. It makes me wonder what else I might be letting slip by me."

"I said I was sorry," she protested.

"You made two children cry," he said implacably. "You caused immediate emotional distress to families who were looking for a nice day out on the water, enjoying the majesty of nature. Some of those same families have been to SeaWorld or Atlantis to enjoy the majesty of nature. They didn't enjoy being told that they were wrong to do so."

Tory opened her mouth to speak, then paused, closing it again. He wasn't going to give her back her job; she could see that. When she'd crossed the line this time, she'd done it conclusively. She still hadn't thought he'd *fire* her. She took a breath in through her nose, let it carefully out, and said, "Whether they enjoyed it or not, they needed to hear it. Those whales are being held captive against their will. They have a right to be free."

"And I have a right to not have customers come rushing in demanding refunds, but here we both are." Jay shook his head. He was a big man, soft from years spent on land, although his shoulders and neck were still thick with muscle from his time as a fisherman. He was an imposing figure when he stood, which was the reason he gave for staying seated almost all the time: he wanted to delight people, not intimidate them. "You've been a good guide. If you want to reapply next summer, I'll consider you. But for this season, you're a liability. You're done."

Reapplying would mean coming in at entry level: half the pay and all the worst boats, the ones no other marine biologist wanted. The thought burned. Even worse, by next summer, she'd either be defending her dissertation or looking for a new adviser, either of which would leave her too exhausted to jockey for a new place in the pecking order. "I'll keep that in mind," she said, hoping her unhappiness wouldn't come through in her voice, even though she knew full well that it would. "Should I see Christine for my last paycheck?"

Jay frowned. For all his good points, he didn't like paying his employees even a second early—or, quite honestly, at all. There'd been a bit of a scandal a few years back, when he'd tried to convince college students to intern on his boats for the "experience." That had been shut down quickly by students and universities alike, but the memory clearly still stung. "I'll mail it to you."

"If I don't have it by the end of the week, I'll have to come back and ask about it," said Tory, in her sweetest tone. "I guess I might wind up talking to some people about whales."

"That's blackmail."

"You just fired me. I think I've earned a little blackmail."

Jay exhaled hard. "You can't talk to your bosses like this in the real world."

"I'm not planning to go into the real world. I'm going to work in marine conservation. As long as I'm not dangling from the ceiling, people will take me seriously as a scientist."

"I'll get Christine to set up your deposit and provide you with a receipt."

"Thank you," said Tory. She took one last look around the Dream Dives offices, taking in the maps of the Monterey Bay, the awards from local polls and contests, and the framed pictures on the walls. Her entire life was on these walls, from her childhood as a passenger to her gawky teenage years as a deckhand, all the way to her time as an adult subject matter expert. She had grown up here, measuring things one summer at a time.

When she looked back to Jay he was watching her, a strangely gentle look in his eyes. "You still chasing mermaids, Vic?" he asked.

"I've never been chasing mermaids," she said. "I've only ever been chasing Anne."

Jay nodded solemnly. "Well, then. I hope you find her."

Tory drove along the road that would take her home, trying not to dwell on the meager size of her final paycheck. It had been enough for a few weeks' worth of groceries, or to buy access to another set of private camera rigs. The oceans were still the great unknown: with so many fledgling marine biologists switching to climate science and meteorology when the die-offs began, and with so many others going straight into conservation, the ones who remained didn't have the manpower to chart everything that was out there. Cameras were smaller and cheaper every year, and there were video networks sunk through the entirety of the open sea, but almost all of them were privately owned. Passes were sold by the season, since most of the people requesting access were trying to map the increasingly unpredictable weather patterns of the world's oceans.

Tory could have done guided whale-watching tours for years without saving enough to buy camera time on one of the really exclusive networks, the ones sunk around volcanic vents or in the spawning grounds of the great white sharks. That was fine. The cameras she needed were smaller, less reliable, and almost entirely pointed at the Mariana Trench. She checked the amount of the deposit twice before sending off requests for access to two more of those networks. Food was less important than footage. She'd lived on ramen noodles and dried seaweed sheets before. Doing it again was no problem.

Monterey was still a beautiful city, even after closing on twenty years of drought, wildfires, and other complications. The fires had never reached the city, although they'd come close a few times; Tory would never forget the first evacuation, huddled on the beach, wrapped in a thermal blanket while she watched the sky turn red. She'd been nineteen at the time, Anne less than two years gone, and the thought of losing her home so soon after she'd lost her sister had been enough to trigger a full-blown panic attack, sending her weeping into her father's arms. But the city hadn't burned. The firefighters had stopped the fire before it could get that far, and Monterey had endured, becoming a little bit more of a period piece masquerading as a tourist town with every passing year. They'd always been haunted by the ghosts of Steinbeck and Cannery Row, those two great icons of the Great Depression. Now they were also haunted by the coastal towns that hadn't been so lucky, by all the pieces of a dying way of life.

What people didn't understand was how hard Monterey worked for its own survival. They hadn't been able to stop or slow climate change, but they had been blessed with a high concentration of scientists, drawn by the Monterey Bay Aquarium and its many conservation programs. Faced with the idea of losing that research site, those same scientists had set themselves against the problem with an iron will. They had chased funding, pursued grants, and encouraged innovation. As a result, while the rest of the state was falling into despair, the people of Monterey were building as fast as they could, throwing lines into the future and hoping they would hold.

Desalination plants dotted the coastline like fairy towers, their solar-paneled roofs glittering in the California sun. They were closely monitored by marine biologists and conservationists, watched for signs of negative environmental impact. That was just a formality. The city needed the tax breaks provided by the state in exchange for them waiving their groundwater rights. The city needed the food produced by local farmers. The city needed *water*.

Tory was grateful for the desalination plants, like every other child of California, but that didn't stop the shiver from running up her spine when she looked at them. The waste produced by the desalination process was proving invaluable to scientists, letting them catalog pollution, document plankton, even analyze salt levels to determine the scope of the dilution effect triggered by the still-melting glaciers. The water that went back to the sea went back clean. Fully two-thirds of the desalination plants were also devoted to water purification, removing pollutants before restoring the salt level and pushing the cleansed water back out to sea. The ocean's potential to supply humanity with freshwater seemed limitless.

But the rain forests had seemed limitless once, as had the redwoods. It was hard not to look at the plants and guess at the shape of an as-yet-uncharted future looming out of the fog, too distant to see clearly, but coming closer all the time.

Tory took her eyes away from the coast and focused on the road.

There were three kinds of people in Monterey: the idle rich, who'd moved there when it became clear that this small jewel of the Pacific wouldn't burn like Lake County or wither into desiccated silence like Santa Cruz; the scientists, who lived in subsidized housing and kept the complex system of desalination, solar power, and grant-bearing research going; and the remainders of the old Monterey, the people who weren't going anywhere, no matter how much they were offered, no matter how broadly the research organizations hinted.

Tory's parents had been fresh out of the Coast Guard when they purchased their home, bright-eyed newlyweds with a decent amount in savings (and an even more decent amount in Katherine's trust fund, left by a wealthy relative who would never have called it a dowry, even though it functionally was). They had fallen in love with the little Colonial-style house overlooking a remote strip of beach with no convenient parking lots or access roads. Their small, well-maintained property would fetch four million dollars in today's real estate market. They intended to live there until they died.

Both her parents' cars were in the driveway. Tory pulled in behind them and took a moment to compose herself before she opened the door, got out, and walked around the end of her father's battered panel van to the open garage door. The buzz of a table saw cutting through hardwood greeted her before her father himself came into view. He was bent over his equipment like a mad scientist bending over a slab, slicing a vast piece of driftwood. His goggles and heavy gloves added fuel to the mad scientist impression.

"Hi, Dad," said Tory.

Brian Stewart looked up. Then he smiled, held up one finger in a
"hold on" gesture, and went back to bisecting driftwood. Tory leaned
against the nearest workbench to watch. Prior to his retirement, her
father had been the manager of one of the local resorts, a position
that paid surprisingly well, thanks to the demands put on him by
his employers and his high-ticket clients. He'd been a troubleshooter,
mediator, and general calming presence for thirty-five years, and had
retired at the age of sixty with a healthy pension and an even health-
ier savings account. Of all the things Tory had to worry about in this
world—and she had plenty, thanks to her fondness for causes anyone
else would have been willing to let go—the future of her parents was
not among them.

The driftwood separated into two pieces, falling to the sides of
the saw blade. Brian pulled his hands away and turned off the saw,
waiting until it stopped spinning before removing his goggles and
taking out his earplugs. Tory hadn't noticed them before, but should
have assumed they were there; years of being a woodworker at home
and a perfectly groomed, coiffed manager at work had left her father
meticulous about anything that could affect either his appearance or
his performance.

"Hello, pumpkin," he said. "Shouldn't you be on a boat somewhere?"

"Funny story," said Tory.

Brian raised his eyebrows. "Suspended or fired?"

"A suspension wouldn't make sense this late in the season," said
Tory.

"Neither does firing their best marine biologist. What could you
possibly have done to make Jay think that this was the best option?"

Tory's cheeks reddened. Brian waited. Living with Katherine
had been preparation for life with Anne and Tory, who never met
a mountain they wouldn't throw themselves against. He was surrounded at all times by strong-willed women, and sometimes the best
way to deal with them was to step back and let them work through
the obstacles they presented to themselves, rather than throwing up
any of his own.

Finally Tory said, "I told a boatful of tourists how unethical and
inappropriate it is to keep orcas in captivity."

"See, I thought you were going to hold out until the next person asked if dolphin was good eating," said Katherine. Brian and Tory turned. She was standing in the doorway that led into the house, drying her hands on a dish towel and smiling. "It's all right. The season was almost over, and you have to go back to school soon."

"I was hoping to earn enough to buy access to a few more networks before I went back," said Tory. "I have blind spots that stretch for *miles*, and every network comes with the associated processing cost. How am I supposed to monitor the water for a large, unknown marine animal if I can't afford camera feeds?"

"Some people would say you're not," said Katherine.

Tory didn't say anything.

The silent standoff wasn't new. Brian busied himself tidying his workbench, stacking the driftwood against the wall and wiping the shavings out of the machinery, leaving it as pristine as he could without breaking out the cleaning oil. They were still standing there looking at each other when he finished. He clapped his hands, the sudden sound making Tory jump and Katherine look at him reproachfully.

"Well, then, we're all here now, so what do you say we head for dinner?" he asked. "My treat. I'd love a nice slice of pizza at the end of a long day."

"Let me get my coat," said Tory, and fled into the house, pausing to kiss her mother's cheek as she squeezed past her in the doorway.

Katherine waited for her daughter to pass out of earshot before she looked at her husband reproachfully and said, "You did that to distract me."

"I did."

"You know she's wasting her potential."

"I do."

"Then why—"

"Because it's her potential to waste." Brian walked over to his wife, putting his hands on her waist and tugging her toward him. She came willingly. "We made her—and God, didn't we do a remarkable job of that?—but that doesn't mean we get to dictate what she does. She's looking for answers. She's looking for peace. If this is what she has to do to find it, let her. Ahab tilted at that whale of his for a long, long time before he found it."

"And it killed him when he did," said Katherine. "Are you sure that's the comparison you want to make here?"

"I don't have a better one," said Brian. He rolled his shoulders in an easy shrug, taking his hands off his wife's waist and pressing them to either side of her face. He smiled, waiting until she smiled back before he let his own smile die and said, "Tory is young and angry and trying to figure out what she wants. Right now, she wants answers. She wants to know what happened to her sister. To be honest, I'm glad. I'd be doing the same thing if I were younger and had her training. Anne... The thought of her gnaws at me. Every night, it gnaws at me, because I didn't save her. I'm her father. I should have saved her."

"If we lose Tory too, what will we have left?" asked Katherine. "She's chasing a dream. She's chasing a hoax. Whatever they're covering up has to be so much worse than mermaids."

"She's an adult. You can't stop her. Learn to accept it, or we might lose her anyway."

Katherine sighed and pulled away. "I hate it when you're right."

"I know," said Brian. He kissed her forehead before letting go. "Let's get ready for dinner."

The pizza was fresh and hot, made with local ingredients by a pizzeria that had been a part of Monterey's landscape for more than thirty years. The price of pork had more than tripled in the last ten years, taking mainstays like sausage and pepperoni to the "deluxe toppings" menu, replacing them with salmon and ground hamburger. Brian looked mournfully at his slice of the daily special—farm-raised shrimp, pineapple, garlic, and mushroom—and said, "I would commit serious crimes for a real meat lover's pizza."

"Then it's a good thing I'm a doctor, and not an officer of the law," said Katherine. "Eat your pizza and stop whining."

"I like seafood pizza," said Tory.

"You like seafood anything," said Brian. "You're no help. You're a traitor to my foodie cause."

"Seafood has less of an ecological impact, and pigs are smart," said Tory. "You shouldn't eat anything that knows how to play fetch. It's rude."

"I'll keep that in mind," said Brian.

The pizzeria was virtually empty. The neighborhood wasn't the sort to attract tourists: most of them would be on Cannery Row, oohing and aahing over the Steinbeck attractions, stuffing their faces at overpriced chain restaurants disguised as local color. Locals knew to stay on the side streets and in the districts well away from the water, where a pizza wouldn't necessarily lead to bankruptcy, and where they wouldn't have to listen to overstimulated, sunburned children whine their way through dinner.

The bell above the door rang. Tory glanced over automatically, and went still as she saw the man standing in the doorway.

Luis Martines was the sort of tall that made basketball coaches sit up and take notice, and the sort of skinny that made those same coaches sit back down in despair. It didn't help that his glasses were too large for his face, giving him the air of a myopic, perennially confused owl. His personal hygiene was impeccable, but his grooming went through a slow cycle over the course of every school year: At the moment, he was clean shaven. By the end of the semester, he would be boasting the sort of big, bushy beard that a mall Santa would envy. As usual, he was dressed in jeans, a T-shirt, and an unbuttoned plaid flannel two sizes too large for his frame. His arms were loaded with folders and loose papers, and he looked like he'd wandered into the pizzeria by mistake while looking for the nearest library.

He spotted Tory and lit up, suddenly all smiles. He was surprisingly handsome when he smiled. "Victoria!" he exclaimed, causing the heads in the pizzeria that hadn't already turned to whip around, looking for the source of the disturbance. He ignored them, wading through the sea of tables until he reached the Stewart family.

Dropping himself into the one empty chair, Luis thrust his armload of papers at Tory. "You need to see this," he said.

Tory took the paperwork automatically. Several years of sharing lab space and research projects with Luis had taught her that if she didn't accept what he tried to give her, he'd let go anyway, resulting in papers everywhere. One cleanup too many had given her a very firm grab reflex.

"What is this?" she asked.

"I finally got those deepwater sonar scans broken down," he said. "You know, the ones centered on the Challenger Deep? I was able to get full analysis of audio signals going back five years—oh, uh, hello, Mr. and Ms. Stewart."

"Hello, Luis," said Katherine, fighting to keep the laughter from her tone. "Would you like a piece of pizza? We have plenty, and sea-food is so difficult to reheat."

"That's because it has a very delicate index of 'done,'" said Luis. "Thermodynamically speaking—"

"Thermodynamically speaking, my partner is an enormous nerd," said Tory, and flipped open the first folder. "Eat pizza, Luis. Enjoy not being in a lab. It's nice to not be in a lab sometimes."

"I went to the wharf first," said Luis. "I thought you might still be on the boat. But your boss said you don't work there anymore. What happened?"

Tory grimaced. She'd known the news of her firing would get back to her lab mates sooner or later—Jason would tell everyone the second he found out, if nothing else, and he *would* find out; he was doing a sampling project that brought him through the harbor twice a week, and he'd eventually notice her absence on the whale-watching boats—but she'd been hoping it might take a little longer.

"I sort of expressed my opinion on keeping orcas in captivity over the microphone to a boatful of tourists," she said. "Jay canned me as soon as we got back to shore."

"Oh." Luis took a piece of pizza. "I guess I can't blame him. I mean, he'd warned you like six times."

"I thought you were supposed to be on my side."

"I *am* on your side," he said, looking stung. "I just brought you something that's going to change everything, if you'd take a second and look at it. You needed to be out of that job, because you need to be free to chase this down."

Tory blinked, slowly processing the words he was actually say-ing, rather than the words her mind kept trying to supply. Finally she looked at the papers in her hands and began to read. The rest of the table went silent as her eyes got wider and wider.

"Oh," she said.

Deepwater sonar was an interesting mix of junk signals and useful readings. Filtering out the inevitable beeps and bloops from military testing, oil pipelines, and other man-made structures was the work of hundreds of hours and sensitively calibrated computer programs. What was left behind fell into two categories: known and unknown. The known noises included whale songs, dolphin chatter, and all the soft, organic sounds of the sea. Even water had a sound, to the people who knew how to listen. The unknown noises were a mess and a mystery, and all too often turned out to be nothing—a military test that hadn't been declassified until after the readings were taken, a submerged glacier collapsing in a novel way.

But there were always a few sounds remaining. Always a few novelties. Always a few mysteries.

Always a few runs of blips that science just couldn't explain.

Tory stared at the peaks and ridges of the sonar readout, feeling her heart struggle to fall out of sync with itself, excitement hastening her breath and tightening her skin. "Where was this taken?" she asked finally.

"Twenty miles east of the Mariana Trench," said Luis. "The ship that snagged the recording wasn't supposed to be there. They dropped a hydrophone for research purposes, since they were off course anyway, and then they answered our standing offer to pay for anything novel from those waters. I think they were sort of laughing at us. I mean, why would a ship's engine that big be running a thousand feet down?"

Brian put up his hand. "Can we get this with a little less intentional obfuscation, for the nonscientists in the audience?"

Tory swallowed hard, trying to force her body to listen to her. Years of therapy and meditation courses had left her with a few tricks; she summoned the sound of the sea, packing it into her ears until she felt her heart rate begin to drop. Carefully, she placed the paper on the table where her parents would be able to see.

"This," she said, touching the top line of waves and curves, "is the standard sonar reading for that area. We've had blips before— surprisingly little whale song, given how remote it is and how rich the water has historically been; we'd expect a place like that to be a popular feeding ground, and it isn't—but most of the time, the water looks like this."

"And what is 'this'?" asked Katherine.

"The song of the sea," said Luis.

Brian raised an eyebrow. "That's surprisingly poetic."

"Studying the ocean forces you to be poetic, because we haven't worn all those ideas and concepts soft around the edges yet," said Luis. "The language is still mired in the maritime, and I don't know that it's going to catch up anytime soon."

"Water sings," said Tory. Luis could talk for hours about the words used to describe the ocean. If she let him get started, they were going to be here for a while, and she wanted to get to the lab as soon as possible. "It's a function of the way it moves. Everything makes a sound, and vibrations hang in water for much longer than they can hang in air. They travel further, too. It's why whales can communicate with each other even when they're miles apart." Air was too thin, compared to water, to really carry sound. There was no such thing as silence in the sea.

"Okay, cool," said Brian, nodding in the way Anne had always called "cool dad." He didn't really understand, but he was pretending as hard as he could. Tory didn't trigger "cool dad" as often as Anne had. Tory had always been more easygoing and less likely to get embarrassed by her parents. But sometimes Brian still brought out the nod, like he was afraid he'd forget how to do it if he stopped for too long. Nothing that reminded them, as a family, of Anne was allowed to be forgotten; she was the ghost at every table, and they'd keep her with them forever if they could.

"So the standard sonar represents the song the water in that area is usually singing. It can tell us things about the currents, the tides, the depth, and more, about the creatures that live there. Not as many marine mammals as we'd expect, for example, since there aren't many of their songs embedded in the profile." Tory slid her finger down the paper, to a line marked with jagged peaks and deep valleys. "We got this recording about three years ago." Three years, two months, one week, four days. She would never forget the first time she'd listened to it, the breakthrough it had seemed to represent—or the crushing disappointment it had become when no one else could hear the things she did. "A family of sperm whales wandered into the zone we've been monitoring. It was normal song for a few days, and then they went into distress, all of them. At least six that we've been able to isolate by their voices, possibly more. They screamed for about fifteen minutes. Then they went silent. We've reached out to marine biologists who might have encountered that family either before or after the incident; the pod has never been heard again."

"You think something killed them?" asked Katherine.

"Unless aliens are stealing our whales," quipped Luis.

Tory kicked him under the table. He yelped. "It's the only thing that makes sense," she said, as if she hadn't just assaulted her research partner. "Sperm whales dive deep. They run into things that whales that stick more to the photic zone might never see. There's a chance they disturbed something, and it, well, ate them. But here's the interesting part." She began tapping other rows of sonar readings, finger moving so fast that it was clear she wasn't looking for the data she wanted: she already knew where it was, and was just revealing it to the people around her.

"These recordings were made after the whales disappeared," she said. "There's nothing higher than the mesopelagic zone, which is interesting, because whales have to surface to breathe. There's nothing *new*, either. All these sounds match up to recordings made during the period when we know the whales were present. Note for note, they match. That sort of consistency isn't natural. It's not the way whales communicate."

"Dear, we can't look at little squiggly lines and know what they mean," said Katherine patiently. "What are they?"

"They're blips of whale song, like someone—or something—had been sampling from the whales while they were in the area. And there's nothing new. Whales sing the same songs when they're talking to each other, just like people use the same words. But they inflect them differently. They have tones of voice, rising notes for excitement, falling notes for sorrow…Nothing in the sea is ever identical to what it was five minutes ago."

"Oh," said Katherine. She was starting to look baffled.

Tory moved her finger down to the last line of sonar recording, barely touching the paper, like she was afraid the printout would smear and vanish if she allowed herself to get too close. "This was just taken. These peaks and valleys? This isn't a natural sound. This isn't whale song, or water moving, or anything we've recorded in this part of the ocean. And part of that may be that we don't have consistent, linear audio files; the longest contiguous stretch we've managed to record was less than a week. So maybe this wasn't the first time it happened. Regardless, we have it now. We can see it now."

"What is it?" asked Brian.

Tory looked at her father for a long moment. Then she leaned back, so she could see both of her parents at the same time, and said, "If you showed me this sonar pattern and said it was recorded at the surface, I'd tell you it was the engine of a ship the size of the *Atargatis*. But it wasn't recorded at the surface. It was recorded in the abyssopelagic zone."

"How is that possible?" asked Brian.

"It isn't," said Luis.

Tory didn't say anything. She just looked at the printout in her hands, and thought about her sister, and all the lost and lonely ghosts of the sea.

CHAPTER 3

Monterey, California: July 28, 2022

Dinner was quick, pizza bolted down as fast as Tory and Luis could chew while Tory's parents looked on in amazement. They knew not to interfere when something like this came up. Tory was dancing along the edge of scientific discovery, getting ready for the moment when she would have to trust her instincts and jump into the unknown.

Shoving the last bite into her mouth, Tory stood, already pointed toward the door. A hand locked around her wrist. She stopped, turning to look quizzically at her mother.

"Mom?" she said.

"I know you think this is an answer, and maybe it is; I don't understand the kind of science you do, any more than you understand how the human body fits together," said Katherine. Her voice was grave; her eyes were even graver. "But baby, if it's not an answer, if it's not the piece you've been looking for, don't let it break you."

"It's okay, Mom," said Tory. She deftly extricated her wrist, bending to press a kiss against her mother's temple before she said, "I'm already broken," and followed Luis to the door.

Luis's car was a first-generation Tesla, inefficient compared to more recent models, some of which could run on solar power for a week between charges. It still ran, and buying a new car was a hassle, and so he stuck with the familiar. It was parked at the end of the charging row, no parking permit on the dash. A ticket fluttered there, pinned under a windshield wiper like a butterfly under glass. Luis plucked it and shoved it into his pocket, where it would wind up too crumpled to read. His family came from old tech money, Silicon Valley startup royalty stemming from the age of Microsoft and IBM; he could afford to ignore his parking tickets, knowing the apps monitoring his police record would pay them dutifully and in a timely manner.

Tory envied his casual relationship with money. As long as something didn't crest the mid-five figures, he could pay for it on a whim—and often did, keeping their lab outfitted with all the latest toys, subscribing to all the relevant journals, and guaranteeing neither of them would starve while takeout was an option. The only things he *didn't* pay for were the data bands, partially because he was less obsessive than she was—he already had years of data to collate and review—and partially because they'd agreed that once her penny-a-piece scans began bearing fruit, he'd throw their entire research budget behind whatever feeds would serve them best.

He'd offered to take up the subscription fees for the feeds she had already deemed necessary. Several times. But for now, this was the way Tory could contribute and not feel entirely dependent on him. It was something. It was small, but most of the time, it was enough.

"I'm okay with this as long as you're taking blind stabs at the target," he'd said. "But as soon as you narrow it from 'the ocean' to 'this stream, right here,' I'm going to start paying for whatever we need."

Tory had been narrowing ever since. Years of narrowing, of eliminating other trenches, other dead spots, focusing more and more on the fifteen-hundred-mile-long geographic feature known as the Mariana Trench. It had been inevitable, in some ways. The Mariana Trench had been the last known location of the *Atargatis* before communication stopped. The ship had been found some distance from there, but that could have been a matter of drift; there were strong currents in that part of the ocean. Her answers were waiting in the Mariana Trench. She knew it.

Luis looked at her worriedly as he unlocked the car. "You're making the scary face again."

"Which one?"

"The one that says you're going to burn down the world if that's what it takes to get what you want."

"It's good to know I'm easy to read." She opened the door and slipped into the car, buckling her belt and waiting for Luis to join her before she continued, "I'm so close, Luis. I'm *so* close. Anne's out there, and I'm going to find her."

"Tory…Anne's dead. You know that, right?" Luis put a hand on the wheel, making no effort to hide his concern. "She died before I met you. Figuring out what happened to her isn't going to bring her back."

"I know." Anne's bones were at the bottom of the Mariana Trench, if they hadn't been devoured by some creature of the deep, recycled into the body of the living ocean. Tory would have been content for her own final resting place to be in the belly of a giant squid, but her sister? Her land-loving, bright-eyed sister who'd only ever wanted to make a name for herself? No. Anne deserved better. Anne deserved a pine box in an ecologically sound graveyard, lying under six feet of nutrient-rich soil, going back into the ground. Anne was never going to have that. The least Tory could do was solve the mystery of why not.

Anne was supposed to have been famous, to have been bright and beautiful and worried about getting old. She wasn't supposed to be *dead*, or intrinsically linked to what most people believed was a massive maritime hoax by a corporation with more money than morals. If Tory couldn't make Imagine apologize for taking her sister away, she was damn well going to make sure the world knew the truth. Anne hadn't died for nothing. She hadn't died because the crew fucked up, or because *she'd* made a mistake.

She'd died because Imagine had discovered mermaids, and, upon finding them, hadn't been able to control them.

"Do you really? Because sometimes it seems like you think there's going to be a quick and easy answer to this question."

"I want there to be. But quick and easy both passed us by years ago." Tory shook her head. "I know we have a lot of work to do. I know we're not even halfway there. Most of all, I know we can't stop looking just because it seems like it's too much."

"Hey, now." Luis smiled, allowing his worries to melt away in the face of the sheer joy of scientific progress. "I never said *that*."

He hit the accelerator. Tory watched long enough to be sure they weren't about to back into one of the other cars in the parking lot before allowing her attention to turn to the printouts she was clutching in both hands.

The data was open to interpretation. She knew that. All data was open to interpretation, and there would always be people ready to disagree with any theory that arose, ready to argue that the water on Mars didn't count because it was the result of slow geologic processes and not weather patterns, ready to argue that the bacteria clustered around volcanic vents was not proof of extremophilic life. Scientists liked to argue about discoveries almost as much as they liked to make them, and arguing about someone *else's* discoveries was the best game of all.

And yet.

And yet it was difficult to see what those peaks and valleys could be, if not the evidence that something deep below the pelagic zone was mimicking a sound heard on the surface: some sort of undersea echo repeating the roar of an engine that had died years before, going silent forever.

And yet it was impossible to look at the lists of disappearances in the vicinity of the Mariana Trench—so many that they rivaled the fabled Bermuda Triangle—and not see the claw of some unknown predator at work. The number of people lost in that slice of the sea was startling, but the ocean had never been gentle where humanity was concerned; sailors were forever being washed overboard, passengers were forever being surrendered to the weather. Ships sank in storms. The seas of the world were a vast and interconnected graveyard, every inch riddled with bones and haunted by the ghosts of the lost. Every mile of every ocean could be marked as the site of some "surprising" or "unexpected" death; humanity sailed, and the sea punished it for its hubris.

And yet. The number of whales, dolphins, and other marine mammals lost in and around the Trench was more than startling; it was unreal. Older pods tended to avoid the waters around the Mariana Trench, unless blown there by bad weather. Even some of the older sharks would go miles out of their way to avoid swimming through those waters. It was difficult to say what sort of memory a shark had, but they knew enough to stay away.

Something was down there. Something that could slaughter sperm whales and leave research vessels floating abandoned and unmanned. Something that mimicked the sounds it heard, using them to lure its prey. Something that defied belief. And whatever it was, Tory was going to find it, and make it pay for what it had done to her sister.

During the semester, Tory and Luis worked out of a lab at UC Santa Cruz. For the summer, Luis had taken a research position at the Monterey Bay Aquarium, not far from the wharf where the whale-watching tours docked. Both worked on their respective dissertations whenever possible, meeting to compare notes and verify that their research was still coming up with the same—or at least similar—results. Luis was seeking proof of hidden deepwater megafauna, for whales without eyes and dolphins adapted to dive so deep that the pressure should have burst their air-filled lungs inside their chests, for surviving megalodon and the source of the kraken myth. He pointed to diving bell spiders and geological off-gassing as proof that there could be air breathers in the deeps that never came to the surface. He used Tory's sonar readings to argue that there were things down there, beyond the reach of even unmanned scientific vessels, with no need to seek the light.

"Sure, it's not likely, and sure, it would throw a lot of what we think we know into question, but we have strong enough evidence that it's worth chasing," he said when pressed, expression calm and voice untroubled. This was a speech he'd been giving for most of his adult life. He had it down pat. "The ocean is the last great mystery in the world. We may as well pursue every clue it contains. We'll have all the questions answered soon enough, and things are going to get very boring after that happens."

Both Luis and Tory knew that it was his father's money that made his theories even halfway palatable to the academic community; sure, he was chasing monsters, but he was funding more practical research almost as an afterthought, using it to create the structures and framework he needed. As long as he kept signing checks and doing solid lab work, the fact that his version of marine biology owed a great deal to philosophy and folklore could be overlooked.

Tory wasn't so lucky. Since acoustic maritime camouflage wasn't a recognized field, her official area of research was acoustic marine biology, using unusual sonar readings to create an accurate census of the population of the oceanic trenches and valleys. Geothermal imaging made topographical maps of the seafloor common, and they grew more precise by the year. Geothermal imaging couldn't account for things like coral growths, shipwrecks, or cold currents, and it certainly couldn't predict where the animals would be. Sonar could. Bit by bit, Tory was constructing a model of the living ocean, one that could shave decades off research and exploration. If that had been all she was doing—if that had been her focus and her passion— she could have written her own ticket to any research facility in the world. Privately held, military, scientific, it wouldn't have mattered. They would all have wanted her.

Sadly, her passion was elsewhere, and everyone in her admittedly specialized field knew it. She was as much of a monster chaser as her partner, and she didn't have the pedigree to make her seem respectable.

Luis pulled into his parking spot behind the Monterey Bay Aquarium, managing to fit mostly between the lines this time. There were only a few other cars present, and Tory recognized them all: they belonged to researchers and wildlife rescue workers. Anne-Marie was raising a group of orphaned baby sea otters, and they needed her at all hours of the day and night, causing her to virtually move into her closet-size office. Dmitri was tracking the long-term impact of desalination on the local plankton, expressing a very real concern that they were throwing the balance of the sea off, one filtered gallon at a time. His work required him to take water samples according to a rotating five-hour schedule, slowly shifting him around the clock and forcing him into a world of catnaps and constant caffeination. Bo just hated sleep, and avoided it in favor of the lab whenever possible. They were her people, in love with the ocean, forgiving of its foibles, protective of its boundaries.

To a point. None of them had lost as much as she had. She loved the ocean—she always would—but it needed to give back as much as it had taken from her, even if it could never return her sister. Tory looked at the sonar readings in her hands, tracing a line of data with her finger. The ink was dim under the parking lot lights, but she didn't need to see it anymore. She knew what it said.

"What if this isn't what we think it is?" she asked, and her voice was small and timid, the voice of a child who'd never been allowed to say goodbye, rather than the voice of a woman on the verge of a discovery that could change her life.

"Then we'll keep looking until we find something that *is* what we think it is," said Luis. "I know the answers are out there."

"Thanks, Mulder," said Tory, aiming a friendly punch at his arm.

Luis grinned and said nothing.

They had keycards and passcodes for building access after hours. The lights came on as they walked down the hall, then turned off again behind them. (The motion sensors were a bone of contention within the administration. The marine biologists wanted them set to the highest sensitivity possible, to allow them to track runaway seal pups and escaped octopi. The accountants wanted them turned down as far as they could go, keeping the building from being lit up like Christmas every time someone sneezed. The result was something that pleased no one, with the sensors set to notice the presence of "average" humans but nothing smaller. Some of the shorter researchers couldn't get the lights to come on, and had to be escorted to the bathroom after closing time.)

The door to Tory and Luis's lab was ajar. The pair stopped dead, looking at the gap between door and frame like it would explain itself.

"Did you leave the door open?" asked Tory finally.

"No." Luis sounded more baffled than offended, but there was offense there too; he'd grown up so certain of his own privacy that it had taken him a while to realize that an unlocked lab was a lab at risk. Supplies were always running low, and people often "borrowed" things when they thought they could put them to better use. Since those things sometimes included data passes for the feeds, or supposedly confidential test results, locking everything was the only way to be safe.

"I was on the boat all morning, and I went straight home after I got fired."

"I know."

"So there's no way—"

"I *know.*" Luis reached to the side, gesturing as if he were going to push Tory behind himself. "I'll go in first."

Tory rolled her eyes. "Oh, please. I'm the one who *passed* her self-defense class, remember? If we have an intruder, they'll leave you with a broken arm and I'll be carrying everything for the next three months." Her voice only quavered slightly. She'd been tackling waves too big for her and problems beyond her pay grade since she was a child. She wasn't going to let fear take her now. "Get behind me."

Luis kept protesting as she surged forward and slammed the door open. The motion sensors snapped on, illuminating the room.

The man who'd been sitting patiently at her desk, so still that the room had forgotten he was there, smiled. "Ah," he said. "Finally."

Tory froze again, staring at him. Luis stepped into the room and stopped in turn. The man continued smiling.

He was handsome, in an expensive way: everything about him looked more designed than natural, as if he'd been refined in a factory for creating lovely, forgettable men. His teeth were white; his jaw was strong; his hair was dark and thick; Tory thought she would have trouble picking him out of a lineup after five minutes away from him. The only remarkable thing about him was the color of his eyes, a bright ice blue that would have seemed more ordinary on a sled dog. Even they might have been contact lenses, a flash of something spectacular to distract from the predictable whole.

His suit was clearly bespoke, and just as clearly expensive, fitting him like he'd been born in it. His polished leather shoes were a few shades darker than the briefcase beside his purloined chair. His hands were folded on one knee, a casual, easy pose that did nothing to make him seem more human.

"I'm surprised," he said, in a conversational tone. "I was expecting you nearly an hour ago. Did you get distracted by some bright new discovery, one worth postponing the opportunity to change the world?"

"You're trespassing," said Tory. Anger flared in her like a lit match. Her eyes narrowed. "Who *are* you? This lab is private property. You can't be in here."

"You're correct that the lab is private property. It belongs to the Monterey Bay Aquarium, which does not fund your research but, as I understand it, is willing to let you conduct your work here in exchange for a healthy donation from Mr. Martines's parents"—the man nodded toward Luis—"and in the hopes you'll discover something that can benefit this institution. If you read the fine print of your contracts, you'll find the aquarium reserves the right to allow anyone access to your lab at any time, providing they are confident the individual or individuals in question are not here to interfere with your research in any way. I assure you that I'm not here to interfere."

"So why *are* you here?" Luis's inflection mirrored Tory's almost exactly.

The man rose, extending his hand for one of them to shake. He didn't seem concerned about which of them it was. "My name is Theodore Blackwell, and I'm here as a representative of Imagine Entertainment."

Tory stiffened, the blood draining from her face so fast it left her reeling. For one terrified moment, she was afraid she was going to collapse, leaving Luis to deal with this—whatever this was—alone. The moment passed. Her heart, while beating too fast and too hard against her ribs, did not go out on her; her lungs continued to fill. She was still standing.

"Get out," she said, through clenched teeth. The soothing sound of the sea seemed impossibly far away.

"Miss Stewart, you've been asking—begging, cajoling, and occasionally ordering—Imagine to send a second expedition to the Mariana Trench for the past seven years, and for the past seven years, Imagine has been refusing. There was insufficient data to make a second voyage viable. As I'm sure you understand, Imagine remains in a highly precarious position where the events of 2015 are concerned. On the one hand, there is no one who wishes for answers more devoutly than my employer—no." His voice hardened on the last word. "I see you preparing to contradict me, to cite the loss of your sister as proof that no one has suffered as much as you have. I concede that you've suffered. I do not dispute that you've paid a greater price than anyone anticipated. But your sister was not the only one lost at sea."

Mr. Blackwell took a step forward. "There were dozens of Imagine employees on that boat. People I'd worked with for years. People I considered personal friends. My losses are greater than yours in volume, and again, I'm not the only one. Each of those people had a sister, Miss Stewart, or a brother, or a lover, or a parent. So yes, we want to know what happened as much as you do, if not substantially more. But there is always the other hand to consider. The hand which answers to shareholders and the court of public perception. The *Atargatis* was a tragedy—one the world has, by and large, allowed to be forgotten. The footage is dismissed as false; the tragedy becomes an unavoidable accident. The word *hoax* overtakes the much less pleasant *slaughter*. There was no hoax. The footage is real."

"We knew that," said Luis softly.

Mr. Blackwell spared Luis a tight smile before returning his attention to Tory. "Going into those waters for a second time will reopen old wounds and bring all the old accusations and armchair experts flooding back into the light. To use the maritime metaphors your people seem to be so fond of, we'll be throwing out chum, and the sharks *will* come. A second voyage can only be undertaken under the most specific and particular of circumstances."

"What are those?" asked Tory. Her jaw felt like it had locked in on itself. It was beginning to ache. It was oddly difficult to see that as a bad thing. If she was focusing on the pain, she wasn't going to hit the man from Imagine with a chair.

"We must have new information that would allow us to get *answers* from sending another ship. A crew that will be careful, cautious, and invested. And absolute secrecy, of course. That goes almost without saying." The corner of Blackwell's mouth twitched. "Imagine will film everything for release if we're successful—it could bring peace to those who've been questioning for the past seven years—but if we fail, or if what we find is less than savory, nothing will be said. We need people who understand that."

"So you decided to sit in our lab like a creeper because you wanted to gloat at Tory about how you were never going to make her feel better?" Luis stepped up next to his partner, hands balling into fists. "I don't know how you do things at Imagine, but where I come from—"

"Where you come from, disputes are settled by calm discussions in beautifully appointed boardrooms, while the people having the discussions pretend they've bucked the old trappings of the business world simply because they no longer need to wear ties. I know where you come from, Mr. Martines. You cannot frighten me by playing on the idea that you might commit violence. I know better."

Luis frowned. "That's not how this was supposed to go."

Again, the corner of Blackwell's mouth twitched. "My apologies. Next time I'll have my office call ahead for a copy of your script." He returned his attention to Tory. "I'm not here to toy with you or waste your time. I'm here to make you an offer."

"What's that?" she asked, warily.

"Imagine has been taking an interest in your research," he said, still calm, still unruffled. "We find your approach to the mystery of the Mariana Trench fascinating. Sonar, for the depths where light cannot go. Ingenious, if unlikely to produce any truly useful results— but unlikely is not, as they say, impossible. Your findings have been remarkable."

Tory's eyes widened. She hugged the printouts to her chest, finally finding her voice as she demanded, "How do you know what I've found?"

"We've been monitoring the same data feeds. We've even been instrumental in convincing some of the feed holders to reduce their fees for you. Without informing you, of course. We didn't want you to feel beholden to Imagine."

"I would never!"

"We're aware, Miss Stewart." Blackwell shook his head, lips pressed into a thin line. "The filming aboard the *Atargatis* was never expected to be hazardous. If it had been, we would never have been there in the first place. We're an entertainment company. We never wanted anyone to die. Had we possessed the slightest inkling that there might be something real out there to find, we would have handed responsibility for the mission over to a research group that could handle the more dangerous aspects of the project. Errors were made. People were lost. Some of their associates have attempted to blackmail the company, even after Imagine was found innocent of intentional wrongdoing. Not you. Not your family. You've never taken a dime from us—"

"I would *never*," said Tory again, more hotly.

"—*voluntarily*," said Blackwell. Again, that twitch of his mouth, like it was all he could do to conceal his amusement. "Imagine has been interested in your research for some time. Mr. Martines has provided enough financial support that our contribution has been ... masked, shall we say. We've been able to slip certain necessary items to guide your professional development into the gaps he would otherwise have left."

All those years. All those times when a data feed would become accessible exactly when it was needed, when a piece of equipment she would have sworn Luis didn't care about had suddenly appeared in the lab, letting her work progress. Even the ease with which certain applications had been approved by committees infamous for their slowness and reticence to consider research not focused on feeding people or relieving the increasingly global droughts...Tory had taken all those things as a consequence of Luis's family wealth, or her own status as a victim of the *Atargatis* tragedy, or both. Suddenly she was seeing them in a whole new light, and she didn't like it.

"I can see this distresses you," said Blackwell. "I knew it would. I recommended to my superiors that you be left out of this project. I was outvoted. Apparently, there are those who believe your expertise is key—or at least, that your presence on the vessel, as one of our scientific experts, will prevent rumors of hoax."

"Project?" said Luis.

"Vessel?" said Tory.

"The *Melusine* sails from San Diego in three weeks' time; preparations have been under way for years, only waiting for the science to catch up with the ambition. You have the sonar reports. You know how the equipment works. We—by which I mean the board of the Imagine Network—want you on that vessel when it launches. It will travel to the Mariana Trench. It will use its dynamic positioning system to settle itself in the best possible place. And it will, God willing, finally answer the question of what happened to the *Atargatis*. The entire voyage is being funded by Imagine, with support from several other interested parties. It will cost you nothing but time. It might provide the answers you seek. So." Blackwell paused. "Will you set sail with us?"

"I don't even see how that's a question," said Tory.

Blackwell nodded and reached for his briefcase. "Excellent," he said, although his tone implied that it was anything but. "As it happens, I have the paperwork right here."

CHAPTER 4

Berkeley, California: August 3, 2022

T he mermaid."
The slide showed an elegant woodcut of a woman, naked from the waist up, scaled from the waist down, sitting on a rock and staring toward a city on the nearby shore. Her face was turned away from the viewer, but she was lovely, with long, flowing hair and gently sloping breasts.

"The earliest entries into the mermaid monomyth were recorded in ancient Assyria, twenty-five centuries before the Common Era, when the goddess Atargatis supposedly flung herself into the sea in grief over the death of her human lover, a shepherd, whose name has been lost to antiquity. The theme of human women being transformed by the combination of grief and drowning continued in the myth almost to the present day."

The slide changed to a shot of Disney's iconic little mermaid, hair blazing red and enormous blue eyes turned toward the distant surface. The longing implied in the woodcut was fully realized here: the animated princess yearned, *ached*, for whatever was above her, straining toward the forbidden.

"When Hans Christian Andersen wrote 'The Little Mermaid' in 1836, he inverted the old mermaid stories. No longer were women going to the sea: instead they wanted to leave it, to explore the clearly superior wonders of human society. The majority of mermaid stories written after this fable took root have shown this same sensibility—the idea that somehow life on land is superior. Please note that I said 'the majority.' I've been teaching this class for some time now, and I can assure you that I've seen every exception to the rule. Writing and self-publishing a novel to prove me wrong is a viable use of your time, but you should be aware that six people have gotten there before you for specifically that reason."

Laughter swept the darkened lecture hall, some of it sincere, some of it nervous. The room, which could seat three hundred, was full, with TAs and interested auditors standing against the back wall. The lecture was being streamed into another two hundred homes, for the sake of the distance learners and the students who were unable, for one reason or another, to attend.

It would have been nice if they'd all been there to witness her genius. Dr. Jillian Toth knew that most of them were there to see the village fool dancing naked in the square. She was a quack, having been written off by everyone outside her admittedly specialized field—sirenology being an offshoot of marine biology, with aspects of physiology and cetology mixed in—and regarded as the scientific equivalent of a tabloid reporter. But she kept speaking, and she kept working, and someday, she was sure, she would show them.

She would show them all.

It was hard for the audience to see her with the lights as low as they were; she was a shadow, a silhouette, a conversation that began and ended in comfortable darkness. Even when she'd been held in higher regard by the academic community, Dr. Toth had never been inclined to seek the spotlight. Instead she kept to her podium, her online forums, and her growing body of essays, which many dismissed as the ramblings of a woman whose crackpot theories could thrive only in academia, where concept and execution were sometimes so divorced as to bear no relation to one another.

In the light, she was a tall, strongly built woman of mixed English and Hawaiian descent who managed to seem angular and rounded at the same time. From her father she had inherited strong legs, brown skin, dark hair that required little more than regular brushing, and an absolute conviction that those who challenged the sea would eventually get what was coming to them. From her mother she had inherited a tendency to freckle a darker shade of brown, a certain emotional distance from the people around her, and pale green eyes, like chips of sea glass that had somehow missed the shore and washed up in her face instead. Her admirers said she was beautiful, confident, and clever. Her detractors said she was fat and loud and took up too much space. All of them were, within their limited spheres, correct.

The slide changed again, this time to a screenshot every person in the class recognized. That didn't stop the vague murmurs of discontent as people realized what they were looking at.

In the picture, the creature—the mermaid—was facing away from the camera, pulling itself along the *Atargatis* deck with clawed hands. Its tail was broad and flat, more like an eel's than a dolphin's, and while the substance growing from its scalp could have passed for hair under the right light, it was clearly something…else.

"The *Atargatis*, 2015," said Dr. Toth. "This picture was taken prior to the disappearance of all hands on board. People have spent the last seven years with this image and the others like it, devoting their time to the effort to discredit the so-called 'mermaid mystery.' Apparently, it's more believable that the *Atargatis* had a complete special effects lab manipulating the film as it was created than it is to say that perhaps mermaids—or something terribly like them—are real."

"The film could have been manipulated after it was taken but before they were lost," said a voice. The speaker didn't yell, but his voice carried surprisingly well in the silence left by Dr. Toth's last statement.

"And all copies of the unmodified footage were somehow successfully wiped from the *Atargatis* systems, to the point that the navy's computer science experts have been unable to retrieve them?" Dr. Toth turned to face the room. If she was perturbed about being interrupted, she didn't show it; she still sounded effortlessly calm, almost sedate. "If the Imagine Network had released this footage as one of their television specials, I'd be right there with the skeptics, arguing that this couldn't possibly be real—if we can't figure out how the trick was done, it simply means they've been stepping up their game. But they didn't. The Imagine Network fought the release of this footage tooth and nail. They wanted it to disappear. The United States Navy started the leak. Without them this might be a tragic footnote, forgotten by all except for the families of the victims. The film is too comprehensive, too complete, and too flawed to be anything but real."

"Shouldn't flaws make you question more, not less?" The voice sounded amused now, like it had found the weakness in her entire thesis.

Dr. Toth wasn't taking the bait. "Some flaws create questions. Why does the monster have a zipper; why did the ghost of Lover's Lane wait until new construction was announced before attacking. Some flaws are the key to a Scooby-Doo mystery. Other flaws are necessary for a thing to be realistic. The film from the *Atargatis* is internally consistent. Objects do not appear or disappear without cause. People talk in a realistic way, repeating themselves, stuttering, stumbling over their own words. There are individuals we only know by name from the passenger roster, because they are never called by name on film. Reality is much less convenient than fiction. People don't introduce themselves every time they see someone that they already know. Mascara doesn't magically reapply itself between takes. The flaws in the *Atargatis* video are the flaws that appear in reality."

"So you're saying perfection is the enemy of the truth."

"I'm saying this is my classroom, and you're disrupting it. The veracity of the *Atargatis* footage is not up for discussion at this time. Please hold any further questions until the end of the lecture."

"Why did the navy release the footage?"

For the first time, Dr. Toth stopped cold. For the first time, she actually looked displeased. Then she took a breath, and the world resumed.

"The *Atargatis* was captained by a woman named Jovanie Seghers. Her father, Lieutenant John Seghers, was retired navy. He had contacted his former colleagues as soon as his daughter stopped responding to his messages, asking them to check up on her. Without him the *Atargatis* might not have been found for substantially longer, if it was found at all. Someone on the ship which found the *Atargatis* also found some or all of the footage. They watched it, realized that Imagine was likely to bury it, and released it before any official cease and desist could be issued. Imagine was still cleared of all charges. The footage was deemed both falsified and illegally released. So far as I am aware, the only person to suffer actual consequences was the seaman who chose to upload it."

"Have you spoken to him?"

"That is not your concern. Now." Dr. Toth cleared her throat. "The Mariana Trench has long been considered a likely spot for the existence of 'real' mermaids. Deep, isolated, and on several historical shipping lanes—"

She was still talking as the shadowy figure of a man detached from the wall and walked up the stairs to the door. She continued talking as he made his exit, and it was anyone's guess whether she saw him go.

It was no real surprise when, after the lecture concluded, Dr. Jillian Toth returned to her office to find a well-groomed, remarkably forgettable man sitting in the chair she kept for visiting students. She walked past him, shaking her head, to drop the thumb drive holding the day's lesson into a fishbowl filled with similar drives in varying sizes and colors. All were labeled in her private shorthand, making it virtually impossible for anyone else to make sense of her filing system.

"I thought I told you not to come here," she said. "Whatever you're selling, I'm not interested."

"I believe your exact words were, 'Damn you, Theo, unless you've convinced that boss of yours to send another boat, don't even bother talking to me,'" said Blackwell. He looked at her fishbowl of thumb drives, allowing one corner of his mouth to twitch upward. "I see you've been busy. I remember when you could fit them in a saucer."

"Yeah, well, the field of mermaid science is booming, in that 'she's clearly insane but the students love her and she works for peanuts' sort of way. I may not have any credibility, but I have tenure, and that's more than I can say for you." Jillian opened the fridge next to her filing cabinets, withdrawing a bottle of violently red liquid. "Are you planning to leave like a nice little corporate shill, or do you need me to contact security? Because I'd *love* to contact security. You never need to get me another birthday present if you make me contact security."

"You've returned every birthday present I've given you in seven years."

"I wouldn't return this one. I would treasure it." She opened the bottle and took a long drink of the contents. They smelled of fruit punch and hibiscus.

Blackwell waited for her to finish. When she lowered the bottle, he said, "We're sending another boat. By your own terms, I believe that means I'm allowed to be here."

Jillian paused before putting the cap back on the bottle and returning it to the fridge. Then she stopped, hand grasping the handle, eyes on the faded snapshots taped to the freezer door. Someone with a good eye for skeletal structure might have been able to recognize the laughing, black-haired man with his arm around her shoulders as Theodore Blackwell; he had the same ice-blue eyes, like chips out of a living glacier. But the man in the picture was at ease, casual, relaxed. The man in her office now didn't look as if he knew what relaxation was.

"Don't toy with me, Theo," she said, addressing the picture, like she trusted the man she'd known more than the man she knew now. In a very real way, that was true. The Theodore Blackwell who'd protested whaling practices with her, surfed with her in the waters off Hawaii, and proposed to her on Oahu, that man was dead and gone and surrendered to the sea. This man, this virtual stranger...he was something different. Something dangerous.

The best predators always learned how to masquerade as things that wouldn't seem threatening. That was how they got close enough to strike.

A glimmer of what sounded like genuine offense slipped into Blackwell's voice as he said, "I can't believe you'd think that of me."

"What, that you'd use me to promote your own agenda? Or that you'd tell me lies? Or wait, that you'd dangle something you knew I wanted solely for the sake of convincing me to go with you?" Jillian turned to face him. "You did all those things when you still loved me more than you loved your work. I forgave you then, because my love for you was stronger than my sense of self-preservation. I grew up."

"We have a vessel. A research ship, larger than the *Atargatis*. Every luxury, every amenity. Hulls designed to stand up to torpedo impacts, shields and supports and a hundred other safety features. Built-in electrical systems capable of supporting radar arrays like you've never had access to. We can detect motion hundreds of meters down." Blackwell stood. "We're ready."

"Really? Because that sounds like a lot of untested technology in the hands of a media corporation. How many of those systems actually *work*?"

Blackwell ignored her. "We can pinpoint a single jelly drifting on a submerged current. We have some of the best scientists in the world ready to sail with us. But we don't have a sirenologist."

"I hate that word," said Jillian.

"You didn't hate it when you were doing the talk show circuit, talking about everything Imagine had done wrong on their first voyage. I believe I have video of you defining the term. Several times. 'A marine biologist who specializes in the scientific study of mermaids, their feasibility and probable reality,' wasn't that your line?"

Jillian broke eye contact first, glancing down at her sensible shoes. "That was a long time ago. We all did things in the wake of the tragedy that we aren't necessarily going to be proud of now."

"Yes, I suppose we did." Blackwell looked at her calmly. "You told me if we ever sent out another ship, you would be on board."

"I didn't go out with the *Atargatis* because Imagine demanded too much ownership of my research." And because she'd been afraid. Afraid that they would find exactly what she'd said they'd find; afraid that when faced with the reality behind her theories, she would learn that she'd been right. About everything.

And she had been.

Blackwell, who knew the truth behind her words almost as well as she did, let the pretty fiction stand. "The terms are different this time. Any research you conduct will belong to you, completely. Imagine requests only that they retain right of first publication of proof of the existence of mermaids. They guarantee publication within six months of returning to shore, and will place the entire Imagine media engine behind you to promote your findings. They have their own publishing wing, you know. You wouldn't have to go out on submission if you didn't want to. Their standard terms are quite generous."

"They'd have to be, if they want to lure in authors who could as easily go elsewhere," said Jillian. She was starting to sound dazed, like she couldn't quite wrap her head around what was happening. "They would have to acknowledge the footage of the original trip."

"If we find proof, they will."

"I'd want that in writing."

"You'll have it."

If the *Atargatis* footage was conclusively proven not to be a hoax—if it was acknowledged by the corporation as real—everything would change. All those questions finally answered; all those grieving families allowed to find their peace. All her research... "Are you serious? Imagine is funding a second expedition? What in the world could convince them to take that sort of risk? I know you didn't talk them into it."

"It wouldn't have been my place," said Blackwell, tone cooling. "The initial motivation behind this second voyage is above my pay grade, and frankly, I'm glad. There's always the potential for something to go wrong. The *Atargatis* taught us that."

"Not just the *Atargatis*," muttered Jillian.

Blackwell ignored her. "If something should happen, God forbid, I need to be able to say, without fear of perjury, that the motives behind the trip were pure. So far as I'm aware, they are. Technology has advanced. We have better tools, and we know what we're looking for. Scientists have been analyzing the *Atargatis* footage for seven years. While there's much about the biology of these creatures that we can't know for sure without getting our hands on one, we are so much better prepared than we were."

"Imagine is finally taking the position that the mermaids on those tapes are real."

"Officially, Imagine's position remains the same as always—for now. But you're not blind, you're not stupid, and you're the one who told them what they were looking for. You knew those things were real the second you saw the recording. Even if Imagine had wanted to make up a monster story to cover for the loss of a very real group of people, they wouldn't have been able to do such a good job in such a short amount of time. CGI ages poorly. That technology, too, has marched on. If there was something in those tapes for the world to discredit, it would have happened already. The fact that it hasn't should be proof enough of what happened on the *Atargatis*, no matter what Imagine says to the media. It wasn't a stunt, it wasn't a mistake, and there's been no cover-up. The world just doesn't like the answers we've been able to provide."

"So why is Imagine going out there again?"

"Because we want closure." Blackwell squared his shoulders,

a small, almost unconscious gesture that most people would have taken for formality.

Jillian frowned. "Is your back bothering you?"

"My back's always bothering me, Jillian."

"Dr. Toth."

"Dr. Toth, then. Yes. My back is bothering me. Nerve damage doesn't go away simply because one takes a desk job. I need your answer. Will you sail with the *Melusine*, and help Imagine provide answers to the people who've been waiting for the last seven years?"

"The *Melusine*." Jillian snorted. "That's a little on the nose, don't you think?"

"If we're successful, there will be a documentary. My employers are very good at managing the details."

"That's true." She sobered. "I'll need a copy of the contract. I'm willing to sign an NDA, but I need time to review both the NDA and the contract with my lawyer."

"The contract will be provided after your lawyer has approved the NDA. I assume you'll be using William?"

"He still represents me."

"Excellent. He's as unbiased as anyone you pay can possibly be. We sail in two weeks. Can you be ready?"

Jillian's smile was sharp and full of teeth. "I've been ready to make amends for my past sins for seven years, Theo. What's a few weeks on top of that?"

Theodore Blackwell walked calmly across the visitors' parking lot. He did not hurry. He seemed to be a man with only one speed, a ground-eating pace that was nonetheless slightly stilted, like something was out of sequence with itself. He also did not look back. He knew he presented an odd sight on a campus like this one, a liberal school, ecologically minded and populated by young radicals who truly believed their generation would somehow repair the damage done by all the generations before them. They were bright eyed and ambitious and looking toward the future, and if there was anything in the world that he envied anyone, it was their confidence that they'd succeed.

(That was a generalization, of course; he knew anxiety and uncertainty bred in this new generation just as prolifically as it had in his own. Perhaps even more so. Each new wave of humanity found itself crashing onto a beach that was a little more cluttered from what had come before, a little more damaged from the carelessness of others. If these students seemed motivated and determined, it was because they'd seen the writing on the wall. Earth would survive whatever humanity did to it. Humanity might not. These children, and their children, were making the last-ditch effort to bring the planet back from the brink. He wished them well in their fight, even as he was grateful that his time on the front lines was over. He was a clerical worker now, support staff at best, and he would never be a warrior again. Circumstances had seen to that.)

By the time his car came into view, he had lost all feeling in his right thigh. He kept walking, using that practiced stride to get him through the process of unlocking the door and sliding into the driver's seat. The car's autopilot wasn't good enough to trust on unmapped surface streets, but the university routes had been among the first programmed into the commercial models; it could get him back to the highway, and from there it would be fine. Relieved, he flipped the switch to give the car total control, pressed the button to inform local law enforcement that the driver was medically impaired and unable to reclaim control of the vehicle, and reached for his briefcase.

The damage to his spine was extensive. In another time, before medical science caught up with human need, he would have been paralyzed from the waist down. Advances in nerve regeneration—ironically, partially due to compounds isolated from certain jellyfish, which did not age, did not die of natural causes, and seemed to hold the key to immortality—had allowed doctors to regrow and reconnect portions of his spinal cord, coaxing them through fused bones and shattered pathways. He could stand. He could walk. He'd never be a runner, but then, he'd never been a runner to begin with.

The constant pain was a side effect he could live with, given the alternatives. Most of the time, it was manageable, save when the damaged and regrown nerves began firing wildly, sending messages of agony shooting along his spine. Sadly, those periods were unpredictable; sometimes he could be fine for days, dealing with the sort of low-grade pain that would have been unimaginable once, but was now merely the cost of doing business. Other times, he'd be unable to stand without screaming.

The car pulled smoothly out of its slot and moved at a measured pace toward the exit. Autonomous cars stuck precisely to the speed limit in the absence of other vehicles, and used the prevailing speed of traffic to determine a safe rate when other drivers were present. Initially they'd been too safe, adhering to traffic laws with a precision that made them dangerous to the humans on the road. A certain amount of lawlessness had been necessary to make them ready for wide distribution.

Even an autonomous car could break the law. But under most circumstances, no tickets would be issued, especially in the case of someone like Theo, who would have been a genuine threat to himself and others if he'd tried to take the wheel. With shaking hands, he opened the briefcase and withdrew a small leather case. The numbness in his leg was temporary; if he didn't move quickly, it would transition into shooting pain that could make it difficult to inject the medication he needed with any degree of accuracy.

The numbness was beginning to take on a burning tingle as he withdrew a syringe and snapped an ampule of medication into it. It would have been cheaper to measure and mix his doses one at a time, but given how narrow the window between onset and injection often was, he was happy to pay for the security of knowing he wasn't going to accidentally kill himself. The surface ampule was clear, showing the reassuring golden tint of the liquid inside. Botulism toxin, mixed with a blend of sea snake and cone snail venom, along with other, synthetic ingredients. It was a noxious cocktail, fatal in large doses. It didn't impair his senses—not that his doctors had ever been able to determine—but he was still considered legally intoxicated for fifteen minutes following a dose.

Theodore slid the syringe into the meat of his burning thigh, barely noticing the sting, and pressed the plunger home. The ampule emptied into his flesh with a familiar biting, chilling sensation, like he was being swarmed by ants dipped in liquid nitrogen. He closed his eyes, counting backward from ten.

By the time he reached five, the pain was down to a manageable level.

By the time he reached zero, the pain was gone. He opened his eyes, taking a gasping breath as he tried to settle back into his own skin. The syringe still protruded from his leg. Gingerly, he pulled it free and went through the process of removing the needle and spent ampule, placing both in the biohazard bag in his passenger-side foot well. It wouldn't do to need to go through the needle-replacement process while hurting; he attached a fresh needle to the syringe before replacing it in the medical kit and returning the whole thing to his briefcase.

With the car on automatic, it was safe to get back to work. He withdrew a headset from his pocket and attached it to his left ear. "Dial Mr. Golden," he said.

"Dialing," said a female voice. The word was followed by several neutral chimes, less aggressive than ringing or beeping, designed to soothe the nerves of the caller.

Theodore had no nerves. He couldn't feel a thing.

"Blackwell," said the voice of James Golden, founder of Imagine Entertainment and still CEO, despite multiple attempts to oust him from his position. His age was catching up with him; his voice shook in a way it hadn't only a few years prior, a way that would have been unthinkable before the *Atargatis* incident. His time in the golden seat was coming to an end. The *Melusine* expedition was his last attempt to secure a legacy built on more than terrible science fiction movies and rumors of deaths at sea.

The poor fool didn't realize that nothing was ever going to eclipse the *Atargatis* in the public consciousness, no matter how compelling. Prove that mermaids were real and the conspiracy theorists would swarm out of the woodwork to paint the lost voyage as a sacrifice in the name of greater ratings, holding up the old footage and screaming about how it had been buried under the label of "hoax" and "special effect," conveniently ignoring the fact that their hands had been the ones to hold the shovel. Prove that mermaids weren't real, and well...

That simply didn't bear thinking about. "Here, sir," said Theodore.

"Well? Is your batty ex in?"

Jillian wasn't his ex; the divorce papers had never been signed, by either one of them. And she wasn't "batty." The loss of the *Atargatis* alone would have been proof of that. Everything else was merely support of the fact that her theories had been right from the beginning.

Theodore took a deep breath, shoving those thoughts to the

bottom of his consciousness, and said, "I believe so, yes. She had the conditions we'd anticipated and prepared for."

"Good. We need her."

And Jillian needed Imagine. Her presence would convince the cryptozoological and skeptic communities that there was no hoax, while also allowing the more legitimate scientists taking part in the voyage to excuse their involvement as an opportunity for a free cruise; once the existence of mermaids had been proven, her inclusion in the process would validate her life's work to the people who'd been writing her off as a crank for the past decade. Everyone would benefit from Jillian being on the ship.

"She raised some valid questions about the *Melusine*. The shutters are still unreliable, sir. They failed in three of the last five tests."

"Which means they succeeded in two. We're not going to need them. This ship sails with the best security money can buy."

In Theodore's experience, money was not the thing that made good security. Neither was managing your hiring quietly and through a casting agency, with aesthetics taking a higher degree of consideration than actual experience. "Still—"

"We got the Abneys to sign on. Those damn fish won't know what hit them."

Theodore resisted the urge to sigh. "If you say so, sir."

"And the Stewart girl? She's prepared?"

"She understands the restrictions placed on her research, and is willing to abide by them in exchange for being able to answer her questions about what happened to her sister. She'll be ready when we raise anchor."

"Good. Good. She's going to put our ratings through the roof." Golden sounded almost reflective, like he was leaving the real conversation for a parallel conversation that existed only in his own mind. That had been happening more and more frequently of late. There were times when Theodore worried about senility, about Golden losing his grasp on the present and retreating into the past, when he'd been young and strong and the touch of scandal had never come anywhere near him. It had to be tempting.

Golden sighed. "I didn't want to do this," he said. His voice was still distant; he might not be continuing his retreat, but he wasn't coming any closer to reality while he had any choice in the matter. "You know that, don't you?"

"I do, sir. This was the best choice for the company." That it would help others—giving Victoria Stewart the closure she needed, validating Jillian's research, doing similar things for the dozens of other people who were to be included on the voyage, improving their lives in ways both great and small—was almost beside the point. Imagine was Golden's legacy, and he'd do whatever he had to in order to protect it from the scolding eyes of time.

Everyone above a certain pay grade within the corporation knew that the *Atargatis* hadn't been lost; she had been attacked. They knew that the video footage was real, and unaltered. Had Imagine been able to control its release, that might not have been the case. They could have added a few zippers, a few inappropriate shadows, and allowed people to assume that some half-finished horror film had been leaked under the wrong name, while the *Atargatis* had been the victim of some more normal incident at sea. But Imagine hadn't been first on the scene. Imagine's people hadn't been the ones to find and view the footage, or the ones to release it. The United States Navy had done that. By the time spin control had been invited to the party, it had already been far too late.

Most people believed the footage to be false, which worked in the company's favor: it painted them as monsters who had tried to capitalize on a maritime disaster, but not as incompetents who had sailed blithely into danger. It also prevented others from attempting to capitalize on a discovery that rightfully belonged to the corporation.

The creatures that wiped out the *Atargatis* were real. They were unknown to science, their presence indicated by folklore and mythology around the world, and now that the seas were changing and humanity was looking to them for the hope of salvation, the chances of those creatures being found again—found officially, on the record—were increasing by the day. Discovery was inevitable.

Imagine needed to control that process.

That was where Golden's legacy would come into play: with an entertainment company so dedicated to the question of what had happened to its people that it was willing to risk another loss in order to bring about a greater discovery. Golden would get the honor of naming the creatures, of putting his stamp on the future, and he could die knowing he'd left Imagine in the best situation possible. The *Melusine* would sail because there was no other option. Perhaps there never had been.

"Everything is almost ready."

"Yes, sir."

"Are you sure you won't reconsider?"

"I am, sir."

"I'm not sure you understand how important you are to the day-to-day operation of my office, Theodore. I am . . . concerned."

"Jeanne is perfectly capable of taking over my duties on a short-term basis; I wouldn't want to hand her the job indefinitely, but I've documented my tasks for the next quarter, and she has more than enough support to get her through my absence." Theodore kept his voice calm, trying to sound as if his investment in this were purely professional. "It's essential we have someone on the *Melusine* who understands the importance of this voyage, and who will guide the researchers to the correct paths."

"I don't want to lose you."

"We're not expecting a repeat of the *Atargatis*, sir. Everything will be fine."

"When will you be back?"

"I should be in your office within the hour."

"Good. We'll discuss this further then." The line went dead.

Theodore sighed. Working for a media mogul at the end of his career had proven more stressful than he'd expected—and he'd gone into this career change with his eyes open, expecting to work harder than he'd ever worked in his life. Going from the deck of a fishing vessel to a desk job was a change, and a necessary one. With his injuries, the sea was no longer his to claim.

Except for this one last time. The *Melusine* was going to sail, and he was going to sail with her, come Hell or high water. He owed that much to the man he'd been and the woman he still loved.

Closing his eyes, Theodore Blackwell surrendered to the numbing effects of the painkillers washing through his system. There'd be time to worry about the future soon enough. That was the thing about the future. It didn't wait.

No matter how hard you tried to run, it always caught up with you in the end.

CHAPTER 5

Berkeley, California: August 6, 2022

The students who knew Dr. Jillian Toth only as a force of nature on the UC Berkeley campus wouldn't have recognized her. She'd left her car at home, taking BART into San Francisco. She'd paid for her ticket in cash, even though she had a perfectly good Clipper card; this was one trip she didn't want logged in anyone's computer. Once news about the second voyage broke, there would be unethical "journalists" looking for every angle they could find, looking for people to point at and mock. She'd be out of their reach. That wasn't true of the person she was on her way to see. Anything she could do to prevent being followed was worth doing, because soon she would be relevant again. Whether she wanted to be or not.

She got off the train at Embarcadero, then took the back stairwell to the surface. The cameras there were almost always broken, increasing the chances she could avoid having her face recorded. The air was stale and smelled of human urine and ancient marker fumes; she breathed shallowly, trying to focus on anything but the smell. One of the fluorescent lights was out of order, adding a horror movie flicker to the journey that she could have done without. There was such a thing as taking a motif too far, and that was exactly what this was—a motif. The people who were trying to preserve their privacy in an increasingly unprivate world often used tricks like this, creating unappealing zones where the people responsible for maintaining the cameras would be less likely to go. The blind spots would never get any bigger, but they could be sustained, if people were willing to work for them.

She'd come this way before; she knew how to hit her beats. No one bothered her as she walked from the station to the water, where wharfs and lightly decaying buildings replaced the streets. A surprising number of them were original construction, survivors of the battle against gentrification, now slowly losing their battle with the sea. Pier 39 had been the sacrifice to the tourist trade, sold off and turned into a theme park version of itself, complete with a standing antique carousel that still ran on the weekends. The rest of the waterfront was as it had always been: damp, sea-struck, and smelling of fresh fish, brackish water, and salt. Jillian paused and breathed in deeply, letting the Pacific fill her bones. She loved her teaching position at Berkeley, and the faculty housing that came with it, but sometimes she wished, desperately, that she could still live by the sea.

Lungs filled and soul finally content, she resumed her walk.

There had been a time when the San Francisco Bay was second only to Monterey in pounds of fish dredged out of the water. The whole city had eaten off the backs of the men and women who sailed here. These days, between die-offs and toxic algae blooms, the only boats left were the hobbyists and the lifers: the people who didn't really depend on the sea and the ones who'd been depending on it for so long that they'd rather starve behind the wheel than eat with dry land under their feet. Jillian's father had been a lifer, although he'd fished a different bay, and he'd died as he had lived, at the helm of his vessel, swallowed by the unforgiving waves. It had been hard to even mourn for him. It was the only way he would have ever wanted to go.

The wharf creaked underfoot, settling deeper into its foundations. The wood was slightly spongy. Not enough to feel rotten, but enough to soften her footsteps, keeping them from echoing. There were only a few vessels docked. A private sailboat, gleaming and pristine, probably owned by one of the few remaining tech millionaires; an old fishing tug, weathered and rusted but still functional, strewn with tangled, hand-knotted nets; a scientific vessel owned by the Academy of Sciences, its deck swarming with college students preparing to take samples from the body of the Bay. And a newer, sleeker fishing boat, well cared for, too new and bright and expensive for this place, for this time. It belonged twenty years in the past or fifty years in the future, when it would have been part of a fleet, not a relic reminder that once, things here had been different.

Jillian stomped as she got closer to the boat, trying to give some small warning that she was on the way. "Ahoy the ship," she called, stopping short of actually setting foot on the deck. "Is anyone home?"

There was a rustling noise from below deck. Jillian stayed where she was, waiting, until a head popped into view. The young woman had features similar to Jillian's own, open and expressive and lovely in the right light, currently contorted into a puzzled frown. Her dark hair was cut short, and she had her mother's sea-glass eyes, so green they looked artificial.

"Mom?" she said.

"Hi, Lani." Jillian smiled. She couldn't help herself. Excuses to visit her daughter were less common than she would have liked, and neither of them had it in them to seek out contact without good reason; that had never been their relationship, not even when Lani was a child. Growing up with her own hypervigilant parents had left Jillian relaxed, ready to let her only daughter take her own risks and her own chances. That was the only way to learn.

"Mom." Lani finished emerging from below deck, pulling herself stable with the rail. She had her father's height and wiry build; it would have taken two of her to make one of Jillian. "What are you doing here?"

"I wanted to see you."

Lani raised an eyebrow. "We both know that's not enough reason for you to come to San Francisco."

"May I board? There's something we need to discuss."

Lani hesitated, and in that hesitation, Jillian could see the last ten years of her life. Theodore's accident and the subsequent slow death of their marriage; Lani being forced to choose between her parents and finally, inevitably going with the father who seemed to need her more. Of the three of them, Jillian sometimes thought her daughter was the only one not foolish enough to hold out hope of a reconciliation. Lani had seen the worst of what they could be together, and she wanted no part of it.

Finally, almost grudgingly, Lani said, "Permission granted," and vanished back into her hole.

Jillian sighed and followed her. This never got any easier. Maybe that too was a good thing; maybe easy was too much to ask. But God, sometimes she wanted it.

Lani kept a clean ship, especially considering that the *We Remember* was a privately held fishing boat, designed for short trips out onto the Bay. Jillian politely didn't say anything about the cot against one wall. She knew Lani had lived on the boat before, and probably would again, if the economy continued the way it had. As long as her daughter was healthy and reasonably happy, she would leave well enough alone.

"Coffee?" Lani pushed past the folding table that dominated the living space, heading for the hot plate and battered stainless steel pot on the counter. Brewing in glass was dangerous when there was a chance of high winds coming up and blowing everything out of place.

"No, thank you." Jillian sank into a folding chair, managing not to wince as the bolts on the side bit into her thighs. She was proud of her daughter for finding her place in the world, but sometimes she wished that place were slightly less narrow. "Have you spoken to your father recently?"

Lani froze. Then, slowly, she said, "No. I haven't. I know he's been busy with his work." *As have you*, was the silent accusation.

Jillian nodded, accepting the unspoken criticism without complaint. Objecting to the truth did no good. "Imagine is assembling another voyage to the Mariana Trench. Mr. Golden seems to want to validate his legacy by proving that what happened to the *Atargatis* was outside of his control. He wants to prove that mermaids exist. I've been invited to accompany the researchers."

"Will you?"

"Yes." Jillian looked levelly at her daughter. "I think I owe the world that much, don't you?"

Lani said nothing.

The assumption in most circles was that the Toth-Blackwells had separated because Jillian couldn't handle the changes in Theodore after his accident. Jillian hated that people thought of her that way, as someone so shallow that she'd give up on the man she loved simply because he was no longer capable of running down the deck of a moving ship with a net in one hand and a live lobster in the other. She let the assumption stand. It was, in its own way, less damaging to her, both personally and professionally. No one wanted to be the person who would give up on a loved one for such a petty reason, but everyone was, on some level. People *understood* the idea that Theo's accident could have driven them apart.

What people wouldn't understand or forgive her for was what she'd done.

Imagine had funded much of her early research, and those studies had been the basis for the *Atargatis* mission. She had been the one to pinpoint the Mariana Trench as the most likely spot for mermaids to not only exist, but exist in large-enough numbers that a sighting—that interaction—might be possible. She hadn't sailed with the voyage, in part because she'd still been trying to be a good wife, to help her husband adjust to his new circumstances, and in part because Imagine's contracts would have left it in control of far more of her research than she was comfortable with.

And on some level... She'd reviewed legends and sightings from around the world to settle on the Mariana Trench. She didn't consider herself a credulous woman. She studied mermaids because she *knew* they existed, that they were going to be brought to the surface in her lifetime, and that she was probably not going to be the one to discover them. She was uncomfortable in tight spaces, which meant she was never going to live a submariner's life, and that was where the action was. Down, deep down, below the photic zones, in the places where only the most powerful and specialized equipment could go. So she'd looked at each recorded sighting with open eyes, studying them for commonalities, considering the cultural differences behind the features the stories focused on, and in the end she'd been able to come to only one conclusion:

Mermaids weren't mammalian. They couldn't be. Too many sightings focused on their "slender backs" and "narrow waists"—features that seemed reasonable to modern readers with modern beauty standards, but which made no sense for an Italian fisherman during the plague years, or a Puerto Rican swimmer in the 1920s. If the mermaid had been an idealized projection of a human woman onto a marine mammal, she would have looked different every time, fat during some eras, thin during others, not consistently slim to the point of freezing in oceanic waters. The people who described mermaids were describing a real creature, something that wasn't mammalian, but looked mammalian enough to make a tempting lure. And why would anything lure sailors, if not as a form of sustenance?

Imagine had offered her a contract she hadn't wanted to sign, and so she hadn't signed it, but she hadn't attempted to negotiate it either. She hadn't suggested changes, or involved her lawyer, or done anything to get herself a place on the *Atargatis*, because when she came right down to it, *she hadn't wanted one*. She'd looked at her data, everything she'd derived from primary and secondary sources, and she'd seen the shadow of a creature she hadn't wanted to meet. Not then, not now, and not ever. Certainly not in the middle of the ocean, with no high ground to run for.

She'd given Imagine the map to the mermaid, and she'd shown them the shadow of the mermaid, and when the time had come to set sail, she'd said, "No, thank you," using intellectual property as an excuse, and stayed safe at home. Everyone knew she'd consulted on the voyage—anyone who'd ever whispered the word *mermaid* during a scientific conference had consulted on the voyage in one way or another—but few people realized how deep that consultation had gone. Or how many people had died because of the answers she'd been in a position to provide.

Her career was a shipwreck. At least it was a shipwreck that she had, thus far, managed to survive. That was more than she could say for the ones who'd sailed upon the *Atargatis*. But the guilt, ah . . .

The guilt was the reef upon which her marriage had crashed, combining with all the other factors to make their love unsustainable. Sometimes she thought she was still crashing there, drowning inch by inch under the weight of what she'd done. If she had the chance to swim out and free herself, why shouldn't she take it? Why *wouldn't* she take it? Her daughter was grown. Her husband was gone. She was only living for her work, and none of her colleagues could look at her without smirking anymore. Go out with the second ship, see the shadow of the mermaid, and get . . . something back. Not her life. Probably not her reputation.

Maybe her peace of mind.

"We sail in two weeks," said Jillian. "Imagine has assembled another research team. I imagine I'll know a few of them. I imagine most of them will know me, by reputation if nothing else. It should be a fascinating journey."

"Does Dad know?"

"He's the one who invited me to go."

Lani laughed, short and bitter. "Wow. I can't tell if that's his tomcat way of giving you a dead mouse so you'll love him again, or if it's him trying to get you killed so he can move on. Want to take a bet?"

It was Jillian's turn to say nothing and look silently at her daughter. Lani looked away first.

"I'm sorry," she said. "That was mean."

"Something being mean doesn't mean it isn't true. You know your father and I love each other. We always will. Sometimes loving each other isn't enough to make up for all the things you know about another person."

She knew Theo had sold his freedom, his integrity, and even his original face to Imagine, allowing them to sculpt her rough-and-tumble eco-warrior husband into the perfect, poised assistant, not a hair out of place, not a harsh word on his lips. He knew she'd sent the entire crew of the *Atargatis* to their deaths while she stood safe on the shore, blissfully removed from the carnage. What was the point in finalizing their divorce? They would always be married where it counted, in the horrors they had shared.

"You're really going to go?"

Jillian nodded. "I have to. This is my chance to set things right. If I don't take it, I might as well go home and sign those divorce papers right now, because I'm never going to be this brave again."

"*Mom.*" Lani closed the distance between them and looped her arms around her mother's shoulders. After a second's surprised blinking, Jillian embraced her daughter in return, pulling her close, breathing in the good, salty smell of her skin, so like the sea, so unlike anything else in the world.

They held their embrace for what felt like forever, Jillian relaxing until the world was right for the first time in years. She was with her daughter, the floor rocking beneath their feet as a steady reminder that they were at sea. Lani had grown up on boats like this one, refitted whaling boats, scientific research vessels, yachts—anything that would set sail, that would get their little family away from the land

and out to sea where they belonged. All the good memories Jillian had of her family had taken place at sea.

"Be careful out there," Lani said, pulling away. "I know you want to make things right, but I don't...If you have to go, I want you to come home again."

"I will, sweetie," said Jillian. "You know I will. I'm a scientist, remember? Imagine knows what's out there this time. I'll be fine."

Her words hung between them, holding every hallmark of a lie. There was no way to prove it, and so they simply smiled at each other and let the moment go.

ZONE TWO: PHOTIC

Are mermaids real? Yes. Are mermaids friendly? No. Why is this so hard?

—Dr. Jillian Toth

Mankind has a responsibility to the sea. We owe it our lives.

—Theodore Blackwell

...by placing responsibility for the failure of the *Atargatis* mission on the members of her crew, or better yet, on mechanical failure, Imagine might have been able to avoid being tarred in the eyes of the world. After all, the company had hired the best of the best to sail that ill-fated voyage; they could hardly be held responsible for what happened to the ship after it was outside the range of easy rescue. They could have gotten away clean, had they been a little less devoted to doing the jobs that we, the public, had asked them to do:

We had asked them to entertain us. They were dedicated to doing exactly that. To putting the world on film and casting it in a fantastic light for our amusement. In order to accomplish this, there were no fewer than a dozen cameras running on the *Atargatis* at any given time.

There was no chance Imagine could avoid culpability in the matter of the *Atargatis* mission. The courts might have been willing to forgive them, but the people never did. For James Golden, prison might have been kinder.

—From *Imagine: Fall of an Empire*, by Peter Giles, originally published 2019

What you have to understand about the mermaid legend is that it's universal. No matter where you go, the mermaids got there first. Even inland, if there's a big-enough lake, I guarantee you there's a local community with a story about women in the water with beautiful voices who lure men to their deaths.

Where there's water, we find mermaids. Maybe it's time we started asking ourselves exactly why that is.

—Transcript from the lecture "Mermaids: Myth or Monster," given by Dr. Jillian Toth

CHAPTER 6

San Diego, California: August 18, 2022

Sunrise painted the sky over the San Diego harbor rosy pink and dandelion gold. The sea was a burnished sheet of silver, motionless to the naked eye. A few sailboats dotted the horizon, but it was otherwise an abandoned frontier, waiting for the *Melusine* to get under way.

Like most vessels of her size, the *Melusine* bore a striking resemblance to a floating hotel. The staterooms facing the water—some intended for occupation, others for use as labs during the voyage—were set back from the hull, creating balcony-like "halls" separated from the sea by intricate railings. Each deck's ceiling was the next deck's floor, until the top, with its wide open spaces, put an end to the wedding cake–esque assembly. It was huge and grand, designed as much for stunning presence as for functionality.

Two figures stood on the fourth deck. A slender, unsmiling slip of a woman, pale blonde hair blowing in her eyes, a microphone in her hand, and a tall, cheerfully chubby man with a handlebar mustache, holding a camera. The woman was all in white—white slacks, a white corset top, white high-heeled shoes utterly impractical for her shipboard setting—while the man was more relaxed in board shorts and a Hawaiian shirt.

"We're good in five, four, three..." The man counted off the last two numbers on his fingers.

When he hit "one," the woman's face blossomed into a welcoming smile that invited viewers to ask about her day or tell her about their D&D characters. Olivia Sanderson, geek goddess and current professional face of the Imagine Network, had been honing her image for years and knew exactly what balance to strike in order to get her point across.

"This is Olivia, coming to you from the deck of the *Melusine*. This mighty research vessel has been constructed for a single essential purpose: to return to the Mariana Trench and finally answer the question of what happened to our friends, our companions, and our idols those seven years ago." She paused, letting her expression go wistful, feeding the camera several seconds of empty space.

(That empty space was a calculated choice on the part of her editors, who had asked for it specifically. It would be replaced with a clip of the original research team waving to another camera, in another time. Connect to the past but represent the future and the world can be yours.)

Returning to the present, Olivia summoned back her smile, which was even brighter this time. "What is the *Melusine*, you might ask? As the largest privately owned research vessel in the world, this floating city has a crew of over two hundred, and an occupant capacity of almost a thousand. We're sailing with only four hundred people, a mixture of crewmen, scientists, researchers, animal behaviorists, and, of course, our camera crew. I'll be your guide through this voyage, translating our findings for the layman, while Professor Pixels back at headquarters will be taking you through the science. You're a part of this journey as much as any of the people on board, and with your help we can answer the mystery of what happened to the *Atargatis* once and for all."

She stopped, still smiling. Ray flashed her a thumbs-up.

"You're clear," he said, lowering the camera. "Good work."

"I didn't sound too treacly?"

"Not at all. You didn't sound like you were about to start ripping out throats with your teeth either. You found the balance, and you held it." Ray hit the button to upload his footage to the cloud, where the techs at Imagine could grab it and start getting it ready for prime time. Nothing would be released until they had proof the mermaids were out there, but once they did, the programming directors wanted to be ready to roll. Imagine would be all-mermaid, all-the-time before the non-Imagine media had a chance to catch their breath. "You want me to get you some establishing shots of the dock? People should start getting here anytime."

"Just give me a second," said Olivia.

Ray nodded. "All right. I'll be checking light levels on the water if you need me." He wandered a few feet down the deck and pointed his camera at the ocean, giving her the space she needed.

Olivia was grateful, even as she knew Ray would tell her she didn't need to be if she mentioned it. She was always grateful. He'd been assigned to her when she did her first San Diego Comic-Con report, a skinny nineteen-year-old dressed like Emma Frost, trying to get people to talk to her microphone and not her tits. She'd been terrified, right until she'd realized that somehow her genial, nonthreatening cameraman had pulled himself up another foot and developed the sort of shoulders that would give a linebacker pause. He was her protector when she needed one and her friend when she needed one of those even more.

Ray was the reason the two of them had been the first non–crew members to set foot on the *Melusine*. One of his cousins worked for the company supplying the mess, and he'd been able to talk their way into their cabins a day early. That gave them a night to walk the ship without fear of tripping over someone who was trying to do serious work. Half of the news was about being prepared.

The other half was about looking good on camera. Olivia pulled out her compact, checking that her lip gloss was even and her eye shadow was unsmudged. She needed to make a good first impression with the people she was about to sail with. Speaking of...

A black town car pulled up at the barrier established by Imagine security. The rear doors opened and two people climbed out. The woman was gawky in that seaside way, like she was more comfortable on a surfboard or a ship than she'd ever be on land. She wore khaki slacks and a white polo shirt, and had tanned skin and brownish hair in a ponytail. There was something familiar about the shape of her face, even at this distance.

"Hey, Ray," said Olivia. She pointed. "Why do I know her?"

"Because that's Victoria Stewart, Anne's sister," said Ray, moving to stand beside her. "I think she goes by Tory, or something like that. She's our sonar specialist."

"The man with her?" He was taller, skinnier, and darker skinned, with shaggy black hair and a distracted expression. His clothes were almost identical to Victoria's, which either meant they came from the same university, or they shared a closet. Given how much longer his legs were, the former seemed like a better bet.

"That's Luis Martines, her research partner."

"Another sonography guy?"

"Not quite. Third-generation American, son of Silicon Valley billionaire Antonio Martines and his wife, Marianna Martines. One sister, Angela. He could buy this boat, if he wanted it. He's less about sonar and more about oceanic megafauna."

"Oceanic...?"

"Big fucking animals below the surface of the sea. Whales and elephant seals and colossal squid. I read his paper on the probability of a surviving population of megalodon, including predictions of where they'd be found if extant. He's good. A little immature when it comes to concluding arguments, but he's got potential."

Olivia rolled her eyes. "Could you sound more pretentious if you tried, do you think, or have you reached the limit of your powers?"

"You have yet to see the limit of my powers," said Ray, and boomed laughter.

Olivia rolled her eyes again, but she was grinning. "I've seen a few."

Ray laughed again, less loudly, and began filming the people below them, resting the camera on his massive shoulder.

Before he'd become a cameraman, Ray had been a mixed martial arts fighter, good enough to make it to the international finals on multiple occasions. He'd been considered a contender for the big titles and the big money that came with them—the sort of money that came with a permanent "get out of jail free" card, the kind that could buy lawyers and mansions and accountants good enough to keep most of it in the pockets of its earner. Then he'd blown out both his knees during a fight, badly enough that it had taken most of the money he'd already socked away to pay for reconstructive surgeries. Oh, his insurance was willing to do enough of the repair to make him *functional* again, but he didn't want *functional*. He wanted to walk and dance and run and live his life as painlessly as possible.

The end result was a miracle of modern medicine, the sort of semibionic implant that would have been a fantasy a decade ago—and which was, amusingly enough, partially funded by grants from Imagine. The company had been investing in medical research since before the *Atargatis*, paying for the sort of advances that would never make enough money to be viable for publicly traded medical companies, which preferred to focus on wider-spectrum applications. But Imagine was in entertainment. If it wanted to invest in loss leaders and philanthropic therapies, it was welcome to do so. The results were bionic knees and nerve regrowth and genetic treatments for autoimmune disorders, and even though everyone knew the fading health of James Golden was the driving force behind those choices, the world reaped the benefits, and Imagine made millions, while repairing a few of the cracks in its public image.

Ray had finished physical therapy, been certified healthy if no longer fit for the ring, and made his way straight to Imagine headquarters in Burbank, California, to apply for a job. Any job. Whatever they wanted him to do, he was happy to do it, as thanks for the second chance he'd been given. (It didn't hurt that he'd spent so much of his savings on his new knees that he *needed* a job that didn't involve kicking people for money. Something cushy and low impact. After his previous career, anything would have seemed cushy and low impact.)

Some people, seeing a mountain that walked like a man step into the office, would have called security. Others would have smiled and explained that unfortunately, they did not have any job opportunities for natural rock formations. But Theodore Blackwell, smarting from his own most recent surgery, had been at the recruitment desk the day Ray Marino arrived to look for work. He'd looked at the man, at the skills on his résumé, and he'd thought about Imagine's latest generation of professional faces, the ones who'd been chosen through website participant vote, the ones who trended small and sylph-like and terrifyingly breakable.

"It says here that you took a cinematography class in high school," he'd said. "Did you enjoy working with the camera?"

"I did," Ray had replied, surprised. "Why do you ask?"

And Theo had smiled.

Now here they were, years and assignments and Imagine-funded training courses later, and Ray was one of the most in-demand cameramen in the company. His eye for composition was unique and still surprising to viewers, without crossing the line into being difficult to follow. He had a unique visual "voice," and could have left Imagine for a career in more reputable media. He might have done it too, if not for Olivia. She needed him. She needed the security of a cameraman who understood her, who wouldn't be put off by her little idiosyncrasies, like her fervent attempts to get to any given site at least a day early. He wasn't even sure most of the company knew she did that. He'd seen her paying for their first hotel nights on a separate card, one that didn't bill to Imagine, with a look on her face that was almost ashamed. He hadn't said anything then, and he wasn't going to say anything now. She was Olive, she was his partner, and he was going to stay with Imagine for as long as she needed him. Even if it was forever.

Some Imagine porters appeared below, assisting Victoria and Luis with their bags. The town car must have been bigger on the inside than the outside, because the luggage just kept coming, from the expected suitcases and duffel bags to a series of hard-shelled cases that clearly contained scientific equipment.

Next to him, Olivia whistled, long and low. "That's the case for a Serranko-brand handheld mass spectrometer," she said. "Those things cost a quarter of a million dollars, and they're accurate to point zero one parts per *billion*. If you fed it the DNA for a specific snake, it could find one scale in a gallon of swamp water."

"That is some distressingly specific scientific knowledge you're throwing down, Olive," said Ray, giving her a sidelong look. "You planning to switch careers on me?"

"Ex-girlfriend used to talk about the Serranko series like they were sex toys," said Olivia. "I sort of memorized their product catalog for pillow talk. Which means they still send me catalogs. Paper catalogs on this thick, glossy paper that you *know* costs almost a dollar a page. It's amazing. It really is science porn."

"That makes marginally more sense," said Ray.

Another car pulled up next to the first. A tall, imposingly built woman in a UC Berkeley sweatshirt got out, holding a valise in one hand. She turned toward the *Melusine*, and not even the distance between them could disguise the hatred in her face. Olivia's eyes widened.

"Whoa," she breathed.

"Okay, that's somebody I don't want to meet in a dark corridor once we're out in the middle of the ocean," said Ray. "I think she might murder someone with a fishhook."

"Don't even joke."

"I'm not even joking."

Victoria had spotted the newcomer. She was approaching her with hands that were visibly shaking, even at this distance, while Luis trailed along behind.

"What do you think that's about?" asked Ray.

"*That* is Dr. Jillian Toth," said Olivia. She stretched onto her toes and leaned forward, gripping the rail tight, until her feet were on the verge of leaving the deck. Ray fought the urge to grab her and force her feet back down to the ground. She was a big girl. If she wanted to do something ludicrously dangerous, she was allowed.

He *did* subtly reorient his camera to capture her balancing on the rail like some strange white bird preparing to take flight. Footage of Olivia being whimsical was rare enough to be money in the bank, even if it would have to be stripped of all context before it could be used.

"They're shaking hands," reported Olivia. "Victoria looks like she's about to pee her pants, she's so excited. That makes sense. Dr. Toth is kind of a big deal."

"Dr. Toth being...?" Ray prompted. "Talk to the camera, Liv. The camera needs to hear from you."

"World's foremost scientific expert on mermaids—no, really, that's an actual thing an actual human decided to do with their life, and I guess I'm not one to talk, since I'm out here dressed like an off-brand Emma Frost to avoid Marvel's copyright lawyers—and pretty much the only person who turned down a spot on the *Atargatis*, which means she's also incredibly sane. If this ship starts going down, get next to Dr. Toth. She'll glare the water into staying away from you."

"I don't think that's physically possible."

"But won't it be fun to find out?"

On the dock, Dr. Toth had extricated herself from Victoria and was handing her equipment to the porters. More cars were appearing, faster now, like the first two arrivals had broken some sort of invisible seal. Victoria kept hold of her mass spectrometer like it was her baby and she was terrified of what anyone else might do; Luis annoyed the porters by trying to help them, and Dr. Toth...

Dr. Toth paced toward the *Melusine*, hands by her sides, eyes raking along the sides of the great ship. Whatever she saw there didn't seem to impress her; her scowl never wavered, as etched into her face as the lines between her eyebrows and at the corners of her mouth. Ray zoomed in on her, trying to get a decent shot. The light must have glinted off his lens when he moved the camera, because Dr. Toth turned to look directly at him, raising an eyebrow in silent judgment before she calmly, deliberately flipped him off and walked back toward Victoria and Luis.

"Shit," said Ray, lowering the camera. "We've got a postproduction problem child."

"Hmm?"

"Dr. Toth just gave me the bird."

Olivia wrinkled her nose. "Oh. Well. Isn't that just dandy."

Imagine wasn't a cheap company; it was, as it had always been, willing to throw money at projects that needed it, providing the need was genuine and not a case of mismanagement or embezzling. That didn't mean the accountants appreciated spending money when they didn't have to. Postproduction problem children did things on camera to make it harder to use the footage. They swore or made obscene gestures or exposed parts of their body that weren't supposed to appear on prime-time network television. They required that footage be censored, whether it was with beeps or blurs, and that took both time and money, and could call down the wrath of the programming directors. Especially when those problem children appeared on a supposedly "unedited" program, like this one. Every blur was a reminder to the audience at home that this "unfiltered reality" was as carefully staged and managed as any scripted show.

It wasn't good. If Dr. Toth was one of their senior researchers, she was going to have to appear on camera, and if she was going to make a habit of flipping off the lens, she was going to need to be managed.

"Isn't this going to be fun?" muttered Ray, and kept filming.

Car after car arrived on the dock below the *Melusine*. Imagine porters swarmed from vehicle to vehicle, grabbing luggage and equipment, tagging it with the appropriate markers—green for private bags, which would be piled up in the dining hall for individual passengers to collect once they knew where their bunks were located; red for public labs; yellow for private labs—before dragging it away, leaving the people behind. There was a horrifying amount of luggage. Everyone Imagine had selected to sail with the *Melusine* was a professional, from chemists and biologists to radar and sonar technicians. There were analysts, technicians, even administrative assistants who'd be helping to coordinate the research being done on the boat. That didn't mean any of these people had known exactly what to pack for a task of this size, or really knew what they were getting into.

A battered Jeep pulled up to the staging area, disgorging two people in khaki uniforms that would have looked more reasonable on a jungle safari than they did at a suburban dock. The shorter of the two slammed the driver's side door, put his hands on his hips, and eyed the ship speculatively.

"Think she'll float?" he asked. He had a French-Canadian accent to go with his fish-belly complexion, and the easy stance of a man who'd never met a challenge he couldn't handle, one way or another. A slouch hat dangled halfway down his back, held in place by a rawhide cord.

"If she doesn't, this'll be the easiest payday we've ever had," said his companion, a striking woman of Japanese descent. She was easily a foot taller than he was, and her hair was cut in a no-nonsense buzz. Her accent was Australian, thick enough to smear on toast. She removed a long case from the back seat of the Jeep before waving the porters imperiously toward the vehicle. "Careful not to drop anything, all right? About half of it explodes if you annoy it, and it's all been sanctioned by Imagine, so no 'accidentally' forgetting to carry my grenades."

The nearest porter stopped in the act of reaching for a box. "Which one has the grenades?" he asked, in a strained tone.

The woman flashed a gregarious smile. "Not telling," she said. "If you don't drop anything, it shouldn't matter."

The porter blanched and grabbed the box, scurrying away. The woman laughed as the man gave her a reproachful look.

"Now, Michi, what did we say about torturing the hired help?"

"That it's damned funny, and I'm not going to stop unless I'm given a solid reason to do so."

The man opened his mouth like he was going to say something. Then he stopped and grinned. "Oh, right," he said. "That's exactly what we said. Let's go meet the locals." Together, they turned and started toward the *Melusine*, leaving the porters to carry their things. They had enough weapons on them to survive until they were settled. They always did.

Jacques and Michi Abney weren't the best big game hunters in the business. The best would never have considered going on television, allowing their faces to be plastered across vidscreens and billboards the world over. Every year brought another layer of pointless regulations to the hunt, and sometimes having a recognizable face was the difference between successfully bribing a guard to let you into the wildlife preserve and being arrested on sight as a poacher. It was all a bunch of tree-hugging bullshit as far as Jacques was concerned. The big game would be gone outside of zoos in another twenty years whether he took some of it home or not. The white rhino was proof of that. All the conservation efforts in the world, and for what? So the last wild male could die of old age, surrounded by armed guards he couldn't understand, as much a captive of mankind as any zoo-bound specimen? At least the animals in the zoos didn't know what they were missing.

No. Better to give the beasts the honor of a good, clean death while the wild was there to witness it. If there was a heaven for lions, Jacques had sent six of them there all by himself, and he fully expected to send another dozen to join them before he got too old to deal with the expense and difficulty of the veldt. It was the least he could do for the big animals that had brought him so much joy and given so much purpose to his life.

Michi wasn't as much of one for lions and the like. She was allergic to cats, and thought safaris were unhygienic. Her passion was for the sea. She came from a whaling family that had hunted whales off the coast of Japan for centuries. It was only during the last hundred years that foreign do-gooders had insisted the whaling industry cut back, triggering a series of events that had led her parents to immigrate to Australia, where she'd grown up surfing, swimming, and shark fishing. Bringing in a great white wasn't the same as taking down a blue whale, but it was close enough. And now the bastards were trying to restrict that as well, saying the seas were in a delicate phase and needed humanity to act as "stewards" to the animals that remained.

They'd met on a fishing expedition, her angling for her first orca, him looking to bring home a leopard seal. It had been love at first sight. Michi was open about and proud of her hunting background, and it hadn't been long before Jacques was right there with her, trading anonymity for celebrity and the opportunities it carried. He might never sneak into another restricted wildlife park, but he'd been called by quite successful zoos to put down violent or unneeded animals—and with the amount of security in most remaining animal sanctuaries, a hunt through a good animal habitat could be better than the real thing. It was like using porn in place of traditional foreplay. Sure, it might ruin you for the old way, but since when had mankind ever been focused on the old way? Onward and upward, that was the ticket.

Imagine was paying them half a million dollars, each, to be on board the *Melusine*, talk to the cameras, and take out anything that attacked it. Best-case scenario, nothing happened, and they walked away a combined cool mil richer, making mocking noises about mermaid hunters who liked to throw their money away. Worst-case scenario, monsters from the deep tried to take out the ship, and they got famous beyond their wildest dreams for being the first humans to kill a mermaid live on camera. (It was difficult to call that outcome "worst." Jacques had actually salivated at the thought of killing something out of myth, and the sex they'd had the night they signed their contracts had been incredible. This trip was going to be good for them.)

Luis and Victoria were still standing, talking to Dr. Toth, when the bounty hunters walked by. Luis's head whipped around, eyes narrowing in wary disbelief.

"Luis?" Tory touched his arm. "What's wrong?"

"I know them," he said. "They have a web series about killing things."

Dr. Toth rolled her eyes. "Of course they do," she muttered. "God forbid Imagine send out a second ship without making a show of force. The first voyage had women paid to dress up like mermaids, ours gets hired killers. Ever wish you were on the *Atargatis* instead?"

"Every day," said Tory.

Luis was just getting warmed up. "They crashed a Bigfoot

convention last year. Came in with a dead orangutan and started laughing at everyone for being stupid enough to think we could share a continent with a hominid primate without them catching and killing it. People were shouting, crying, one guy threw up...It was a mess. It was just a mess. Why are they here? They shouldn't be here."

"They're here to kill mermaids," said Dr. Toth. "Imagine lost one voyage. They're not going to want to lose a second. It would look like carelessness, and if there's one thing James Golden doesn't want to be remembered for, it's carelessness. It's—" She cut herself off in the middle of her sentence, eyes going wide and face going pale. "Excuse me," she said, shoving her valise at Tory.

Caught off guard, Tory took the valise. She held it awkwardly as Dr. Toth ran across the dock, weaving around porters and passengers alike, toward a man who was getting out of his car. He was tall, handsome in a carefully average way, wearing a tailored suit—her own eyes widened in unconscious parody of Dr. Toth's expression.

"Isn't that the man who broke into our lab? Mr. Blackwell?"

Luis squinted. "Looks like it," he said.

"What's he *doing* here?"

"Whatever it is, Dr. Toth doesn't look happy about it." She was yelling and gesturing emphatically. They were too far away for her words to carry, but they didn't need to: her posture was telegraphing her displeasure. Luis wrinkled his nose. "I would *not* want her looking at me like that. Think she's going to ask us to help her hide a body?"

"Maybe. I hope not. But maybe."

Mr. Blackwell said something to Dr. Toth, raising his hands, palms outward, in what may have been intended as a soothing gesture. She responded by slapping them away, pointing to the *Melusine*, and continuing to yell.

"Think they know each other?"

Tory snorted. "If they don't, I think they're about to."

"Seriously, though, that's not the way you yell at some corporate shill. I've seen my dad yell at plenty of people who work for him, and there's a different tenor to it. Like, he's mad, but it's not personal. This is personal." Luis frowned. "And now they're coming over here. Swell."

"Yeah, swell," mumbled Tory. With Dr. Toth's valise in her hands, they couldn't flee for the safety of the *Melusine*—not without either dropping the other woman's things on the dock or sort of stealing them. Neither seemed like a good idea.

Mr. Blackwell limped. Not severely; it was more of a hitch in his stride than anything extreme. But everything else about him was so carefully calibrated and designed that it stuck out, a flaw in an otherwise perfect machine.

"Thank you," said Dr. Toth, holding her hand out for her valise. Tory surrendered it willingly. "Theo tells me he's already met both of you, so introductions are unnecessary. Theo *also* tells me he's planning to come on this voyage. This is proof that even smart people can be wrong."

"Imagine's insurance carriers were reluctant to approve another sea voyage after what happened to the last one," said Mr. Blackwell. Tory couldn't think of him as Theo. When she tried, it was like her brain shied away from the idea. "In order to get them to sign off, we had to agree to send a corporate observer on the trip. I am Mr. Golden's right-hand man. It only made sense that it would be me."

"You're Golden's chief flunky, which is why it makes *no* sense for it to be you," countered Dr. Toth. "He needs you landlocked and accessible, not riding herd on this bucket of wet cats. Don't you dare get on that ship."

"You don't have the authority to tell me what to do, Professor," said Blackwell. There was a note of unfamiliar teasing in his voice, like this was a conversation the two of them had had many times. Tory and Luis exchanged a look.

"I *do* have the authority to push you off the pier," muttered Dr. Toth.

"That may be so, but you won't do it." Blackwell nodded to Tory and Luis. "Glad to have you aboard." Then he walked on, heading for the *Melusine*. After a moment's glaring, Dr. Toth followed.

"What do you think *that* was about?" asked Luis.

"I think this is going to be an interesting voyage, that's what," said Tory. "Come on. We don't want to miss orientation." She started toward the ship, Luis beside her. If she kept her eyes focused straight ahead, she could pretend that Anne was there too, walking on her other side, ready to crack the biggest story of her career, ready to solve the mystery of what had killed her.

CHAPTER 7

San Diego Harbor, California: August 18, 2022

The *Melusine* was a luxury research vessel, outfitted with the latest in cutting-edge equipment. It had also been designed by one of the largest entertainment companies in the world, with people who understood what audiences wanted to see involved with every stage of construction. That was why, when they arrived in the main dining hall and assembly space, more than a few of the passengers gasped, looking around in wide-eyed amazement.

(Ray and the other cameramen were already there, waiting to catch the wonderment on camera. Some reaction shots could only be taken once. It was possible to stage a lot of things—more than most people would have believed possible—but genuine surprise and amazement didn't work that way. People could tell when they weren't real.)

The dining hall was easily the size of a high school gymnasium, taking up the equivalent of two floors at the center of the *Melusine*. It wasn't just for show: that raised cathedral ceiling reduced the vessel's overall weight by creating a bubble of open space at its center. The polished oak walls were filigreed with swoops and swirls of shell inlay that occasionally, seemingly at random, formed the Imagine logo. Each panel could be reversed to reveal a touch-sensitive work screen, allowing scientists to stream video, share data, or even call home; the *Melusine*, unlike the *Atargatis*, was equipped with the latest

94

in data streaming and cloud technology. The ship could vanish without a trace and not a scrap of research would be lost.

Bit by bit, the room filled with the specialists, researchers, and technicians Imagine had tapped for this historic journey. Some of them knew each other already: old friends, old lovers, old rivals. "The seas are huge but oceanography is small," as Dr. Peter Harris once said, before he became a victim of the *Atargatis* disaster. Many of them were already laughing, seeming to treat the experience as more of a pleasure cruise than a serious scientific expedition.

Tory stuck close to Luis, grimacing as one of those familiar faces walked by: Jason, alongside the professor who was supervising his graduate work in photosynthesis below the photic zone. It happened—the mere existence of chlorophyll-bearing plants on the seafloor confirmed it—but as it happened in the absence of visible light, no one was sure exactly *how*. Jason was pursuing chemical alternatives. His advisor was pursuing a Nobel Prize for stabilizing the world's seaweed farms. Jason didn't seem to believe that his advisor's ambitions posed any danger to his own work, and after they'd stopped dating, Tory had given up on explaining it to him. Let him get his research stolen because he was too arrogant to cover his own ass.

A pair of redheaded women entered, their hands flashing in rapid ASL.

A heavily tattooed, incredibly pale man in a lab coat walked in, eyes fixed on his tablet. He looked like he was supposed to be bouncing drunks at a bar in West Hollywood, not ambling around the *Melusine*. Maybe that was the reason for the lab coat: it made him seem more like a part of the scene and less like someone who'd gotten lost on his way to a riot.

More and more people appeared, until the sheer size of the voyage began sinking in. Even with conversation at a minimum, the noise was appalling. Whispers, sneezes, even breathing all seemed amplified by proximity.

There was a stage at one end of the room. A man in white slacks and a button-down white shirt walked onto it, a captain's hat perched on his head and his attire carefully calculated to give him a military air without crossing the line into stolen valor. A woman in a floral dress followed him, hanging back a few feet, like she wanted to avoid drawing focus.

The man stopped at the center of the stage, folding his hands behind his back. The woman stopped in turn, still a few feet behind. When the crowd did not immediately fall silent, he cleared his throat. Microphones in the ceiling picked up the sound, amplifying it until it was audible in every corner of the large room.

Everyone stopped talking except the two signing women. They continued to argue until the lights flashed. They lowered their hands and turned toward the stage.

"Welcome to the *Melusine*," said the man. Behind him, the woman in the floral dress signed in rapid translation. She was a sign language interpreter, then, presumably there for the sake of the two women.

"I will be your captain for this voyage; my name is Marcus Peterman," said the man. "You can call me Captain, or sir. I am responsible for everything pertaining to the safety and operation of this vessel, and in those areas this voyage is entirely under my command. For all other purposes our sponsor, Imagine Entertainment, will be directing our journey. The woman behind me is Hallie Wilson, who will be providing sign language interpretation during our voyage. Should you need her to assist you for any reason, please make your request through the Wilson twins, as she is primarily here to help you communicate with them."

The redheaded women waved to the people around them, unnecessarily identifying themselves as the Wilson twins.

Captain Peterman continued: "Most of you are sailing with us for the purpose of continuing and completing personal research. Any contracts you have are between you and Imagine. I will not be assisting with the interpretation of those contracts. My crew is not available to assist with your research, although they will be glad to help with any problems relating to the well-being of this vessel. Like you, we are employed by Imagine. Unlike you, we are here to make sure everything goes smoothly, and that you return safely home." He didn't need to mention the *Atargatis*. The ghost of that earlier voyage was all around them. The *Melusine* was a haunted house. She had been since the day she'd been commissioned.

"Meal schedules will be posted daily outside the dining halls. Your food preferences, allergies, and dietary restrictions have been logged. Kosher food is being prepared in a separate section of the kitchen which has been cleaned to rabbinical standards. Gluten-free food is being prepared in a closed room to minimize risk of cross contamination. If you have any questions, please feel free to ask. And welcome, all of you, to the *Melusine*."

Everyone applauded. It seemed like the thing to do. The captain left the stage while they were clapping, and Theodore Blackwell took his place. The clapping stopped. Some people looked confused; others wary. Theodore Blackwell was a known quantity around Imagine, James Golden's cold right hand. If he was here . . .

"Greetings," he said. The amplifying effect that had carried Captain Peterman's voice to the back of the room picked up his, making it impossible to ignore. Hallie remained behind him, hands flashing as she relayed his every word. "I am Theodore Blackwell, and I will be on this voyage with you as a spy for Imagine."

A nervous ripple passed through the room, half laughter and half gasp. Theo smiled.

"Come now," he said. "You can't think I'd try to hide it, can you? You're some of the smartest people in the world. Top of your respective fields—although admittedly, some of you are working within a field of five. In those cases, all five members are probably on this vessel. Good luck figuring out who's on top."

This time the laughter was more sincere.

"We sail to answer a great mystery of the modern maritime age: what happened to the *Atargatis*? The question is deeply personal for many of us. The answer will not heal our wounds, but it may begin the process of healing. We will hopefully answer a greater, older mystery at the same time: are we alone on this planet? Elephants, dolphins, even crows have exhibited signs of what we recognize as intelligence, but they are not our equals. They aren't the elves or fairies or, yes, mermaids of legend. If we can find a mermaid, if we can prove these lovely ladies of the sea are more than just stories, we can answer a question humanity has been asking for millennia. We're not just here to right a wrong. We're here to make history. Thank you for making it with us."

This time, the applause was sustained, accompanied by a few cheers and whistles. Ray captured it on camera, Olivia standing silent next to him. She lived in crowds but she didn't like them; they were too large and chaotic for her to find them comfortable. Give her a camera and a script and she could change the world. Give her something like this and she withdrew.

Jillian wasn't clapping either. She watched the stage through narrowed eyes, arms crossed. She didn't think most of the people around her realized they were already moving. The *Melusine* was large enough to be steady on the water, and her engines were advanced enough to be almost imperceptible. Jillian had been on more than her share of ships, and she knew what the vibration in the soles of her feet meant.

Why didn't Imagine want us to know that we were pushing off? she wondered. *What don't they want us to see?*

Theodore was speaking again. She took advantage of the room's distraction to step back, out the nearest door, and slip away.

Almost everyone was gathered in the assembly room: the few crew members in the ship's halls were easy enough to avoid. No one tried to stop her as she made her way up the stairs, down the hallway, and finally onto the deck.

The dock was dwindling in the distance, far enough behind them that she couldn't have swum back to safety if she'd wanted to try. A few trucks that hadn't been present when she'd gone inside were parked there. It was too far for her to make out the logo on their sides. She pulled out her phone and snapped a few pictures anyway, getting a long shot before blowing up her lens to the greatest magnification possible and taking a series of pictures of what she hoped would prove to be the logo. Imagine was hiding something. She wanted—no, she *needed*—to know what it was.

Even at her phone's greatest magnification, the logo was barely the size of an eraser head. She zoomed in as much as she could, reducing it to a smear of meaningless pixels. Nothing.

Nothing...except for the fact that she was on a vessel filled with scientists, some of whom worked with advanced visual processing software for the sake of getting clear shots of creatures that lived half a mile below the surface of the sea. Someone would be able to tell her what she'd just taken a picture of, and why Imagine didn't want them to see it. It was just a matter of finding someone with the appropriate equipment and convincing them to help her out. That wasn't going to be any problem at all.

Theo, on the other hand...Theo knew her. He knew she didn't trust Imagine as far as she could throw it; that in fact, part of her motivation for coming on this trip was keeping Imagine from burying any results that it didn't approve of. He'd be watching her like a hawk. Anything she was going to do would need to be done while he wasn't looking. That meant finding allies, and quickly, among the people he'd helped to hand-select—many of whom viewed her as either crackpot or competition, if not both.

"Isn't this going to be fun," she murmured, to the sounding sea, and turned to go back inside.

The speeches were over when she returned to the main room. About half the people were gone, while the rest circulated around the buffet and the open bar. Drinking heavily on the first night of a long voyage seemed like a bad idea to her—although, to be fair, drinking heavily later on could interfere with getting actual work done, whereas now, it would just mean the world's least pleasant hangover. Maybe the boozehounds had the right idea.

The two redheads were among the people remaining. They had resumed their silent argument, their hands flashing so fast that it was like the world's most aggressive game of patty-cake. Jillian stopped a few feet away, watching them talk. ASL was a beautiful language. It was also a language she didn't want to sneak up on; the idea of being accidentally slapped in the face by a particularly vehement point didn't appeal.

The translator in the floral dress was nearby. She offered Jillian a friendly nod.

"Hi," said Jillian. "I know I'm supposed to talk to them, not you, when I'm talking to them, but do you know how I can get their attention without getting punched by mistake? I want to say hello. I don't want to visit the infirmary."

"They're not fighting *that* hard," said the translator.

One of the two redheads began making a violent, repetitive sign directly in front of the face of the other.

"They don't usually hit strangers," amended the translator. "Hang on." She signed something complex, holding her hands up so the redhead she was facing could see.

They both dropped their hands—ending the discussion midsentence, as it were—and turned to Jillian. Jillian waved. The two redheads waved back.

"Hello," said Jillian. "I'm Dr. Jillian Toth. I just wanted to say hello and find out what you're going to be doing on this voyage."

The first redhead signed something rapid while the translator said, "We know who you are. I'm Holly Wilson. I'm an organic chemist. I'm going to be doing surface and depth analysis at the Mariana Trench, to determine whether there's something unusual going on with the chemical makeup of the water."

Jillian recognized science simplified for the layman, and she didn't push. Organic chemistry was so far from her own field that it was an essentially alien discipline. She could make Holly explain—scientists were usually eager to do just that, and she'd been working in academia long enough to know how to phrase her questions, to make it seem like she really *cared*—but it would be a waste of both their time.

"I'm Heather Wilson," signed the second redhead. "I'm a submersible operator."

Jillian blinked. "Really?"

Heather scowled. "Why are you surprised? Is it because I'm deaf?"

"No, it's because I'm claustrophobic," said Jillian. "What sort of submersible?"

"I have a one-body Minnow pod," signed Heather, shoulders relaxing. "It's configured to my body weight and specs, and all systems are designed with visual signaling prioritized. It talks to me better than a hearing person's could ever talk to them. I'm rated for depths of up to twenty-five thousand feet, although my equipment can handle depths up to forty thousand. I'll be going down once we reach the Trench."

Holly's hands flashed. "You know forty thousand feet is pushing it. You're not going into the Challenger Deep."

Heather shrugged.

"It's a pleasure to meet you both," said Jillian. "May I ask an etiquette question?"

"Better asked than assumed," signed Holly. Both of them laughed.

"Is your translator related to you?"

The twins exchanged a look before Heather signed, "Why do you ask?"

"Because her name is 'Hallie,' and she looks somewhat similar."

Substantially taller—Hallie had nearly a foot on the twins—and with clearly artificially blonde hair, but similar, especially in the face.

"Hallie?" signed Holly.

"I'm their older sister," said Hallie. "You're *allowed* to talk to me, as long as you're not ignoring Holly and Heather. I'm also on this ship as a scientist."

"What kind?" asked Jillian.

"I'm an acoustician and sign language expert."

"The mermaids!" Jillian slapped her forehead, an exaggerated gesture she hoped would make her seem bumbling and harmless. She wanted to make friends with these people. She wanted them to trust her. "I've seen the videos. There are shots where it looks like they're communicating via some sort of sign language."

"I've seen them too," said Hallie. "It doesn't just look like they're communicating. They *are* communicating. They have a language. If I can get more footage, I'll be able to start learning it. I've already picked up a few signs." Her hands were never still; she was constantly translating for her sisters. It was impressive. She probably had a grip of steel.

"I look forward to seeing your results," said Jillian.

Holly signed something, looking suddenly shy. "I've read your book three times. Could we get a picture?"

"Of course," said Jillian.

Holly handed her phone to Hallie, and the twins clustered to either side of Jillian, striking a quick, practiced pose. They were so tiny it made Jillian feel like a giant, an orca swimming among dolphins. She smiled, and the camera clicked, and it was done. The twins returned to their original places, Holly taking the phone back to check the picture, while Heather resumed signing.

"It's a pleasure to be working with you," was the translation.

Jillian, who recognized a dismissal when she heard one, nodded. "Same. I'll see you around the ship." She turned to go, and nearly walked straight into Theo.

"Walk with me," he said, offering his arm.

There was no way out. "Of course," she said, fighting to keep her tone from turning grudging, and slipped her hand into the bend of his elbow.

Theo led her across the room to a doorway she hadn't noticed before. There was an elevator on the other side. It had been waiting; the doors opened as soon as he pressed the button, and it was a matter of seconds before they were descending deeper into the body of the *Melusine*.

"I should have known you'd notice when we got under way," he said, in a conversational tone. "I would have warned you, but you seemed displeased enough by my presence that I didn't want to push my luck when we were close to shore."

"Why? Were you afraid I'd throw you overboard?"

"The thought did cross my mind."

"Your mind knows me too well." Jillian pulled her hand out of the crook of his arm, eyeing him suspiciously. "What are you doing here, Theo? How did you get your doctors to approve this?"

"I'm not an invalid, Jilli," he said. "I was for a little while, but those days are long past. I'm perfectly sound for a sea voyage, as long as I take my medication and monitor my physical activity. This vessel is fully accessible. There are elevators in place of stairs to get from level to level, ramps graded for wheelchair use on the main decks—we could use the *Melusine* for a chronic illness convention and not worry that any of the attendees would be unable to take advantage of the opportunity."

"There are so many 'if's in that sentence," said Jillian. "*If* you take your medication. *If* you monitor your physical activity. What will you do if what happened to the *Atargatis* happens again? You can't run."

"If what happened to the *Atargatis* happens again, none of us will be in a position to run." The elevator stopped with a faint chiming sound, accompanied by a single strobe of the overhead light. Catching Jillian's confused look, Theo smiled and said, "For the Wilson twins. Of course we wanted the ship to be fully accessible anyway, and we knew we'd need at least one sign language interpreter to work on the mermaids' language. Finding one who was not only a scientist, but traveled with a pair of deaf siblings who worked in oceanographic fields, was like winning the lottery. If these mermaids are intelligent, we'll learn to communicate with them."

"Before or after they swallow our faces?"

"One hopes before, but beggars never can be choosers."

The elevator doors opened. Theo stepped out, with Jillian close behind him, her eyes going wide and round with awe. He smirked, saying nothing. Let her take a moment to drink it all in. Once she had, perhaps she'd be better prepared to talk like a reasonable person.

Many of the passengers aboard the *Melusine* were aware of the pool on the lower level that sampled and purified water. It had been included in the description of the vessel, advertised as part of the ship's exercise facilities. It was unsafe to swim in the open sea, and the decks that would have been used for pools and waterslides on a cruise ship were devoted to research stations and docking ports. With the number of swimmers in the crew, some sort of compromise had been necessary.

Knowing something existed and seeing the scope of it were very different things. The pool was easily two-thirds the size of the room above, large enough to be used for anything short of Olympic conditioning. "Twenty feet at the deep end; three at the shallow," said Theodore. "Salt water, of course, but purified to such a point that it should be fairly mild against the eyes. The hot tub is freshwater. Taken from the same source, but desalinated before heating. We use the same desalination pumps for our drinking water, so we'll know instantly if anything breaks down. The water cycles constantly. We could all pee in the pool at once and it would be gone in under a minute."

"What a charming image," murmured Jillian. Her eyes flicked from wall to wall, taking in the dimensions of the space. The docking area for the submersibles took up one corner, slicing off a section of the room; the showers occupied another. That didn't account for certain quirks in the layout.

Theo waited patiently. Jillian had been a genius when they'd met in college, and she'd grown more brilliant with each passing year. The bitterness that had accompanied her growth was a sad consequence of being a bright light in a dark world. If any of the people on the *Melusine* would suspect and then divine the pool's secret, it would be her.

"This room's too small," she said finally. "The pipes on the ceiling connect to the purification system but not to the pool. What are you doing with the extra space, and where is the water going?"

"Two minutes," he said fondly. "I knew you were still the brilliant woman I married. This way." He started across the strip of dry floor between the pool and the locker area. There were no privacy walls; if people wanted to use the facility, they needed to be comfortable with nudity or change in their quarters. It was a small but necessary evil: by omitting changing rooms, the ship's designers had blocked Imagine from placing cameras in the pool area. Most filming licenses still refused to grant consent for even nonsexual nudity.

There was a door in the far wall, locked with a keypad and a card reader. Theo produced his card from his pocket, punched in his code, and swiped them through.

The door opened to reveal a small room, the dim lighting making the bright water of the glassed-in diving tank all the more startling. Three bottlenose dolphins swam easily there, darting over and around each other as they played. A control panel to one side offered multiple screens, showing the dolphins from various points below the surface.

"The truck you saw was loading them onto the ship; the logo belonged to a large marine entertainment concern," said Theo calmly, while Jillian gaped. "We feed them through a hatch. They'll mostly be receiving fresh-caught fish, although Twitter—the female—prefers frozen shrimp."

"Theo, you...I...How could you?" Jillian stared at him. "You've been protesting exploitation of marine mammals for as long as I've known you. You broke your damn spine trying to stop a whaling ship! This is—"

"Necessary," said Theo. "We have submersibles and cameras, but those are machines; they can't navigate like the dolphins can. These are well-trained, happy animals. They're not being abused or used for entertainment. They have a job to do."

"A job that's taking them into waters they would never enter voluntarily, where we're looking for an apex predator capable of *ripping them apart*," said Jillian. "You're signing their death warrants if you release them near the Mariana Trench. How could you?"

"How could I not?" Theo shook his head. "Science has costs. We've sacrificed so many people in the name of this discovery. What's three dolphins added to the existing tragedy? There will always be risks. I can't say with absolute certainty that all three of these animals will be coming home. But if there's a chance that letting them scout for us will save human lives, I'm going to take it. I have to take it. This is so important, Jilli. This trip could change everything."

"Why? Because if we find mermaids we'll have something intelligent that has hands and looks vaguely like us, and maybe then we'll respect it? We have that. Chimpanzees, great apes, orangutans—they have hands, they look vaguely like us, and they're intelligent enough to be considered people in a court of law. Dolphins don't get that courtesy solely because they look more like fish than like the girl next door. Mermaids split the difference. Finding them won't make us treat the oceans any better, and it won't magically turn them into a protected species. If anything, it's going to make them the competition."

"If you feel that way, why did you agree to look for them?"

"Because I owe the people who sailed on the *Atargatis*, using information I provided. Because mermaids have always been the competition when it comes to the sea. They've been luring us and drowning us for centuries. I want to see their faces. That's all. I want to see them, and know I was right every time I said they were out there."

"The film—"

"The film." Jillian scoffed. "Imagine brings back proof, irrefutable proof, and what do we get? We get to hear how many ways the world can say *hoax*. I am going to be eyewitness testimony. I am going to make those people eat their words."

Theo looked at her solemnly. "The dolphins will help."

"Everyone else on this ship volunteered. The dolphins didn't."

To her profound surprise, Theo laughed. "I see," he said. "Is that your issue? That the dolphins didn't volunteer?"

Jillian nodded tightly.

"Let me set your mind at ease. You know dolphins can communicate, yes? That they have a language?"

"Yes. Of course."

"We have a cetologist on board who specializes in marine mammal communication. We're hoping he'll be able to work with Dr. Wilson—the hearing Dr. Wilson—to establish the parameters of the mermaid 'language,' assuming they have one. All three of these dolphins are here of their own free will. They've been offered release into the open sea after the voyage is done, in exchange for their services now. These dolphins are buying their freedom. I'd expect you, of all people, to be pleased by that."

Jillian looked at him coldly before she said, "I knew you'd changed. A man has to change when he goes from riding a deck to riding a desk. They're not the same thing, and you can't be the same person when you move between them. But somehow I thought you'd still have a sense of ethics."

"Jillian—"

"You're hiding this, which means you don't want me shouting it to everyone else on board this ship, and I'm fine with that; if I keep your secret, you owe me. Stay out of the line of fire, Theo. Make yourself look good on the cameras, impress your employers, but for God's sake, keep yourself safe. We have a daughter who loves you, even if I don't always understand why, and I won't have this voyage making an orphan out of her. Just leave me out of your bullshit justifications for selling your ethics to the highest bidder. I've heard them before, and they're tired. So am I." She turned and started for the door.

"Jillian—"

The door didn't have any special security on this side. Jillian let herself out.

Theo stood in the dim room, the dolphins endlessly circling behind him, and wondered when, exactly, things had started to go so very wrong.

Olivia moved through the crowd of scientists with an ease that would have stunned the people she'd gone to school with, who remembered her as the timid, socially awkward girl from the back of the classroom, the one who read too many comic books and never made eye contact.

Now she was poised and confident, having traded her corset and pants for a white sundress that made her look young, innocent, and harmless. She directed her microphone with a fencer's ease, eternally going in for the point. She still never made eye contact, not directly. She had just grown more adept at faking it.

Some things never changed.

"What are you hoping to gain from this voyage?" she asked Jason, smiling winsomely at him. "Do you believe the mermaids are real?"

"No," he said. The word was flat and nonnegotiable. "None of us do. If something like that existed, we would have discovered it decades ago."

"Then why did you agree to go on this voyage?"

"With the equipment and freedom Imagine is providing, we can push our own research forward incredibly, and as they only claim ownership of data directly related to something that doesn't exist, this was an opportunity none of us were going to pass up."

"Aren't you worried about damage to your reputations?"

Jason smirked. "There isn't a scientist on Earth who would blame us for going where the funding was. We'll be fine. And who knows? Maybe I'm wrong, and we'll find mermaids, and we'll all get rich."

"Here's hoping," said Olivia, and smiled again before moving on to find her next target. What she *really* wanted was a quote from the Wilsons, if she could get one. They were photogenic, striking, and unusual enough to make good B reel.

Almost all the scientists had been drinking since the speeches wrapped up, and their tongues were nicely loosened. She couldn't use things like Jason's flat denial of the existence of mermaids, which went against the narrative Imagine was hoping to craft, but the rest of it could be edited into something serviceable. Everything could be helpful, providing it was massaged the right way.

The girl with the brownish ponytail—Anne Stewart's sister— was near the buffet, looking disinterestedly at a tray of cold cuts. Olivia angled toward her, already smiling.

"Hi," she said, once she was close enough. "I'm Olivia Sanderson, from Imagine. I was wondering if I could have a moment of your—"

"No," said Tory, and turned, and walked away.

Olivia stared after her.

"Well," said Ray, stepping up next to her. "I think I'm in love."

"At least this is going to be interesting," said Olivia, and the *Melusine* sailed on, out of safe waters, into the uncertain sea.

CHAPTER 8

The Pacific Ocean: August 24, 2022

The passengers—loud, enthusiastic nuisances that they were—had finally made their way back to their rooms, and Captain Peterman was alone with his crew.

"Check the doors," he said.

One of the engineers nodded understanding before making a circuit of the room, verifying that each of the outward-facing doors had been securely locked. It wouldn't do for a passenger to wander in on this discussion. Elsewhere on the ship, he knew the Imagine security crew would be having a similar meeting, discussing its plans for the journey to come.

As if this sort of thing could be planned for. They would sail, and they would either find what they were looking for or they wouldn't. Captain Peterman would never say so out loud, not on a ship with this many recording devices, but he hoped they didn't find anything. The *Atargatis* was lost. Let her stay that way, and let the rest of them live.

"Locked, Captain," said the engineer.

"Excellent." Folding his hands behind his back, he turned to face the crew. "All right, everyone: we are on the maiden voyage of an untested research ship built to the specifications of an entertainment corporation."

"Did you see their security goons?" demanded one of the

navigators. She snorted, making an exaggerated cupping gesture with her hands. "None of them have any training, but damn do they look good. It's like they were all hired out of a casting catalog. Models with guns."

Another navigator laughed and mimed shooting a gun before striking a pose. Captain Peterman cleared his throat, waiting for the levity to die down. On a voyage like this one, a little nervous energy was only to be expected. They were being paid well for their time and expertise; they would all be set for at least a year when they made it back to shore.

If they made it back to shore.

Gradually, the laughter faded, and the captain began to speak again. "We are currently sailing under the ship's automatic systems, which will get us past occupied waters before we need to begin manual navigation. Shifts have been posted in the break rooms, as well as sent to your individual mailboxes. Please remember to wash your hands and not to use the passenger restrooms."

A general shudder ran through the assemblage. Ships were basically enormous petri dishes for disease, and no matter how educated or adult the passengers seemed to be, there was always one who wouldn't wash their hands if there was a gun to their temple. Mermaids were one thing. Norovirus was something entirely different, and far more believably dangerous.

"This ship is outfitted with an armored shutter system, designed to be manually deployed in the event of an attack," said the captain. "The code can be inputted from either of two authorized terminals: one in my quarters, one in the main control room on the top deck. Once the code is entered correctly, there will be a ninety-second countdown before the ship is sealed."

One of the engineers raised his hand. "Sir, have these shutters been tested?"

"Only in dry dock," said the captain. "We will be running an operational test tonight at midnight."

"What about redundancies?" asked another engineer.

"Imagine didn't see fit to provide any," said the captain. "We have the shutters. We have the guards. That is intended to be enough. Now to your posts, everyone. We have a long voyage ahead of us."

*   *   *

By bedtime, everyone had realized the *Melusine* was under sail—an archaic misnomer, since the great ship didn't have so much as a mast. Even her lifeboats were battery powered, with lithium-based engines good for six days in open water. She moved across the water like she was being towed by an invisible hand, silent and steady enough that it was possible to forget she was a moving ship, that land was already leagues behind them and growing more distant with every moment that passed.

'What do you think?' asked Holly, sitting on the edge of the bed she'd claimed as her own. The three sisters had one of the largest staterooms on the *Melusine*, the sort of suite that could have held a whole family of tourists (and probably would, when the *Melusine* was inevitably repurposed as a luxury cruise ship).

'Most of the people we're going to be working with are competent,' Heather replied. She yawned, covered her mouth, and continued, 'I don't know if I'd trust them with my baby, but I don't have to. The other submersible operator has his own pod.'

'Is he rated as deep as you are?' asked Hallie.

Heather beamed, making a pair of V's with her fingers and knocking them together before delivering a definitive pinching motion. 'Fuck no.'

Holly laughed. It was the first sound any of them had made since closing the cabin door.

Virtually everything about Holly and Heather Wilson was identical, from their faces to their fingers. Even their hearing loss matched. Both had been born deaf. The precise cause of their deafness had never been identified. The girls were healthy, happy, and well adjusted; the family had already lived near a good Deaf school when they were born. The question of cochlear implants had been left until Holly and Heather were old enough to answer it for themselves, and by the time they'd been asked, they hadn't wanted the surgery. They enjoyed themselves and their reality as they were.

Hallie was three years older than her sisters. She had been fascinated when her parents explained that the new babies couldn't hear. They had already used some baby sign with her, taking advantage of the fact that in most infants, hand dexterity developed faster than vocal acuity. It was a small thing to keep teaching her, bringing in a tutor twice a week while Holly and Heather were still in their crib. By the time they'd started signing, there had already been a willing translator standing excitedly by.

The three of them hadn't always been a unit. Holly had gone to graduate school for organic chemistry; Hallie had spent three years translating in a public high school as part of her extended thesis; Heather had gone to a private institute to hone her skills behind the wheel of a submersible. Her beloved Minnow had been paid for by the institute, putting her millions of dollars in debt. She was still buying it back from them, one component at a time, funding her loan payments with deep-sea footage, recordings, and more concrete discoveries. One private donation had totaled a quarter of a million dollars, and all the donor had wanted was some seashells guaranteed to have come from the bottom of the sea. People were strange.

People were also wonderful. The call from Imagine had brought them together at last, giving them an excuse to ply their various trades in the same space. Heather was under a six-month contract; if the *Melusine* returned to shore before her time was up, she'd be doing underwater cinematography for the Imagine files, to be used in whatever terrible science fiction movie the film division decided to cobble together next. Holly and Hallie were only under contract for the duration of the voyage, but that nice Mr. Blackwell had made it clear to both of them that if they wanted to stay with their sister, Imagine would find them a place.

'I really do want to go down into the Challenger Deep,' signed Heather. There was a wistful, almost dreamy look on her face, like she was thinking about a handsome man or a delicious cake.

Holly threw a pillow at her. 'You are *not* going into the Challenger Deep! I don't care how highly rated you are! People don't come back from there!'

Hallie sighed. 'Is there a chance we could go five minutes without fighting about the Challenger Deep?'

'It's only the deepest spot in the *whole ocean*,' signed Heather, expression still dreamy. 'There have been four descents ever, and only one of them was manned. That was a long time ago, too, before we knew there might be mermaids there.'

'Wait—if people have been down there, how could they *miss* the mermaids?'

Heather shrugged broadly. 'Not my department. Maybe mermaids migrate? Anyway, the submersible that went down there before was big and slow. It was a down-and-up. I can move like a fish. I can see what the bottom of the ocean really looks like.'

'You can pop like a grape from the pressure,' signed Holly. 'You're *not* going down there, and that's final.'

'You're not my mother.'

'No, I'm your twin, and I think I get some say in whether you risk your life!'

Heather started signing faster and Holly signed back, their fingers flashing almost too fast for even Hallie's practiced eyes to follow. Not that it would have mattered. Like so many twins, they had their own language, a form of streamlined, truncated ASL that left out most of the connective tissue of conversation. They could get their points across at dizzying speed, making it impossible for anyone outside their small closed unit to decode. Hallie rolled her eyes and got out of bed, heading for the door.

She paused long enough to sign, 'I'm going to find the hot tubs.' The twins ignored her, still arguing. She sighed, exasperated, and let herself out.

Orientation had included directions to the spa facilities on each floor. There were three "wet rooms" per occupied level of the ship, divided into male, female, and coed rooms. The coed wet room was by far the largest and nicest of the three, with large hot and cold tubs, as well as sinks and showers. It made sense. Most people didn't care about gender-essentialist bathrooms, but they *did* care about bigger hot tubs.

Exhausted and overstimulated, Hallie made straight for the coed bathroom. She would normally have chosen the women's room when she was this tired, hoping it would be less populated and hence less likely to force her into a social setting, but the ship had just gotten under way. The party was over, and this crowd didn't seem like the type to move it to the hot tub. (Actually, most of this crowd seemed like the type to take water samples from the hot tub and tell her exactly what sort of terrifying bacterial soup she was soaking in. Holly had done that several times before she'd moved away from home. Sometimes having an organic chemist for a sister was a trial.)

As she'd hoped, the coed wet room seemed deserted. Hallie

undressed, placed her things in a locker, and grabbed a towel. It only took her a few seconds to shower—more sluicing off than actually trying to get clean—and head for the hot tub.

Someone was already there. The little blonde who'd been doing interviews on the foredeck during orientation. Her hair was paler than Hallie's, ice white instead of wheat, and it looked natural, unlike Hallie's own. (All three Wilson sisters were natural redheads. But red hair drew attention, and ASL interpreters were supposed to blend into the background, not pull focus from the people speaking. She'd been dyeing her hair since she was sixteen. She no longer knew what she looked like as a redhead.)

"Hi," said Hallie gingerly, approaching the water. "Do you mind if I join you?"

"The water's free," said the blonde. She didn't open her eyes. She had relaxed completely, a towel propping up her head to keep it from grinding against the marble edge of the tub. "Hot, though."

"I'll take that under advisement." Hallie eased herself into the hot tub, unable to stop herself from hissing as the water enveloped her. "Okay. Not kidding about the hot. Good, but...holy crap, that's warm. I'm Hallie, by the way."

"The sign language interpreter." The blonde still didn't open her eyes. "I know who you are. Your file was pretty impressive. I'm Olivia. I'm one of your assigned media personalities."

"What's a...?"

"A media personality is someone who's famous for being famous about being famous. We live in the shadow of our own tautologies." Olivia sank a little deeper. "I report for Imagine. Sometimes I do photo shoots from the set of whatever series they're getting ready to launch. I moderate panels at big conventions and get my picture taken with people who're famous for actually having done something, and then people look at those pictures and they assume I must be more famous than I am, and I get more famous by association."

"That sounds—" Hallie stopped. It sounded awful and appealing at the same time, and the exact opposite of her own intentionally shadowed existence.

Olivia cracked open an eye and smiled wryly. "I know how it sounds," she said. "It started as a therapy thing, believe it or not. Debilitating social anxiety and self-image issues. My therapist was a comic nerd. She recommended cosplay as a way to step outside myself and see me the way other people did. One of the people who saw me was a scout for Imagine's web network. They needed correspondents who looked good in a corset, I needed something to focus on that wasn't how uncomfortable I was, one thing led to another and now here I am. I'm pretty cool with it. I like what I do, and I'm good at what I do, and I'm going to keep on doing it for as long as I can."

"Huh," said Hallie. "I actually hadn't started judging, but that's good to know."

Olivia's smile faded a bit, losing some of its wryness, replacing it with a vulnerability rendered surprising by the brevity of their acquaintance. Then again, they were both naked; that was usually good for shortcutting a few social conventions. "I didn't think you were judging," she said. "It's just that people make assumptions, and sometimes it's easier on me if I can...skip past them and get to what comes next."

"Makes sense to me," said Hallie. "People make assumptions about me too."

"Really?" That coaxed Olivia's other eye open. She looked much younger when she was paying full attention, like she was expecting to be graded. "Like what?"

"Well, I don't know if you noticed, since I was standing way back on the stage, but I'm almost six feet tall."

"I did notice that," said Olivia. "It sort of stood out."

"Exactly. I'm tall, I'm curvy, I'm a natural redhead—I know people who assume I should have been a lingerie model or a centerfold. Not that there's anything wrong with nudity, if that's what you want to do for a living. It's just weird sometimes to realize how many people start out their first conversation with me imagining what my tits look like under my clothes."

Olivia blinked. "You're naked *now*."

"So you don't have to imagine it." Hallie shrugged. "I'm tall and hot and I decided to go into a profession where most of the time, it's my job to be unobtrusive. Clearly I must have hit my head."

"The possibility exists," said Olivia. "Your sisters seem nice."

"My sisters are brilliant and obnoxious and I have ceded our room to them until they stop yelling at each other."

Silence fell. It extended for several seconds as Olivia tried to find a way to ask the question that was clawing at her throat without seeming inappropriate. Finally she blurted, "How are they *yelling*?"

"Even ASL has a yell mode," said Hallie. "It involves a lot of waving and slapping of hands, and it's distracting as hell, especially if you've been trained to pay attention to signing. I can't tune them out and I don't want to eavesdrop, so I came for a nice soak."

"Well, it's nice to meet you, fellow soaker," said Olivia.

Hallie smiled. "You, too."

Elsewhere on the *Melusine*, similar scenes played out—some clothed, others not, depending on the participants. Scientists set up equipment. Porters carted boxes and suitcases from level to level. In the galley, kitchen assistants prepared the next day's breakfast, taking rashers of bacon from the freezer and kneading the dough that would become the morning's cinnamon rolls. And some people, of course, slept, confident in the knowledge that their journey had begun, that soon they would be making history.

In her cabin, Tory paced, restless, unable to chase the specter of her sister away long enough to relax. Anne had sailed on a ship like this one. Anne had cut across these same waters (no, not the same; the *Atargatis* had set sail from Seattle, not San Diego; she had sailed the same sea, but she had sailed on other tides, borne ceaselessly toward a watery grave), had slept in a bunk like this one, had tried her best to make it home.

"I'm coming for you, Anne," Tory whispered, stopping by her cabin window and looking out on the dark water. The reflections of the running lights that dotted the sides of the *Melusine* twinkled like stars against the sea.

"I'm coming to make sure everyone knows what really happened," she said, and everything was silence. She crawled into bed.

It was hours before she slept.

The first active shutter drill began at midnight.

It ended two minutes later, in failure.

The *Melusine* sailed on.

CHAPTER 9

The Pacific Ocean: August 29, 2022

Life on board the *Melusine* fell into a rhythm that was familiar to everyone who'd been part of a research expedition before, and faintly baffling to the rest of them. Meals were served from six to nine, noon to three, and six to nine again, accommodating the admittedly eccentric schedules of the scientists and technicians who swarmed the decks, monitoring their projects, stealing one another's clipboards, and generally getting in the way.

Jacques and Michi Abney staked out a place on the rear deck, running fishing lines off the back of the ship and celebrating each catch with a degree of enthusiasm that bordered on the obscene. They had a portable barbeque and would cook portions of their catches. Whatever they couldn't eat would be thrown back into the water to attract bigger fish.

(Their position at the rear was a compromise. They had originally been planning to fish off the side of the ship, until the people in charge of water sampling and analysis objected. Apparently the presence of lightly barbequed fish in their samples could throw off their results.)

The security teams, as yet unneeded, spent their time drinking coffee and working on their tans. Quite a few crew members "accidentally" wandered into those tanning sessions. The captain didn't stop them. Shirtless, well-oiled men were good for morale. Even

Michi Abney seemed to think so, and would sometimes deliver platters of barbequed fish to the men. The lack of women on the security team seemed like one more clear indication that they had been chosen on the basis of their looks, and not for anything related to their qualifications.

Tory's lab was toward the rear, close enough for her to smell the Abneys' grilling and as far as possible from the engines. She had run various microphones and sensors from the sides of the *Melusine*, anchoring them with magnets to keep them from being lost as the ship moved, and spent her days analyzing her recordings, looking for signs that they were passing over something—anything—that didn't sound like the sea was meant to sound. She was bent over her keyboard when there was a knock at her lab door.

"Enter," she said, not turning.

"Really?" The voice was female, unfamiliar, and surprised. "I thought you'd ask who it was first. Are you sure you want me to come in? Because I will, but then I'll be in, and you'll have to live with that."

Tory spun on her stool. The lithe blonde she'd seen doing pickup interviews with the other scientists on board—the one who had tried to talk to her at the welcome banquet, the one she'd been dodging since they'd left the dock—was standing in the doorway. As seemed to be her norm, she was dressed entirely in white, this time a white sundress with ruffled straps that would have seemed more natural on someone ten years younger than she looked. (Knowing Imagine and the way it did its casting, that probably meant she was fifteen years too old for that dress. They always went for the ones who looked young. It meant they could stay on the air for longer.)

"Oh," said Tory, in a strangled voice. "I didn't realize..." She stopped. Anything else she said would have been insulting or flat-out rude, and no matter how much she didn't want to talk to this woman, she had to share a ship with her. The *Melusine* was huge. At the same time, it was a closed community. There was no escaping.

"I figured," said the woman, with a small, unhappy moue of her lips. "I know you have good reasons to avoid me. I'm not here to ask for an interview or shove a camera in your face. My contract says I have to at least try for an interview with everyone on board in a research capacity, but it also says that if I can get half of a research partnership, that's enough, if the other half doesn't want to talk to me. Your partner was really sweet. We chatted for an hour to make sure I wouldn't be required to talk to you."

"So why are you *here*?" Tory couldn't keep the whine out of her voice. This was the situation she'd been dreading since she'd realized an Imagine-funded voyage would, of necessity, have someone to fill the role Anne had filled when the *Atargatis* sailed: to chronicle and frame the complex, confusing process of oceanic research in a way that the audiences at home would be able to not only understand, but appreciate. Scientists were almost stock characters to people who didn't have to deal with them directly; everything they said sounded scripted and foreign, because they were speaking a part of the language that was no longer commonly used at home. If it ever had been.

"Because I know who you are, and I know why you've been avoiding me, and I know you can't keep avoiding me forever, so I figured I might as well come down here and clear the air before we reach the Mariana Trench," said Olivia. "Once we're there, everything moves to the deck—as much as possible—and I'll be running around with a camera crew, trying to make sure we're present for any major discoveries. I can't do that if it's going to make you so uncomfortable that you can't focus on your work."

"If you know who I am, you know why I don't want to talk to you."

"I'm not your sister."

Silence fell between them, heavy as a stone. Tory narrowed her eyes. Olivia's cheeks flushed a deep, painful-looking red, like an internal sunburn.

"I mean . . . Oh, fuck. Oh, fuck me. I mean, just because I'm doing the job she did on the *Atargatis*, that doesn't mean I'm trying to take her place. I've seen her reports. She was really good, but we don't have the same reporting style, we don't focus on the same aspects of a situation, we don't even have the same inflections. She spoke French and German, I speak Klingon and Quenya."

"Quenya?" asked Tory blankly.

"Uh, Elvish. From Tolkien. My point is, we're different kinds of nerd who just happened to luck into being conventionally pretty and having a decent amount of presence on camera. I didn't know you'd be here when I took this assignment."

"When did you take this assignment?"

"About two months ago."

That made sense. Imagine must have been working on the *Melusine* long before the ship reached the point of being ready to go, and even if Tory's research had been the last thing the mission needed, the company would have been getting the crew ready all that time. There were Imagine-funded scientists on board. Their research had been going on substantially longer than a month. There were porters who knew every inch of the ship—and the *Melusine* hadn't been built overnight. Of course there were people who'd known before she did what they were signing up for.

That didn't make it feel any less like a betrayal to know that her sister's replacement had known about the journey before she did.

Tory swallowed, trying to put her personal feelings behind her. It wasn't working. She wanted to yell, to rage, to tell Olivia she didn't belong in this lab, that if anyone was going to be the face of the voyage, it should have been Anne. There was archival footage. There were recordings that hadn't been used. There were all the videos Anne had sent home, videos that Tory knew had to be preserved somewhere on Imagine's servers, alongside everything else that had been transmitted from the *Atargatis*.

But this was already a haunted house. Would giving Anne's ghost a face really have made it any better?

"I'm sorry," said Tory, swallowing again. "I'm just...I've been avoiding you, and I'm really grateful that you've let me, and I'm not ready for this."

"Are you ever going to be?"

Tory paused before she said, "I don't know."

"I need you to know, because my job says I have to be on that deck, and so does yours." Olivia looked at Tory solemnly. "I want to respect your pain. I want to give you the space you need. But I'm going to be honest with you: I don't respect your pain enough to let it cost me my job. I don't respect *anyone's* pain that much, not even my own."

"At least you're honest," said Tory. She felt numb more than anything; like the world was slowly, softly slipping away from her, leaving her suspended in nothingness. It was an interesting sensation. She couldn't say she liked it. "I know you're not Anne, and I know you didn't take this job out of some weird desire to shit on her memory. I mean, intellectually, I've known that from the start. Imagine didn't stop hiring people to be professionally pretty just because they lost one. That would have been silly."

"Silly, and not very profitable," agreed Olivia. "Not too good for me either. I took this job because people scare the hell out of me."

Tory lifted an eyebrow. "How does that work?"

"I'm scared of you, but there's a camera between us. That makes you safe. I talk to you, and the camera catches everything you say, and I can review it later, at my leisure, when there's no pressure to say the right thing or react immediately."

"But don't you have to do that while we're talking *for* the camera?"

Olivia shrugged. "Sure. It's just that you're not talking to for-real Olivia when that's happening. You're talking to camera-Olivia, who is essentially fake and exists only so for-real Olivia can buy nice things."

Startled, Tory laughed. "Who am I talking to now?"

"I'm not sure. I think mostly for-real Olivia, because there's no camera. But I *am* using some of the breathing exercises my therapist taught me to keep from freaking out."

"I don't do breathing exercises."

Olivia's shoulders hunched.

"My therapist taught me to think about the sound of the sea instead. It helps."

Olivia's shoulders relaxed. She even smiled as she took a look around the lab. "This is where you work?"

"Yup." Tory finally pushed her chair back from the monitor, enjoying the way the wheels rolled across the tile floor. She waved her arms, indicating the whole space. "Luis has his fancy radar over there, and I have my fancy sonar over here. When I get a result that seems like it could actually be something, he reorients his sensors and takes as many readings from the same area as he can. I'm looking at sounds and he's looking at shapes."

"Oh, I know what you're recording," Olivia said, looking embarrassed. "I go over all the video footage every night before sending a highlight reel to Imagine. I can usually arrow in on what's going to play well with our audience."

"Right," said Tory. She took a deep breath. "I can't promise to be your new best friend. I'm trying to find out what happened to my sister, and you're always...I mean, you're just so *present*. You're doing the job she should be doing, and isn't."

"Because she's dead."

Tory sputtered for a moment before she asked, "Are you always this blunt?"

"When I have to be." Olivia shrugged. "I have a job to do. Will you let me do it?"

"I'll try."

"Thank you. That's all I wanted to know." She turned to head for the door.

"Wait." The word was out almost before Tory had consciously formed it. Olivia paused, looking back at her. Tory stood. "I know you've been to most of the labs on board. Do you want a tour of this one?"

Olivia looked surprised. Then, almost shyly, she smiled.

"I would love that," she said.

Below the *Melusine*, the living ocean drifted by.

They were miles from any major landmass, off the shipping routes and away from all targets of military interest, sailing through waters that saw few vessels in the average year. They were skirting the Mariana Islands, never coming close enough to encounter the fishing boats that skated around them like bugs on the surface of a pond. The locals knew the *Melusine* would be coming through, had been warned both as a courtesy—a ship this size would frighten away most of the usual fish—and to keep vessels that didn't want to be caught on film from crossing their path.

It helped that there were apparently local superstitions about Imagine, and the *Atargatis*. People had always disappeared in the waters over and around the Mariana Trench, but those disappearances had increased in number since the first, failed attempt to confirm the existence of mermaids. Yachts had been found drifting, no crew or passengers present; fishing boats had washed up on shore with holes in their bellies and nothing in their holds. That alone had been enough to guarantee them relative solitude.

At the surface, the waters here looked like the waters everywhere else in the world. The scientists clinging to the decks of the *Melusine* sampled the water as they passed over it, analyzing the organic compounds present, charting the levels of pollution. (More comprehensive readings were being taken by the ship itself, as she cleansed hundreds of gallons of water hourly, pumping them in, purifying them, and pumping them out again. Some of the chemists were concerned about this throwing off their readings. Others felt that this afforded an excellent excuse to sunbathe until they reached their destination, lying on deck chairs and reading lurid novels on their tablets. Both groups were correct, in their own way.)

Jacques and Michi continued fishing off their stretch of deck, but they weren't the only ones sampling the bounty of the sea. Several scientists whose work wouldn't begin in earnest until they reached the Trench had taken to fishing off one of the lower decks, making a competition of who could bring in the most, or the strangest. The kitchen staff had proven remarkably tolerant, as long as the scientists frying fish on their stoves were willing to clean up after themselves. It seemed as if the *Melusine* was a hot point of life and vitality in an otherwise empty world.

That could not have been more incorrect. The *Melusine* floated at the very top of the photic zone, in the pelagic, or open sea. The farther she got from shore, the more packed with life the water became. They had sailed well away from the polluted "dead zones" that popped up near the shore; they'd even sailed outside the range of the worst of the radiation from the 2011 Fukushima disaster, which had left great swaths of the Pacific between Japan and California tainted. The waters here were as close to clean as remained in the world, and were getting cleaner as the *Melusine* sailed.

They were also getting deeper. With no continental ridges to shove against each other, forming submerged mountains technically taller, if not higher, than anything in the dry world, the seafloor was free to reach depths no unprotected human would ever see. The fish that thrived here were ancient, strange, and, all too often, unknown. Mankind's exploration of the oceans had been going on for centuries, yet had barely scratched the surface, leaving much of the depths uncharted. This trip would hopefully change that, in some small ways...if the people made it back alive.

On the deck of the *Melusine*, a scientist yanked on her rod too hard and too fast, causing the line to snap. While she cursed and her compatriots laughed, the green bumphead parrotfish she had been trying to reel in swam straight down, away from the light, away from the threat posed by sharp hooks that fell from the surface of the water. It was not an intelligent creature; it moved out of instinct, fleeing what it couldn't comprehend. It wouldn't have been in these waters at all had it not blundered into a current that its dim instinctual memory told it should not have existed; the sea was changing too quickly for the long, slow knowledge of the fish to keep pace.

Adult parrotfish could survive easily at depths of up to thirty meters, well below what any of the casual fishermen aboard the *Melusine* were capable of reaching. The fish swam until all was darkness, until it felt it was safe. Then it stopped, hanging in the water, going still as stone as it waited for signs of danger. It wasn't sure which way to go. Instinct would eventually see it safely back to the shallows, but eventually was not now, and while it was not a clever creature, it knew enough to be afraid.

Light flickered below it. Light meant the sun, the surface, and the warm shallows of its youth, where it had been small and swift and surrounded by the bodies of its cohort. Parrotfish didn't have nostalgia as mammals measured such things, and it had abandoned those shallow waters of its own volition, following instinct into deeper places where it could reach its full growth. It was still a schooling fish, preferring the company of others of its kind, but it no longer swam in such teeming numbers. That was for the young. Still, light was a temptation. The parrotfish swam downward, following the light.

The water around it cooled, slowly enough that the unwary parrotfish didn't notice. It was following the light. Every instinct it had told it that this was safe, this was the way home. It was not a deepwater fish, to understand the risks of bioluminescence, the things that could hide behind a glittering glow. It was already at the very bottom of its natural range, and it was still swimming downward.

An adult bumphead parrotfish can weigh more than a hundred pounds. This one tipped the scales at slightly over seventy, larger than a human child. But when the thin, strong hands reached up from below and dragged it down, it didn't break away. It couldn't. It had gone too deep. The water roiled for a moment with its struggles, then was still as the hunter that had claimed it dove down, deeper still, heading home.

The bubbles created by the parrotfish's final moments broke the surface as the fish never would, obscured by the *Melusine*'s wake, and quickly lost.

Two more shutter tests were performed, both at midnight, when fewer passengers would be awake to notice.

Both failed.

CHAPTER 10

Western Pacific Ocean, above the Mariana Trench: September 2, 2022

The *Melusine* sat motionless in the water, held in place by heavy chains and suspended anchors. The seafloor was so far beneath them that traditional anchors would never have worked; they had to depend on counterweights, and hope no storms blew up while they were here.

As Olivia had predicted, the deck had transformed into a veritable science city as soon as the ship came to a stop: workstations and lab benches had popped up almost instantly. Most were clustered near the rails, barely leaving space for people to move, while those who didn't *need* immediate access to the sea—and who had been too slow to race up and stake out their space—were packed near the walls, grumbling about their luck. Fishing lines hung from every deck, attached to sensors and microphones and lures as often as they were attached to hooks. The business of science was getting under way.

(Every level of the ship was getting into the act. The swimming pool had been closed to human use, becoming a "tidal pool" where live-caught fish could be deposited for study. Vacuum tubes attached to the bottom of the ship were extended, pulling in still more fish and depositing them in the pool. There had already been an incident involving someone's prized squid and a deeply confused juvenile great white. More such incidents were expected, and indeed, highly anticipated; several of the scientists who didn't care for the sun had brought their computers down to the poolside, treating the pool as their private aquarium.)

After four days in place, the easy parts were over. Now was when the serious work could begin. The fact that very few of them were actually looking for mermaids was almost inconsequential; with this much oceanography happening in a narrowly focused area, if there were mermaids out there to find, they were going to be found.

Tory paced the lowest public deck, watching the RIBs being prepared for launch. Each of the rigid inflatable boats had the capacity to hold six people joyriding or four people doing serious science—although with so many conflicting kinds of science being done, most boats had been reserved by groups of two or three. The sign-up sheets had gone out to the passengers the night before, and she and Luis had been lucky enough to get their names at the top of the list.

"What is *taking* so long?" she asked, for the fifth time.

"I'll sedate you," said Luis. "I know how to set your microphones. If I set your microphones while you have a nap, no one will ever know, and if they did know, they wouldn't blame me." He was leaning against the rail, expression remarkably calm.

Tory stopped pacing to glare. "You had six cups of coffee with breakfast this morning. I *watched* you."

"Yes, but what you didn't watch was my good night's sleep, or the incredible sex I had before going to bed. We should have gone to floating science camp years ago. You know what gets oceanographers horny? Being in the middle of the ocean. It's amazing."

"You're a pig."

"I am not. I'm a gentleman."

"Who did you sleep with?"

"I'm not going to kiss and tell," he said, mock-affronted. "And besides, it was nobody you'd be interested in. I stay away from the kind of girls you like. They're always so high-strung. Which brings us back to you needing to calm down. Go to the hot tubs tonight and see if you can find someone to give you a backrub." He waggled his eyebrows. "Maybe that lady in white. Olivia? She's hot."

"She works for Imagine."

"They're the ones who say to imagine the possibilities."

"Room on your boat for one more?"

They turned toward the voice, Luis pushing away from the rail while Tory tensed, clearly fighting the urge to resume pacing. Dr. Toth was walking toward them, her valise in one hand. She was wearing a black peasant top that left her shoulders bare, and looked less like a scientist at work than a tourist getting ready to go for a pleasant sail.

"I didn't want to pilot solo, and by the time I'd gotten around to trying to find a team, most of the RIBs were full," she continued. "I won't get in the way, and what I need to do isn't disruptive."

"What *do* you need to do?" asked Tory. It was impossible not to sound wary. Most of the scientists aboard the *Melusine* had come to an understanding about their research and results: "publish or perish" was still a driving motive for many of them, and no one wanted to see their hard work appearing under someone else's name.

"Water samples." Dr. Toth held up her valise. "If there are mermaids in the area, and they've been coming to the surface to hunt, there should be some signs in the water. We know some of what to watch for from the *Atargatis* incident, and I have theories about the rest."

"The ship does water sampling throughout the day," said Luis. "The winches are going, like, *constantly*."

"Yes, and I've been watching those results, but I want some surface readings. I think the sheer size of the vessel is probably keeping the mermaids at what they consider a safe distance while they decide what to do with us. Remember that the *Atargatis* didn't have any immediate sightings, and the *Danvers* didn't have any confirmed sightings at all. Just lights on the water." The *Danvers* had been a military ship. Her crew had been the ones to find the *Atargatis* drifting. The *Danvers* had remained for several days, searching for survivors, only to move on when the sailors began reporting strange, unsettling lights in the water. None of the reports had said anything about mermaids.

"So you think they're watching us?" Luis glanced over the rail. The water was very dark and very clear at the same time, like looking through a window into infinity. A cold hand seemed to run along his spine, sending chills all through him.

"Mr. Martines, I *know* they're watching us. The only question is from how far away." Dr. Toth smiled thinly. "I'll ask again: is there room on your boat?"

"There is, as long as you're willing to remember that we're the ones who signed up for it; we don't move on until we get the readings we need, and we come back when we say it's time to come back." Tory took a step forward. "Is that acceptable?"

"That's dandy," said Dr. Toth.

The RIBs were almost ready. Tory, Luis, and Dr. Toth lined up for the first available boat, climbing in when motioned to do so by the crew. As the only one of them who'd grown up using vehicles like this one, Tory took the helm, listening intently as a crewman gave her a quick rundown of the controls. They were mostly as she'd expected; boats this size didn't really allow for a lot of customization, not without losing their easy interchangeability and flexibility. Push the throttle to go forward; pull back to reverse; turn the "wheel" to turn the RIB. There were no brakes. To stop accelerating, she would stop pushing forward.

"If there's an emergency, hit this," said the crewman. He indicated a flat red button set off to one side, well out of the range where it might be hit by ordinary motion. "That will alert the ship that there's a problem, and activate your tracking beacon. We'll be able to send someone to intercept you. Please reserve for actual *emergencies*."

"Running out of beer doesn't qualify?" quipped Luis.

The crewman leveled a flat look on him. He shrank back in his seat.

"No," said the crewman. "If we thought you were taking this vehicle out for recreational purposes, we'd need to request you leave. There's a long list of people who want the RIBs for actual research."

"We don't have beer," said Dr. Toth, settling on the RIB's rear bench. She placed her valise between her feet, anchoring it with her ankles. "We are boring scientists, off to do boring science things. Thank you for helping us get under way, Marty."

The crewman offered her a dry smile. "I have to go through the prelaunch checklist with everyone, Professor. You know that."

"I do, but since I believe we've heard all the salient bits, can't you give us a little push and trust us to come back in one piece?"

His smile faded. "In these waters, I don't trust that about anybody. You be careful out there, Professor. You too, kids." He took a step back before Tory or Luis could object, turned to the woman manning the crane controls, and hollered, "RIB six is ready for launch!"

"Confirmed!" the woman shouted back. "All hold!"

Shouts of "All hold" ran up and down the deck as the other

crewmen acknowledged the launch. The pulleys activated, and the RIB was lifted into the air, sliding over until it hung suspended above the water. It was a twenty-foot drop at most; they would probably have been fine if the clamps had simply let go. Wet, but fine. Instead the pulleys whirred and the RIB was lowered slowly and deliberately toward the water. When they were a foot or so above the surface, the clamps released, surrendering their magnetic moorings on the prow and stern of the inflatable boat. The drop was negligible, barely lasting long enough for the passengers to notice. Then they were afloat, finally separate from the great body of the *Melusine*.

After the stability of the *Melusine*, the rocking of the RIB in the water was almost a shock. Tory laughed, delighted. Luis made an unhappy face.

"This, right here, is why I took a Dramamine before we launched," he said. "There's something wrong with you."

"I could say the same," said Tory. "Everybody seated?"

"Aye, aye, Captain," said Dr. Toth. Her tone was dry as dust, but she was smiling. Like Tory, she seemed to be taking pleasure in the motion of the small boat, enjoying it in a way that would have seemed impossible to someone who hadn't grown up effectively at sea. Children of islands and the coast went one of two ways: they learned to fear and respect the water, or they learned to live for it.

Tory hit the throttle and the RIB rocketed away from the *Melusine*, out into the wide blue world.

On the *Melusine*'s lowest deck, a similar departure was being prepared—similar in that someone was planning to leave the ship for something smaller, less secure. Different in every other way.

Heather was dressed in a skintight wet suit. Knowing this moment was coming had kept her away from the dessert tables at the dinner buffet, had kept forcing her into the pool right up until it became an aquarium, and still drove her to the gym on deck three. Her Minnow was calibrated to her body weight and size, sensitive to within a five-pound range, and could refuse to launch over any discrepancy. It was a safety function, and while she was capable of overriding it if necessary, the pod's systems made a record of every override, and too many of those could endanger her funding.

Holly helped her sister check the closures on her wet suit, and tried not to think about the fact that its coloring—charcoal gray and electric orange, with bright blue running stripes—was designed to make her body easier to spot if something went wrong and she wound up floating to the surface of the water, unprotected, unable to light a signal flare. They had had their arguments about Heather's choice of profession; had started having them when they were teenagers and Holly realized what she wanted was the lab, while what Heather wanted was the world.

(People who thought they were identical simply because they shared a face and a height and a hairstyle weren't paying close enough attention. Heather had been swimming competitively since the age of twelve, and had the muscled arms and lithe build that came from her athletic choices. Holly, in contrast, was slim instead of sinewy, and often needed to ask her sister to open jars or lift boxes for her. They knew their differences inside and out, had been charting them since the day they began to deviate from their simple synchronicity. Let them be taken as identical in the eyes of the world. They could never fool each other, and that was all that mattered.)

'I wish you wouldn't do this,' signed Holly.

'I'm on this ship *because* I can do this. Imagine hired me to do this.'

'I thought you were going to go down after they'd already checked the water. To make sure it was...' Holly waved her hands helplessly for a moment, not signing, just expressing her frustration. 'Safe. They were supposed to make sure it was safe.'

'Lots of people have gone diving here. Some of them have even gone into the Challenger Deep. None of them were eaten by mermaids.'

'None of them were here *looking* for mermaids, and none of them have been here since the *Atargatis*.'

Heather sighed.

It was true there had been no major dives in the area since the loss of the *Atargatis*. Most research funding was happening in places that were being harder hit by climate change and pollution: the Mariana Trench was remote enough not to be of major interest to the private concerns currently making up the bulk of the research opportunities. There had been a few small private dives, usually funded by skeptic organizations seeking to debunk the *Atargatis* film, but none had gone deeper than thirty meters, and none of them had found anything.

'You can't just do a scan and declare a piece of ocean safe,' Heather signed. 'You know that. Things move in the water. Just because there isn't a shark right now doesn't mean there won't be a shark later. I know my job. I'll be safe.'

'I still don't like it.'

'I know.' Heather caught her sister's hands, effectively silencing them both. It would have been phenomenally rude to do to a stranger, but this had been part of their communication since childhood. She met Holly's eyes, smiled, and waited.

Seconds ticked by. Finally Holly smiled back, leaned in, and kissed her cheek.

Heather let go of her hands. 'I'll bring back your samples,' she signed, and turned and walked away, neither saying nor waiting for goodbye.

Holly stayed where she was. Sometimes she felt like she was still in middle school, standing in the hall, watching her sister go. They had gone to a private school for deaf children and their family members; Hallie had attended with them, part of the small cadre of hearing children who flocked through the halls like strange birds, mouths moving in a parody of communication. But up until the day the swim team had held tryouts, it had always been Holly and Heather, Heather and Holly, the Wilson twins against the world. And then Heather had been called to the water, and Holly had remained on the shore, dry and waiting for her sister to come home.

Holly sighed, turning to walk out of the room. She could help Heather get ready. She couldn't watch her go. Some things were just too much to ask.

The launching station for the Minnow was built into its own cubby. Heather had signed on late in the construction process, and part of what had landed her the job was the fact that her submersible was the correct size for the launch already designed for the *Melusine*. She had required no adjustments or revisions to their plan. She was grateful for that. Too many places didn't want to hire her, claiming her lack of hearing was a liability that would put an unfair burden on their insurance. Never mind that she traveled with a submersible designed to her parameters, signaling all alarms and issues with flashing lights and pressure changes in the fabric of her seat; they were uncomfortable about the idea of working with a deaf woman, and while the Americans with Disabilities Act made it harder for them to refuse her employment, it didn't make it impossible. There would always be lawyers who specialized in keeping the disabled out of the workforce, especially when the jobs they wanted to do—the jobs they were trained to do—were difficult or dangerous or otherwise complex.

But the *Melusine* had been built around the idea of a Minnow, and Heather had a Minnow. More, Heather had one of only three privately owned Minnows in the world rated for depths like those in the Mariana Trench. All the others came with steeper fees and more difficult operators. All she needed was a place to dock and permission to descend.

The three engineers responsible for maintaining the launch and monitoring the Minnow gave her the thumbs-up. They had learned some basic sign for when she wasn't in the submersible; once she was inside, they would be able to communicate via the translator overlay on her control panel. A flashing light would alert her to any messages, and they'd type whatever they needed her to know. It was a simple, reasonably elegant solution. More than once she'd had an engineer tell her, in halting ASL, that it was better than the verbal way; they didn't need to worry about distracting her during a complicated maneuver, and distance never led to distortion. In the soundless depths, she was perfectly at home.

Heather offered them an amiable nod and walked to the open hatch of her Minnow. It was more manhole than door, barely wide enough for her to wiggle through. Earlier versions had been even tighter, requiring her to go without eating or drinking for a full twenty-four hours before the trip. That had been...less than ideal. Blacking out from hunger while hundreds of feet below the surface of the sea was a good way to wind up a statistic, one more name on the long list of lives the water had claimed as its due.

She grasped the bar above the hatch and slid, feet-first, into the comforting snugness of her pod. There was room inside for one person, and she was small enough that she did most of the minor maintenance herself; finding an engineer who could get through the entrance was virtually impossible. Anything more complex was either done by machine or required cracking the hull, a maneuver that would put the Minnow into dry dock for up to six months. Heather had become extremely skilled at keeping her systems up and running. The last time she'd been grounded for six months, she'd driven everyone around her out of their mind with her fussing. No one wanted that to happen again.

Settling into the seat, she locked her feet into position, bare heels flush to the metal of the pedals, and fastened the four-point harness that would keep her from being knocked around during her descent, before beginning the slow, methodical process of checking and verifying that all systems were working as well as the technicians thought they were. A single red light would have been enough to abort the descent. Anxious as she was to get to work, she was even more anxious to stay alive.

As each switch was flipped, toggle was pressed, and button was pushed, the associated light came on, deep blue and steady. She pulled the submersible's keyboard over and tapped out, 'All systems clear down here. Up there?'

'No problems: showing good to go,' was the reply. 'Ready for launch?'

'Absolutely.' She added a smiley face. It was unprofessional, but without tone of voice to tell the techs what she was feeling, she needed to take her shades of meaning where she could find them.

'Sealing the hatch.'

She couldn't hear the clang as her submersible's hatch came down—although she'd been told by Hallie that it was remarkably loud, a clang that echoed through the entire room—but she could feel the air change around her. The Minnow was being pressurized to sea level, and would stay there throughout her descent, saving her from the need to worry about the bends when she surfaced. She knew how to control for decompression sickness, but it was better if it could be avoided. The pressurization would also make her hull more difficult to puncture. She was a fully inflated sphere dropping into the darkness, and anything that wanted to get to her was going to have a fight on its hands.

'Pressure is steady,' came the message. 'Are you ready to drop?'

'Ready,' she replied.

'Launch in five...four...three...two...'

The *one* was never transmitted. It was assumed. Heather braced herself, hands on the sticks that would control her depth and orientation, and felt the shock run though the Minnow as the *Melusine* released the connecting cables. For a single dizzying moment she was sinking like the lifeless thing she was. Then she pushed down with both feet, triggering the exterior lights, and the water came alive around her. She pulled back on the sticks, stopping her descent, leveling out, and hung there, suspended no more than ten feet below the *Melusine*'s hull.

It was easy to forget how big the ship was when she was aboard it. She tilted the submersible, letting her lights play along the bottom of the *Melusine*. A few fish swam there, exploring the limits of their world. No mermaids, of course.

She snorted. "No mermaids, of course" would probably be the epitaph for this mission. Most people assumed the *Atargatis* video was a hoax. Heather knew better—everyone who worked for Imagine knew better—but she had spoken to evolutionary biologists, had read all Dr. Toth's papers on the subject, and had come to her own conclusions. Yes, mermaids were real. That didn't mean they were going to be caught twice in the same spot. For them to have gone undetected for so long, they had to be migratory, and they had to be cautious. Imagine wasn't going to find mermaids. They'd be lucky to find anything.

That was fine by her. She was being paid to dive and explore one of the remotest, least documented spots in the world, all in pursuit of something that wasn't going to be there, which meant she couldn't be blamed when she failed to find it. She was going to find something else instead: she was going to find the bottom of the Challenger Deep. She was going to do what no one else had ever done, or even really dreamed of doing, and she was going to do it as a one-woman diver with a disability.

This would change the world. Maybe not in the big, flashy way Imagine wanted, but it would be enough for her, and for every deaf girl with a dream who came after her.

Heather pushed down on the sticks and dropped into the dark.

CHAPTER 11

Western Pacific Ocean, above the Mariana Trench: September 2, 2022

Tory steered the RIB to a stop. The *Melusine* was a speck on the horizon, so far away that it was impossible to guess at her size; she could have been a tugboat or an aircraft carrier, or even a toy, waiting to be picked up and carried away by some unseen child. There was nothing else. No land, not even the hint that land might exist somewhere beyond the water. The world could have flooded completely and left them none the wiser.

"Luis?" she asked.

"On it." He began unclasping cases, revealing their waterproofed contents. He was a blur of motion as he assembled his microphones and clipped them to small drone systems.

Tory, meanwhile, braced her back against the controls and opened her laptop. Less water resistant than the microphones, but protected by as many layers of shielding and plastic as technology could manage, it would continue to work as long as she didn't actually drop it into the water. "I'll have the software up in a minute," she said. "You're clear to do your drops anytime."

Dr. Toth leaned back against her seat and watched them. "The two of you make me tired just looking at you," she commented mildly. "Kids are great, but holy shit, am I glad I'm not one anymore."

Tory glanced up for a heartbeat—long enough to see that Dr.

Toth was serious—before returning her attention to the screen, saying, "We only have the RIB for a few hours, and even if we had it longer, there'd be no guarantee the weather would stay good enough to let us get our readings. We have to move fast."

"Besides, science should feel urgent every once in a while," said Luis. "It makes up for the parts that drag on and on." He dropped a microphone over the side. "You know, half the time we're saving the world in slow motion, but days like this, we get the chance to run."

"That doesn't make it any less tiring to watch." Dr. Toth stretched, turning her face toward the sun. "It's a beautiful day. The ocean isn't going anywhere."

"Truer words," muttered Tory, and kept typing.

Luis frowned. "Except it is. The ocean we have today isn't the ocean we had ten years ago, and it's definitely not the ocean we're going to have ten years from now. Pollution, global climate change, nuclear runoff..."

"You know what I like about the ocean we *do* have?" asked Dr. Toth. "The part where we've dumped so much crap into it that it would be justified in becoming something out of a horror movie, and yet the horror movie it's giving us isn't related to any of those things. Not really."

"What do you mean?" asked Tory.

"I mean if the mermaids are real—and they are—and if the mermaids are smart enough to be watching us—which they also are—they don't have anything to do with humans. They evolved on their own. They stayed in their own environment until we started sending ships into their living room. To them, we're the myths. We're the monsters. We appear out of nowhere, we've probably snagged more than a few of them in fishing nets and trawler rigs, and half the things we have on us at any given time are going to be incomprehensible to a preindustrial society with no concept of manufacturing. They aren't our fault. We didn't mutate some flatworm into a murderous new form, and we didn't melt a glacier that freed a prehistoric predator. They exist because they exist. That's nice." Dr. Toth smirked. "I'm so used to humans being responsible for everything that it's a pleasant change when we didn't do it."

"Humans are the worst," deadpanned Luis.

"You said it, not me," said Dr. Toth. "What are you kids doing?"

"I'm setting up a microphone array to get an auditory snapshot of the area, and Victoria's getting her software online so that she can pick it apart," said Luis.

"We think the mermaids communicate verbally, in addition to signing," said Tory. "We know that they're mimics."

"How do we know that?" asked Dr. Toth.

Tory paused. Dr. Toth's tone and attitude were familiar: she'd seen them from dozens of professors. But sometimes those professors were trying to guide her to an obvious conclusion, while other times they didn't care about her results; they just wanted to keep her running in circles so that they wouldn't have to do any actual work.

Dr. Toth wasn't responsible for her final grade. Tory took a breath and said, "Mr. Blackwell recruited us for this voyage because of the focus of my research. How much do you know about sonar mapping?"

"It can be used to get a topographic picture of something we can't see, like the inside of a cave or the bottom of an undersea cavern."

"Well, what I do is *biological* sonar mapping. I record the sounds of living things and pick them apart to learn more about the creatures that made them. I can identify every known species of kingfisher by call, and while I'm not an ornithologist, I've been able to supply recordings to actual ornithologists that may help them prove certain species aren't extinct after all." Tory returned her eyes to her screen, typing as she continued, "Think of Times Square. Someone who did ambient noise recordings there would get so much more than they'd be expecting. Not just cars and trucks and buses, but the subway underground, and the planes overhead, and the *voices*. Thousands of people, hundreds of languages. People singing, screaming, laughing. Music. Recorded advertisements. Police loudspeakers. There'd be so *much*. But if you have good software and a lot of patience, all that information turns into archeology."

Tory had started speeding up halfway through her speech, words tumbling over each other in her excitement. "How many languages are there? How similar are they? Figure that out and you know how far people have come to be in this place. Languages that evolve in similar places tend to have similar sounds; you can get an idea of how widespread the species as a whole is from how dissimilar the words are. Look at the ambient noise. Is it bouncing off high structures? Is it coming from different levels? You can even learn things about the biology of the people you're listening to. Labored breath, sounds of pain, crying... There's so *much*. Unsnarling an afternoon in Times Square could be the work of years. The coral reefs are the Times Square of the ocean. So many species, so many sounds, so many things to untangle and learn."

"We're a long way from the coral reefs now," said Dr. Toth.

"I know. The Challenger Deep is more like setting a microphone array in the middle of a cornfield in Iowa and waiting to see what the wind brings you. I have days and days of essentially dead air. The water moves, the fish swim by—I can hear those too, once I know the water in an area well enough—but mostly, things are quiet. It's just that when they're not quiet, they're a lot noisier than they ought to be. The water down there *rings*."

"You think you've been eavesdropping on the mermaids."

"Yes, and I think they've been eavesdropping on the world." Tory glanced up again. "A pod of whales comes through in December; we hear that same pod singing half a mile down in June. Note for note, the same whales. How? We know they aren't here anymore. Echoes don't last that long. A boat goes by, we hear its engines from the same level. And on and on and on. The mermaids steal sounds. Why, we don't know. But the thing that got us a spot on the *Melusine* was the *Atargatis*."

Dr. Toth frowned. "How's that?"

"We found a recording of the *Atargatis* engines," said Luis. He threw three more microphones into the water. They floated for a moment before their weight dragged them below the surface. He hit a button. A brief cascade of bubbles appeared as the engines attached to the microphone shafts whirred to life, driving them deeper. "As in, we found a recording that claimed the *Atargatis* engines were in the Mariana Trench, right now, operating at full power."

"They mimic," said Tory. "Why, we don't know. Maybe it's a hunting strategy. Maybe it's part of their mating rituals. Maybe they enjoy making different sounds with their mouths. Dolphins play."

Dr. Toth said nothing, her face stony and her eyes unreadable.

"It doesn't really matter," said Tory, once she was sure Dr. Toth wasn't going to contradict her. "We know they're here, because there's nothing else that could explain what I've already recorded. Now we need to figure out if that's part of how they *communicate*."

"What do you think?" asked Dr. Toth.

"I think they're smart enough to have a language, and I think we need to figure out how it works. Dr. Wilson can handle the visual component. I've got the sound."

"Hence my part of the plan," said Luis, throwing three more microphones into the water. He pitched these farther out, driving them downward at an angle. "I get her the best possible auditory snapshot of the area, she pulls it apart and uses it to tell us how these things work. It's like hyperspace modeling, but with living organisms, and it's going to win us every prize in the book. They're going to need to invent new medals just to tell us how awesome we are."

"I see," said Dr. Toth, and finally unlocked her own valise. It opened like a gleaming stainless steel and glass flower, tubes attached to small drones gleaming in the sunlight. Both Tory and Luis turned to look, unable to suppress their curiosity. Dr. Toth smothered a smile. Science was all about curiosity. It was a world where the kids who touched hot stoves and poked sticks down mysterious holes in their backyards could get better tools, protective gear, and bigger holes to poke at. Asking scientists not to look into an open box was like asking cats not to saunter through an open door. It simply wasn't practical.

"These are autonomous drones—probably cousins of yours," she said, picking up one of her gleaming contraptions and nodding toward Luis's remaining microphones at the same time. "They're designed to dive, take their samples, and return. As long as they can find the homing signal, they'll find their way back to me."

"Why couldn't you release them from the ship?" asked Tory.

"For the same reason you couldn't set your microphones there," said Dr. Toth. "We're tainting the water by sitting in it. We create an artificial dark spot, which is interfering with plankton and algae in the area surrounding the ship. We're filtering the water we take in for the pool. That means the wildlife density is changing, too. If I want a clean picture...Well, if I want a clean picture, I need a time machine and access to preindustrial waters. Since I'm not going to get that, I need to take the next-best option, which is distance. Besides, it's a beautiful day. I couldn't spend it cooped up on a ship."

"Yes, because spending it crammed into a RIB is so much better," said Luis.

Dr. Toth looked at him. "Yes, it is," she said. "Out here, we're free. We can go our own way. The fact that we're planning to return doesn't matter. Right now, if we wanted to, we could choose to run. We could hit the gas, angle toward the islands, and get the hell out of here. See the world. See something other than this patch of blue."

"Is that what you want?" asked Tory.

Dr. Toth shook her head. "I'm in this for the long haul. I just want to get my samples. But not wanting to be free and not wanting to *feel* free aren't the same thing. When you get to my age, you'll learn to hold on to any illusion of freedom you can get."

Tory's laptop beeped. She looked at it before smiling, half in satisfaction, half in relief. "Software's ready," she said. "Luis?"

"On it," he said, and tossed the rest of the microphones into the water. The waves swept over them and carried them away.

Most people thought the lights on Heather's submersible were surprisingly soft. Given the depths to which she was descending, deep places where the sun never reached, they expected her to be packing floodlights, powerful things strong enough to send a vampire scurrying back into its grave. Instead, her light array cast a soft white light, more like a glow than anything else. They had been calibrated that way so as not to alarm the fish. As she sank deeper, she would switch to red light, which was virtually invisible to most of what she was likely to encounter.

Cameras on the Minnow's hull filmed everything around her, transmitting it to the *Melusine*, where one of the technicians was monitoring the feed. If she saw anything they wanted a better look at, the message would come down, and she'd find herself spending half an hour following some exotic fish around the ocean. Not the most exciting part of her job, but not the worst, either. There were sampling tubes built into the bottom of the submersible, allowing her to bring back water and live specimens. It was best to avoid sampling on the way down if possible. Better to increase her weight when she was already on the way back up, and didn't need to worry about putting an excessive strain on her engine.

A school of silvery fish flashed by, bodies glinting in the light. Heather turned the submersible to track their progress, then turned back to the real business at hand: descending. Even in a submersible pod designed to withstand the crushing depths, descent was a delicate business, best taken slowly, methodically, and with the utmost respect for the drowned world around her. This was not where she belonged. This had never been where she belonged. Humanity had chosen the land over the sea millennia ago, and sometimes—when she was letting her mind wander, when she was romanticizing what she did and how she did it—she thought the sea still held a grudge. Breakups were never easy, and while humanity was hot and fast and had had plenty of time to get over it, the oceans were deep and slow, and for them all change had happened only yesterday. The seas did not forgive, and they did not welcome their wayward children home.

The waters grew darker as she sank, one eye on the view port, the other on her controls. The "glass" she looked through was a specially treated blend of titanium and clear metallic compounds. She didn't understand its chemical composition—she was a pilot, not a chemist or engineer—but it had been designed to withstand crush depths even deeper than those the rest of her sub could withstand. A window was a frivolous design element in a research sub. For a documentary setup, like hers, it was necessary. Much of the development budget for the Minnow had come from companies like Imagine. At least one large entertainment concern was hoping to turn the submersible into a unique theme park ride, one where guests could descend into the dark of specially designed and maintained "oceanic vents," seeing deep-sea fish in a parody of their natural habitat. Another company, this one specializing in romantic couples cruises, wanted to turn the submersible into a strange new date location, one where champagne could be shared while a silent driver steered lovers into the abyss.

With all that money coming in from sources that wanted—no, *demanded*—a show, it had been essential the view port be made capable of withstanding the depths. It was frivolous and silly, and privately Heather was grateful. She liked the cool mystery of the deeps, but it was nice to be able to see where she was going without depending on the cameras. Mechanical failure was always a risk, especially when she was cruising hundreds of meters beneath the surface of the sea. If something happened to breach her hull or compromise her window, she'd die almost instantly. If something happened to her cameras, on the other hand...

Every submersible operator knew the stories of the ones who'd gone down but never come back up, the ones whose engines had stalled or whose cameras had gone wonky, telling them everything but which way to go if they wanted to survive. Not all of the missing submersibles had been recovered. Some of them were still out there somewhere, metal coffins resting at the bottom of the sea, unfindable thanks to the depths where they had settled. A window couldn't go to rolling static and unanswered questions. A window showed you what was there.

A red flash from the console caught Heather's attention. She glanced to the text scroll.

'Everything good?'

'Fine and dandy,' she replied. 'About to drop again. Some fish, but no mermaids so far.' She added a winking emoji. Her operators would appreciate that. They were a good bunch of people, not humorless bureaucrats like the ones she'd worked with when she was doing drops to check for precious minerals on the seafloor. All things considered, if she couldn't be doing purely scientific work, she'd take entertainment over government contracts any day. At least the people who worked for Imagine knew how to laugh, and didn't treat her like some sort of affirmative action hire. She had her job because she was *good* at her job. Not because she was a woman, or a twin, or a redhead, and certainly not because she was deaf. But try telling that to some of those assholes. As far as they were concerned, she'd either been hired because her ears didn't work, or because her tits did.

'Keep an eye open!' came the return message. A light turned green above it. She was good to continue her descent.

Heather flipped a few switches and tilted the nose of her submersible down, easing her way into the depths. The water continued to darken. The fish grew stranger with every meter of her descent, flattening, lengthening, acquiring a profusion of teeth and tendrils and glowing fins. There was nothing in the world like the deep ocean, where life was rare and its hold was tenuous but tenacious, refusing to let go. She breathed deeply, letting the canned, slightly stale air of the submersible fill her lungs. She was a surface creature where surface creatures had no business being, and it delighted her.

Down she went, down and down and down, until sunlight seemed like something from another world, impossible and easily forgotten. A jellyfish drifted past, diaphanous tendrils dangling, and for a moment she could see the outline of a human form in the way its membranes pulsed, the ghost of a drowned girl forever doomed to haunt the restless sea.

When Heather and Holly had been young, still learning the way to navigate their closed, silent world, Holly had been the practical one and Heather had been the dreamer. There were people who thought those positions had been reversed as they'd grown, with Heather going into the concrete solidity of engineering while Holly moved into the fluidity of organic chemistry. Those people couldn't have been more wrong. Holly was a scientist to the core, focused on the practical, the achievable, and the understandable. Heather was still a dreamer. She'd known she could never be an astronaut since she was a child, that no one would put a deaf girl into a rocket and tell her to reach for the stars, so she'd looked around until she'd found the next best thing, and then she'd done what she had to do to make it her own. She was one of the best in her field, and a lot of that was because after giving up on one dream, she'd be damned before she gave up another.

Machines beeped and buzzed around her as she dropped into the dark, leaving the last of the mesopelagic layers of the ocean behind her. She heard none of it. When something needed her attention it flashed, green or red or amber. In that regard she was already a creature of the deeps. Light, more than sound, caught and held her focus. She couldn't be distracted unless she wanted to be. Everything she was, she focused on the drop, and on the promise of the Challenger Deep.

The light at the front of her submersible touched the trench wall. She had reached the first milestone. From here she would be moving through barely charted waters, passing through channels that virtually no human eye had ever seen. Certainly no human eye protected by a machine as sturdy and nimble as hers. She could spend a year exploring this trench without ceasing to discover things that science didn't know. She was breaking new ground. She was answering the unanswered questions.

'Dropping,' she typed one handed, and pulled back on her steering wheel, heading down, down, down into the dark.

CHAPTER 12

Western Pacific Ocean, above the Mariana Trench: September 2, 2022

Tory climbed out of the RIB and nearly walked into Olivia. She stopped, blinking. Olivia—dressed today in white jeans and a faux corset—blinked back.

"Uh, hi," said Tory.

"Hello," said Olivia, cheeks coloring faintly pink. She paused before asking, "Did your science go well?"

"Oh. Uh, yes. Very well." Tory resisted the urge to rub the back of her own neck. She was here for science—she was here for *Anne*—not for some schoolgirl crush on a woman who couldn't stop bleaching her laundry.

Honest.

Olivia smiled, blush fading. "Excellent. Hello, Luis."

Luis, who had just stepped off the RIB, offered Olivia a jaunty wave. "Hey. Where are you off to?"

"Heather Wilson is making her first descent into the Challenger Deep. I was heading for the lower deck to watch the video feed. Did you want to come?"

"I'm good, but you should take Tory." Luis pushed his partner's shoulder, knocking her forward, ignoring her glare. "She loves a good dive, don't you?"

"I hate you and everything you stand for," said Tory.

"That means yes," said Luis, and turned to help Dr. Toth out of the boat.

Olivia bit her lower lip, looking at Tory for a moment before asking, "Did you want to come?"

Tory reviewed her possible excuses quickly before throwing her hands up and saying, "Why the hell not? Lead the way."

Olivia's smile was quick as she turned and resumed her walk. Tory followed.

They didn't speak as they walked along the deck and took the elevator down to the pool deck. They weren't the first ones to show up wanting to watch the dive; when they got there, Holly and Hallie were already standing next to the monitors, so close together that their shoulders were touching.

"Hey, Hallie," said Tory, stepping into position. Olivia stopped a foot or so away. "What's going on?"

"Heather's on a deep dive. Holly came to get me so we could watch." She shook her head. "It's always tense."

Holly kept her eyes on the monitors and didn't say a word.

Hallie sighed.

Hallie sometimes thought things would have been easier if she, and not Heather, had been a twin. Let everything stay the same except for birth order. She could still have been the translator for her sisters, but she would have been the one with a constant friend, companion, and busybody glued to her side, while Heather could have gone off and lived life her own way, not worrying about upsetting Holly.

The leftmost monitor was set up with a caption crawl along the bottom, relaying Heather's conversation with the operations team. Hallie recognized the typos as belonging to her sister; this was a live feed.

"Hey," said Olivia, leaning forward to see Hallie around Tory. "The two of you feel like being interviewed about Heather's descent?"

Holly's eyes were fixed on the captions, wide and bright and frightened. Hallie glanced at her before shaking her head apologetically.

"Maybe later," she said.

Olivia nodded. "Ray's supposed to be taking a nap anyway. He was up late last night, getting footage of the midnight research team."

"Of which I was one, so if I can be out of bed, he should be too," said Tory primly.

"Shut up." Olivia leaned over to bump Tory's shoulder with her own. "It's not his fault that you're a biological sport who doesn't require sleep."

"It's his fault that he isn't," said Tory.

Hallie signed the whole time, more out of habit than from any belief that Holly was paying attention to her hands. Holly's eyes were glued to the screen, watching the fish swim by, seeing what her twin saw as she went down, down, down into the dark.

Heather was ten meters past the mouth of the Mariana Trench and descending. The pressure outside her submersible was such that if she'd opened the hatch—if the machinery keeping it locked had allowed her to open the hatch—she would have been crushed before she had the opportunity to drown.

On the surface, thirty feet was nothing. She could walk thirty feet for a cup of coffee, moving horizontally, making no real effort. Underwater, everything changed. Every foot she descended was another foot of water piled on top of her, another foot of weight and pressure and danger. She was far past the depth that the greatest free divers in the world could survive. She was approaching the depth that had, for decades, been the deepest mankind could safely go— not that there was anything safe about what she was doing. Safety had been left far behind her, and she was flying.

Nothing had passed her cameras in almost five meters. The last thing she'd seen had been some sort of squid, glowing pearlescent under her lights, moving fast enough that it was almost as if it had registered and was objecting to her presence. Things this deep usually didn't care about her. She could startle them with sudden motions, but a calm, controlled descent was something for them to ignore. The squid had been fleeing.

'Getting an audience up here,' said the display. 'Both your sisters came to see the show.'

'Tell them it's just getting started,' she typed back. At this depth, there was going to be a several-second delay on each end: she could respond instantly when something came through, but she had no way of knowing when the first message had been sent. She pulled gently on her controls, forcing the submersible deeper into the black.

The Challenger Deep was ahead, and with it, sights no human eye had ever seen. She was going to be the first. She was—

Something flashed by her window, moving into the light and then out again too quickly for the eye to follow. She pulled back, stopping her descent, and hung suspended in the water as she typed, 'Did you get that? Can you slow it down?'

The reply would take at least thirty seconds: time for them to get the request, slow the footage, watch it, and send back an answer. Heather began to turn slowly, lights bouncing first off the wall of the trench itself, and then off the nothingness beyond, illuminating absence. The water was crystalline and clear, lacking most of the high cloudiness of the photic zones. It was a lack of plankton and larval animals, which accounted for much of the usual distortion. Down here, it was just her, and the sea, and whatever had swum past.

Her console flashed. The answer was coming through.

'Heather,' it said.

'Heather, please,' it said.

'Heather, please remain calm,' it said.

Heather frowned. This piecemeal method of communication was nowhere near good enough. They'd have to drop some sort of signal booster for her next descent, something that could bounce the wireless between her and the ship. This sort of stuttering delay did no one any good.

'Heather, please remain calm and return to the surface,' said the full message.

Heather's frown deepened. She hesitated with her fingers above the keys, trying to decide on her reply. If she said 'no,' they would argue. If she asked 'why,' she'd be as good as agreeing to return. And she didn't *want* to return. It had taken time and effort to get this deep, to enter the stretch of sea that she'd been dreaming of since the day she signed on for this mission. She could descend again, but there was only one first dive in any one location. One chance to make a first impression. Without a clear and obvious danger, she didn't want her first impression of the Challenger Deep to be undefined motion on a monitor and fleeing like a scared puppy with her tail between her legs. She wanted to *know*.

Heather pulled back her hand. The communication channels

were bad enough, attenuated and stretched thin by the water, that it would be at least a minute before anyone could say for sure that she wasn't responding. She could cover a lot of ground in a minute.

Heather hauled on the controls, and her Minnow continued its descent.

The only real difference between the Challenger Deep and the Mariana Trench was the light. Heather had thought she knew what darkness looked like; had believed the waters of the trench were as dark as it was possible for a place to be. As her submersible slipped below the surface of the Deep, dropping downward at a pace that skirted the line between conservative and ambitious, she realized with slow and dawning wonder that she had never known darkness in her life. Nothing that lived on the surface had.

Humanity had feared the dark since time immemorial, and yet humanity had never *experienced* the dark, because it wasn't until recently—the age of cunning hands and clever machines—that the dark had been anything more than a whispering legend, a rumor of a nightmare. Biologists and the laws of evolution on Earth said humanity had started, like everything else, in the sea. Maybe that explained fearing the dark. An ancestral memory of this sort of all-consuming nothingness would have been enough to terrify anyone.

The dark pressed around her like it had physical weight, like it accounted for more of the crushing danger of the deeps than the water itself. Her submersible's lights pierced it like spears, so bright that they seemed unbelievable, yet unable to illuminate more than a few feet on every side. She could have turned on every light she had, lit every emergency signal, and still not done anything to brighten the Challenger Deep. This was where darkness went to live forever, growing deeper and more powerful as the eons passed it by.

Heather was not claustrophobic—couldn't be, with her job—but as she looked into the blackness around her, as she felt it pushing down against her skin, her heart stuttered in her chest, becoming heavy and awkward as it tried to get back into rhythm with itself. She took a deep breath, shunting the panic aside. There was no point to it. All it could do when she was this deep was get her killed. Then, with a single sharp, decisive motion, she turned the submersible's lights off.

The dark surged in like a living thing, extinguishing the world.

It had her surrounded in an instant. Heather's heart lurched again. She took a deep breath, forcing herself calm, and waited for...what? Not for her eyes to adjust. This wasn't the tame dark of a city street or a suburban home. It wasn't even the slightly wild dark of a forest or a secluded beach. Moonlight, starlight, lightning, they were always there, always lighting up some fragment of the world. They were beyond her here. So she wasn't waiting for her eyes to come to terms with what surrounded them. She was waiting, if anything, for her heart to catch up with the rest of her.

Slowly the fear subsided, and her heartbeat resumed its normal rhythm, so familiar that she could ignore it. Heather smiled before powering the console lights back on. There were no new messages. Either the *Melusine* was still waiting for her reply or she had traveled outside of communication range. It didn't matter. They couldn't demand that she come back.

A few flipped switches and her research lights were on, casting a soft red glow. These lights were designed to be as unobtrusive as possible, not frightening the fish. Truly deepwater species found their own ways to make light, or gave up on it completely, consigning it to whatever served as ancestral memory for fish. Down this deep, it seemed like whatever didn't glow in the dark didn't have eyes either, like evolution had written off sight as a useless skill.

(Which begged the question, she sometimes felt, of whether there were senses humanity, blessed as it was with light and air and a relatively pressure-free environment, had given up on as useless. She and Holly got by fine without hearing; the only time they were really inconvenienced was when they had to deal with people who *could* hear, and who inevitably thought the twins were suffering in some way because they couldn't. What else might people have given up, and never noticed was missing, since it was virtually impossible to define an absence?)

She hung there, suspended, while she recovered her bearings, and watched the water around her come alive. It wasn't the fast, teeming life of the surface. But from time to time something would move in the shadows, a jelly drifting past or a fish coming to investigate her lights. She watched as a long, thin ribbon of something that might have been an eel swam past, too far away for her to get a good look at it, too close for her to avoid the impression of limitless teeth bursting from its cavern of a mouth. The laws of nature were different here.

Heather took a deep breath and resumed her descent.

She had been slow before; she was glacial now, turning her submersible in an effort to record everything around her, every scrap of motion and distant, shadowy glimpse of the walls of the Deep. She didn't want to bring her running lights all the way up until she reached the bottom—and she *was* going to reach the bottom. This was her Everest, and she was taking her time to make sure she made it all the way. The video feed of her descent would prove it had happened. The video of her ascent would tell the scientists on board where they wanted her to go next, when she went for them and not for herself. This drop, this descent, this was all for her. This had always been for her.

Being a twin sometimes meant going to extremes to find a way to distinguish herself from her sister, especially since they had so many labels. They weren't just twins, they were deaf twins, attractive deaf twins, attractive deaf twins with naturally red hair, attractive deaf twins with naturally red hair working in STEM. Sometimes she felt like they were so labeled that they should have collapsed under all the competing expectations. Instead they pressed on, and they found ways to set themselves apart from one another. Holly took the surface of the sea, and she? She got the bottom.

She was finally taking what was hers.

The message light on her console blinked. Heather glanced at it, interested.

'HEATHER COME BACK TO SURFACE NOW,' it said. Apparently, it had taken longer to come through because it was coming through complete. Interesting. The packet rate must have been scrambled by the water.

Quickly she tapped, 'Too deep for swift ascent. Finishing mapping pass. Surfacing on schedule,' and pressed SEND. Let them yell when she got back to the ship. There was no way she was cutting this mission short for anything but a natural disaster. She turned her eyes back to the viewing window, easing herself farther downward.

The natural disaster swam toward her with a sinuous rippling motion, cutting through the water like it possessed no resistance at all. Heather took her hands off the controls, eyes going wide and chest going tight. When she signed up for this mission, it had been with her eyes on the Challenger Deep, not because she'd believed, for even an instant, that she was going to *find* anything.

The mermaid was the size of a small thresher shark or an adult human, swimming with the up-and-down thrust of a dolphin or a person in a mermaid costume. For one dizzy moment Heather's brain seized on that idea, turning it around and trying to present it as the solution. Imagine had paid professional mermaids to accompany the first voyage to the Mariana Trench. They could have done it again. They could have...

No. Science, logic, reality, they all said no. The mermaid wasn't wearing any protective gear. Its hips were too narrow to belong to an adult human, much less be shrouded by a pressure suit to keep it from being crushed. It couldn't be a person in a costume. No matter how much her mind wanted it to be, it simply. Wasn't. Possible.

It was long and lean, narrow boned, more like a fish than a mammal. It had fleshy buttocks, but only in comparison to the lean outline of its hominid back, the almost fleshless curve of its long eel's tail; it could sit, she was sure of that, assuming the classical pose of Andersen's Little Mermaid on her rock. A primate pelvis, then, or something that mimicked a primate pelvis, for whatever strange evolutionary reason.

Its face was something like a viperfish's and something like a mummified ape's and something like the shadows that sometimes chased her through her dreams. Its eyes were wide and round and fixed on the submersible, set above a mouth that seemed too full of teeth to be possible. A cloud of filmy "hair" surrounded its head, the individual strands somehow too thick, each of them glowing at the end with bioluminescent light.

It slowed a few feet from the submersible, the question of those primate-like hips answered as it flipped to hover upright in the water, long arms making smooth circling motions to keep it stable. Its hands were webbed, almost like fins that had been accessorized with opposable thumbs.

It was looking at her.

Heather swallowed, staring into the mermaid's eyes. She wasn't scared. She should have been—she knew that much—but in the moment all she could feel was numb shock slowly giving way to wonder. They were real. They were *real*. The *Melusine* had come to the Mariana Trench to find mermaids, to answer the question of what had happened to the *Atargatis* once and for all, and now here was a mermaid, looking at her. Right at her. Belatedly she realized that if the mermaid was looking at her, and she was looking at the mermaid, that she'd done it: she had made first contact. She was going to go down in history as the person who, after centuries of legends and fairy tales, had gone to the bottom of the sea and proven that mermaids were real. Mermaids existed.

More of them were coming. Her throat got tight as movement in the water around her resolved into more approaching mermaids, all roughly the same size as the one hanging suspended in the water in front of her.

Seen like this, she could start to find the differences between them. All were gray, fish colored, but some had white stripes on their tails while others had black stripes interspersed with bands of paler gray. A natural variance? Some sort of deepwater cosmetic? Or a sign of age and maturity, appearing and changing as they grew? Humans didn't have those sorts of marks, but many other mammals did, as did many fish. Were they fish or mammals? They had no breasts, only a slight curve to their chests that could, at a distance and in shadow, be taken for cleavage; they seemed to have little to no body fat. They must have been eating constantly, never slowing their pursuit of calories. It was the only way they could possibly survive in waters that were so deep, and so cold, and so unforgiving.

The message light was flashing again. Heather didn't look at the screen. She had more important things to worry about.

I wish I were a biologist, she thought. She would have been able to understand more about what she was seeing, if she'd been a biologist. But then, maybe it was best that she wasn't. She could look at them and just see *mermaids*, rather than trying to pick them apart with her eyes. The cameras were still transmitting. The biologists back on the ship would have plenty to work with by the time she made it back.

The first mermaid swam closer, eyes fixed on Heather. She held her breath, not daring to move as the mermaid reached out and pressed one hand against the viewing dome. With its fingers spread, it was even more apparent how delicate they were, how finely boned. The webs connecting them were almost as thick as the fingers, reinforcing the impression that the mermaid's hands had started their existence as fins.

Then the mermaid pulled back its other arm and punched the window.

Heather jumped. It was a reflex; she couldn't help herself. She stared as the mermaid pulled back and punched again. It was a small show of hostility. It wouldn't have mattered...but there were so *many* of them, and more were coming all the time.

'No,' Heather signed, heedless of the fact that the mermaid couldn't possibly understand. Her skin felt too tight, her heart hammering again, this time driven by perfectly reasonable fear. The mermaids could survive down here. The mermaids were *designed* to survive down here, crafted into perfect denizens of the deep by millions of years of evolution. They were alien, yes, but they were aliens of Earth, clearly cousins to the viperfish and eels that moved through these unforgiving depths.

More mermaids moved toward the submersible. Somehow she had made the transition from "curiosity" into "danger," and now they were on the attack. Unable to think of what else to do, Heather hit the button that would activate the submersible's external lights— all of them. They flashed on, and the water around her lit up like midday in comparison to the absolute blackness of only a moment before. The mermaids recoiled as Heather gawked, unable to move her hands in her shock.

Mermaids surrounded her on all sides. Hundreds of mermaids, more than should have been possible, more than the Challenger Deep could possibly have sustained. There was no way, there was just no way, and yet there they were, thin arms thrown up to shield saucer eyes. Then, as she watched, they lowered their arms and looked at her. It was difficult to ascribe human emotions to their inhuman faces, and yet it was impossible to look at them and not see hatred in their eyes.

Heather grabbed the controls and began to ascend.

Ascent, like descent, was meant to be controlled, managed as carefully as possible to avoid decompression and the damage that could come with reducing the pressure on the hull too quickly. There wasn't time to worry about that now. She hauled and the submersible responded, climbing through the water ten times faster than the safety protocols allowed. The message light was still flashing, and she kept ignoring it; there was no time to worry about what the mission control team was trying to say, and she didn't have the time to type a response even if she'd wanted to. She needed to focus.

Motion out of the corner of her eye told her she was being pursued: the mermaids, far from being put off by the light and motion, were chasing her. They cut through the water seemingly without effort, moving fast enough to make her throat go dry. She needed to keep going. She needed to—

The impact came from the left, hard enough to rock the submersible sideways in the water. Heather barely had time to steady herself before she was hit again, this time from the right, the blow shaking the entire pod hard enough that her stabilizers flashed red, begging for her immediate attention. She was shooting upward at an unsafe speed, and still she was being hit from all sides, and still the mermaids were all around her.

According to the depth gauge on her control panel, she was more than two hundred meters below the surface. Too deep for her to survive if something broke through the wall of her pod. Too far for her to swim; even if she ejected, she'd never make it to the surface. The deepest a human could hope to dive and come up with a chance of survival was about seventy meters, and she wasn't going to reach that for—she spared a glance at the meter. For another forty-five seconds, and that was pushing her engines in a way she didn't like and didn't trust.

Forty-five seconds was nothing on land. In the air and sunlight, where the pressure was negligible, it was *nothing*. Here, hundreds of feet below the surface of the sea, forty-five seconds was an eternity.

The impacts continued, coming from every side, slamming into her with a regularity that jarred her bones and rattled her teeth in their sockets. She kept her hands on the controls, trying to ignore the lights flashing all around her, more with every impact, like the submersible itself was screaming. The alarms she'd never heard were going off, she knew that much, and part of her wondered, with an academic detachment that she recognized as shock, how hearing people could *stand* it. It was bad enough to have the submersible shuddering around her and the lights threatening to blind her: if there had been another sensory input on top of all that, she might have snapped, no longer able to cope with what was happening. Sometimes isolation was the only armor she had.

Messages scrolled across the screen too fast for her to read. Every member of the monitoring team seemed to be typing at once, and she wouldn't have been surprised to learn that her sisters were there too, slamming their hands down on the keys, trying desperately to connect.

I'm so sorry, she thought. *I'm so, so sorry.*

The impacts stopped.

The lack of shaking was as stunning as its beginning had been. Heather's eyes widened, her lips parting as she dared to take a shaky breath. The mermaids were marine predators. They must have attacked because she had wandered into their territory; they were trying to defend themselves against something unknown and potentially dangerous. When she had fled rather than attacking back, she had shown she wasn't a threat. They must have stopped following her as soon as she'd passed outside the waters they considered "theirs."

With a trembling hand, she reached for the keyboard, and tapped out, 'I'm OK. I'm on my way back up. I'll be there s'

The impact from above was enough to drive the submersible more than ten meters down before Heather had fully registered that she'd been hit. The engines strained. The alarms she couldn't hear screamed. The hit came again, harder this time, and with a profound shudder, the submersible's systems stopped fighting.

The lights went out.

The water outside was so dark that for a few seconds, Heather could see nothing at all. Only blackness. Her heart was pounding so hard that she was starting to feel sick, like her cause of death was going to be heart attack, and not asphyxiation.

The submersible was sinking. *I'm going to see the bottom of the Challenger Deep after all*, she thought dizzily. Her bones would rest there. She closed her eyes. *God, Holly, I'm so sorry.*

People always said twins were connected, that they could feel each other's thoughts across great distances. Heather had usually dismissed those claims as bullshit and hocus-pocus, but now she found herself wishing she could believe. She didn't want to go without telling Holly she'd miss her. More, she didn't want to go alone. She'd come into the world as part of a pair. She shouldn't be leaving it solo.

Opening her eyes, she fumbled for the control panel and began flipping switches, trying to find the combination to restart the engines and give herself a second chance. She knew it existed. If her engines weren't physically damaged—if they'd just been overwhelmed by conflicting signals and the surrounding pressure—they could be rebooted. She could get out of this. It would be a funny story in a few years. That time she'd almost drowned in the Mariana Trench. That time she'd almost been killed by mermaids. They would laugh and laugh and never stop laughing. They would. They *would*.

The first flickers of bioluminescence moved past the window. Heather ignored them as best she could, feeling for the controls that would return her to the world where there was light, and air, and her sister, waiting patiently for her to come back and start apologizing.

She was still trying to restart the engines when there was another impact from above. This time it was accompanied by a trickle of water falling down to strike her shoulder, shockingly cold and impossible to ignore.

Heather closed her eyes.

When the final impact came, when the water flooded into the pod and took the rest of the world away, she didn't fight it. It would go faster if she didn't fight it.

It could never have gone fast enough.

CHAPTER 13

Western Pacific Ocean, above the Mariana Trench: September 2, 2022

Holly's screams were deep and primal, unshaped by her ears; they came straight from her gut, the cries of a wounded animal that knew, all the way down to its bones, that it could never be whole again. She threw herself at the startled engineers, clawing for the control panel, and it was only Hallie's arm around her waist that pulled her back. Heather's final words were still flashing on the screen, that unfinished sentence trailing into nothingness...

Hallie thought she would be seeing those words every time she closed her eyes for the rest of her life.

"What the *fuck*?!" demanded one of the bystanders, a scientist she didn't know by name. She thought it was one of the theoretical biologists. She honestly didn't care. He looked like he'd sink if she threw him into the pool. She wanted to throw him into the pool. She wanted to do a lot worse than that.

"She can't hear herself," Hallie shouted, a lifetime of explanation, of translation, of shielding her baby sisters from the world kicking in and taking over. It was almost a relief. Maybe if she translated her sister's grief, she'd find a way to handle her own.

There are only two of us now, she thought, and her stomach clenched.

Holly jerked out of her arms, pushing her way to the controls. Hallie let her go. The scream had died, replaced by a deep, absolute

157

silence that should have seemed familiar, and instead felt even louder than the sound that had come before it.

Hallie tapped Holly on the shoulder. Holly turned, eyes wide and wild.

'We have to go down,' she signed, fingers flashing. 'We have to get another submersible. We have to go get her. We have to save her.'

'We can't,' Hallie signed. 'We can't. She's gone. They lost contact. Her hull ruptured. Holly...Heather's gone.'

Holly stared at her for a long moment before flinging herself, weeping, into her older sister's arms. Hallie bore her up, but barely; her own knees were threatening to buckle, to dump her to the deck.

Nearby, Tory watched with her hands pressed over her mouth, fingers clamped so tightly that they were going white around the edges. She jumped when someone reached over and pulled her hands down, turning to stare, wide-eyed, at Olivia.

Even with everyone running and panicking around her, Olivia seemed calm. The skin around her eyes was tighter than usual, but apart from that, she could have been preparing to go on the air. She had Tory's hands firmly by the wrists, keeping them away from her face. She might as well have been carved from marble, for all the yielding she seemed capable of in that moment.

"Don't hurt yourself," she said, in a low voice. "It won't do anyone any good, and we have someplace we need to be."

"I wasn't going to hurt myself," said Tory automatically. Pain flared at the corner of her mouth. Olivia still had her hands hostage; she felt the pain with her tongue, and tasted blood. She had pulled an old split on her lip open. She winced and amended, "More than I already had. Where do you think we need to be? Heather is *dead*—"

"That means the mermaids *are directly under us*." Olivia let go of her hands and took a quick step back, like she was afraid of reciprocal grabbing. "We're going to wind up shutting down half this damn boat for the rest of the day because everybody's sad and there's nothing immediately apparent for us to take revenge on. But you—"

"I could pick up the sonar from the entire school," breathed Tory, eyes going wide with something other than shock or sorrow.

Olivia nodded. "So move."

They moved, leaving behind the mourning masses around the

launch point. They could feel bad about it later; right now, there was science to be done, and only a short time in which to do it.

There were those who considered scientists heartless, or cruel, or uncompassionate, because of moments like these: anyone who could turn their back on a tragedy to chase down something seemingly inconsequential like a sonar rig was clearly somehow less than human. What Tory would have explained, if she'd been in a position to do so, was that curiosity was part of what made them *absolutely* human. Curiosity was the reason humanity had come down from the trees and spread across the world. Sadness was tempting. Sorrow held more charms than most people liked to think, and it would swallow her whole if she let it. She had been dancing with sorrow since the *Atargatis*. But that was what made it so important that other things happen even when the sad things were already going on.

She couldn't bring Heather back. She couldn't change the past. That didn't mean she couldn't avenge Heather, and her own sister, for the sake of the people who'd been left behind. Sometimes science was the closest thing to the sword of an avenging angel humanity was ever going to get.

"Luis!" She slammed the door of their lab open so hard that it rattled in its frame. Her partner jumped in his seat and spun to face her. "Focus any microphones you aren't using on the space below the ship, and repurpose everything you *are* using! We need audio, and we need it five minutes ago."

"What are you—" He stopped at the sight of Olivia, an unreadable expression sweeping over his face. "What is she doing here?"

"Chasing a story," said Olivia. She followed Tory across the room, watching the taller woman settle at her computer. There was something like hunger in her eyes. "They're right under us."

"They . . . You mean the mermaids? We *found* them?"

"Right," snapped Tory, hands already in motion, twisting dials, setting new parameters. "Heather Wilson went down. We got some incredibly clear visual feeds, but she wasn't recording anything more than *very* raw audio."

"Well, she's deaf, so I guess she wouldn't think about what those settings ought to be," said Luis automatically. He stopped, eyes bulging in their sockets, before he managed to squeak, "Wait—*what*? We have video confirmation that they're down there? Like, actual video confirmation? Not just 'Looks like an eel, let's call it a mermaid so we can justify this shit-show'?"

"They killed her," said Tory, not taking her eyes off her screen. Her hands kept moving. They never slowed, never stopped.

But Heather's had. Heather's hands had been her connection to the world, the way she spoke, the way she defined herself as a part of the greater mass of humanity, and now they were still. They were going to be still forever. It was hard to focus on her typing, and not on the things that Heather's hands would never say.

Luis was gaping. Olivia turned to face him, smoothly sliding into her position as professional go-between as she said, "Heather was piloting her submersible into the Challenger Deep when unknown aquatic hominids surrounded her vessel and attacked. She fled, they pursued. They were faster. She was lost at sea."

Luis closed his mouth in favor of blinking before asking, "What the fuck do you mean, 'unknown aquatic hominids'?"

"Haven't you watched any of my reports on the inboard feed? You've been in half a dozen of them." More often than any other scientist on the ship, except for Tory, who had been featured almost a dozen times. Olivia kept waiting for someone back at corporate to catch on to the reasons behind that. No one ever did. Sometimes the obliviousness of people was her only refuge.

"Why would I watch them? I was there when you were making them."

"Because there's bumper text, to give context, and—oh, never mind." Olivia pulled out her tablet, swiped her fingers fiercely across it, and offered it to Luis. "Look. Mermaids."

Luis took the tablet. The recording from Heather's Minnow was playing, mermaids swimming out of the deep dark and into the brighter water around the submersible. The alien lines of their anatomy hurt his eyes. If they were mammals—they couldn't possibly be mammals—their evolution had followed a path unlike anything else on the planet. If they weren't mammals, if they were fish or reptiles or something older and stranger and lost to the march of science, then they were mysteries and marvels.

"Oh my God," whispered Luis. His fingers tightened on the

tablet, like he was afraid she was going to rip it away from him. "This is...I mean...Is this footage going to be on the public servers?"

"If it's not, I can have it sent to you," said Olivia.

"This changes everything. There's no way anyone can claim Imagine faked this. There's no way—this is *real*."

"I know." Olivia looked over her shoulder to Tory, whose attention was consumed by her own machine, her own efforts. "It always was."

"I have to get to work." Luis spun to face his computer. He didn't give back the tablet.

That was all right. Olivia would get it later, after she'd cleared the footage for him and recorded her report about Heather's death at sea. By now, Imagine's lawyers would be getting involved, summoned from their boardrooms and their beds to begin enforcing their iron-clad accidental death clauses. There was no one on the *Melusine* who hadn't signed papers stating that they understood the danger. Even if the ship was lost with all hands, this voyage would not be a repeat of the *Atargatis*. Everyone knew the risks that they were taking. They had chosen to take them anyway, risking their lives in the name of scientific progress. But that didn't change human nature. There was always a chance someone connected to Heather would see her death as a way to make a quick buck, trying to balance a loss that could never be balanced with a bigger bank account.

Eventually her phone would beep and she'd be summoned to hair and makeup so they could get her ready to go on camera and record a segment about the death of Heather Wilson. Transparency was the Imagine watchword for this voyage: document everything, don't conceal anything. They wanted to show the blood and sweat and tears, because those would put the ratings through the roof when this footage went public. Those were what *mattered*.

Olivia felt like the people who controlled the programming were missing something. It wasn't Heather's death that mattered; it was her life, the way she'd favored her left side when she signed, even though she was right handed, because she'd learned to talk with one hand and steer a submersible with the other. It wasn't what Tory could write down that mattered; it was the curve of her neck and the slope of her shoulder, and her unending anger at a world that refused to be exactly, enduringly the way she wanted it to be. Every person on this vessel was a story in the process of telling itself, and all of them were fascinating, and all of them deserved to be heard.

Content that Luis was working, she drifted closer to Tory. The other woman's screens were consumed by different sonar frequencies and long chains of sound-mixing panels, each of them filtering and running through a different data feed. "What are you doing?" she asked, as casually as she could manage.

Tory kept her eyes on the screen. "I'm running a sound isolation program on the audio feed from Heather's submersible, to take out the engine noise and the other human-made sounds, and I'm enhancing what's left, trying to find the mermaids."

"How do you already have—"

"Heather and I talked yesterday, when she got the go-ahead for today's launch. She set me up with a private relay, in case Imagine wanted to get weird about the video. I needed the audio as fast as I could get it." Tory didn't turn, but the muscles around her eyes tightened in a way that spoke of self-satisfaction, albeit a bitter example of the same. Heather had paid too high a price for the files, and everyone knew it. "I don't have the visual feed at all. Her contract wouldn't allow it. But wouldn't you know it, they didn't push the deaf girl about the audio."

"Sneaky," said Olivia.

"Smart," said Tory.

"Sometimes they're the same thing."

Luis whooped. Olivia turned. He was spinning in his chair, arms thrust straight up like his team had just scored a touchdown. Seeing Olivia looking his way, he lowered his arms and shrugged almost apologetically. He kept smiling. It seemed like he was unable to stop.

"Sonar is picking up a large, dense mass directly below us, about ninety meters down. I've got the mermaids. I've got them on my feed. I can *track* them."

"Wait." Olivia frowned. "I thought Tory was doing sonar and you were doing...whatever it is you do."

"We work together because we both use sound. She uses recorded sound, for analysis and study. She wants to know what mermaids and the like do when they're at home alone. Do they sing like whales, or chitter like monkeys? Do they talk like humans? How do they communicate amongst themselves? I use sonar imaging to take 'photos' of things in the water, so we know where to point the microphones. Sometimes her recordings tell me where to look; sometimes my pictures tell her where to listen. Right now, we both know where we're going, so we're both going to get useful results."

"And are you?"

"I know where they are now." Luis turned back to his screen. "I can track them in real time, now that I have a fix on them."

"Can't they just dive and lose you?"

"They could, if I didn't have relays seeded through the water from here to the top of the Challenger Deep. I've been dropping beacons since we got here. I'll need an hour with a magnet and a recall signal to clear them all out before we leave, but right now, I could follow a sardine to the bottom of the ocean and not worry about losing it."

"Wow," said Olivia, hoping she was infusing the word with the right mixture of awe and delight. The scientists on the ship lost her often and easily once they started talking about things like sonar relays and tracking systems. She could report on them, once someone else had broken the science into bite-size chunks, and she could muddle through if she absolutely had to, but in the end she found that for the most part, she simply didn't care. Mermaids were real, and they were deadly. All the scientific knowledge in the world wasn't going to change that. What mattered was how they were going to make the people at home understand that this wasn't a joke, it wasn't a hoax, it wasn't an attempt at better ratings. The world was bigger and stranger than people thought, and things that were big and strange could also be fatal.

On Luis's screen the spreading circles of the sonar array remained static, providing a grid for the information being displayed. Everything within the circles might change, but the circles themselves would stay the same, patient and unyielding.

Far from the lab, beneath the *Melusine*, powerful speakers put out quick bursts of ultrasonic sound, receiving the echoes as the sound bounced off whatever was in its path, and using those echoes to model the obstacles. The result was not the photo-realistic imagery of science fiction, but rather the imprecise estimates of science fact. Something roughly the size of a human being was swimming hundreds of feet below the ship, in the company of dozens of other somethings, all of approximately the same size. They were holding their position, staying in the deep black, not coming up to the level where cameras could have captured a useful image. Without something like Heather's Minnow, equipped with its own bright lights, they might never have been seen at all.

"They like to stay deep, until they don't," said Olivia.

"What's that?" asked Luis.

"Nothing." But she'd meant it, hadn't she? The footage from the *Atargatis* was disjointed and difficult to watch in places, but the timeline was clear. They had dropped a sampling device over the side of the ship, something designed to go deep and come back with water samples, allowing them to start the slow, arduous process of charting chemical and biological changes between water levels. What was found in the pelagic would not necessarily be present in the abyssopelagic, and so on. The presence of light and plentiful organic material changed everything.

Only the sampling device had returned with more than just water. A mermaid had come along for the ride, hitching its way to the surface, and it hadn't shown any real signs of distress when it was pulled into the air. In fact, it had seemed perfectly at home there, showing all signs of breathing easily until it chewed the face off of a molecular biologist and pulled him over the side of the ship. His body, like the rest of those lost in the disaster, had never been found.

The mermaids liked it down in the deeps, of that there was no question. The deeps were their home. But when they needed to come up...

"They can," whispered Olivia, and watched the shapes forming and breaking up on Luis's screen, and wondered what was going to happen when the sun went down.

On the other side of the ship, someone else was asking the same question.

Jacques and Michi Abney had their own cabin, large enough to host a family of five, complete with a Jacuzzi tub that had been used every day since the *Melusine* left port. What was the point of living the high life on someone else's dime if they weren't going to take advantage of every amenity?

(Besides, as Michi pointed out shortly after the ship got under way, Imagine wanted to minimize their contact with the rest of the crew. Fishing was all well and good, and it passed a certain number of hours, but time spent behind closed doors was even better, and came with even less risk of unwanted contact. They weren't going to get in trouble for sequestering themselves. If anything, they were going to put themselves in line for a bonus. Her logic was impeccable. Better yet, it aligned with what Jacques already wanted to do. He was generally happy to go along with Michi's wishes, but found it so much more pleasant when she wished to do enjoyable things.)

At the moment the tub was empty, and every available space in the cabin was piled with military-grade weapon cases. Michi held a tablet, scrolling down the list of their inventory, while Jacques moved around the room, verifying her list.

"Grenade launcher?"

"Yes."

"Grenades?"

"Yes."

"How many tranquilizer rifles do we have?"

"Six: three set for human-sized targets, two for walrus, and one for orca." Jacques smiled, fast and feral. "We can sedate anything that comes as far as the surface, and with the punch on these things, *surface* is a negotiable term."

"Excellent. Rated for shark?"

"All of them." Their tranquilizers were a proprietary blend developed by a multinational fishing concern that needed to be able to sedate and live-capture large sharks without making a fuss about it. People were so oversensitive to the supposed overfishing of sharks— as if it wasn't the height of hubris to decide humanity needed to be put into the position of custodian to the world's apex predators? God had made man to fight and defeat His other creations. Why else would He have made his chosen children physically weak but mentally strong? In the battle between man and shark, the shark should always have won. That it didn't proved only that man was intended to be victorious, and should be allowed to kill whatever he could before he, in turn, was killed.

These tranquilizers didn't fuck around with animal safety. No chemists had monitored their effects on heartbeat or respiration. Something shot with one of these bad boys would go down hard, and would either get back up again or not, depending on its individual biology. Kill the weak, preserve the strong. Create a challenge for the next generation. What was the point of winnowing the world, if not to make a better fight for the children?

"What's the status on the security teams?"

Michi smiled, slow and feral. Jacques felt his heart flutter, the way it always did when she looked at him like that. There had been times when he'd despaired of ever meeting a woman who understood the hunt. Now that he had her, he was never going to let her go. They would die together, gored by a bull elephant or torn to pieces by a pod of hippos, and he would go out with a smile, content that he'd spent his time on Earth in the company of his opposite and equal, something he would never have thought possible.

"They're ready to go at our word," she said. "Blackwell understands he can't stop us. This is, as they say, the cost of doing business."

Jacques nodded. "Good. Let's get ready. If the last contact was anything to go by, the fish-women will surface when the sun goes down. That's when the fun begins."

"Then we have a few hours," said Michi, with a meaningful glance at the small slice of bed not covered by boxes and bullets.

Jacques opened his arms. She set her tablet aside, and went to him.

The news was filtering out to the rest of the *Melusine*. Many would have said there was no such thing as privacy on a ship like this one, that any information would inevitably be shared by all, simply because it couldn't be avoided. They would have been wrong. There were secrets aplenty on the *Melusine*, kept close to the chests of those who held them. But something like this, the loss of one of their own caught on camera for a viewing audience that numbered in the dozens...that couldn't be concealed. No matter how much it would have helped things to keep Heather's death hidden until a response could be formulated calmly and clearly and without emotion getting in the way.

That was never going to happen. Heather was dead, and mermaids were real, and the ship's population was split between sorrow and elation, the two seemingly inimical states sometimes sharing the same shadow, the same skin. Even those who'd known and liked Heather couldn't fully swallow their joy. Mermaids were *real*. The mission was already a success. Anything they discovered from here was only going to enhance their scientific value—and they'd be able to write their own tickets after this. They'd be able to set their own price.

Fear was a tight undercurrent through everything, but it was tempered with relief. No one could have missed the security teams moving along the decks, checking everything, and the shutters were there if anything truly bad happened. Imagine would protect them.

Dr. Jillian Toth, the world's foremost expert on mermaids, the woman without whom the *Atargatis* would never have been able to set sail, stood on the top deck. She wore a thick sweater, and her hair was a tangled mess, whipping around her ears, tying itself into elaborate knots that would be easier to cut out than to comb. Her eyes were fixed, not on the water, but on the horizon, and the distant, drawn-out promise of safety.

Footsteps beside her warned her that she was no longer alone. "This is my fault, you know," she said.

There was a pause before Theo asked, "How did you know it was me?"

"You limp. Not always, but when you haven't taken your medicine, you limp. And you wouldn't have taken your medicine if you were calling James to tell him the bloodbath was getting under way." Jillian looked from the ocean to her estranged husband, expression all but daring him to contradict her. She was itching for a fight, *dying* for something to give her an excuse.

Theo had been married to her for more than twenty years. He knew better than to give her what she wanted. (Oh, once, he would have risen to the bait, a fish willingly pursuing the hook; he would have thrown blame in her face until she started biting down on it, and they would have screamed at each other for hours, until they were both exhausted, until they could start to see the pathway out of their problem and into a solution. But that time was in the past, when they'd been better at loving each other, and worse at getting in one another's way.)

"Why do you say that?" he asked, mildly.

"Because I try not to lie to myself when I can help it. To the rest of the world, sure, but to myself? That's a bad business. Better not to start." Jillian turned back to the water. "All of this is my fault."

"Did they elect you God when I wasn't looking? I suppose that would be a paradox, if you think about it. God is a middle-aged biology professor who exists in God's own creation, only to go back to the beginning and make it for herself. Although I'll be honest. If you're God, I want to have a talk with you about my accident." Theo

167

joined her at the rail. Where her eyes were fixed on the horizon, he fixed his on the roiling sea. "Having a little fight is no reason to try to crush me to death with the hull of a whaling ship."

Jillian's laughter was bitter. "Sometimes I would have told you differently."

"But those times, you didn't have phenomenal cosmic power." Theo leaned over to nudge her shoulder with his own. "Why is this your fault, Jilli?"

"Because I'm the one who said there was truth behind the legends. I'm the one who insisted there was something to find, until some damn programming director listened and convinced your boss I might be right, or at least that I might be amusing. Without me beating the drum, the *Atargatis* never sailed. Without the *Atargatis*, we never sailed, and if we never sailed, then Heather isn't dead. All of this comes back to me."

"Everything comes back to someone. If Lani shoots a man, is that on us? Is it on our parents? How far back do we follow the consequences of free will?"

"Until the guilt goes away."

"Then we're going all the way back to the apple every single time. Do you really want that kind of responsibility?"

For a long moment, Jillian said nothing at all. Finally she leaned to the side until their arms were pressed together, holding each other up, and said in a soft voice, "We're out of time. You know that, don't you? The sun's going to go down, and whatever damned secret plan you're trying not to tell me about—whatever made you bring those dolphins, and those bastards with their overly large guns—is going to start, and a lot of people are going to die. A *lot* of people are going to die. Maybe even us."

"Maybe," Theo agreed noncommittally. "But we got to sail together one more time. Wasn't that worth the risk?"

"For you and me? Maybe. For everyone else on this godforsaken vessel?" Jillian shook her head. "It never was. It never could have been. And this is all my fault."

This time Theo didn't contradict her. They stood together, and watched the sun sink lower in the sky, creeping inch by dreadful inch toward sundown.

ZONE THREE:
APHOTIC

There are some challenges that are worth risking everything.

—Heather Wilson

Nothing is worth the risk of being lost at sea.

—Dr. Holly Wilson

It is the belief of this commission that the "mermaids" sighted in the vicinity of the Mariana Trench are not, in fact, representatives of a previously unknown genera of fish or marine reptile, but are instead a previously unknown form of deepwater dolphin or manatee. This would explain all documented aspects of their physiology, without contradicting known science as regards these creatures.

It is further the belief of this commission that if there is any veracity to the claims that disappearances in the area are due to these "mermaids," the disappearances are more likely to be the fault of sailors or onlookers becoming confused by the sight of something so unexpected, and falling consequentially overboard. There is simply no possible way a purely oceanic species could be attacking something so far out of their natural environment without damaging either the vessel or themselves. The mermaid, whatever she truly is, is a myth and a treasure, and cannot be held accountable.

—From the newsletter of the International
Cryptozoological Society

Mankind needs the mermaid to explain why we left the sea in the first place. If you look at the aquatic ape theory—discredited what, six times now? But it keeps coming back, like a bad penny veiled in a sheet of bad science—we should have been the masters of our watery abode. We should have been kings of the sea. Orcas and leopard seals and other aquatic predators exist, but so do lions, bears, all manner of terrible things on the land; they should not, on their own, have been enough to drive us from our home. Sharks exist, implacable, cold blooded, and terrible. That's true. At the same time, I'm not going to stand here and tell you the crocodile is any real improvement. Everything that threatens us in the sea has its counterpart on land, with less of the gravity-defying freedom the water offers. So what could have driven us away?

171

Nothing more nor less than an equal. One whose mastery of the waters outpaced our own, and left us with the choice to flee as predators, or to live as prey...

—Transcript from the lecture "Mermaids: Myth or Monster," given by Dr. Jillian Toth

CHAPTER 14

Western Pacific Ocean, the Mariana Trench: September 2, 2022

The shell had been strange but not unknown, no, not unknown; shells had come before. Some had been left to pass unmolested, watched as they drifted downward, doing whatever it was shells did. They never cracked themselves open, but extruded limbs and tentacles, snatching small things foolish enough to wander into reach. There had been close calls before, when one of the youngest thought to go and see the shell, consumed by childish curiosity, but those close calls had always ended with strong arms around weak shoulders as the shell drifted past in blissful ignorance. There was no point to starting a fight with the unusual, which didn't even smell of food, when it could be avoided.

Ah, but that had been long ago, before the waters changed. The fish had dwindled in number season on season, until the rich feeding grounds were all but gone, replaced by nothing to fill a belly or strengthen an arm. Half the young had been consumed to sustain the mature. Virtually all the old had been consumed as well, swimming into the deepest dark and not surfacing again. There were appetites to be sated, no matter how cold the water became, no matter how strange the sea turned. As long as there were bellies, they would need to be fed. As long as there was life in the sea, there would be teeth. The past shells had drifted through a sea full of life on their

173

unknowable shell errands. This one had dropped into a sea filled with death.

It had been desperation as much as territorial rage that led them to attack the shell, to drive it downward, looking for the crack in its surface. Still, it might have escaped, had not the noise and unusual activity attracted the attention of one of the eldest, who had risen, majestic, from the depths, and driven the shell down, down, down into the dark, where it had cracked and spilled its contents into the waters, delicate and delicious and already dead. The eldest had devoured the shell's inhabitant almost before it could be seen, but it had been seen, oh yes, it had been seen, and it had been *recognized*. They *knew* this thing, and others like it. They had seen this thing before.

Where there was one of these things, there were always others. The delicate, delicious things that died so easily never traveled alone. Their schools varied in number from few to many, but they *never* traveled alone.

Deep beneath the waves, the hungry turned their eyes upward, toward the promise of plenty, and began to prepare.

News of Heather's death had spread throughout the ship: there was no one aboard the *Melusine* who didn't know they'd suffered their first fatality. That was a cold comfort, especially given that most of the scientists, however hard they tried, were more interested in the circumstances of Heather's death than in the reality of it.

Was it true she'd died trying to cross into the Challenger Deep? *Trying to flee from it, actually, but yes, that had been her intent.*

Was it true that she had managed to capture clear, unedited footage of the aquatic entities they were here to find? *Yes, before they killed her.*

Was it true the entities had attacked? *Heather was dead, and her bones were never going to be recovered—was that true enough? How dead did she have to be before people stopped asking the question?*

Well, what had she done to provoke them? *Because mermaids were beautiful mermaids were peaceful and gentle and kind, mermaids were fairy tale creatures given flesh, and who cared about the* Atargatis *video? Who cared about the blood already on their hands? Heather must have done something.*

Because if Heather hadn't done something, they would need to consider the fact that they were floating in the middle of open waters, sitting ducks for anything that might decide to surface and begin the slaughter. The crew was already preparing for the worst, doubling and then tripling security patrols, while the scientists tried to go about their business as if they weren't moving toward the end of the world.

Holly had stopped making eye contact when people spoke to her, taking refuge in their assumptions and prejudices about the deaf. If she couldn't see them she couldn't "hear" them, and maybe they'd stop talking. When that didn't work she retreated to her cabin and closed the door, sequestering herself from a world that wanted to talk endlessly about her sister's death without ever pausing to acknowledge that her sister, her *twin*, the other half of her heart, was gone.

Hallie had followed Holly for a little while, until it became clear that she wasn't welcome either: for this short time, she had been lumped with the rest of the world as "not Heather," and wasn't going to get anything out of her surviving sister but motionless hands. She was used to silence. Heather and Holly laughed and grunted and made all the other sounds that came with being mammals—Holly snored something awful, which had always struck Hallie as funny—but they didn't do it on purpose. A refusal to sign, on the other hand…that was something new, and painful, and too much to be borne.

She had left a note on the whiteboard they used for long-term communications, letting Holly know she'd be in the cafeteria if she was wanted, and then she had fled the room where the ghost of one silent sister haunted the survivor. Some things hurt too much. Some things needed to be delayed as long as possible.

Their parents were never going to forgive her. They'd always tried to treat the twins the same way they treated Hallie, supporting instead of coddling, encouraging them to experience the world in their own way and on their own terms, but Hallie knew damn well that her parents would always consider the twins her responsibility. No one who responded to the birth of deaf children by turning their eldest child into a translator—a transformation Hallie appreciated, even enjoyed, but hadn't been given much of a vote in—was going to accept that three daughters had gone out and only two had come back.

Assuming any of them came back. The mermaids were real, the mermaids were below the ship, and the *Melusine* was making no move toward leaving. This was what Imagine had been hoping for.

This was the worst-case scenario described in their contracts, in the fine print that said that even in the event of injury or loss of life, the mission would be carried out to the best ability of the surviving crew. Heather's bones would be picked clean and scattered long before Hallie and Holly made it home.

Maybe that was better. Maybe they could get through the worst of the mourning and return to shore ready to start the process of healing, recovering, getting *better*.

"And maybe somebody has a bridge they'd like to sell me," muttered Hallie, picking up her empty mug and heading for the coffee machine. She'd already had five cups of coffee. Caffeine thrummed in her veins, bright and stimulating and almost enough to chase off the loose-limbed lassitude that threatened to rise and overwhelm her. She needed to stay alert. For Holly, in case her sister needed her.

"Dr. Wilson!"

The sound of her name was surprising enough that she jumped, slopping coffee over the lip of the mug and onto the skin of her hand. She sucked a breath through her teeth as she turned. That Canadian man, the hunter, was behind her. As always, he was dressed in khakis, like he thought this was a safari, or the goddamn Disneyland Jungle Cruise, and not a sea voyage to the ends of the known world. He even had a slouch hat, pushed back on his head so as not to muss his perfectly groomed hair. Who *did* that? Who went around dressed like the *GQ* idea of the big game hunter?

His eyes were cold, glaciers set into a human skull and left to play the part of windows to a dark and terrifying soul. Hallie hesitated, revising her first impression. Maybe the point of the theatrics was to distract from those eyes, which had more in common with what little she'd seen of the mermaids before they attacked than they did with anything human.

"Yes?" she said, cautiously.

"We need you." His tone was brusque, proprietary: he was clearly taking her attention as a given.

"We who, exactly?"

"My wife and I. We were told you are the voyage acoustician, and we need your skills."

Hallie hesitated. It should have been nice to have someone

remember that she was a trained scientist, as qualified to be here as anyone else on board. Under the circumstances...

"What do you need me for?" she asked, trying to keep the quaver out of her voice.

"Trying to get a head count on those beasties down there. It seemed to follow that if we had someone who understood the behavior of sound give it a go, we might be able to isolate one voice from another." Jacques looked at her expectantly.

Hallie stared at him. "You want me to listen to—well, for lack of a better term, *crowd* noise, in what is effectively an open-air amphitheater with unknown acoustics and no floor, and tell you how many *people* were speaking? When there's no way of knowing whether most of the people present were speaking at all?" Tory could have done it. Tory had a different specialization.

"I wish you wouldn't call those things *people*." Jacques scowled. "They're beasts at best, creatures at worst. Can you help or not?"

"I'm sorry, but I think the answer is 'not.'" It was a relief to hear those words come out of her mouth and know they were the truth. She wasn't lying; she couldn't help, not with those starting conditions. Maybe if she analyzed the video first...

No. No, and no, and all the no in the world. Her sister was dead. That video might become Heather's legacy, might be the thing she was remembered for, but Hallie wasn't going to start studying it until she had to. Certainly not for this man, who looked at her with eyes like ice and had a bulge in the pocket of his shorts that spoke of gunfire and violence.

Jacques's face hardened still further. "I was under the impression that all the scientists assigned to this journey were meant to help when asked."

"Not at the expense of our own research, and not outside our fields of expertise," said Hallie. "I can't help you, because underwater modeling is not my field. Give me a crowd inside a man-made structure and I can pick it apart for you. I can tell you a hundred things about those people and what they're saying and why. But I can't map the entire Challenger Deep, and I can't predict population density when I don't know what the population sounds like, or how widely distributed it is. You need a statistician, and an acoustic engineer, and I don't know, a marine biologist."

He glared at her. "I thought you would be more eager to avenge your sister."

Hallie looked levelly back, refusing to give him the satisfaction of seeing how uncomfortable he made her. "I am. But this is not the way I'm going to do it."

There was a long pause. It stretched out between them like a tether, until Hallie tensed, afraid of what would happen when it inevitably snapped. No one else was coming into the cafeteria: all the other scientists were focusing on their work, and all the nonscientists were preparing for whatever was going to happen next. If Jacques wanted to grab her, there would be no one there to see.

(In an odd, distant way, she hoped he *would* grab her. She had taken several self-defense courses in college, preparing for the time when she'd be expected to take care of her sisters. A normal translator wasn't meant to serve as a bodyguard, but a normal translator didn't answer to her parents. If something had happened to one of her sisters because Hallie wasn't able to stop it, they would never have let her live it down. They were never *going* to let her live it down. She didn't want them to.)

Finally Jacques shook his head, a brisk motion that made Hallie itch to step away from the implied threat in his posture. "Fine," he said. "But I'll remember this, and pray you do not find yourself in need of assistance before our time aboard this ship is done."

He turned and stalked away, leaving Hallie alone with a mug of coffee in one shaking hand. Carefully, she set it down next to the machine. She didn't really want it anymore. The thought of drinking something—of drinking anything—made her stomach turn and bile rise in the back of her throat.

"That was unpleasant," said an unfamiliar voice.

Hallie turned. The man behind her was tall, solidly built and covered in tattoos, with long brown hair and an amiable face. It was the sort of face that begged to be told stories, constructed by nature to listen. He was wearing tan slacks and a white button-down shirt, and while there was no possible way he could be a recent arrival on the *Melusine*, he didn't look familiar in the slightest.

"I'm sorry," she said. "You are...?"

"Dr. Daniel Lennox," he said. "I'm sorry we haven't met before this. I've been working on a project that's kept me fairly stationary, and there hasn't been time for the proper pleasantries. But I'm excited to finally have this opportunity, even if it's under terrible circumstances."

"Oh." She blinked. "You know who I am."

"I do." His expression smoothed, becoming solemn. "I'm sorry for your loss. I know how much this has to hurt. That's part of why I'm approaching you now. Psychologically speaking, you're in shock; you'll be able to work for the next few hours, even if you freeze up after that. The situation hasn't become fully real for you yet."

"Work on what?" asked Hallie blankly.

"I'm a cetologist. We're going to figure out how the mermaids talk to each other, and then we're going to figure out how to talk to them. Will you help me?"

Hallie hesitated, looking over her shoulder in the direction Jacques had gone. One man wanted her to help kill the creatures that killed her sister; the other wanted her to help him understand them.

In the end there was no question which it was going to be. She would help him understand them. She would help *them* understand *her*, and when she told them why they had to die, they would know it was their own fault. "Of course," she said, turning back to Dr. Lennox. "Where's your lab?"

Dr. Lennox smiled.

"I think I have it."

Luis and Olivia both looked toward Tory, the one with guarded optimism, the other with confusion.

"Got what?" asked Olivia.

"The mermaids—we need a better word for them as an aggregate; we don't know their genders, we don't even know if they *have* gender in the human sense of the word—have a hybrid language. Look, see?" Tory pointed to the video looping in one bottom corner of her monitor. "They sign, just like they did on the videos from the *Atargatis*. Part of their language is silent."

"Makes sense," said Luis. "Sound carries underwater, and everything we know about these assholes tells us they're predators. You don't want to warn everything around you that you're coming."

"Right," said Tory. "So they sign, and that lets them communicate when they're close together, and then, when they need to talk over long distances, they—"

"Do they sing?" blurted Olivia. "Like whales?"

"They do sing," said Tory. "Or at least they hum, and they click, and they shout to each other. It's just not as smooth as the signing. I think they reserve the singing for when they can't relay things silently."

Luis paused for a long moment, looking at her gravely. Tory nodded. Olivia frowned, looking between the two of them, trying to find the key to the things they weren't saying.

Finally she couldn't take it anymore. "What?" she demanded. "What is it?"

"If they have a language—not just one language, but two languages, one spoken and one not—and if the complexity of their spoken language is anything like the complexity of their signing, they must be sentient," said Tory. She sounded reluctant, like this was the last thing she wanted to be saying. "There's no way they're not."

"Cats meow and know what they're saying," said Olivia. "Birds sing. That doesn't make them smart."

"There's a lot of difference between a song that basically says, 'Hey, come fuck me' over and over again and a distinct, signed language," said Luis. "Especially one that didn't get abandoned as useless after they migrated from shallow waters into the depths."

"Assuming they ever lived in shallow waters in the first place," said Tory. "There's nothing about them to indicate that there was a migration. Maybe they evolved in deep waters. That makes a language based on gestures an even bigger sign of intelligence."

"How could they—" Olivia caught herself. "Bioluminescence. They glow enough to see themselves talking."

Tory nodded. "Exactly. I don't think we can say, with any sort of certainty, that the mermaids *aren't* intelligent. And if they're intelligent, then we have to be very careful about how this goes from here."

"Even if they attack the ship?" asked Luis. "The last time we encountered them, they attacked in a matter of hours. There's no reason to believe that won't happen again."

Tory looked quietly miserable. Luis, who had known her for years, knew she was thinking of her sister again, and how easy revenge had looked when she was standing on the shore, thousands of miles from here, with no real choices to make. Here and now, on this ocean, in these waters, she had decisions in front of her. No matter what she chose, it was going to hurt.

"I hope they attack us," she said, in a small voice. "If they attack, we can fight back, and maybe the Wilsons don't have to live with what I've lived with. But we *can't* go after them. We just can't. They're intelligent creatures, and we don't . . . we don't have the right. Even after everything they've done, until we know that they know they've been hurting people, we can't go after them."

"So what are we supposed to do?" asked Olivia.

Tory looked at her. "We tell the captain about their language," she said, in that same small voice. "We tell Mr. Blackwell, which is basically the same as telling Imagine. We don't hold anything back, and we let them decide what happens next. We document everything that happens."

"After that?" asked Luis.

"We tell them that we need to get the hell out of here before we all get eaten," said Tory. "And when people say that decision is above our pay grade, we pray we'll live to see the shore."

The fourth shutter test was conducted in the middle of the day, where success would be immediately obvious to the passengers.

Like the others before it, it failed. Quietly, faces grim, the engineering crew spread across the ship. The fault in the system had eluded them this far, but they were out of time. If they couldn't fix the shutters, they were all going to die.

CHAPTER 15

**Western Pacific Ocean, above the Mariana Trench:
September 2, 2022**

Jacques stormed into the cabin. Michi looked up and frowned, hands stilling on the rifle she'd been reassembling. "I thought you went to retrieve the acoustician," she said, making no effort to keep the accusation from her voice. "What did you say to her?"

"Nothing," he spat, pushing past her to the table where their small, private sonar array chuckled to itself, spinning endlessly as it chased the sounds beneath the sea. It was a primitive thing compared to the sophisticated equipment used by the *Melusine*'s scientists, but that was part of its value: it could be dropped, jostled, drenched, and continue working as if nothing had happened. It was a poacher's tool. While it lacked the power to pinpoint a single voice in a pod of whales—something more advanced, more delicate equipment could do with ease—it could *find* the pod, and for people like Jacques and Michi, finding the pod was all that was required.

Once they had located the whales, the rest was child's play.

"You must have said *something*," said Michi. "Did you tell her we needed her help? That we were going to hunt the creatures that slaughtered her sister like a dog? She should have beaten you here."

"Yet clearly she didn't," said Jacques. "She said what I was asking was an impossibility—but that's not why she refused me. I saw the revulsion in her eyes. She thinks of us as killers, and she wanted nothing to do with us."

"To be fair, she's not wrong." Michi slotted the last component into place and leaned forward, looking down the barrel with a practiced eye. It was a custom job, designed for picking birds out of the sky over Tokyo. Like most snipers' rifles, it was balanced to her exact specifications. It would be a lethal weapon in anyone's hands. In hers, it stood a chance of killing gods. "We're killers. Embrace that. Let it make you stronger."

"I would rather have made this easier on the both of us. It could have *been* easier on the both of us, if she'd just been willing to do her damn job."

"She's a scientist. We were warned when we took this job that most of the scientists wouldn't want anything to do with us." Michi put her rifle aside, rising. She walked to her husband and draped her arms around his neck, pressing herself against him. "We're going to go down in history as the first hunters with a confirmed mermaid kill. That's worth more than all the money in the world."

"But not worth enough to make me refuse the money," said Jacques.

Michi snorted. "With all the bullets a million dollars can buy? I'd shoot you myself if you tried."

"Good," he said, and kissed her. Michi made an approving noise, molding herself against him as he slung an arm around her waist and scooped her off her feet.

Most of the bed was covered in weaponry. They still found room.

The pool deck was dim, lit only by the lights filtering through the water. It cast everything in an eerie blue light, unbearable and strange. "I don't want to be down here."

"I know," said Theo, exiting the elevator. His leg ached. He needed his medicine, preferably before the nerves caught fire, but he wanted to sit down before injecting himself. Some things were safe to do when walking. This wasn't one of them.

"I mean it." Jillian glared at the back of his neck. "I don't like that you have these dolphins here. It's not right, it's not fair to them, and I don't want any part of it."

183

"You've made that perfectly clear."

"Then why—"

"Because the mermaids are here, and that means it's time to start putting the rest of the pieces into play. That includes the dolphins. Really, I'd expect you to be pleased." The corners of Theo's mouth twitched in what looked more like a death's-head grimace than a smile. "I told you, they were offered a choice, just like the human members of this voyage. They had exactly as much opportunity to refuse as the rest of us."

"Not all the rest of us," said Jillian quietly.

Theo, who had long since learnt that there was no point in arguing when she got like this, said nothing. He kept walking, trusting his increasingly unsteady legs to carry him a little farther. Once he reached a chair he could give himself the injection, let temporary, transitory wellness sweep away the shakiness and the pain. Until then he needed to focus on the future, looking ahead to the place where he'd be able to call this mission either a success or a failure.

The door to his private lab slid open, revealing two people already at work. The blonde woman with the red roots was immediately identifiable as Dr. Hallie Wilson. The other person was less familiar. Jillian frowned, following Theo inside.

Behind the glass, the dolphins swam and twisted, performing their endless acrobatics for an unappreciative audience. It must have been difficult, being a captive-born dolphin, trained all their lives to perform for the amusement of capricious humans, and now thrust into a world where that kind of show was no longer considered politically correct or appropriate. It would have been better not to have them captive at all, but if they were, there should have been something for them to *do*.

You're going to be doing something now, thought Jillian, and felt instantly guilty. The dolphins had earned a lifetime of leisure, if that was what they wanted, and a release into the big blue sea, if that was their preference. Cetologists had been able to converse with dolphins for almost a decade. It should have been easy to determine what, exactly, the dolphins wanted to do.

Primatologists had known the great apes were capable of conversation for longer than that; had been, in fact, carrying on conversations with them for almost fifty years. That hadn't stopped zoos or poachers or private collectors from pulling them out of the wilds and putting them on display. Humanity was cruel. Of that, more than anything else, Jillian was sure. Humanity was cruel, and if you were prepared to try to find a bottom to that cruelty, you had best be prepared for a long, long fall.

"Dr. Wilson; Dr. Lennox," greeted Theo. The two looked up, Hallie seeming briefly surprised to see Jillian before she straightened and folded her hands behind her back. Theo continued onward, heading for his chair. "You know Dr. Toth, I assume?"

"Only by reputation," said Dr. Lennox. He took a step forward, extending his hand. "I've read all your papers, Dr. Toth. Your thoughts on mermaids were revolutionary even *before* we knew there might be something out here. I always believed you. Even when it got me laughed at, I always believed you."

"You're the cetologist," said Jillian, taking his hand. It was easier to observe the niceties than it was to spurn them. It always had been. She'd had colleagues who didn't want to, over the years, and had observed as their careers suffered from seemingly unrelated snubs and misconceptions, all of which could be sourced back to the time they refused to shake a colleague's hand. Her own career had suffered for larger reasons, but she had never refused a handshake. "I knew you were on board. I'd expected to run into you by now."

"I've been down here, mostly," said Dr. Lennox, freeing his hand from her grip. "The dolphins and I have been playing a very slow game of chess. Twitter is better at long-range thinking, Cecil understands the game, but Kearney is *good* at it. Could probably play professionally, if he wasn't a dolphin."

"The bylaws actually have something to say about dolphins?" asked Jillian.

"Not specifically, but they have something to say about robots, aliens, and the necessity that all players competing on a given level be human." Dr. Lennox grinned lopsidedly. "Chess players turn out to include more than their strictly fair share of nerds. Who would've thought?"

"Everyone who's ever met a chess player," said Hallie, and gigglesnorted at her own joke. The other three turned to look at her. She looked back, unembarrassed. "What? I am a delight."

"Fair enough," said Jillian. She returned her attention to Dr.

Lennox. "What are the pair of you doing down here? Other than playing chess with the dolphins."

"Dr. Wilson has just joined me. With the new audio footage we were able to...recover"—he paused, looking briefly abashed, before continuing—"we've been able to start figuring out how their language is structured."

"The mermaids."

"Yes, the mermaids."

"Even though they're not cetaceans? There's no way those things are mammals."

"They might be," said Theo. He was unpacking his kit, preparing the injection to steady his leg. His hands still weren't shaking too severely for him to deliver it to himself. Jillian averted her eyes. She didn't care about the needle; she cared about the betrayal in his face every time he caught her looking. This was something he didn't want to share with anyone, but especially not with her.

"Once someone brings me a body, I'll be able to tell you with certainty, but I can say with *virtual* certainty that there's no way anything that moves like they do, and has the build they do, and lives as deep as they do, could possibly be a mammal," said Jillian. "The endothermic metabolism simply won't support it."

"Not all mammals are endotherms," said Hallie.

Everyone turned to look at her. She shrugged.

"The naked mole rat is an ectothermic mammal. It regulates body temperature externally, not internally. Nature is bigger and weirder than anyone ever wants to think it is. The standards for being considered a mammal are narrow, and very specific: lactation, hair, and three bones in the inner ear. Nothing else is required."

"That's oddly disturbing," said Theo. "What about live birth?"

"The echidna," said Dr. Lennox.

"Warm blood?"

"Again, the naked mole rat," said Hallie. "It's also a hive organism, self-organizing in ways that would be more 'normal' in bees or termites. Some marsupials lactate through their armpits, by the way, and there's even been debate as to whether intentionally premature live birth should be considered the same as full-term live birth. Like the snakes that do the live-birth thing."

Theo frowned at her. "Now you're pulling my leg."

"It's in no condition to be pulled, dear, and she's serious," said Jillian. "There are snakes that lay their eggs internally, incubating them inside their bodies to protect them from predators. They hatch inside their mothers, finish gestating without the benefit of either eggs or placenta, and are born alive and fully formed. So is that live birth? Is it oviparous birth? Or is it something completely different? Dr. Wilson is correct: the problem with trying to define nature is that nature is bigger than we are, and nature doesn't care whether we know how to define it. Nature does what nature wants." She paused. "But I still don't see how they can be mammals. Whatever they are, they're something new. They're *not* skinny whales with fingers."

"No, they're not," said Dr. Lennox. "But they *are* deepwater creatures with a spoken language, which means they're similar to whales in one regard: they have to account for fluid dynamics when they're trying to speak."

"Which is where I come in," said Hallie. "We knew from the original footage that at least half of their language is signed. The new footage supports that, and makes it clear how intelligent they have to be. They're using at least thirty words during the time we have them on film—and that's just what they're doing with their hands."

"How long have you been analyzing their spoken language?" Jillian asked, looking to Dr. Lennox.

"Since we left port," he said. "I started with the *Atargatis* tapes, which are all from above water—not good, for someone who specializes in analyzing sound as it carries *through* water. But Victoria Stewart—the sonar specialist—has been doing dumps of the ambient oceanic noise since before we started this excursion, and once she signed on, I got access to her research." He paused, grimacing. "I'd feel bad about that, if she had any interest in the specifics of how they communicate. She's been working on isolating their speech, figuring out how it works, figuring out how it all hangs together—she wants the machinery of their speech. I want the filigree."

"Sounds like a lot of pretty self-justification for stealing what should have been her Nobel Prize for first contact with an alien race, but hey, who am I to judge? Everyone on this boat is studying mermaids now, because I managed to convince somebody with a checkbook that they were real." Jillian hooked a thumb toward the tank. "You still haven't justified the dolphins."

"The mermaids communicate through a mixture of signed and spoken language," said Dr. Lennox. He was starting to look less certain of his place in the conversation. Jillian had that effect on people, especially when she was gearing up to becoming a human avalanche.

That had been one of the things Theo had liked best about her, back in the days when their marriage was stable and her anger had never been aimed at him. The trouble with having a bear sharing your bed was that one day, the bear was going to notice that you were there; one day, the maimings would begin in earnest.

"I am aware," said Jillian coldly.

"Most of their spoken language is in the band of sounds dolphins can reproduce, and as we mentioned, these are smart dolphins who really want to work with us."

"They're learning to speak mermaid," said Hallie. Jillian turned her attention to the other woman, who didn't flinch. "We're teaching the dolphins common phrases from both recordings and from Miss Stewart's research. They should be able to open the channels of communication. If we can talk to them—"

"They'll still be the creatures who killed your sister, and Miss Stewart's sister, and a lot of good men and women I was once proud to call colleagues." Jillian's voice was, for once, not hard or aggressive; she sounded almost apologetic, like she hated to be the one bringing reality back into the science of the moment. "Also, what in the world makes you think opportunistic oceanic predators capable of taking down a *submersible* wouldn't eat dolphins? They're going to look at your little friends as an offering of delicious treats. There's not going to be a free and open exchange of ideas. There's going to be a bloodbath."

"Why did you come on this voyage if you were only going to discourage every attempt we make at a nonviolent solution?" asked Theo.

"Because you asked me to come. Because I know more about mermaids than anyone else on the planet. Because you were going to get yourself killed, and at least this way, I'll know I did everything within my power to prevent it." Jillian folded her arms. "Because I missed my first shot at seeing them, and by God, that wasn't going to happen again."

"Even if you knew it could kill you?"

"Even if I knew it already had." She turned to Dr. Lennox. "What's your first name, kid?"

Daniel Lennox had three degrees in marine biology: one general, one focused on whales and dolphins, one focused on other seagoing mammals. His time on the protest vessels and the sabotage ships had come after Jillian and Theodore's had ended, but he'd heard stories about them from the older hands, who spoke of Theodore like he was a Spartan hero, and Jillian like she was a cross between the Devil and Helen of Troy. He didn't know whether the time he'd spent in their company was proof that one shouldn't meet one's heroes, or proof that one absolutely should. They didn't know him from Adam. They never would. All their heroics had come before he had been a part of the picture, before he had left the classroom for the big wide world outside. It was freeing. There was room for him in his own story.

But at the same time...Jillian Toth had been sailing the seas while he was trying to figure out whether he wanted the lab or the field. She had held a harpoon in her hand and screamed expletives at a whaling crew, salt in her hair and blood in her eyes, while he was arguing about his thesis with a bunch of bloodless advisors who saw no need to get passionate about anything that didn't feed into their own research. She had been a demon of the sea, and she still was; he could sense that much. Let her wear all the sensible sweaters she wanted to, let her hide her fury under polite frowns and her compassion under sharp words; he saw through it. She was still, and would always be, his Helen of Troy.

"Daniel, ma'am," he said.

"Good. I hate thinking of people younger than my daughter as Doctor. It seems dehumanizing. Yes, you did the work, and I'd never take that away from you, but I'm not stealing the rest of your life for the sake of your degree." Jillian straightened, squaring her shoulders like she was shaking away some unseen shadow, some clinging phantom of those earlier journeys. "Hallie, I'm sorry for your loss."

"Thank you, ma'am," said Hallie. Her eyes were bright. Too bright. It was like she had a fever consuming her from the inside, something neither contagious nor curable.

Although it might well prove to be contagious in the days to come. Depending on where the world went from here. Depending on the waters ahead.

Jillian looked at her steadily. "I know you don't want my advice, but here it is," she said. "Get out of here. Go upstairs, find the sister you still have, and hold her. You're her voice when she needs to speak to the rest of the crew. More than that, you're her anchor to the world. Without you she'll drift, and if she drifts too far, you're never getting her back. Don't let that happen to her. Don't let that happen to you."

"All due respect, ma'am, you can go fuck yourself if you think I'm going to do that." Hallie signed as she spoke, habit and anger conspiring to move her hands, and her gestures were so broad and so sharp that it was clear to everyone around her that she was shouting, screaming her displeasure into the soundless world. "Heather is *dead*. Heather is *gone*. Those *things* took her from us. I can't even bring a body home to my parents. They trusted me to keep my baby sisters safe, and I failed in the biggest way possible. I *lost* one of them. I am damn well going home able to tell my parents I avenged her."

"Then why, for the love of God, are you trying to talk to them?" Jillian demanded.

Hallie's eyes were still bright. Maybe that was the worst thing of all. "Because I want to tell them why," she said. "I want to look at them, and know they're *listening* to me, whether they're doing it with their ears or their eyes or something else. I want them to hear me when I tell them we're going to kill every fucking one of them, and I want them to know why. I want them to know they did this to themselves."

"Conservation—" began Daniel.

"Screw conservation," said Hallie. "I'll help you learn their language. I'll help you tell the dolphins what to say to make them understand that we want to talk. And then I'll help you blow them out of the water."

"When a man undertakes a journey of revenge, he needs to dig two graves," said Theo, interjecting himself back into the conversation. The others turned toward him. He stood, and his leg was no longer shaking.

He looked between them, one after the other, and his face was calm, like the things they were discussing weren't life and death, but were no more important than the weather. "This," he said, "is how things are going to happen.

"Hallie, I understand that you're distressed. Anyone in your position would be. I am truly sorry for your loss. I do wish to remind you that Heather was aware of the risks when she signed on for this voyage—as were you. However compelled you may have felt by your obligations to your sisters, the fact remains that you signed the same waivers as the rest of the people on this vessel. You knew loss of life or limb could occur in the normal course of our work. We are not, as you so charmingly put it, going to 'blow them out of the water.' We're going to reach out to them. We're going to find common ground. And when we're done, we're going to take them in for study. These are one of the great mysteries of our age. We will not do ourselves or our heirs the disservice of destroying them before we understand them."

"That's exactly what I want," said Daniel. "Mr. Blackwell, it's an honor to know that we're going to be working on one of the last great linguistic mysteries. I promise you, we *will* solve it."

"In the time you have? Perhaps. Perhaps not. Either way, we're going to continue on the course I've charted. If you don't like it, feel free to leave."

"We're on a ship in the middle of the ocean," said Hallie.

"I know," said Theo. "Good luck finding somewhere to go."

Silence fell, broken by the low, steady hum of the ship's engines. Behind the glass, the dolphins continued to circle, waiting for the word to go. They were still smiling. They were the only ones.

CHAPTER 16

Western Pacific Ocean, above the Mariana Trench: September 2, 2022

Little dramas played out all over the ship as the *Melusine*'s residents—the crew, the scientists who'd come to the middle of nowhere to make a name for themselves, or to chase one of the greatest mysteries their field had to offer—whispered and shouted and rejoiced at the news that yes, mermaids were real, yes, mermaids were *here*, yes, they were going to see them. They were going to *see* them. The mermaids were directly below the ship, so deep they could have passed unnoticed, but now? Now there was no way they were getting away.

The ones who had believed in the tape were vindicated; the ones who had believed it to be a hoax, who had sailed with the *Melusine* purely for the scientific opportunities, grumbled and tried to deflect the taunting of their peers. Money changed hands as decade-old bets were settled, over and over, in favor of a myth.

(Hallie and Holly would have been horrified to learn how few of their "colleagues" cared about Heather's death. To them her sacrifice had been a necessary part of the scientific process. She had attracted the attention of the mermaids, and opened a new world of research for the rest of them. Some of them were even almost jealous of her. Sure, she was dead, but her name would be associated with this discovery forever. She might even wind up immortalized in their name, something like *Sirenus wilson*. It was a small price to pay, trading a temporary mortal life for something like that, living forever in the pages of every book on marine biology that was ever going to be written.)

Some people pointed out that their lives were officially in danger. Things that were real could hurt them. They were quickly shouted down by the delight of discovery. Danger was everywhere. You could go out for lunch and get hit by a crosstown bus. Besides, the ship had a fully functional shutter system: they were safe. But *mermaids*...

Biologists made bets on what the creatures would prove to be, fish or reptiles or mammals or something new. One ambitious scientist set himself up in the cafeteria with his monitoring equipment, making the case for a relict population of highly evolved stomatopods from the pre-Mesozoic era. It was such a specific and bizarre theory that amused onlookers had been dropping by for hours, swinging through long enough to grab a drink and a sandwich and listen to him expound on his increasingly detailed ideas.

Chemists grabbed water samples from the surface and from each other, bartering sampler time and probe control with the speed of professional gamblers. An ounce from more than thirty meters down could buy a gallon from ten feet, along with computer time, analysis details, and foot massages. It was like standing on a stock market trading floor, listening to the deals go on, words breaking like waves against every surrounding surface.

While there were still ROVs available, the loss of Heather's Minnow meant there was no submersible on the *Melusine* capable of making it to the bottom. It seemed like an oversight now—a mission this size with only one deep-rated submersible? Whose decision was *that*?—but the fact was, submersibles were expensive and most were privately owned, meaning that unless their drivers had been willing to sign on for the trip, they couldn't be acquired. Remotely operated vehicles were safer and easier, even if they lacked the emotional punch of actually diving.

The two remaining submersibles on the *Melusine* each took three people to crew, and couldn't be launched with less than six hours' prep time. The prep was under way; the prep would be under way for hours. Every twenty minutes of submersion cost something on the order of twelve hundred dollars, and as they were less nimble than the Minnow, the ascent and descent would have to be taken in stages, allowing the pressure time to equalize. It was far from an ideal solution. This did nothing to stop scientists from queuing up for the opportunity to claim the open seats.

The first name on the sign-up sheet was Luis's. Holly's name was written above his, on what wasn't technically a slot. That didn't matter. Much as everyone on the *Melusine* wanted a chance to go down, no one was going to question her right to get as close as possible to her sister. There would be other descents. There would be other chances. The first contact was already over. What came now was the real work.

Michi and Jacques ignored all of this. Their own preparations were finished: rifles assembled, tranquilizers mixed, stun grenades and electric batons checked and ready. They had exhausted each other, working through the last of their nervous energy while surrounded by their armory, two dangerous beasts in the middle of a dangerous world. They lay in a tangle of limbs as the ship pulsed around them, waiting for the call that would tell them it was time for the real work to begin. Jacques ran his fingers up and down the serpentine curve of Michi's spine, and all was right with his world.

All over the ship, engineers worked as quickly and quietly as they could, chasing a mechanical fault that should have been enough to turn them around before they had ever reached this point. Their hands were steady, and their heartbeats were fast, and they knew that everything was riding on them.

No pressure.

Beneath the *Melusine*, in the devouring dark where the sun was a lie and a legend—or would have been, had the creatures in those depths cared about such things—other, simpler preparations were also under way. Even the smallest fry knew the surface was where food was found. Safety and comfort were deep things, dark things, but food? A full belly, a full mouth? Those were shallow things, found where the light sliced through the water like talons through the belly of a shark. They were swift enough, clever enough, to play the line between light and dark like a shield, using it to hunt without becoming hunted.

(There were similarities between the hunting patterns of the mermaids and the hunting patterns of terrestrial lions. Both used their coloration and environment to make their tasks easier; both had a tendency to lie in wait for something to be foolish enough to come close. Once the prey had little chance of escape, they would strike, not necessarily to kill, but to wound grievously enough that flight became impossible. Then they could drag their victims into the deeper dark, where it was safe to linger over food, filling the belly slowly, savoring each drowned morsel. Eating high was faster because it had to be. Too much competition in the high waters, too many things that fancied themselves as predators, would try to catch and keep what was never theirs to have.)

Group by group, they came together, forming hunting parties of sixes and eights, and began to rise toward the light.

"Never seen the water like this before."

"It's just water."

"You looked at it recently?"

A grunt, a shrug. "Been a little busy."

Daryl and Gregory were electrical engineers, normally part of a team of five. With things as stretched as they were, the two of them were working alone, trying to finish their tasks before the sun finished going down. It was going to be close without taking the time to look at the water.

"But—"

"Get over here," said Gregory. "I need more hands."

Daryl didn't move.

The *Melusine* was as self-sufficient as possible for a ship of her size. What most people didn't realize was that "as self-sufficient as possible" wasn't very self-sufficient at all. She sailed with an engineering crew of twenty, and all of them thought privately that she could have sailed with twice that number and not left anyone sitting idle. As it stood, they were down a man almost daily, thanks to cut fingers, scalded hands, twisted ankles, and all the little dangers that came of making repairs to a working ship.

Right now every one of them was working, trying to get those damned shutters up and running before the order came from the Imagine man to turn them on. Most of the engineering team was of the opinion that the *Melusine* shouldn't have been allowed out of port for at least another six months, an opinion that was reinforced every time one of the research teams blew another fuse. They didn't seem to understand that overloading every circuit on the ship wasn't going to get their work done any faster; they plugged their machines into every outlet they could find, and when they blew a fuse, they shrugged, unplugged, and moved on to the next one. Daryl was convinced that the word for a group of scientists ought to be a *blackout*, because that was what the fuckers seemed determined to cause.

Gregory was both older and calmer; this wasn't his first Imagine-sponsored voyage. He'd missed the *Atargatis* by less than a month, thanks to a parasite he'd picked up while accompanying a film crew on a quest for the world's last living dinosaur. (They hadn't found it. They'd found a fuck-lot of nasty biting flies and some exciting fungal infections, one of which still flared up when he forgot his toe cream. He was going to keep working for Imagine until he earned his pension, because by God, it owed him that. It owed him that and more.) He had a tendency to shrug and let it go when the scientists got out of hand.

"They're just big kids," he'd said, time and time again. "They liked to play with toys when they were snot nosed and brownnosing their teachers, and now that they've learned to wipe up both ends, they still like to play with toys. Just more expensive ones. They don't mean any harm, and the way they keep breaking shit means we'll never be out of a job. Let it go."

"Let it go" might as well have been Gregory's life philosophy. Most of the other engineers found him soothing. No matter what was going on—electrical fire, unexplained leaks, missing structural components—he could be relied upon to keep his cool. Normally that was a good thing.

Not right now. Louder this time, Daryl said, "I've *never* seen the water like this."

Gregory paused, wrench in his hand, and turned to look at the other engineer. In a tone of profound weariness, he asked, "You going to let this go?"

"No."

"Not until I look."

"Not until you look."

"Right." Gregory put the wrench down and stood, grimacing as his knees popped. That pension from Imagine wasn't as far in the future as he liked to think. Maybe that should have been a relief—wasn't retirement supposed to be a dream? Something to aspire to?—but really, it was just confusing. Where did his youth go? That strong, straight-backed boy he saw in old pictures of himself, where was he?

Gone to sea, like all the bright-eyed boys, and like all the bright-eyed boys, he was never coming home. Men might return, but the boys? Oh, they never did.

The captain had ordered them to get the shutters working after that Wilson girl went under and didn't come back. The mermaids were real and they were coming. Why they didn't just turn and get the hell out of here was above Gregory's pay grade, but he had some suspicions: a ship this size wasn't made to accelerate on a dime, and if the damn shutters weren't working, who was to say what else might have decided to break?

The security staff was in a tizzy, seeming to have finally realized that they had jobs to do. Amateurs. They'd been hired to look good on camera, not to protect their charges cleanly or well, and not for the first time, Gregory questioned the wisdom of letting an entertainment company call the shots. You didn't let Disney plan a war or Sony run a government. Why the hell would anyone let Imagine supervise a scientific expedition?

Careful of his protesting joints, Gregory moved to the rail and leaned forward enough to look down into the water. The sun was descending, sending bright spears of light slashing across the surface. At first he thought the glitter in the waves was part of that sunset. Light refracted, after all; put light in the water, and it could do all manner of things it would never think of doing in the open air. Water was tricky like that. It could twist a perfectly sensible natural force into something strange and new, and once that had happened, nothing in the world could ever turn it back again.

The glitter moved. Gregory frowned.

This wasn't light reflecting off the water; no matter how strange and new light might seem when it bounced from place to place, following the focus of the tide, it was still light. It had to follow certain rules. One of those was that light refracted through water couldn't move *against* the water. It had to move *with* the water, following the laws of fluid dynamics. This glitter...

It was moving on its own, darting from place to place as nimbly as a fish. And it wasn't at the surface of the water with the rest of the light; it was deep, hanging low, almost on the edge of eyesight. It was mostly visible because the water was so calm, and because it was so *wrong*. It shouldn't have been there, and so it stood out as strange.

Gregory couldn't help thinking that if he'd been alone, he would have convinced himself there was nothing there to see; he had a job to do, and frightening himself wouldn't have gotten it done. He was a calm man because he was a simple one, and he was able to remain a simple man because he refused to contemplate things that would have required him to be complex. Let the younger men be complicated. They were still the shadows of the brave boys who'd set out to sea; they had time for complexity. They'd learn to be simple as they got older. They'd learn that sometimes it was best to let lights in the water be just that, and not ask questions about them, and not look, and not *know*.

"What are they?" asked Daryl.

"Fucked if I know," said Gregory (who was simple, but not prudish). "One of the science kids might be doing something. Robots reflecting the sun or whatever."

"Why would they do that?" Daryl cast him an anxious look. "Couldn't it be one of those mermaids?"

"The captain said the mermaids were all the way down at the bottom. As for the kids, why do they do any of the things they do? There's a girl on deck three who's built a water sampler that looks like a robot shark. She says it's because she wants predators to leave it alone, but that doesn't explain why it chomps its jaws and chases fish. She built it because she wanted a robot shark, and she found a half-decent excuse for doing what she already wanted to do, so she did it." Gregory shook his head. "You could tell me one of them was working on a way to turn the whole ship to sugar, and I'd believe you."

"I guess." Daryl leaned farther forward, looking dubiously at the lights that flashed and glittered in the water. "It just doesn't seem right. Look at how they're moving. Like they're alive."

"The science kids—"

"They like their robots to look like robots," said Daryl. "Anything that looks too alive starts a turf war with the biologists, and then nobody gets any work done. That's almost like...I don't know.

It's like the way anglerfish move. All jittery and bright. Lures. That's what they look like. They look like lures."

"Anglerfish don't swim in schools, and you'd need a whole damn school of them to account for that much glitter," said Gregory. The hairs on the back of his neck were rising, tying themselves into tangles. Something about the situation was wrong, very wrong, and he didn't want to have a damn thing to do with it. He wanted out.

Maybe those devil fish weren't down as deep as he wanted them to be.

"That's still what it looks like," said Daryl sullenly.

"Just because a thing looks like a thing, that doesn't mean that's what it is."

Daryl stopped, turning to look at him. Finally he said, "Worst part is, I followed that. I'm going to go tell the captain."

"If that's what you feel is best." Captain Peterman had authority over the vessel and that was where his command stopped; everything around him had been bought and paid for by Imagine. It was no secret that the captain couldn't scratch his own ass without permission from the corporation. That didn't stop the crew from reporting to him. They'd been raised on the usual structure of the sea, and they knew he should have been able to help them, to protect them, to tell them what to do. Daryl was going to be damned disappointed if he expected Captain Peterman to tell him what was happening with those lights in the water.

But maybe that was for the best. Disappointment was an essential step in burying those bright-eyed boys, and leaving sensible men in their place.

"It is." Daryl bounced on his toes for a minute, excitement and anxiety warring in his eyes. "I know I'm supposed to stay here and help you, but would you mind if I . . . ?"

"Go." Gregory turned his back on the water, relieved in an obscure, unnamable way when he could no longer see the glitter dancing below the surface of the waves. "I can take care of this on my own, and next time we have something to fix that you could handle without me, you can pay me back with an extra coffee break."

"Thanks, man, you're the best." Then Daryl was gone, racing down the deck with the speed that seemed to belong solely to the bright-eyed boys. He'd lose that soon enough. For now, let him have his glory; let him have his fun. The days of the bright-eyed boys were always numbered, and if there was one thing Gregory had learned in his time with Imagine, it was that you couldn't get them back once they were gone. It was kinder to indulge them. There would be years and years to spend with the men they would become.

Something caught his eye as he watched Daryl go. The glitter was still moving through the water, deep and quick and inexplicable. Looking at it made his skin crawl. Gregory turned resolutely away again, going back to his repairs.

When he looked at the water again, the glitter was gone. That didn't make him feel any better. Something like that...If it had disappeared, where did it go?

"Captain?"

On a normal voyage, having a hired engineer—not even an official member of the crew, a man who would be gone as soon as they got back to the dock—intrude without permission would have been enough to trigger a stern lecture, if not actual punishment. But they were all hired hands on this voyage, even the people who had multi-year contracts with the *Melusine*.

(Most of the crew was reasonably sure Imagine had wanted to lock them in before any discoveries were made, so they couldn't go blabbing to the tabloids without breaking some term of their employment. None of them cared. They'd be paid whether or not they were sailing, thanks to the terms outlined in that same contract, and if Imagine wanted to cut checks for their silence, that was fine. The mermaids were too big to stay secret for long. If they didn't talk, the scientists would, and then they'd be able to say anything they wanted, while they got drunk on Imagine's money and didn't do a damn thing between here and their termination dates.)

Right now, the crew was on high alert, and people were seeing mermaids everywhere they turned. Engineers, security staff, everyone under his command was racing to and fro, trying to get the damn shutters working. The ones who lacked the skill to work on the shutters were fixing the little things that had been allowed to slip, or hadn't been tested frequently enough. A little lapse in propriety was only to be expected.

"What did you want, Mr....Cliff, wasn't it?"

"Daryl Cliff, sir. Engineer. Junior, that is. I'm assigned to work with Gregory Richardson."

"I know Gregory," said Captain Peterman. He stood, reaching for his hat. It was a silly affectation, but the passengers felt better when he wore his hat. "Good man. Good head on his shoulders. No one better in a crisis. What's going on, Mr. Cliff?" Gregory had sailed with him before. Gregory had earned the right to have his first name used in casual conversation. This strained-looking young man had not.

Captain Peterman paused, reviewing the last few seconds. The young man *did* look strained. The flesh around his eyes was tight, creating an impression of shock or fear. The corner of his mouth was twitching. Something had given him a fright.

Maybe they had less time than they thought.

"Mr. Cliff?" Captain Peterman repeated, a sharp note in his voice.

"Sir, there's something in the water." Some of the strain vanished, replaced by relief. By telling the captain—by telling the person in *charge*—the young man had rendered this someone else's problem. "Gregory's still there, but he agreed I should come and tell you." That was only half a lie. Gregory knew he was coming to see the captain. He hadn't endorsed it, exactly, but he knew, and that made it true enough to say.

Captain Peterman went cold. Being the first to say the word *mermaid* would be to lose. He would not lose. Voice level, he said, "Something in the water? Son, I don't know if you're aware, but we're in the middle of the Pacific Ocean. There's lots of somethings in the water. This is their home. As far as they're concerned, *we're* 'something in the water,' and they're probably pretty keen on us moving along."

"It's not like that," said Daryl. He stood his ground, even though every instinct he'd developed in three years as an independent maritime engineer told him to back down. It was never good to argue with the captain over anything but the safety of the ship—in part because an engineer who argued over little things was less likely to be listened to about the big ones. There might come a time when the survival of this vessel and her crew depended on the captain listening when he spoke. If he couldn't guarantee that, he might as well turn in his resignation right now.

But the glitter in the water had been wrong. Something about it had turned his stomach in a way he didn't have the words for, had never needed to articulate before; something about it had seemed so inimical that he didn't want to remember what it looked like. When he tried, his mind shied away, presenting him with images of sunlight on the surface, of Gregory frowning at his idle fancies. How could light be threatening? It didn't make *sense*. It was just light, after all. It was just light.

As an engineer, it was his job to speak for the safety of the ship. He was speaking for the safety of the ship now. He knew it all the way down to his bones, even if none of the people who heard him agreed. He was trying to protect them.

On another vessel, another journey, the captain might have dismissed him. But the ship was already in a state of high alert, and Captain Peterman wasn't a foolish man; he hadn't established his reputation by ignoring danger or dismissing people who were clearly in distress. "All right, son," he said. "Let's go see your lights in the water."

Daryl grinned relief. "This way, sir," he said.

They walked side by side along the deck, the captain nodding to everyone who passed. Daryl barely noticed. He was jittery, jumpy, glancing by turns at the water and the sky. The sun was almost down. The water's surface, which had been like glass in the sunlight, was dark, unbreakable; it could have been a foot or a mile deep, and made no functional difference. Anything could be down there. Anything at all.

They reached the stretch of deck where Gregory was working, now using a bulb on a stick to light up the inside of an open panel. The power to that specific stretch of the ship had been cut off to avoid electrocutions while they accessed the shield servos and recalibrated them. It had been a good idea at the time, with the sun in the sky and nothing in the water. Now, Daryl had to fight the urge to shiver, glancing around and trying to measure how much distance there was between them and the water. It was easily twenty feet. Even the lowest deck was ten feet above the waterline.

It no longer felt like enough.

Gregory raised his head at the sound of footsteps, looking only mildly surprised to see the captain. "Captain," he said. "Hope you don't mind if I don't get up. Knees aren't what they used to be, and I think I'm about done kneeling for the day. I stand now, I'm not finishing this."

"As you were," said the captain. "I'm here for a look at Mr. Cliff's mysterious lights. Did you see them?"

The temptation to lie was strong. Daryl could see it in Gregory's eyes, in the way they darted toward the sea and then away again. They were both frightened. Gregory just wasn't showing it as clearly. And now he wanted to lie.

He didn't. Sighing heavily, he turned back to the open panel, allowing his hands to get back to work as he said, "I did. Strangest damned things. It was like some kid had scattered holographic glitter about five, six feet down."

"Could it have been refracted sunlight?"

"That was my first thought, and if I'm being honest, that's what I *wanted* it to be. But it didn't move like sunlight. Moved like something was moving it." Moved like it was alive, was what he wanted to say, and what he desperately did *not* want to say, because saying it would mean acknowledging it, and acknowledging it would give it more power than he wanted it to have. He wanted to forget about it.

Daryl, damn him, wasn't going to let that happen. "Those mermaids," he said doggedly. "Didn't their hair glow?"

"Lots of deepwater creatures have bioluminescence, including the mermaids we're here to study," said Captain Peterman. "But they're not at the surface. The loss of Miss Wilson's submersible occurred in the Challenger Deep." Even swimming at full speed, the mermaids wouldn't reach the surface until well past midnight. That was what the scientists had told them, and with the engineering crew still prepping the security shutters to deploy, that was what he needed to believe.

"Didn't they come to the surface when they sank the *Atargatis*?" asked Daryl.

"The *Atargatis* didn't sink," Captain Peterman pointed out. "She was found adrift with all hands lost. Whatever these creatures are, they're not supernatural, and they can't sink a vessel of this size. Now please, show me this glitter or get back to work."

Daryl moved to the rail and leaned as far out as he dared, eyes scanning the water. There was no glitter. There was no light at all.

203

There was only the deep, boundless sea, lapping against the side of the ship, untroubled by the things going on above it.

"It was right here," he said.

"Now it isn't," said Captain Peterman. "Interestingly, neither is the sun. Looks like it was refraction from the sunset after all."

On the other side of the ship, someone started screaming. And didn't stop.

CHAPTER 17

Western Pacific Ocean, above the Mariana Trench: September 2, 2022

The alert for the ship didn't apply to assigned Imagine filming duties; mermaids or no, Olivia had needed to get a shot of herself in front of the sunset, talking about the dangers lurking beneath. So they'd done it, as quickly and efficiently as they could, waiting the whole time for danger to strike.

It hadn't. Now they were walking back along the top deck through night air that was colder than Olivia would have thought possible, given how warm the days were. Wasn't being in the tropics supposed to guarantee beautiful evenings full of moisturizing humidity, and the opportunity for bellinis on the upper deck? (Mimosas were for morning, with their invigorating orange juice base. Bellinis were for evening, when the sweetness of the peach made it easier to keep drinking them until everything seemed like a good idea.) Sure, the weather occasionally obliged; they'd had their share of golden evenings. But more often, the sun went down and the sea turned cold.

There were probably climatologists in the labs below who could tell her why that was happening, which of the many things humanity had done had caused the temperate tropical nights to turn capricious and cruel. Maybe eventually she'd care enough to ask them. Probably not, or at least not on camera. Climate science was too important to be diverting to the viewer at home. Everyone knew someone who'd been affected by a superstorm or a permanent shift in the weather. People were afraid of what the weather was becoming—what the weather had already become—and so they didn't want it intruding on their entertainment. Anything she learned would be sidelined at best, and used as a mark against her at worst.

So she shivered in her borrowed coat while Ray walked beside her, his big body shielding her from the wind blowing off the Pacific. He looked at her with concern as they moved toward the stairwell, making no effort to conceal his feelings.

"You should tell her," he said.

"Tell her what? That the girl who replaced her sister in Imagine's interchangeable personnel chart is incredibly into her, and would like to hook up?" Olivia shook her head. "I've hinted. I've tried. Either Tory doesn't want me and doesn't know how to say it, or she's not into girls."

"No offense, hon, but you flirt like it's a form of espionage and you'll be executed if you get caught. It doesn't have to be that way."

"It did in my household." Liberal mother; conservative father; autistic daughter learning about social interaction one book and course of practical study at a time. Olivia had figured out flirting from romantic comedies and comic books (although, lacking super-powers, she couldn't use most of the techniques employed by her favorite heroines). She had figured out she preferred the company of women from different books, books with long, scholarly titles and dog-eared pages. Never from her e-reader, no; like most of the kids she knew, her parents checked it regularly to find out what she was reading. Any hint of "pervert" literature would have earned her a smack from her father, followed by a lecture from her mother about how she was special, delicate, and shouldn't worry about such things, since it wasn't like she was ever going to have sex *anyway*. Little autistic girls should learn to masturbate, or better yet, to abstain, because anyone who was deviant enough to want her would be deviant enough to hurt her.

Even at the age of twelve, Olivia had known her mother was as wrong as her father, although it wasn't until she went to college, took her first human sexuality class, and met her first girlfriend (Shoshana, who had fucked like an angel and smoked like a chimney, and was currently headlining her own punk band) that she'd realized both of them had been doing her harm. Her father had left bruises on her body. Her mother's bruises, for all that they'd been harder to see, were proving much slower to heal.

"You don't live with them anymore," Ray rumbled. He didn't have all the details on Olivia's childhood—no one did, including, he sometimes suspected, Olivia herself; there was too much she glossed over, accepting it as normal when it was anything but—but he knew growing up and going away to college had been the best thing that could ever have happened to her.

She wasn't as fragile as she looked, inside or out. He still took his mandate to protect her seriously. She wasn't going to come to harm on his watch, and if he ever had the opportunity to meet her parents, they were going to hear a few things about what he thought of them. If they took offense at that, well, he was going to enjoy demonstrating the more physical side of his job. He was going to enjoy it very much.

"I know. But some habits are hard to break." Olivia kicked the deck. "Everyone I've ever dated has made the first move. They say, 'I'm interested,' and I go along with it. Sometimes even when I don't really want to, just because I'm impressed that they can be so brave. But I don't know how to say it to her, and this isn't the Love Boat. We're not here to make a romantic connection. We're to look good on camera, redeem the *Atargatis*, and do it without getting eaten by mermaids."

"It's a tall order, even without adding dating to the plate," said Ray. "You really like this girl?"

"I do," said Olivia. She sighed. "I'll figure it out. There has to be something I can say to make her understand what I want without me sounding like a total loser."

"I'm sure there is." The horizon flickered red with the remains of the sunset. Ray didn't think he'd ever seen anything so beautiful, or so humbling, in his life. The ocean was bigger than anything he could have conceived. If it swallowed them all, no one would ever know.

Olivia shot him a mock-venomous glare. "You're not *helping*."

"I didn't know I was supposed to be helping. You want me to kidnap her, tie her up, and keep her in a closet until you finish writing a script for your first date?" Ray batted his eyelashes. "I am at your disposal."

"Jerk."

"Yes."

Olivia sighed again. "I shouldn't even bother. What do I have to offer except a lot of therapy over dating a sister surrogate?"

"Dunno. Brilliant, beautiful, good job… You're right. You have nothing to offer."

Olivia scowled. Ray laughed, walking to the rail and leaning against it, resting the bulk of his weight on his folded arms. The wind ruffled his hair. Olivia found herself wishing she were the one with the camera for once; he made a perfect picture, standing there, lit by the soft white bulbs glowing overhead. There was a patch of deck farther down where all the lights were out, due to some routine maintenance task or other, but here, it was perfect. Perfect.

"Have faith in yourself, Olive," he said. "The rest of us have faith in you, and it's time you caught up."

"I'll try." She moved to stand next to him, looking toward the line of the horizon. It was too much and too far. She dropped her eyes, looking down at the side of the ship, and froze.

Someone was clinging to the hull.

"Ray," she said, delivering a quick elbow to her cameraman's side. "Look."

He looked and swore before grabbing a safety hook from the rail. They were fifteen feet long, meant to be used to snag floating debris during a storm, when waves might crest high enough to make them useful. Of all the ship's mandatory safety equipment, the upper deck hooks had always seemed the least useful to Olivia. Now watching Ray lean over the rail and dangle the hook toward the person clinging to the hull, she began to see their purpose. If he could pull whoever was down there to safety…

The hook brushed the person's arm. Olivia saw their head turn, the motion somehow catching glints of light against the hull. Then they were grabbing the hook with both hands, and Ray was pulling them upward, toward the deck, toward the light.

The stranger was almost to the rail when enough of the light reached them for Olivia to see their outline. The grayish skin; the long, stringy hair; the sinuous tail where the legs should have been. *Where the legs should have been.* She didn't think; she just acted, lunging for the hook, intending to rip it out of Ray's hands and send the mermaid plummeting back toward the water where it belonged.

"Mermaid!" she shrieked. "Mermaid!"

Ray was stronger than she was. Hard as she pulled, she couldn't get the pole away from him. He turned to look at her, alarmed by her scream. "Olive, what—"

Maybe it was his distraction, or maybe the mermaid somehow knew it was about to lose its chance, or maybe he'd simply let it get too close. It was a predator; it knew how to strike. While Ray's head was turned, the mermaid lunged, swarming up the pole with a speed that would have seemed impossible if it hadn't been so very, terribly real.

Its head was smaller than Olivia's, due to the fineness of its bone structure, the delicacy of its frame. But that head contained a mouth that seemed to split it virtually in two when opened. She caught a glimpse of its teeth, bristling and needle sharp, before it drove them into Ray's shoulder, biting deep. He howled in agony, the veins in his neck bulging as he tensed against the pain. Olivia tried to lunge for the mermaid, intending to grab those narrow shoulders and yank it away from her friend and protector. He could still be saved. She could save him. She could.

She couldn't. Ray's fist caught her below the solar plexus, knocking her back. Olivia landed on the deck, and could only scream as the mermaid pulled its teeth from the raw meat of Ray's shoulder, hissed in her direction, and closed its mouth over Ray's face.

He kept swinging, kept slapping the thing even as it chewed his flesh away, but it was too late, and had been too late as soon as he'd offered the hook to the climbing mermaid. It bit down harder, sinking its teeth so deep that nothing could have pried them free. Ray stopped hitting. Olivia kept screaming. The mermaid leaned backward, shifting its weight over the rail until it fell, dragging Ray down into the water.

Running footsteps told Olivia someone was coming—not help; help was too late, there was nothing left *to* help—and she scrambled to her feet, still screaming, to fling her arms around the ship's captain. The motion knocked the hat from his head. Startled, he stood frozen for several seconds before closing his arms awkwardly around her.

"There, there, Miss Sanderson," he said, in a strangled tone. "What's wrong? Why were you shouting?"

"She wasn't shouting; she was screaming," said one of the two men with him. He was older, her father's age, thin and sunbaked and

209

rangy. He looked like the sort of fellow who'd offer a hook down the side of the ship if he saw someone climbing there. The thought was enough to make Olivia whimper and cling harder to the captain, who was starting to appear genuinely distressed.

"Captain." The speaker was the other man, the younger one. He had continued walking until he'd reached the place where Ray had been standing. Now he was looking at the deck, eyes getting wider and more dismayed. "I think this is blood over here."

"What?"

"It looks like blood." The young man crouched, touching one of the stains with a trembling hand. His fingertips came away dark, glinting red when he held his hand up for the light. He didn't say anything.

"What is this...?" Captain Peterman took a step forward, dragging Olivia with him. Only then did he seem to remember she was there, that his arms were full of weeping woman, and not holding some shield against whatever force had spilled blood on the deck of his ship. He stopped, looking down at the top of Olivia's head. She had her face pressed against his chest, covering her eyes, keeping her from speaking.

That last part was going to be a problem.

"Miss Sanderson, I need you to tell me what happened," he said, trying to make his voice gentler, succeeding only in pitching it lower in his chest, until it came out as something verging on a growl. The sound irritated him. Comforting silly reporters who had wandered into the wrong story was not a part of his job.

But protecting the people on this vessel was. Heather Wilson had died on his watch, and if the blood on the deck signaled what he feared—something dark and dire and irrevocable—she wasn't the only one. The alternative was that Olivia had slipped and hit her head against the side of the ship.

He'd never wished so hard for someone to have injured themselves. If she hadn't, then the estimates from the scientists had been wrong, and God have mercy on them all.

"Miss Sanderson," he said again. "I need you to tell me whose blood that is." *Please let it be yours*, he thought, half praying. *Please let it belong to the living.*

Olivia mumbled something, voice obscured by the captain's chest. There was a pause as she realized it. She pushed away from him, the gesture turning into a stuttering half step backward. Not, noted Gregory, enough of a step to put her near the stains on the deck where Daryl stood, fingers bloody and face white. She had a feline's instinct for avoidance, keeping herself in the light, and well away from any chance of mess.

"It came up the side of the ship," she said. Her voice was soft, and carried a bone-deep complaint. She was objecting to her own story even as she was telling it. "We were walking on the deck, and it came up the side of the ship. It shouldn't have been able to be on the side of the ship. How did it do that? It's not *allowed* to do that. But it did. It came up the side of the ship."

"What did?" asked Captain Peterman. *Please*, he prayed.

Olivia frowned, expression shifting from confused protest to disbelief. "Why are you asking that? You know what I'm talking about. The mermaid. The mermaid came up the side of the ship. Ray thought it was a person. I did too." Mostly. There had been something off about the silhouette from the beginning, hadn't there? But that hadn't seemed real, not when it was she and Ray and the rail and the thought of someone falling to their death. That hadn't seemed real. After swallowing hard, she said, "Ray offered one of the hooks. The ones we're supposed to use if someone falls. He held it out, and the mermaid took it, and when he tried to pull back, it climbed like it was swimming through the air, like it was so strong it didn't even notice it was going straight up, and then it was *biting* him, and he pushed me away, and—and—" She stopped again, her mouth continuing to move this time, chewing at the air.

The captain looked stunned. Daryl was still staring. Gregory stepped forward, grabbing Olivia by the shoulders and turning her to look at him. He locked his eyes on hers, holding that uncomfortable stare until she turned her own eyes away.

"I'm sorry," he said, voice low, as he let go of her shoulders and allowed her to step back. Somehow, forcing her to look at him had felt like more of an invasion than touching her without her permission. "I'm sorry, but I had to."

"I know," she said.

"Where did it go?"

Olivia was silent for a long moment before she turned her eyes toward the rail, and past them, to the dark and endless sea.

"It took him," she said. "It took him into the water." She wrapped her arms around herself, shivering for reasons that had nothing to do with the chill.

"It took him," she said again.

No one else said anything.

CHAPTER 18

Western Pacific Ocean, above the Mariana Trench: September 2, 2022

Tory glared at her screen. The waves and curves of audio slithered across the display, twining together as they passed their strange messages from one to the other. And she couldn't understand a damn thing they were saying. Oh, she had the basic structures; she knew the underpinnings of the conversation, the places where the sound of the sea met the sound of the *Melusine* met the songs of whales and fish and squid and other deep-sea creatures.

"I can't even tell if the goddamn mermaids are *down* there," she snapped, flattening her hands against the keyboard. It was better than putting her head down. If she did that, she wasn't sure she'd pick it up again before morning. The loss of Heather was echoing through the chambers of the ship, bouncing off the walls, coloring the air. It was in everything they did. It was never going to end.

"I do not think that they will sing for you," quipped Luis.

"Go to hell."

"I have been there, and it is these data feeds." Luis shook his head. "Half the data I'm getting doesn't make sense. It says we're above a huge pod of whales, and there aren't any whales *down* there. There aren't—"

He stopped, eyes going wide. Tory's eyes widened in tandem, but rather than stopping, she started, her fingers stuttering into motion, first tiptoeing across her keyboard and then slamming down with the sort of force that had broken three laptops before she'd turned eighteen. She couldn't be trusted with a touch screen when she was like this; she needed equipment that was built to stand up to tsunamis.

"They're *mimics*, we *knew* they were mimics, we *knew* they remembered what the engines of the *Atargatis* sounded like, of *course* we can't pick them out, because *they don't sound like them!*" Tory kept typing faster, gathering speed. "They have *three* languages! The one they sign, the one they sing, and the one they *steal*, and they use that third language when they're hunting, so the prey never hears them coming! It's genius! You're a genius!"

She paused for Luis's reply. When it didn't come, she spun her chair around, directing a quizzical look at the back of his head. He was sitting very straight and very still, his own hands resting on the desk, motionless.

"Luis?" she asked.

"Do you know what you just said?" He shook his head. She didn't know; of course she didn't know. It had always been about revenge for Tory, but somewhere along the way, revenge had been transmuted into a need to *understand*. She wanted to know why the mermaids did what they did, why they had chosen to leave the safety of the water to hunt prey that should never have been a part of their world. She wanted to hear them. That meant she was willing to listen.

"I said they were mimics," she said.

"No," he said. "You said that they use mimicry *when they're hunting*. They stop using their own kind of sounds *when they're hunting*. What are they hunting now, Victoria? What are they looking for? They killed Heather. They've killed humans before. They know humans come from ships; what happened to the *Atargatis* is proof of that. Between the season and the climate changes, we represent the most food they've seen in one place in God only knows how long. They're hunting. They're hunting *us*."

Tory stared at him. "You can't be serious."

"Nothing else makes sense."

"You're assuming a level of intelligence that—"

"Doesn't seem so far-fetched when you're talking about something with three languages." Luis glared. "Think about your words."

Tory slumped in her seat, face going blank. Luis waited. He'd worked with her long enough to have seen that expression a hundred times; he knew it meant she was combing over her stores of accumulated data, both considered and unconsidered, and using it to draw a functional conclusion.

Finally the light came back on in her eyes, giving way quickly to absolute horror. "We need to tell someone."

"Yes."

"We need to tell Mr. Blackwell." The captain might control the ship, but it was Mr. Blackwell, and Imagine, who controlled the voyage. If anything immediate was to be done, it would be Mr. Blackwell who approved it.

"Yes," agreed Luis. Both of them stood, turning toward the door to their lab.

Olivia was there, small and pale and swimming in a green sweater at least four sizes too large for her. Luis and Tory stopped, bewildered by her sudden appearance. The door had been closed; she must have slipped it open without making a sound. She was hugging herself and shivering.

"Olivia?" said Tory.

"The captain brought me here after the nurse said I was okay, but you were working, and I didn't want to interrupt, so I waited for you to be done, and then I realized I didn't know what to say, so I didn't say anything." Olivia's voice was slow, measured, the voice of a woman who was looking over the edge of the world, and didn't like what she saw. "I still don't know what to say. Do you really think they're hunting us?"

"Yes," said Tory.

Olivia nodded. A tear ran down her left cheek, dropping from her chin onto her sweater. She'd been crying for a while, Tory realized; her sweater was soaked.

"That makes sense," she said. "One of them came up the side of the ship and took Ray. It just... took him. Into the water. Do you think he drowned?"

"No," said Tory, and it was the absolute truth, even filtered through her horror. No, she did not think Ray had drowned. If one of the mermaids had taken him—one of those deep horrors, with teeth like daggers and the hands designed to catch and keep—then he hadn't drowned, because he wouldn't have had *time*. He would have died before his body hit the water.

"Good," said Olivia. She paused before asking, "May I have a hug, please? I don't want to impose. But I very much want a hug right now."

"Yeah," said Tory, and crossed the few feet of floor between them, folding her arms around the smaller woman. Olivia stiffened for a moment, like she had requested the hug without really expecting to receive it. Then she melted against Tory, burying her face against her chest. She didn't sob. All her sobbing seemed to have been used up. She just stood there, shaking slightly, and clung.

Finally Tory asked, "Are you okay?"

"No," said Olivia. She raised her head, not letting go. "Ray pushed me away. He saw what the mermaid was going to do, and he pushed me away so it couldn't get me. I think it would have taken us both, if he'd let it. Why would it do that? He was bigger than it was. What could it possibly want with him?"

"Food," said Luis. Tory winced. He continued without seeming to notice, saying, "Prey is scarce around here, and we know from the footage we've collected so far that they hunt as a group. So it probably took him because it knew it would be able to eat its fill and still support the school."

"Is that the collective noun for a group of mermaids?" asked Olivia.

"It's the best we have," Tory said. She let go of Olivia, taking a step back to give her some space. "We need to go tell Mr. Blackmore what we've figured out. Do you want to come with us? You can stay here, if you'd rather."

"I like to watch old music videos when I'm stressed," said Luis. "I could queue up a bunch for you."

"Thank you for the offer, but no, thank you; I'd rather go with you," said Olivia. "I don't...If I'm alone, I'm going to dwell, and if I dwell, I'm going to retreat, and if I retreat, I'm not sure I'm going to be able to come back. That's what I want the most right now, to go away and not come back, and that's why I'm not allowed to have it, no matter how much I want it. So thank you, but no. I need to go with you."

Luis nodded. Then he hesitated, and turned, and walked back to his desk, beginning to rummage through the piles of paper and small objects that had accumulated there. Olivia blinked after him before turning a blank look on Tory, who shrugged.

"I don't know either," she said. "Luis moves in mysterious ways." Then she winced. "I'm sorry. This probably isn't a good time for jokes."

"No, it's the best time for jokes," said Olivia. She forced a weak smile. "Jokes remind us that we're alive. And that your sense of humor is terrible."

"No contest here," said Luis, walking back over to join them. He held a small black rectangle out toward Olivia. "I thought this might help."

"What is it?"

"Handheld video recorder," he said. "I know Ray was, well. I know he was the one who held the camera for you. I know that's important. So I thought maybe, for right now, you could hold the camera for yourself."

Olivia's eyes widened. She pulled the camera toward her chest like a child with a teddy bear, chin dipping in what seemed like an abortive nod. "Thank you," she said.

"No worries," said Luis.

He waited for Olivia to collect herself, and then the three of them—Tory with her arm around Olivia's shoulders, Olivia hugging the camera—left the lab and walked down the long stretch of deck between them and the nearest stairwell. It was impossible not to look at the sea, that great dark sheet stretching from them to the horizon. Luis had always found that darkness comforting. Who knew what lurked down there, waiting to be discovered? Let deforestation do away with Bigfoot, let sonar destroy Nessie, but the sea would always be deep, always be dark, always be filled with wonders. Every cryptid hunter he knew had turned their eyes toward the sea years ago. That was where the monsters might still be.

Well, he knew something about the monsters now. He knew they were real, for one thing, and he'd been wasting his family's money by looking for them. He should have been using it to build better barriers. Anything to keep them safe from the so-called lovely ladies of the sea.

A few crew members rushed by as they made their way into the depths of the ship. Luis watched them with a weather eye, noting how quick their steps were and how reluctant they were to make eye contact with anyone. The captain had sent out the all-hands alarm after Heather's death, asking people to stay out of the open, to stay in groups, while they prepared the shutters for deployment.

Most of the researchers had remained calm. They were scientists, and a life spent in service to science had an odd effect on the sense of self-preservation. They started out as safety inclined as anyone else, and then they spent their careers learning to run toward explosions, to collect novel toxins for research purposes, to pick up venomous snakes and see the beauty in their alien eyes. Luis didn't think there was much reason to worry about panic among the ship's scientists. As long as their equipment kept working and they weren't actively being eaten alive, they were going to keep doing their research, and keep enjoying the opportunity to do so.

Olivia stayed close to Tory's side. She hadn't loosened her grip on the camera Luis had given her even once. He considered pointing out that a camera was just an object when it wasn't being used, and let go of the idea as a bad one. It was hers now. If she gained comfort from its existence, and not its use, that was up to her. People had their own ways of experiencing trauma, and he wasn't going to interfere.

"Where do you think they're all going?" asked Tory, as they reached the last flight of stairs. This one would take them down to the pool level, where Mr. Blackwell spent the majority of his time.

"If they're smart and we're lucky, to the lifeboats," said Luis.

Olivia frowned. "We'd be lucky if they left us here?"

"No, but I'm betting the mermaids go for small craft first. If they're big enough cowards that they want to desert us, let them get what they deserve, and give us a little extra time to prepare. Maybe the damn things will fill up on the crew, and leave us alone."

Tory looked at him levelly. "You don't really think that."

"We don't know how many are down there, how much they eat, or whether their smarts extend to having figured out a form of food storage." Mermaid larders filled with bodies, preserved by the salt water and growing slowly bloated as they drank in the surrounding sea. And if the mermaids were smart enough to do that, they would be smart enough to figure out that having corpses around would attract other predators, predators that acted on instinct, that couldn't plan; that would be helpless in the face of an organized attack like the ones the mermaids were capable of.

They weren't going to get full. Things like that never did.

"To think, up until today, I wanted to *find* the monsters," he muttered.

The women shot him a sharp look, but neither of them said anything, and he was grateful for that.

They descended the stairs in silence. There were no people around the pool for once, although the saltwater sluice was open; fish swam in the shallow end, darting in and around the artificial coral provided to comfort them. As Luis watched, an octopus snaked out a mango-colored arm and snatched a young parrotfish, sucking it back into its hidey-hole. An adolescent bull shark circled in the deep end, bumping its nose on the walls, never going into water shallower than five feet. But it would. Once it got hungry enough, it would, and the temporary paradise of the shallows would come crashing down.

There were a few engineers clustered around the control station for Heather's Minnow, still taking readings, chasing the ghosts of any mechanical failures that might have made her situation worse. They'd finish their due diligence in the next day or so, and that would be that: Heather Wilson would be officially lost at sea, written down in the history books as one more consequence of man's unending expansion.

Luis couldn't look at them. Neither could Olivia. But Tory turned her head and watched them until they were out of view, marking every hand on every control, every motion and whispered conference.

The door at the end of the room was visible but closed. There weren't many closed doors on the *Melusine*. They tended to slow the free and open exchange of ideas, which was counter to the purpose of this voyage. All of them had been assuming that if they were going to find the mermaids, they were going to do it by working together.

It seemed almost hubristic now, when the mermaids were real and present and dangerous. The *Atargatis* hadn't found the mermaids through a free and open exchange of ideas. The *Atargatis* had found the mermaids because the people on the ship were made of meat, and the mermaids had empty stomachs that they wanted to fill. That was how you found things, in the sea. Be delicious. That was all you ever had to do.

Luis knocked on the door. The sound echoed, almost startling in the open air of the lower deck. He waited, counting slowly to ten, before he knocked again.

"Do you think he's in there?" asked Olivia.

"Mr. Blackwell has been working on something down here for days," said Luis. "I saw him heading for the stairs with Dr. Toth earlier, and when I went to the cafeteria, Holly was there, getting coffee, and told me her big sister was doing something with him. Put it all together, it sounds like a private think tank."

"With an acoustician, a sirenologist, and a bureaucrat? What the hell could they be working on?"

"Brokering a peace treaty with the mermaids to convince them to stop eating us?" suggested Olivia, and giggled, high and shrill. Tory gave her a concerned look. She stopped giggling, cheeks coloring red. "Sorry. I just... I'm sorry."

"It's okay." Tory forced a smile. "You've had a bad night. You're allowed to be a little off."

Olivia, who was staring down the barrel of a lifetime of nightmares, assuming her lifetime extended past this place, this ship, this damned and doomed voyage, said nothing.

The door opened. All three of them jumped.

The man in the doorway wasn't Theo Blackwell, who they would have known how to deal with; it wasn't even Jillian Toth, who could be capricious and unpredictable, but was at least familiar. This man was tall, solidly built—more than solidly; he had the sort of small belly that spoke of healthy meals and a marked enjoyment of mealtime—with long brown hair and sensible glasses totally at odds with his multiple tattoos.

"Can I help you?" he asked.

Luis was the first to respond. He grinned, big and bright, stepping forward and saying, "Daniel, my *man*. What do they need a whale doctor in the basement for? Did you catch something amazing?"

"I'm not a whale doctor, I'm a cetologist, and you are literally the *last* person on this ship I should need to explain that to," said the stranger—Daniel. He frowned. "I repeat: can I help you?"

The name and discipline had been enough of a clue for Tory, who nodded in comprehension and said, "You're Daniel Lennox, our whale expert. That makes sense. The mermaids sing, and you've done groundbreaking work with whale song. Who else is down here?" *Why aren't I down here?* She hadn't known there was a secret think tank to have been rejected by until this moment. It still stung, realizing there was something on this ship that she hadn't been asked to be a part of. Especially if it was related to sound. There was no one with a better understanding of the way the mermaids sang than her.

"I'm sorry, I can't talk about this," said Daniel, and moved to close the door.

Luis was faster. He shoved his foot into the gap before the door could close, smile firmly in place. "I don't think you get to say that right now," he said. "Olivia?"

"Have you spoken to Captain Peterman?" she asked, voice dropping with each word, until it was barely above a whisper.

Daniel frowned. "No," he said. "Mr. Blackwell did, but he didn't tell us what it was about. He said it could wait until later."

"So you don't know." Luis let his smile die. "They're here, Daniel. One of them came up the side of the damn ship and took Olivia's cameraman. Now do you want to let us in, or shall we stand out here and tell the whole story in loud, carrying voices?"

"Let them in," called Theo Blackwell, from the dark behind the door. Daniel only hesitated a moment before opening the door again and stepping to the side.

Luis was the first into the private lab. He stopped, staring at the glass wall beyond which the dolphins circled. Behind him, Tory focused her attention on the workstation where Hallie still stood, great sine curves of sonar and sound patterns dancing on her screen. Olivia didn't look at any of that. She stopped next to Tory, eyes tilted downward, so all she was looking at was the floor. That, in the moment, was about what she could handle processing.

Theo was seated. He looked at the trio with weary eyes and asked, "Well?"

"We were on the deck," said Olivia. "Filming. Sunset panorama. Company orders. Ray saw what looked like someone climbing up the side of the ship." But that wasn't true, was it? No matter how many times she told the story that way, it was never going to be true. *She* had been the one to see the creature; *she* had been the one to call Ray's attention to it. He would never have seen it, if not for her.

The thought that the mermaid would have reached the deck and ambushed someone else hadn't crossed her mind; might never cross her mind. It took too much of the blame away, and that wasn't fair, or right, or true. She deserved to be blamed for this. Any blame she took, she'd earned.

"We knew they could climb," said Dr. Toth. She didn't look concerned, quite; if Tory had been forced to put a name to the look on Dr. Toth's face, it would have been *satisfied*. She looked pleased with herself, like all this was going according to some unwritten, unspoken plan. "There's video from the first mission that shows them on the decks. Imagine should have expected this, and put electrical lines in the railings."

"That happened during the assault," objected Daniel.

Dr. Toth turned weary eyes on him. "That happened during the assault, yes. We know because we have the footage. There were disappearances before the assault. We know *that* because we have the e-mails that made it off the ship before things got too terrible for that sort of documentation. What's to say the mermaids didn't send scouts, hmm? What's to say that some of those disappearances weren't among people who'd gone nowhere near the rail? This is their territory, not ours."

"This is the surface," objected Hallie. "They should know their domain stops where the water does."

"Really? No one told your sister that ours ended where the water began." Dr. Toth's voice was calm. Hallie flushed red and turned her face away. "The trouble with intelligent creatures is that we don't recognize borders that seem completely natural to those who act on instinct. We find ways to make it to the bottom of the sea. Why shouldn't the mermaids do the same? They know there's food here. They know we can live in both places. Why shouldn't they?"

"Because they don't belong here," said Hallie.

"We don't belong there, but there we are, and here they are, and even with everything we think we know about them, we know *nothing*. They could kill us all, with us documenting every step of the way, and we'd still know effectively nothing." Dr. Toth stood. She seemed to loom in the enclosed space. Even Mr. Blackwell turned a cautious eye on her, waiting to see what she was going to say.

"You keep forgetting—all of us keep forgetting—that we're talking about creatures that have appeared in folklore and mythology all over the world. There was a time when these things were *everywhere*. Something drove them from the shallows. Fine. I have theories about that, but since most of them involve industrial revolution and pollution, they're not going to do us any good right now. They retreated and retreated and retreated, maybe because it was easier than fighting us for territory, or maybe because there was a time when we were too much trouble to eat en masse. Ships kept on disappearing. Since the start of man's relationship with the sea, ships kept on disappearing. So assume the mermaids have never forgotten about us. We wrote them off as legends as soon as they were no longer knocking on our front door."

Dr. Toth looked around the small group. Her eyes were burning; her hands were clenched. "We forgot about them, but they never forgot about us. They always knew that somewhere out there they had competition, strange and soft and walking on two legs and defenseless in the water. Most of all, they never forgot that we were delicious."

"So what do you suggest we do?" asked Mr. Blackwell. His voice was as mild as hers was sharp. They balanced each other. Not the way they had when they were younger, maybe, but still, it was balance, of a kind.

"If it were up to me?" She shook her head. "I'd suggest we start this boat and get the fuck out of here as fast as our engines can carry us. If they've moved to scaling the sides to see how much food there is for them here, they're not planning to stop. We're a day, maybe two, from repeating the mistakes of the *Atargatis*. But the *Atargatis* didn't know. They had no way of knowing. We do. If we die like this, it's our own damn fault. We don't get to blame anyone but ourselves."

"We can't leave now," protested Daniel. "Hallie and I are still working on their language. We may be able to talk to them."

Tory stiffened. "That's why we were coming here," she said. Everyone turned to look at her—everyone except for Olivia, who was still looking at the floor. "Before Olivia came to our lab and told us what happened to Ray."

"What?" asked Daniel.

"Can I use your computer?" Tory stepped away from Olivia, moving toward the keyboard without waiting for an answer. Hallie moved to the side, and Tory began to type, rapidly restructuring the data on the screen. The sonar waves moved to the side, piling up in comparative slices.

"Look," said Tory. "When we got here, we had these low signals in the mix. That's their language. When they're just singing to each other, that's what we get."

"That's nothing new," said Daniel.

"This is," said Tory stubbornly. She flipped up a few bands. "The low signals are gone. Where did they go? We know the mermaids didn't go anywhere, so why did they suddenly shut up? You can't say it's a deep dive. We're picking up signals all the way to the bottom of the Challenger Deep."

"What are you saying, Miss Stewart?" asked Blackwell.

"This, here." She indicated a band. "That looks like white noise, but it's not. If you compare it to recordings from the *Atargatis* incident, it's a match."

"To what?"

Tory didn't see the person who asked the question, and that was fine, because it didn't matter: it could have been any of them, even Luis, who knew the answer but wasn't above feeding her a straight line when it would get them to the point faster. "This is the sound made by the *Atargatis* engines. The mermaids are echoing it back at us, because they know it's one of our sounds. That we won't necessarily find it suspect. They're mimics. They have three languages. Spoken, signed, and stolen. When they hunt, they speak in the language that they've taken from their prey. One more form of camouflage. One more way to hide, until they're close enough to strike."

"So they're coming to us." Theodore Blackwell finally stood. His legs were steady. Someone who didn't know better would never have been able to look at him and guess at his condition. "Good. Let them come. We'll be ready. But if they're thieves, it's time we send out some thieves of our own. Dr. Lennox, release the dolphins."

Daniel looked alarmed. "Are you sure that's a good idea?"

"Not in the slightest," said Blackwell. His smile was quick, and cold. "Now, if you would please take it upon yourself to follow instructions, I would appreciate it. They know what they're supposed to do."

"Die, you mean," said Jillian. "If you send them out there, they're going to die."

"Maybe. Maybe not. It's up to them."

Tory's voice was hushed. "You're really going to send *dolphins* out to spy on those things? Have you *seen* how many teeth they have?"

"Dolphins are predators, Miss Stewart. We like to forget that, because we see them as adorable clowns of the sea, but they do just fine without humans to feed them—better, in many ways, without humans to interfere with their choices. They can catch and kill and yes, defend themselves. If the mermaids attack, which we don't know they will, the dolphins will defend. We only need one of them to make it back alive. We know enough of their language at this point for the intelligence they carry to be invaluable."

The rear of the enclosure that held the dolphins was opening, a hatch built into the side of the ship sliding wide, allowing the brightly lit, filtered water in their tank to mingle with the dark, unfiltered water from outside. The dolphins didn't dart immediately for the opening. They hovered, cautious, just inside, keeping themselves contained within the body of the *Melusine* as they discussed their next move.

Daniel twisted a dial on the control panel next to the lever that had freed them. The sound of clicks and whistles filled the air. The dolphins were arguing.

Human-cetacean linguistics were never going to reach a level where either species could understand the language of the other without mechanical help. The human ear wasn't designed to pick up the higher frequencies of dolphin speech; the dolphin mind had trouble processing the lower, slower aspects of human communication. They were two species living at different speeds, in environments that changed the functionality of sound. But no one who had spent any time around dolphins could fail to recognize an argument when they heard one. The dolphins were fighting among themselves, and it didn't show any signs of being resolved.

Blackwell sighed. "The REMINDER button, please, Dr. Lennox."

Daniel pushed a button on the control panel. A prerecorded message began to play, squeaks and clicks and whistles vibrating through the tank. The dolphins stopped arguing to listen. One of them turned black, reproachful eyes toward the glass, looking at the humans on the other side like they had done something wrong.

Next to Tory, Olivia raised her borrowed camera and began filming the dolphins.

"They look so sad," said Hallie.

"They don't want to go," said Blackwell. "They agreed to this before the voyage began. They're research animals, allowed in captivity by loopholes in the environmental laws. Imagine purchased them from their previous owners, explained what we wanted them to do, and acquired their full consent."

"How can you call them animals and say you need consent in the same breath?" asked Daniel. "Dolphins are intelligent creatures."

"Creatures, animals, monsters—it's all degrees, isn't it?" Blackwell shook his head. "If they're animals, we own them, and as this is a scientific research mission, we're violating no laws by sending them out to look at the mermaids, even if we have concerns about their safety. This is within the letter of the law. If they're intelligent beings, then their consent is essential, and we have a contract. One Imagine intends to honor, if they do their part."

"You're sending them to die for their freedom," said Jillian. "Seems harsh."

"Humans have done exactly that for centuries," said Blackwell. "If they want to be treated as our equals, this is part of the bargain."

The speakers inside the tank stopped clicking. The dolphins looked back toward the opening. Then, slowly, with obvious reluctance, they swam out into the open sea. The hatch remained open, a blind eye on the black and bitter waters beyond.

No one said anything. In that moment, in the face of that gaping void of an ocean, there seemed to be nothing to say.

ZONE FOUR: BATHYPELAGIC

Sometimes the mistakes we make can't be taken back. Sometimes those are the worst ones of all.

—Dr. Hallie Wilson

It's my job to keep her safe. I do that, I've done everything I can.

—Ray Marino

Theo—

I know you're aware of the importance of this project. Confirming the existence of the creatures in the Mariana Trench will redeem our reputation; bringing one back for the cosponsors of this voyage will restore our bank accounts. We're not destitute, but we're nowhere near as comfortable as I would like us to be, especially under the circumstances. There are lean times ahead for Imagine, and for all the employees who depend on us. You've seen the same reports I have. You know how much is riding on you.

You have been an excellent right-hand man, Theo. This is your opportunity to prove to me that my faith in you has been well placed. This is your chance to truly serve the company that saved you. Don't let me down.

—Internal memo, James Golden to
Theodore Blackwell, CONFIDENTIAL

I've had people come up to me and say, in so many words, that my life's work is a form of insanity: that by chasing the mermaid from one end of the world to the other, I have lost my grip on reality. That I'm exploiting the tragedy of the *Atargatis*—as long as I continue to appear in front of crowds like this one and plead my case for the lovely ladies of the sea, the victims of that fateful voyage will never be able to rest, because I'll keep reminding people of them. Of the way they died. Of the risks they had no idea they were taking when they decided to go looking for a legend. I, alone, will keep hundreds of people from knowing peace.

I'm okay with that.

I am not the first to chase the mermaid from sea to sea, from the shallows to the depths. I am just the most recent in a long line of scientific Cassandras, looking at the waves and saying, "This is not for us. Be careful, be careful, for this is not ours to claim." If my crime is refusing to be silent, then I'm happy to be a criminal, because believe me, the lovely ladies of the sea, they're out there. They exist. And if we're not careful where we sail, they're going to prove it to us.

—Transcript from the lecture "Mermaids: Myth or Monster," given by Dr. Jillian Toth

CHAPTER 19

Western Pacific Ocean, approaching the Mariana Trench: September 2, 2022

The dolphins moved through the water like bullets shot from the barrel of a gun. They were swift, unflinching, and heading for their target with a speed that would have shocked even their trainers, who had never seen their cosseted, captive-bred subjects move in the open water.

Twitter, as the one with the fastest responses, led the pod. She was a mature female, young enough for her sense of adventure to remain undimmed, old enough to know better than to expect their descent to end well. She'd gone along with the plan in part because she was bored, in part because she was curious, and in part because she'd been promised tropical waters and no more tanks if she was willing to do this one last thing for her keepers. They were good people. Not dolphin-good, but human-good, which was almost good enough. They couldn't fulfill the instinctive needs she had burning in her brain, the ones that told her to find a mate who wasn't her brother or her uncle, to swim, to leap, to *know*. So she was here, with the deep black sea between her and her freedom.

Her brother, Cecil, was close behind, her shadow, as he'd been since he'd followed her from their mother's belly and into the warm waters of the pool where they'd been born. Twins were as uncommon among dolphins as they were among humans, and it had been the intervention of those same humans that had allowed them to grow up safe and healthy and well fed, rather than one of them being taken by some predator while their mother was distracted. Cecil was a good thing in the world, and Twitter was glad for him. He was *smart*. Smarter than the humans who tried to measure and quantify his smartness, even, although they'd never have admitted to that. Of the three, he was the most eager to get out, to explore, and he rode Twitter's fins hard, almost overtaking her.

Kearney, eldest and most cautious of the three, brought up the rear. He had been born in captivity, just as they had; was brother to their mother, who remained safely in her tank, enjoying the lazy life to which she was accustomed. Humans broke the best of his generation, inuring them to captivity, replacing dreams of freedom and the sea with dreams of fat fish in pails and squeaky toys that made the children laugh. (Not all who were broken became clowns for the amusement of human young. Some had turned vicious, all teeth and sullen anger. Those had a tendency to disappear, fading into lie and rumor, forgotten by all but those who had known them. Kearney remembered. Oh yes, Kearney remembered.)

The water grew colder as they continued their descent, down into places where the light never reached, following the sound of their own cries bouncing off unseen walls, unseen dangers. A long fish undulated by, head alive with sparkling lights, and Kearney swung away from the others long enough to snatch it out of its course, letting the taste of it flood his mouth as his teeth broke its skin. It was mostly scale and cartilage, but it was food, and it was food he had taken for himself, taken from the sea as he had been taken, food *no human hands had touched*, and he was never going back, no, not ever.

There was something the humans did not know. They had learned to speak to dolphins during his lifetime, refining their vocabulary until they could speak as infants spoke, all short, declarative sentences and words of firm assertion. Humans could say yes and no and ask for a fish. They could not discuss philosophy, the finer points of religion, the ideas of things that could only be done in dreams. Humans were solid, gravity-bound creatures, with minds suited for solid, gravity-bound things. They could build a ship. They could not write a poem. And they could not have understood what Kearney's parents, who had been taken wild, were talking about when they expressed, again and again, their gratitude to their captors, who had swept them away from the open sea during a time of great slaughter.

Dolphins were good. Humans had the potential for good, although they did not always make the effort. But the creatures born from blending the two, the claw-and-tooth children of the deepest depths...they were not good. They had never been good, would not know how to be if the opportunity was offered to them. They existed only to catch and snatch and devour. They sang no songs of their own, only songs stolen from the victims of their hunger. They were voiceless and cruel and terrible, and if not for them, the dolphins would never have needed to seek the shallows, or put themselves into the path of men, or choose the safety of cages over the freedom of the sea.

Mankind could go hunting for mermaids as much as they liked. The dolphins had known where to find them all along.

Twitter and Cecil sought the mermaids because they'd been asked to, because they thought to buy their freedom with accomplishment. Do a trick, get a fish. Do a bigger trick, get the world. Kearney envied how simple things were through their eyes. He did not try to correct them. He had lived captive and now he would die free, and if he never saw the humans again, that would be fine by him.

They dove. Three together, moving as one, they dove. The pressure of the water slowed their descent. Dolphins were not made to go this deep. Maybe that was what had kept the deep-graspers from destroying them all long ago. The dolphins stayed high and the deep-graspers stayed low, and prey that could not be easily taken was rarely worth remembering.

Twitter's voice called from below. Not an echo, not an answer: her *voice*, singular and strong and sounding as if from her own throat. She stopped in confusion, hanging in the water.

Cecil didn't realize she had stopped quickly enough to do the same. He sailed past her and, finding himself suddenly in the lead, kept going as she clicked behind him, trying to call him back, trying to stop him from plunging into the alien deep that spoke to her with her own voice. Had he been worldlier, more able to be aware of danger, he might have listened. Instead he swam, tail beating against the crushing pressure, and dove, chasing his sister's misplaced voice into nothingness.

Kearney pulled up next to Twitter, hanging there, his sleek gray side nearly brushing hers. She whistled her distress, and he whistled back, reassuring her that this was as it was meant to be. Cecil was chasing a dream into the dark.

His parents, who had been wild caught, had told him of this hunting technique, of the way the deep-graspers, in their thieving, would steal the voices of those who came too close, and how the young and the inexperienced would follow this novelty, fascinated by sounds that should not be, coming from places that should not hold them. They had lost friends and loved ones to the deep-graspers, and when the human ship had come to catch and keep them, their response had been gratitude. Humans meant safety. Confinement, but safety.

It had been a bad bargain. Kearney knew that, even if his parents never had. He would be free. He would live free, if only in this moment, and he would die free, whether now or later. He thought it would be now. He couldn't see a future where it was not now.

A scream from the dark ahead of them, shrill and agonized. It was part whistle and part sigh, and when it stopped, he knew Cecil had stopped as well. No more songs for Cecil, no more games, no more dances. Cecil was free.

Twitter moaned. There was a pause. Kearney could have told her not to move; he could have bid her to be still, suggested she wait to see what the dark would do. But she needed to be free to choose for herself, as he had, as Cecil had, even if Cecil had believed he was following his sister. Kearney was silent.

Twitter turned and swam back toward the ship, moving as fast as she could, moving at a speed that put her earlier sprint to shame. Kearney did not watch her go. He couldn't; the dark was too deep to allow it. All he saw was the faintest suggestion of movement in the water, something that was as much feeling as it was sight. That was enough. He knew she was gone, and Cecil was gone, and he was alone.

The sound of Twitter's stolen song came closer, punctuated by scraps of Cecil's scream. It was a jagged, senseless thing. The thieves knew what to steal, but they didn't know how to put it together in a way that *meant* something. They acted without sense. That was the worst thing. At least the humans, when they tried, were trying sensibly. The thieves just acted.

He hung where he was, not moving, not flinching away. Some things needed to be chosen. Some things needed to be pure.

Twitter was moving fast, but not fast enough to be out of range of his screams. She whipped around, looking back at the empty space where he should have been, the lightless void that did not contain her brother, or her uncle, or anything but the sound of her own voice singing. It was so far away. It couldn't hurt her. It was so far away.

The mermaids that dropped on her from above made no sound. That, too, was how they hunted: sound to enthrall and confuse, claws to catch and close and end the fight.

Twitter had time to scream.

She didn't have time for much else.

CHAPTER 20

Western Pacific Ocean, above the Mariana Trench: September 2, 2022

W e've lost the tracker on the third dolphin." Daniel stared at his screen in horror. "They're dead. They're all dead."

"That can't be right." Hallie started to type. Her fingers fumbled; she backspaced almost as much as she moved forward. "They're *dolphins*. There's nothing out there that should have been able to surprise them enough to take them down."

"I told you." Jillian's voice was calm, virtually serene: she was Cassandra speaking from the walls of Troy, watching her prophecies coming true. "I said this would happen the second you told me what you were planning to do. This is *their* space, Theo. This is their world, and they've had millennia to learn how to use it to their advantage. Dolphins are smart, but this isn't a place where dolphins thrive."

"Dolphins are goddamn geniuses by the standards of the sea," said Daniel. He was still staring at the screen, like he was trying to will the tracking signals back into existence, like he could, through sheer refusal to accept reality, bring the dolphins back from the dead. It wasn't working. The lines where their tracking chips should have been steadily, soothingly beeping, signaling that all was right in the world, remained empty. The chips were off line. The dolphins were gone. "Is there any chance—"

"No," said Luis. Daniel and Hallie turned to him, blinking. It was like they'd forgotten he was there. That wasn't so unusual. Tensions were mounting, and the tenser people became, the more likely they were to retreat into their own heads, into the familiar confines of their own concerns. Luis was a scientific dilettante, a monster hunter who liked to use the latest toys to try to prove his latest theories. The only person here whose concerns genuinely overlapped with his was Dr. Toth, and she didn't *want* to find the things that he was looking for.

"The Marine Mammal Conservation Act of 2019 made it illegal to embed tracking chips in the flesh of cetaceans, even volunteers; there was concern about coercion," he said. To his credit, Theodore Blackwell turned his face away. Luis continued, "The chips would have been glued to the dolphins, attached to their skin with the strongest bio-adhesive Imagine could find—and given Imagine's resources, I'm betting that was pretty damn strong. Even if the dolphins managed to scrape them off, they'd keep transmitting unless they got too deep to be picked up by our scanners. Dolphins can't go that deep."

"Mermaids can," said Jillian. "They're dead. We sent three innocent creatures into a trap, and we did it because we could."

Theo didn't respond. He was staring, wide-eyed, at the tank. Slowly the others turned to see what he was looking at.

Olivia screamed—a short, sharp sound—before clapping her free hand over her mouth, keeping any further sounds from escaping. Her eyes bulged in their sockets even as the blood drained from her head. Tory stared at her.

She looks like she's going to faint, she thought. She'd never seen someone faint before, not even when she'd volunteered at her high school's blood drive, but she'd seen plenty of tourists overcome with seasickness during the whale-watching tours, and many of them had looked like Olivia did right now. The *Melusine* wasn't rocking. Seasickness wasn't the culprit.

Slowly, wishing she didn't have to, Tory turned.

When the dolphins had been released, the door at the back of their enclosure had been left open, in case they wanted to return to the ship. Their freedom was the payment for their service, but there was no reason for them to claim it here, so far from the coasts they knew. The *Melusine* had been prepared to play escort to their final destinations.

The dolphins had not returned. Something else had come in their place.

The mermaid wasn't fully aboard yet: it was hanging in the doorway, its flat, terrifyingly simian face peering over the edge. Every time it moved, its vast cloud of bioluminescent "hair" flared around it. It looked like something from another world, something that had managed to swim out of a dream and into reality. It was clearly cautious, looking around the large, bright chamber with suspiciously narrowed eyes.

Jillian Toth folded her hands over her mouth, almost like she was suppressing a prayer. Like Olivia's, her eyes were wide and round. Unlike Olivia's, they contained neither fear nor dismay. Tears pooled in them, not quite falling, not yet—but that moment was going to come. She was watching her life's work inching into view, and she was overcome. Anyone would have been. Anyone.

"Can it see us?" whispered Hallie, tone caught between horror and amazement.

"Yes," said Theo. He didn't whisper; he spoke in a conversational tone. "I recommend against sudden movements. We wouldn't want to attract more of its attention than we already have."

"Why not?" asked Luis. "Can it break the glass?"

"Unlikely, but would you want to be responsible for frightening it away?" The mermaid was continuing its slow study of the tank. Finally it pushed against the side of the entrance, undulating gently into the space.

Tory gasped.

The footage from the *Atargatis* included several full-body shots of the mermaids above water, taken when the creatures swarmed the decks of the ship. The footage from Heather's submersible showed the mermaids in their natural environment, but was unevenly lit, cutting in and out of focus. This was the first time any of them were seeing a mermaid in the water—where it belonged—without barriers.

"It's *beautiful*," breathed Daniel, and while there were those who would have objected to the reverence in his voice, none of them corrected his statement. It *was* beautiful, in its own terrible way.

So many monsters are.

The mermaid was eight feet long from the crown of its head to the tip of its sinuous tail. It lacked the classic flukes found on its dolphin-esque cartoon counterparts; instead, eel-like bands of fin ran down both sides of its body, starting at the base of its rib cage and continuing to form a fin a foot or so past the end of its cartilaginous tail. The fins were tattered and torn and even missing in some places; enough, presumably, to slow it down slightly, without doing anything to *stop* it. There was no way of knowing whether those small signs of damage had actually done anything to impair the creature. It swam easily, fluidly, with no obvious signs of distress.

The fins rippled and surged with every movement, sometimes propelling the mermaid forward, other times pulling it back. Once it stopped moving it drifted into an upright position, hanging there like the underwater equivalent of a biped. Dr. Toth sucked in a delighted breath, seeing her theories beautifully, if brutally, proven true.

It was difficult to tell whether the mermaid had a pelvis; without a skeleton, or at the very least an X-ray, its inner workings remained a mystery. But there was a swelling at the point where tail met torso, suggesting distinct, if narrow, hips. Its arms and shoulders were simian, and their gray, hairless skin gave them an unnervingly human cast. It had no nipples, no breasts, no belly button; whatever it was, it was not mammalian. It still had a mammal's rib cage and sternum, pushing its shallow chest into a curve that might be mistaken, on a dark night and at a distance, for a woman's bosom.

"Close the door," said Theo softly.

Daniel flinched, his body moving away from his superior and the mermaid in the same motion, like he couldn't decide which direction was the dangerous one.

(In the tank, the mermaid tracked the movement of his body with its round and terrible eyes, watching him; watching all of them, but focusing most on the movement. Movement could mean danger. Movement could mean food. The mermaid hung there like it felt confident in its ability to turn the first into the second, and felt no fear.)

"Sir?" Daniel whispered.

"*Close the door.*" This time Theo's voice was a hiss, filled with a dreadful warning. Failure to obey would end in pain.

Daniel's hand moved.

The door slammed shut fast and hard enough that it would have injured, if not outright killed, anything that had gotten trapped in it. Olivia made a squeaking noise, her hands still clasped over her mouth. Daniel went white.

"If one of the dolphins had been caught in that—" he began, and stopped as the mermaid spun in the water, still floating vertically, to look at the closed door. There was something about the angle of its body, the way its shoulders locked and its long-fingered hands curved into claws, that sent off alarm bells deep in his mind, where the frightened monkey that had come down from the trees still lingered. Instinct told him to fear what he saw in front of him, and so he did, without hesitation.

The mermaid moved so fast it was a streak in the water and began clawing at the closed door. When the metal failed to yield it drummed its fists against it, hammering hard. It made no difference. The mermaid was flesh and the door was steel; there was nothing it could do to free itself.

It stopped hammering and hung in the water, motionless save for the small, apparently automatic motion of the fins along its sides. Then, slowly, it began feeling the wall, dragging its fingers along the steel until it found the seam where the door ended and the rest of the ship began. It started methodically sliding its nails into the seam, worrying at it, trying to pry it open.

On the other side of the glass, Tory took an involuntary half step forward, toward the tank where her sister's killer swam. It didn't matter that *this* mermaid, *this* example of the breed had probably not been involved; all mermaids were her sister's killers now. She stopped when a hand clamped down on her arm, fingers digging in hard enough to bruise. She looked over her shoulder.

Olivia had uncovered her mouth and was holding on to her, as tightly as she could. Her eyes were still too wide, shiny with shock and with unshed tears. "Don't get too close," she said. "Mr. Blackwell said it can *see* us."

Tory looked back to the tank as the mermaid was finishing its examination of the door. It spun, plastering its hands against the metal, and launched itself at the window. The naked eye couldn't follow its movement. One second it was trying to escape; the next it was flying through the water, so fast and so sure that it might as well have been a missile fired from some unspeakable gun. The sound when it impacted with the glass echoed through the room. The mermaid jerked back, disturbingly human mouth opening in a silent scream, exposing an impossible number of teeth.

"They *had* to develop sign language for close communication," said Dr. Toth, sounding satisfied. "Look at that mouth. They can sing, and that's enough to get their point across, but there's no way they would have developed complex speech on their own. And then there's the mimicry to think about."

"The mimicry?" asked Hallie.

"Turn on the speakers."

"Do as she says, Daniel," said Mr. Blackwell, before anyone could object. He was still standing, despite the spreading tremor in his leg. He took a step toward the tank wall, staring raptly at the mermaid. "We need to see what it has to tell us."

"Sir, if we turn on the speakers, she'll be able to hear us," said Daniel.

"That was the point," said Mr. Blackwell.

Daniel flipped the switch.

"We can't be sure the mermaid is a female, even though we keep thinking of them that way," said Dr. Toth. "Look at that skeletal structure. Everything about it suggests a human woman, but nothing about it is going to fulfill that promise. It doesn't have the attributes of a mammal. It doesn't need them. Everything about it is perfect for what it is and what it does. The only things out of place are those lips. You could slap them on any supermodel in the world, and she'd be selling lipsticks five minutes later. Why would something so evolutionarily perfect need those lips? They sing in their throats. They speak with their hands."

The mermaid was looking wildly around the tank, trying to find the source of her voice. Finally it swam to one of the speakers and hung in front of it, head cocked, hair floating around its head in a great black cloud.

"So why would they have lips like that? Lips to purse and pull and shape sound? It's funny. Because parrots can speak, but they don't have lips. They make the sounds in their larynxes. Why didn't the mermaids follow the same path? Mertensian mimicry only explains so much. They could have had faces like knives, an infinity of teeth, and still have spoken to us in echoes of our voices, if they'd done it through the larynx. So why evolve like this? What's the point?"

"What's the point?" said the mermaid. The voice, although distorted and warped by the water, was clearly Jillian Toth's: it bounced off the walls, echoing until it filled the world. "What's the point? What's the point?"

"It's not echolalia; it's fixing on the words that had the most stress on them, which means it's fixing on the words most likely to be a call for help, or an invitation." Jillian walked to the glass and knocked on it briskly, causing several of the people behind her to jump. The mermaid whipped around, staring at her. She didn't flinch. "The speech is a lure, like an anglerfish's light or an alligator snapping turtle's tongue. It's a lure that specifically attracts intelligent creatures. Humans, whales, dolphins—and what do we all have in common? What is the one thing that binds us?"

"We're all mammals," said Luis.

"That's right. We're all mammals." She knocked on the glass again. The mermaid hissed at her. She looked at it impassively. "Mammals. Hot-blooded, hotheaded, never as well suited to the ocean as the fish or the crustaceans...We left and then we came back. The water never forgave us. Why should it? We were the prodigal children, us and our kin, and even if we wanted to come home, home didn't want us anymore. So it made better predators. Things that specialized in the consumption of mammals. Things that could call us across wide distances. I bet this lovely lady of the sea has a whole arsenal of whale songs and dolphin calls and other things she can bust out when she's hunting. Don't you?"

"Don't you?" echoed the mermaid. "Don't you?" Its throat pulsed when it spoke, gills closing for a moment, like it was unable to both breathe and talk.

"They eat fish, because nothing this complex can evolve without becoming an opportunist—there's a reason humans are omnivores. Chimps, coyotes, and ravens, too. We don't have a patent on intelligence. The smarter you are, the more likely you are to want to eat the world. Can you eat seaweed, I wonder, with those teeth of yours?" Jillian leaned closer to the glass. She and the mermaid were face to face, almost nose to nose; they were reflected in one another's eyes.

The mermaid hung motionless, seemingly as enthralled by this look at the face of the enemy as Jillian was. Its mouth was closed, concealing its fishhook forest of teeth; with those fleshy, humanoid lips pursed, it was easier to understand how a lonely sailor could have overlooked the wrongness of the picture, and focused only on what they wanted to be right.

"Seaweed, and fish, and maybe even each other, when the pickings are lean," said Jillian. "But whales, dolphins, lonely sailors... Those are gifts. Take down an orca and your family feeds for a week. They learned to call for us because we wouldn't follow a shiny light or a wiggling worm. They baited the sea with lures, and then they waited."

"Waited," said the mermaid. "Waited, waited."

"If they're so smart and so dangerous, why the hell did they give up the shallows?" asked Hallie. Her voice had dropped, becoming low and tight with anger. "Why did we have to come all the way out here to find them?"

"I don't know, but I'm sure we're going to find out soon enough." Jillian turned her back on her mermaid. She didn't flinch when it started flinging itself at the glass, over and over again, claws scrabbling for purchase as it bit at the water in frustration.

"Um," said Tory. "How strong is...I mean, should we be concerned right now?"

"Not in the least." Theo took a step forward, his leg shaking so hard that it seemed likely to dump him on his face. He didn't appear to notice, or if he did, he didn't appear to care: his eyes were fixed on the wall behind his wife, on the mermaid that thrashed and raged in the water. "This tank wasn't intended to hold a mermaid, but the 'glass' is transparent titanium. The lab that made it assures me that it could take a direct hit from a surface-to-air missile without so much as cracking. The creature stands absolutely no chance of breaking through."

"So we're going to kill it, right?" The voice was Olivia's. Everyone turned to her. She had lowered both her hands. She didn't look angry, exactly; she didn't look anything. She was a perfectly blank slate, something that was as odd as it was unnerving.

"Of course not," said Jillian, before anyone else could recover from their surprise. "This was the plan all along, wasn't it?" She turned to face Theo, who said nothing. Her eyes narrowed. "Wasn't it?"

"I wasn't intending to keep it here—there's another tank below the prow, where we could have transferred a creature after netting it—and I wasn't expecting them to catch the dolphins," he said. "I'll admit that their speed has come as something of a surprise. I thought...Well. It's irrelevant what I thought. When you consider their natural weapons, their clear adaptations to ambush predation, it's reasonable that we expected them to be more passive hunters."

"But you were always planning to catch one for your little menagerie." Jillian shook her head. "I wondered why you would go to all the trouble of isolating the dolphins from the crew. With the number of marine biologists we have here—"

"I didn't expect them to die," he said sharply. "The idea was for them to lure one or more of the mermaids back to the ship. That's all. None of the dolphins were supposed to be sacrificed."

"Just like Heather Wilson wasn't supposed to be sacrificed?"

Theo narrowed his eyes. "I don't appreciate your implication."

"Oh, don't you? I hadn't noticed. Either you're a fool or a monster, and either way, you're not my responsibility anymore. It's time to lock this ship down and get the hell out of here. They're coming. No one is concerned enough about what that means." Jillian narrowed her eyes, gaze locked on Theo. "We have a mermaid. You win, I win, Imagine wins, and now we get the hell out of here."

"You have to understand that isn't possible."

"You're calling the shots, Theo. Anything you want to be possible is possible."

Off to the side, ignored as everyone gaped at either the argument or the mermaid, Hallie moved toward the tank. Her hands were empty. If she was planning some sort of an attack, it was going to be futile. Maybe that was why she was allowed to proceed, why no one stepped in to stop her. What could she possibly do?

'Hello,' she signed to the mermaid. 'Hello.'

The mermaid stopped beating its hands against the glass and turned to look at her.

'Hello,' she signed again.

Slowly, eyes narrowing as it focused on her, the mermaid signed back, 'Hello.' The gesture was imperfect.

'Hello,' signed Hallie. She inclined her head, trying to make the mermaid understand that it had achieved communication. She pressed a hand to her chest, flat, before signing her name.

'Hello,' signed the mermaid.

"Look," breathed Daniel. "I think it understands."

Everyone in the room turned to watch as the grieving sister and the captive mermaid signed back and forth, slowly, seeking connection, seeking understanding across a gulf of space and species and environment, and no one said a word.

CHAPTER 21

**Western Pacific Ocean, above the Mariana Trench:
September 2, 2022**

They had all been forbidden to disclose the fact that a mermaid had been captured. "Think of the unnecessary panic," had been Theodore Blackwell's comment.

"Think of the impending loss of life," had been Jillian Toth's retort.

"We will make an announcement to the crew and passengers regarding the situation as a whole, and what they can do to improve their safety. We'll remind them that they should be staying in their cabins until the captain decides to deploy the shutters, and stress that they should not go out alone." Theo had looked at his ex-wife with something akin to pity. "Dr. Wilson is opening communication channels. Perhaps they will prove open to diplomacy."

"You're a fool," Jillian had snarled.

Luis had said nothing, only looked at the mermaid with hungry eyes. Olivia's hunger had been more vengeful; she had stared at the mermaid like it was a betrayal of everything she stood for, and in the end, only Tory's arm around her shoulders had caused her to look away.

Taking prisoners of war doesn't fix the problem, had been Tory's thought; like Luis, she had said nothing, allowing herself to be escorted from the room, directed to return to her quarters. Silence held until they reached the deck.

Luis kicked the rail. Olivia jumped. Tory didn't.

"Those assholes are going to cut us out. You get that, don't you? Greatest scientific discovery of the century, and they're going to cut. Us. Out." He punctuated his last three words with increasingly vicious kicks to the rail.

Tory rolled her eyes. "Are you done?"

"Yes." Luis scowled at her. "Why are you looking at me like that?"

"Because they're not going to cut us out. They *can't* cut us out. Even if they wanted to, they wouldn't be able to. We're on the ship. People are dying, just like they did on the *Atargatis*. There's no way we can be cut out of this. We're going to be lucky to survive it."

Luis's scowl thawed into something like hope. "Do you really think so?"

"Sometimes I feel like you only listen to me when it's convenient," said Tory. "Yes, I think so. We're trapped on a floating tin can in the middle of the ocean, surrounded by predators smart enough to communicate and plan, and no one's doing anything to get us the hell away from here. We're not going to get cut out. We're going to die."

"I'm going to the lab. I want to see if their communications shifted after Mr. Blackwell took that one captive."

"You do that," said Tory. She stood where she was as Luis turned on his heel and trotted down the deck. Only then did she look at Olivia and ask, "Are you okay?"

"Ray's dead," said Olivia. "I don't know what I am anymore."

Tory laughed, strained and brittle. "You'll figure it out. Do you want me to walk you to your cabin? You shouldn't be alone."

Olivia hesitated before shaking her head. "I don't want to...I'm not sure I *can* be alone right now. I don't know what to do with my hands."

"Oh." Tory took a breath before offering her hand to Olivia. "Hold on to me."

Olivia bit her lip and slipped her hand into Tory's. Her fingers were cold. Tory clutched them a little harder than was strictly needful, in part to warm them, in part because Olivia wasn't the only one looking for something to hold on to. The world was changing. Some of the changes were things she'd been dreaming of for years, while others...others she could have gone a lifetime without. Mermaids were real. Mermaids had killed her sister. These things were facts, grains of traumatic sand she had long since embedded in her psyche. Every aspect of her life was built on the scar tissue of those two statements.

But the mermaids were intelligent. The mermaids were hunting because they were hungry. They had been bothering no one out here in the middle of the Pacific—and if that wasn't quite true, at least they were staying in their own territory, and only bothering the people foolish enough to trespass on the lovely ladies of the sea. The mermaids were minding their own business. Based on what she'd seen belowdecks, Imagine had commissioned this second voyage knowing that, and not caring. They were here to disturb something deep and ancient and cold, something that was better left alone.

Belatedly Tory realized they were walking toward her cabin. She glanced at Olivia, whose pale hair glowed in the moonlight. The mermaids glowed too, bright and cold and implacable. Their light seemed unnatural to her, as a daughter of the land, who had grown up surrounded by things that did not bioluminesce. Even her knowledge of marine biology couldn't change her revulsion at the sight of them. But Olivia...

Olivia's hair was lovely, softly silver, like all her color had been stolen away. She was a black and white shadow of a woman, eyes downcast, trusting Tory to lead her to whatever came next. Tory realized she wanted to protect her, and that she had no idea how to do it.

"Where's your cabin?" she asked, in a soft voice, trying to sound gentle, trying to sound like she wasn't a threat. "I'll walk you there."

"I'd rather not be alone." Olivia slanted a glance in her direction, sizing her up through the silvery fall of her hair. "Is it all right if I spend the night with you?"

There were layers upon layers to that question, giving every word a double or even triple meaning. Tory swallowed hard. "I don't mind if you sleep over," she said.

"Oh," said Olivia, looking faintly disappointed.

"I wouldn't mind sleeping with you either," said Tory. "I just don't want it to be because you're upset and need someone to comfort you. I'm not that kind of girl."

Olivia's feet stopped moving, like they were suddenly rooted to the deck. Tory continued for a few more steps, before the rigid line of Olivia's arm jerked her to a stop, giving her the choice between letting go and staying where she was. She chose to stay, turning to look at Olivia, still lovely in the moonlight, now staring at her with wide eyes.

"What did you say?" she asked.

Tory flushed. "I'm sorry. I may have been misreading the signals. I thought…I sort of thought you'd been flirting with me. I didn't say anything because I wanted to be sure, and because I wanted—I wanted to prove the mermaids were down there. I wanted to do it for Anne. I felt like I had to do that much for her, after all the promises I made her, before I did something for me."

"No, I meant…What did you say?" Olivia shook her head. "I don't always understand…I mean, signals are hard. Especially about something like this. People don't say what they mean. They say things that live in the same neighborhood as what they mean, and then they look at me like I'm stupid because I don't pick it up instantly. I'm not stupid. I'm just not that specific kind of smart."

"Oh." Tory didn't let go of Olivia's hand; instead she adjusted her grip, turning her fingers so she could step closer to the other woman without bending her arm at an uncomfortable angle. She stopped when they were almost nose to nose, her chin tilted slightly down, Olivia's tilted slightly up. "Normally I'd ask you out before inviting you to spend the night. Coffee, maybe, or a movie, or a trip to the aquarium to watch them feed the otters." Although the only real difference between the otters, adorable as they were, and the mermaids was scale, wasn't it? If the otters had been big enough, they would have eaten their trainers without hesitation. The sea had little room for sentiment.

"Oh," said Olivia, her tone turning the word into a revelation instead of just an echo. "So when you said sleeping with, you meant sleeping with. You like me?"

"I like you," said Tory, with a hint of amusement—not mocking, quite, but definitely laughing somewhere deep under the words. "I didn't at first, because of what you represented, but the more I've gotten to know you, the more I've liked you. And under the circumstances, I don't think we need to stand on ceremony."

"What about your work?"

"My work?" Tory laughed openly this time—openly and bitterly, like she couldn't believe any of this was really happening. "My work is happening without me, in a room I'm not welcome in. Luis will keep watch on the sonar, but there's nothing for me to do. Not until they let me back into the conversation about mermaid language."

"Do you think they're going to?"

"Honestly, I don't know, and I don't know whether I want them to. I don't know much of anything right now. This is what I've been trying to prove for my whole life, that these things exist, and now they do, and I...I just don't know." Tory ran her thumb along the side of Olivia's hand. "But I know we're here. And I know I liked you even when I didn't want to like you. And I know I don't want to be alone either."

Olivia didn't say anything. Olivia just stepped closer and kissed her. After a moment's surprised hesitation, Tory kissed her back, and for a while the world made sense again.

Luis wished he could leave the lab door open, partially so anyone walking by would know he was in there—and might be willing to talk; would *probably* be willing to talk, especially if they had coffee—and partially so he'd be able to hear what was going on outside. It was impossible to spend as much time as he had with Tory and not develop a healthy respect for the way the world *sounded*. It could tell him so much more than anyone thought it could. Even silence told a story.

(Before Heather had died, he and Holly had gotten into several good-natured debates about the nature of sound and silence, and whether what he learned from the first was greater than what she learned from the second. Hallie, who had inevitably been recruited to translate these fights, had started throwing up her hands and ordering them to get a room after the third round. He wondered where Holly was. He wondered whether she was holding herself together. But there was the ultimate betrayal of their natures: without Hallie to act as go-between, they couldn't understand each other. He knew half a dozen signs; she could read his lips with limited accuracy, if he spoke slowly and they were both patient. He wasn't patient right now. He suspected she wasn't either.)

Luis cracked his knuckles, sat, and began typing.

Tory focused on audio recordings; she wanted to know what

was being said fathoms below. She wasn't a linguist. She was a code breaker, treating the elements of language as pieces of a puzzle. It was a necessary part of the task of translating something as alien to human ears as the voices of the sea: she could filter the things that *weren't* language, setting them to the side, and present the people who could actually do the translation with coherent data. Back at the aquarium she'd worked with cetologists and marine biologists to try to figure out what she was listening to. At least at the beginning, she'd been doing that here as well, turning to the other scientists recruited by Imagine and letting them bolster her work as they progressed with their own.

She knew she was a publicity stunt—the grieving sister of a member of the *Atargatis* crew, setting sail for answers—and she'd come anyway, because anything else would have been letting Anne down. Luis had known it was not only a publicity stunt, but a publicity stunt aimed at *someone else*, and he'd still signed up without hesitation. Where else was he going to get this sort of opportunity? Because while he was on the self-awareness train, he also knew his work was a joke at best and a waste of time at worst. He was a cryptid chaser lucky enough to have been blessed with access to essentially unlimited funds, and he was frittering away the family fortune chasing things that might or might not exist.

He'd tried, on several occasions, to make himself feel bad about that, to find it in his heart to pursue another passion, something more immediately beneficial to humanity. In the end he kept coming back to the things he loved, and to the calm understanding that even if his *work* wasn't going to save the world, the things it created might. Tory's recording equipment had improved a thousandfold because of him, and those recordings didn't just help her; they were used by hundreds of marine biologists, climatologists, and statisticians. When he'd paid for a hundred trackers to be put on colossal squid, for the sake of determining whether something even *more* colossal might be devouring them, he had funded a dozen research products and created a pool of data that was still being mined for its practical applications.

The human race had always created dreamers whose seemingly frivolous dreams forced the creation of infrastructures and innovations that benefited everyone around them. He was just the latest in a long line of people who, by wanting something they could never have, dragged the rest of the world kicking and screaming into a new phase of the future.

Luis called up the sonar readings, spreading them across three monitors with an artist's skill. Each greenish screen showed the sound waves radiating as a faint ring of vibration, breaking into sketchy outlines when they hit something. He checked all three windows several times as he calibrated his settings. The sonar pulses weren't his—those were a part of the *Melusine*'s standard array of sensors—but he had access to the data they were returning, and he was grateful for that. Getting Heather to drop sonar probes for him before she did her dive would have been both expensive and time consuming. Worse yet, it could have led to her encountering the mermaids even sooner, when they had less data, and less of a chance of learning the things they still needed to know.

Two people were dead. At least two people; for all he knew, half a dozen more could have been pulled off the sides of the ship during the last hour, while he was staring at a creature out of his dreams (out of his nightmares) and wondering whether she'd ever be able to admire him the way he admired her. Two people were dead, and three dolphins were dead, and he was still going to be a hero when he got back to California, because he was a cryptozoologist who had actually gone out and *found* something. He'd argued for the existence of mermaids, and by God, he had *found* them.

The whole world changed when you *found* things.

One by one, he flipped the camera feeds on, letting them roll until they stabilized. There were lights mounted on the bottom of the *Melusine*, but he lacked the authority to activate them: they could be activated only by someone with full system access. He assumed the captain could do it, but the captain had other things to worry about, and besides, what would he say? "Hey, can you turn on the lights so I can get a better look at the fish"? No. It wouldn't do him any good. Other methods had to be used.

Some of the cameras utilized red lights, letting him see the marine life without disturbing it. Others were set to show motion and temperature differentials. They were more useful when observing mammals than when trying to get a clear look at fish, but they were better than nothing. One by one his windows into the underwater world flickered on, showing him the sea.

The water was dark and calm. Even in heavy storms, deeper water remained undisturbed; there were currents, there was natural movement, but storms were, by and large, a concern for the surface. There was something important in that. The things that could swamp ships and drown sailors were almost unnoticeable a few meters down, where the water did as it would and paid no attention to the turmoil. A few fish flashed by, and he followed them from window to window, automatically making the mental adjustments to recognize them in each visual frame. It had taken a long time to learn how to do that, but after years spent interpreting the input from differently calibrated cameras, it was no longer conscious.

Fish. More fish. A drifting squid; he would have thought it was dead if not for the occasional pulses of its mantle, propelling it away from the ship.

And there, in the depths, a spray of glittering light, like someone had lit a sparkler fifteen feet down and without access to the air. Luis sat up straighter, watching the specks of light dance and swirl. They weren't moving very fast; he wouldn't have been sure they were moving at all if not for the fish that shared the frame, higher up and darting quickly out of the way. That gave him a frame of reference, and confirmed that yes, the specks were rising, slow, slow, cautious as anything.

His hands moved on the keyboard, redirecting three cameras in the area, moving one of the downward-facing probes up a few meters and shifting it toward the lights. Moving the cameras was a complicated matter. Most were motorized; some were attached to drones he could move in the water, anchored to the ship by thin cables, assuming they were anchored at all. If he moved them too fast, he risked snapping the cables. Worse, he risked startling the things he was attempting to film. What good was it to reorient the cameras if he lost the target in the process?

Holding his breath, he drove the probe closer to the lights. More of the lights appeared in the frame; they were covering each other, ducking in and out of view. He could see the thin threads of "hair" connecting them now. It was a mermaid. He was sure of that. But mermaids were like lightning; they moved fast enough to catch dolphins in the open sea. Why was this one moving so slowly?

Maybe it was hurt. Maybe it was dead. If he could retrieve a dead mermaid, their biologists would have something to work on, and he would be there again; he would be in the room, because it would be *his* mermaid, his great new find. The lights continued to drift. Luis nudged the probe closer.

The mermaid turned its head, looking directly into the lens.

Luis gasped, slamming back in his seat. There was no way the creature could see him—no way it could even know he was on the other side of the camera—but that didn't matter; again instinct was taking over, telling him this was the bigger predator. Telling him to *run*.

Intellect overrode instinct. Fascinated as always by the mechanics of the mermaid, he leaned forward to get a better look.

The body of the mermaid was obscured by water; the lens could only contain the face and drifting cloud of "hair," the bright points of twinkling light that tipped each strand moving in and out of view like stars on a cloudy night. It was beautiful. It wasn't human—it wasn't anything like human; a manatee would have been closer, since a manatee would at least have been a *mammal*—but it was beautiful. The slope of its forehead, the angle of its cheekbones, the soft, distressingly human pout of its lips...

The lovely ladies of the sea weren't what anyone had expected or wanted them to be, but they were still amazing. Something about them spoke to a thousand years of cultural literacy and conditioning, reminding him of all the stories of sailors who'd found their true loves beneath the waves. The fact that this creature would have eaten him as soon as looked at him didn't matter. It was in its element, it was moving as fluidly and easily as the water itself, and it was incredible.

It tilted its head, studying the camera. After a moment's contemplation, it reached out and tapped the lens, setting the camera rocking in the water. The motors that drove it had internal stabilizers, designed to keep it as steady as possible (and based on the motor function of a chicken's head and neck). They couldn't stand up to an actual impact. The picture moved, bouncing with the lens.

The mermaid tapped the camera again. Luis frowned.

"What are you trying to do?" he asked.

The mermaid leaned closer, lips opening to show those terrible, inhuman teeth. It was still beautiful. It was just easier to dismiss that beauty, because this thing—this *thing*—was no sailor's dream. It barely qualified as a nightmare. He could see tiny shrimp moving in the mermaid's hair, white, eyeless things no more than an inch in length, claws picking at the strands, cleaning them, grooming them. No simple hairbrushes or shell combs for this creature; like all that lived in the sea, it had found biological solutions to its needs.

The mermaid surged toward the camera, moving with sudden intent. It swatted the camera away. The servos kicked on, trying to move the camera back into its original position. The mermaid hit it again, driving it farther down. The signal crackled into static before dying. The window that had been displaying its feed snapped closed, the other windows shifting to fill the gap it had created. They presented a picture of the mermaid moving through the water, moving toward the ship, ceaseless and unrelenting.

There were no others. Only the one, rising by itself. Luis checked the feeds, angling the lenses so as to chart the mermaid's ascent. It was going to come up on the port side, not far from his lab.

"This is stupid," he said to himself, as he stood and reached for his digital camera. It was next to a dart gun, designed for tagging fish and squid as they dove. He grabbed that as well, stuffing it into the waistband of his jeans. It was an unfamiliar weight. There were probably people in the world who found carrying a gun to be comforting, even necessary to their peace of mind. He wasn't sure he wanted to meet any of them.

Jacques and Michi probably qualified. They walked like people who were ready to shoot the whole world to get what they wanted. He tried to avoid them as much as possible. He didn't want them near the mermaids, either, although the deaths—two so far, and first contact was only just now being formally made—were enough to explain why they'd been asked to come along. Imagine had known from the start how contact was likely to go. It had seen it before, after all.

Not for the first time, he wondered how much of the footage from the *Atargatis* incident had never been released to the public. Something must have been held back, some telling piece of damning documentation that made it possible for Imagine to come out of the situation with clean hands. Clean*er*, anyway. There was no way any of them were walking away completely clean. Not the first time, when the seas had run red and the ship had become a haunted house. Not this time either.

Luis stepped out of the lab and onto the deserted deck, pausing with his head cocked, listening. No alarms were ringing. The ship's engines were a low, steady hum, so constant that it had become inaudible over the course of the journey. He only noticed it now when he was actually looking for it, or when he was adjusting the equipment to balance it out. He was sure the engines drowned out many smaller, subtler sounds near the surface, but since he and Tory were almost always looking deep, it didn't matter as much for them as it might for some of the other researchers. Anyone who wanted to do shallow-water work on a ship like this one was guilty of thinking small, and probably deserved the distortions they would get.

Under the engines were the other steady sounds—the whistle of the wind, the lapping of the water against the hull, the things that kept the ocean from being truly silent. No dynamic system could be soundless without existing in a vacuum. The *Melusine* was a part of her environment now. Man-made and artificial, yes, but subject to all the same rules as everything else around her.

Luis wondered whether the mermaids knew what a coral reef was, whether their normal migrations ever brought them into waters shallow enough to support that sort of ecosystem. He wondered whether they looked at the *Melusine* and saw a sort of floating reef, something that served the same purpose for its air-breathing inhabitants as the coral structures did for those beneath the sea. It was a charming, whimsical thought, and it would have seemed a lot more reasonable if the mermaids hadn't turned out to be flesh-ripping monsters that wanted to eat everyone in sight.

Oh, well. Couldn't win them all. He stayed where he was, wishing he dared close his eyes, and kept listening.

There: a soft slapping sound, coming from about fifteen yards away. Hand on the butt of his tagging gun, Luis started cautiously in that direction. He was following a hunch as much as he was following the sound, hoping what he'd observed so far would pay off in some small but measurable way.

He came around the bend in the hall. The sea spread out in front of him, framed by the metal poles that supported both this deck and the deck above it. Parts of the ship were more like a grid than anything else, a fine lattice of interconnected walkways that looked impossibly delicate, like they would be lost in a matter of seconds if a real storm blew up. The whole vessel seemed impossibly delicate at times. In reality, the *Melusine* had plated shutters that could be closed from the control deck if necessary. With the entry of a code and the press of a button, the ship would become an armored fortress, impervious to attack from outside.

The mermaids weren't going to get them the way they got the *Atargatis*. That had never been a risk. A few people might die—a few people always died when there was a discovery to be made, and every single one of them had signed contracts indicating that they understood precisely that—but the ship would survive, along with almost everyone on board. There was something comforting about that.

A hissing sound told Luis he was on the right track. He walked along the deck, getting as close to the rail as he dared, and looked along the line of the hull to the water.

The mermaid, which had already managed to climb more than halfway up the side of the ship, clung there glaring at him. It didn't have human eyes, but it could still make itself understood. It was angry. It was looking for something to take that anger out on.

He would do.

"Howdy, Ariel," said Luis, and held his camera over the rail, snapping several pictures. He didn't bother to turn off the flash. These were the first out of water pictures taken of one of these creatures since the *Atargatis*; they were going to be the first pictures accompanied by a living photographer who could attest to their authenticity. They were *going* to be clear.

The mermaid snarled before echoing, "Howdy, Ariel, howdy, howdy," in a passable imitation of his own voice. It began climbing faster, swarming up the side of the ship like it was on a mission.

To be fair, it probably was. It just wasn't a mission Luis had any intention of going along with. He danced back along the deck, trying to estimate how long it would take the now-enraged mermaid to make its way to the rail. He'd just finished counting down from eight when a hand reached up and grasped the metal. He took several more pictures, zooming in on the knuckles, which bent in a way that was subtly *wrong* to his eye. The ichthyologists were going to have a field day with this one.

So were the cryptid chasers of the world, and he was about to become their king. Out of everyone on the planet, Luis Martines was the one who'd gone out and *found* something. Every scrap of additional material he got now was icing on the cake of what he had already accomplished.

Let Tory have her vengeance and Mr. Blackwell have whatever he was looking for. Let all of them have whatever they wanted. He was going home at the head of his field, and every choice he'd ever made was going to be justified by this moment.

The mermaid's arms looked wiry and weak, but they pulled it over the rail with surprising strength. It hit the deck with a sick slapping sound, like a barrel of dead fish being emptied. It was still for a moment. Luis wasn't sure whether it had actually hurt itself or was just lying in wait. Then it rolled over, making a retching noise, and vomited what must have been a gallon of water onto the wood.

He took pictures of that, too. It told him more about the creature's biology than he would have thought possible. The gills in the mermaid's neck were still half-open, pulsing with every breath it took; at the same time, the mermaid was visibly breathing through the narrow slits of its nose, which pulsed in time with the gills. It was probably an excellent method of fighting off aquatic parasites. Anything that tried to attach to the mermaid's gills would be either blown loose when it exhaled, or would suffocate, unable to deal with the change between water and air.

Everything about the mermaid was a biological miracle, designed to take advantage of its environment. It had no reason to become anything other than aquatic, but it wasn't the first fish to learn how to deal with oxygen. The snakehead, the lungfish, those had pioneered the art of moving between environments. Its hands, its arms, the strangely simian curve of its spine, all those things had precedents elsewhere in the sea. But like the human body, which collected some of the best innovations evolution had come up with for the land, the mermaid combined them in a new, and terrifying, way.

As Luis watched, the mermaid got its arms under itself and braced its hands against the deck. It had no dorsal fins to speak of, but the small fins on its sides waved constantly as it oriented itself. Whether that was a function of movement or something automatic didn't matter.

It turned its head. It saw him. The lights around its face danced and swayed with the movement of its hair. It would have been easy to see the mermaid, at any sort of distance, as something out of a fairy tale. Something to be idealized and pursued.

It opened its mouth. "Howdy, Ariel," it said, still using his own voice. It was an oddly disturbing sound. Even knowing that the mermaids were mimics couldn't stop him from feeling violated when it didn't stop.

The mermaid moved.

It should have been slow, graceless, unwieldy: all the things he'd always assumed of marine animals on land. The few that were actually fast were terrifying. He'd seen a video once, of eels in a billabong in Australia that had learned to hunt birds. They were like arrows, launching themselves skyward, their tails anchored in the mire. They moved faster than anything aquatic should have been able to move in the open air. He'd watched that recording and silently swore he'd never go anywhere near a billabong, never go anywhere near creatures that could think like that and hunt like that, in ways no fish had any right to hunt or think.

The mermaid moved like those eels were its ancestors, like it had studied at their fins and learned how best to take advantage of the change in its circumstances. It didn't slither so much as it undulated, pulling itself along with its hands while its lower body somehow found traction on the slippery deck. Luis gaped in openmouthed awe for a split second before he realized it had closed more than half the distance between them, and was working fast on the rest of the gap. He turned and ran.

The sound of the mermaid's hands slapping the wood pursued him as he fled. He turned the corner, heading for the enclosed hallways where the sea was out of sight, acting on some deeply buried instinct that told him he might be safer if he got away from the water. Amphibious or not, the mermaid was a creature of the sea. It wouldn't pursue him too far from its natural habitat.

A man stepped into his path. Luis shouted something unintelligible as collision seemed inevitable. Then strong arms were reaching out of the nearest doorway, jerking him out of the way as the man— Jacques, his features becoming visible as he took another step forward, out of the shadows—raised his sidearm and fired three times. The mermaid screamed, its voice still unnervingly like Luis's own.

He turned his head and found himself looking into Michi's eyes.

They were brown, cold, and surrounded by impeccably applied winged eyeliner. He had time to wonder who took the time to do their makeup before coming out to hunt mermaids before she was shoving him away, a disgusted expression on her face.

"Really, mate, what were you hoping to accomplish?" she demanded, her accent painted broadly across every syllable. She sounded like the pure distillation of Queensland, Australia, all sunny skies and brutal murder. "If you were looking to kill yourself, there are easier ways."

"It's dead," said Jacques, stepping into the room. He looked at Luis and sniffed. "Little boy, are you a fool, or are you too stupid to know when you're taking unnecessary chances?"

"Hold on a second," said Luis, scowling. "I didn't take any unnecessary chances. I knew the mermaid was coming, I went to have a look at it."

"Carrying this?" Michi held up his tracker gun. Luis's hands flew to his waistband. Michi looked at him with open pity. "Please. I got it off you while you were trying to decide whether or not my breast was touching your arm. This thing doesn't even have *bullets*. It was never going to save you."

"It's a tracker gun, and I'd like it back." Luis held out his hand. He was proud of the fact that it wasn't shaking. Under the circumstances, he felt like that was a victory.

"What do you track with it?" Michi dropped it into his palm. She looked almost bored.

"Mostly squid and big fish."

"You wanted to track the mermaid?" Jacques snorted. "We know where the fish-women go. They go down to Davy Jones's locker, and they take you along for the ride."

"What are you *doing* out here?" asked Luis, tucking the gun back into his waistband. It was less reassuring now than it had been. Guns were always less reassuring once it was clear how easily they could be taken away.

"We should have stayed in our, how did that nice marine biologist put it? In our 'senseless fish slaughterhouse.'" Jacques sniffed. "We are what nature designed us to be. Carnivores. Children of the veldt. We take what the world offers."

"We're not actually required to stay away from the rest of you," said Michi, putting a hand on Jacques's arm. She smiled—the first sign of true warmth she had shown—before turning cool eyes on Luis and saying, "Mr. Blackwell feels we make people nervous, and that it's best for us to stay out of the way when possible. As we'd prefer not to circulate with people we don't care for anyway, we've stayed mostly isolated. That doesn't mean we haven't been keeping an eye on things. And once the security teams were activated, so were we."

All the data feeds for the ship were shared. Sampling data wasn't, necessarily; Luis knew several projects were being managed under veils of partial to complete secrecy, letting the researchers who were conducting them feel secure sharing their results. Someone who sent a probe to gather water from the surface of the Challenger Deep, for example, could expect a certain measure of privacy. But the microphones that studded the hull and dangled from the body of the ship, the cameras, like his, that buzzed through the water... All of those used the *Melusine*'s Wi-Fi to transmit their information back to the people controlling them, and all of those feeds could be sampled at will.

Most people didn't care about things like Luis's cameras, which were small and idiosyncratically oriented when compared to the cameras being operated directly by Imagine. That didn't mean that *no one* cared.

"You were spying on me," he said dully.

Michi waved a hand dismissively. "You say 'spying,' we say 'following the closest thing we have to a native guide in these waters.' When we hunt lion, we find a local who can lead us to where the prides are. When we hunt whale, we find someone who understands where they like to roam. We're hunting mermaid. Dr. Toth is not a good guide. She never tried to find them. Not once since we got here. You know why?"

"I know why," said Jacques. "The lovely doctor does not look for her sirens, because she always knew they would come to find us. She made us the lure for her line, and she sat back to wait. How does it feel to be a wiggling worm, hmm? I think you know the feeling well."

"Did anyone ever tell you that you have the social skills of a hyena?" asked Luis.

"I love my husband; you insult the hyena," said Michi. "Yes, we watched your video to see where we'd be most needed. Unless you relished the thought of having your face chewed off by a horror from the deep, you owe us your thanks."

"I was doing fine," protested Luis.

"No," said Michi, with absolute, unshakeable calm. "You weren't."

Luis opened his mouth to argue. Then he stiffened, realization slamming through him like a lightning bolt. "You *shot* it," he breathed, and whirled, running into the hall.

There was the mermaid, sprawled on its face, three large holes blown in the flesh of its back. The meat they revealed was a dark, disturbing pink, like salmon or fatty tuna. Luis rushed to its side, not hesitating as he dropped to his knees in the viscous slime that had spread out to surround the body, and hoisted the head.

Its eyes were filmed over, its mouth hanging open, revealing a graveyard of jagged teeth. It didn't move at all. From the pliancy of its flesh beneath his hands, there was no question that it was dead.

"We have a dead one," he breathed, and suddenly everything was good again.

CHAPTER 22

Western Pacific Ocean, above the Mariana Trench: September 3, 2022

Midnight had come and gone with Dr. Toth still gazing at the mermaid on the other side of the glass. The mermaid stared back, unblinking. It had eyelids, but used them rarely; she supposed they were an adaptation to protect the eyes from debris in the water, and possibly also to protect them from the open air. Which came first, the amphibious outings to the surface or the functional eyelid?

"Chicken and the egg, my dear," she said.

"Chicken," said the mermaid. "My dear." Its imitation of her voice was improving. If she kept talking to it, it would be able to fool her own daughter. The thought was fascinating. Had they been ambush predators, back when the tall ships sailed more frequently through their territory, back when men were easier to catch and consume, as long as the mermaids were willing to be patient?

The rise of steamships must have changed so much about their hunting techniques. For humanity, the industrial revolution had been the start of an era of booming prosperity and comfort. For the mermaids, it must have seemed like one of their most reliable sources of food had dried up effectively overnight. Add in the rise of the whaling industry, and it was a miracle they'd been able to find enough to survive.

"You should have been the mascot for Greenpeace," she said.

"They would have loved you so much." At least until the mermaids started eating the activists. That would have been a bit difficult to explain.

"I wish you'd stop taunting the thing," said Theo mildly.

"And I wish you'd order the captain to deploy the shutters. You promised me."

"The shutters aren't... precisely prepared for deployment."

Something in his tone made Jillian turn and frown at him. "Meaning what, exactly?"

"Meaning..." Theo paused and sighed. "Meaning they've failed every systems test. We cannot currently deploy the shutters."

"Of course we can't," said Jillian, with a small, bitter laugh. She turned back to the tank. "What's your game, Theo?"

"My game is above your pay grade," said Theo. "Leave the mermaid alone. You're not learning anything. You're just playing with it."

"That's where you're wrong," said Jillian, aware that she was being distracted but unable to stop herself from rising to the bait. "Listen to its echoes. It's *learning*. Maybe not what it's saying, but how to match my inflections more closely. If it followed us for a week, it would be able to call you from the water and make you believe, beyond the shadow of a doubt, that it was me calling you. It's adapting."

"It's not adapting that quickly."

"It's matching the sounds made by a human throat while completely submerged," said Jillian. "It shouldn't be able to *do* that. Human speech underwater doesn't sound like human speech. It sounds like something dead and drowned and distorted. Whether it's thinking about the adjustments or doing them automatically, it's matching something it shouldn't be able to match. That's incredible."

Hallie and Daniel glanced up from the workstation where they were attempting to connect the mermaid's hand motions to the ones on the video. If they could crack the surface of its language, they had faith they would be able to start building a working vocabulary. That was what mattered: finding a place where their two worlds would meet, a form of commonality between their two species. Without that, they were going to remain predator and prey, separated by a thin glass wall.

"We got lucky, in a way," said Daniel.

Hallie's head jerked around. She stared at him like she was trying to understand who he was and what he was doing in her presence. Then she shook it off, and asked, "How do you mean?"

"At least the mermaids have something we recognize as language. I was always afraid that when we met truly intelligent nonmammalian undersea life, it would be...I don't know, a species of giant cuttlefish that communicated via light pulses. You know. The kind of thing where we'd never be able to translate, or where the translation would take a decade. Just long enough to find out that they'd been counting down to the invasion the entire time. Sign language is relatively easy."

"Spoken like a man who's never tried to navigate the disconnect between two different types of sign language."

Daniel blinked at her. "There's more than one kind of sign language?"

Hallie swallowed a groan. She was exhausted, overwhelmed, and still numb from Heather's death—a state she knew wasn't going to last forever. Eventually her heart would thaw enough to let the pain in, and she was going to collapse. Part of her wanted to work as hard as she could, as fast as she could, to make sure her place on the research team was justified—to make sure she could be there when they told the mermaids, "You killed a good woman" in a way they could understand. The rest of her just wanted to lie down and let the hurting come. It was going to happen. Putting it off wasn't going to do her any good.

She wished Holly were here, or that she were with Holly. Even though Holly had made it clear that she wanted to be alone right now, it was hard not to feel guilty about leaving her sister surrounded by people who had never made any effort to learn how to communicate with her. For most of them, signing began and ended with an extended middle finger. Anything else was too hard for them to bother with.

"There are multiple forms of sign language," she said, voice tight and temples throbbing. "ASL has its own grammar, which does not match English grammar. Hearing professors started getting angry when Deaf students who were native speakers of ASL didn't follow English rules in their writing, and started pushing more and more for something called SEE—Signing Exact English—which forced Deaf students to learn a whole new grammar in order to make things easier on their hearing instructors. The whole world is set up to be easy on hearing people, but that wasn't good enough for us. We had to find the one corner that wasn't designed to cater to our needs and take it over, and fuck the people who already lived there, who had a perfectly reasonable way of talking to each other, who didn't need us to 'fix' them."

Daniel blinked. "Um," he said, after a long pause. "Okay. I guess that means that yes, there are multiple forms of sign language."

"All over the world," snapped Hallie.

"All over the world," said the mermaid, its voice somewhere between Hallie's and Dr. Toth's.

Hallie froze. Until the mermaid had spoken, she hadn't considered that she was talking out loud: Daniel wasn't the only one who could hear her.

"I'm sorry," she said.

"Don't be." Dr. Toth waved a hand. "Knowledge that can be imparted loudly and with passion always lasts longer than knowledge that has to be whispered. You care. That's a good thing. Now figure out how to talk to my mermaid."

"Yes, ma'am," said Hallie.

Mr. Blackwell raised an eyebrow. "*Your* mermaid?" he asked.

"I know she belongs to Imagine, and you'll have your own swarm of clever scientists—we know they're clever; they were smart enough not to sign on for this voyage of the damned—on shore to take custody of her, but right here, right now, she's mine." Jillian's eyes returned to the mermaid, tracing the outline of its body. "Right now, she's the answer to every question I've ever asked, and a few hundred that I haven't stopped to think of yet. I'm going to enjoy her while I can."

The phone rang.

It was an odd, archaic sound, all the more so because it came from an actual wall-mounted receiver. It looked like the sort of thing that should have been placed in the president's private quarters in a Cold War movie. All four people in the lab turned to look at it, some with confusion, others with contemplation. Mr. Blackwell actually looked annoyed, as if this was the last thing he'd been expecting.

"Aren't you going to get that?" asked Jillian. "How many people have the number for your secret lab?"

"The captain," said Theo, starting for the phone. "The head of security, who may also be the only member of the security team who actually knows which end of his gun is which. Jacques and Michi Abney. They're only supposed to call in the event of an emergency."

"I'm curious, what's your definition of an emergency? Two people were dead *before* we took one of the mermaids hostage," said Jillian. "Do you think they understand revenge? They may be coming to get their sister back, which means they could come here first." She didn't look particularly worried. If anything, she looked interested, like this would be something remarkable to watch.

"That's horrible," said Hallie.

Jillian shrugged. "That's nature."

Theo didn't say anything. He just removed the phone from the wall, holding it to his ear and listening before he said, "I see. Thank you for letting me know." There was a pause while he listened. "I see. I'll inform her."

He hung up the phone and turned to find the others watching him intently.

"Jillian," he said. "That was Michi Abney. Apparently one of the scientists had a little run-in with a mermaid on the deck of the fourth level, and she and her husband had to shoot it. The mermaid, not the scientist. They're preparing for a necropsy in the wet lab, and I thought you might like to supervise."

Jillian, who had started for the door as soon as he said the words *shoot it*, didn't reply. She also didn't look back. The door slammed behind her, and for a moment, everything was silent.

"Supervise," said the mermaid, in a passable imitation of Theo's voice.

None of the humans said anything at all.

The *Melusine* had been designed using many systems and principles developed by the cruise companies: soundproofing, stabilizers, a thousand small comforts intended to make the experience of sailing halfway around the world more pleasant than it had ever been in the past. Her passengers were, by and large, less appreciative than they could have been; even the ones who'd spent enough time at sea to notice how steady the decks were, how the vast ship almost never seemed to rock, had long since forgotten their surprise. This was just how things were now. Stable. Serene.

Tory slammed into the door of her cabin, shoulders hitting a split second before her butt, her left hand fumbling for the handle. The locks were set to her biometrics, keyed to her thumbprint—another feature borrowed from the cruise ship industry, which had long since learned that drunken retirees looking for a little afternoon delight were not in the mood to fumble for their keys. Most of the lab spaces used more traditional hardware, but the cabins were locked to their specific occupants, and to those who had been granted explicit permission for entry.

Tory wasn't thinking about that. Tory was thinking about Olivia's mouth on hers, Olivia's hands traveling across the skin under her shirt, clever fingers tracing the topography of her skin. It had been a long time since she'd had sex, and longer since she'd had sex with a woman. Jason had been her most recent lover. His arrogance had carried into the bedroom, where he'd been happy to insist he knew how to please a woman, even as he consistently failed to make sure she was satisfied before falling asleep.

Breaking up had been as much about her libido as it had been about her pride. If he'd been good for either one, she might have been able to stick it out. As it was...

But Jason was in the past and Olivia was in the present, and she might have felt bad about how raw Olivia was—how likely she was to be bleeding inside from the loss of her friend—if it hadn't been for her own wounds, which had opened the day Anne died and still hadn't scabbed over. For the first time, Tory felt like she might have found someone who knew what it was to hurt. They could learn to heal together. Even if it was only for one night, they could learn to heal together.

The handle clicked under her hand. The door swung open, dumping them both onto the floor, where they landed in a tangle of limbs that froze for a heartbeat, stunned into motionlessness. Then Tory's mouth was seeking Olivia's again, reestablishing the connection between them, sealing the loop, and Olivia's hands were startled back into motion. Tory kicked the door. It swung shut. The cabin was dark enough that with the door closed, she couldn't see anything, but she didn't need to; the human body was a predictable playground, one line leading into the next.

Olivia giggled. Tory gasped.

The dark came down hard.

After a small amount of time had passed—long enough for them to remove their clothing; long enough for them to feel their way to the bed, Olivia giggling every time she put her hand on something unexpected, Tory laughing in response, like joy was an infection—they lay curled together under the sheets on Tory's bunk. Olivia's knee was pinned between Tory's thighs, keeping them both quietly captive.

"It's dark in here," said Olivia.

"I know," said Tory. "I grew up on the beach. I never got used to a lot of ambient light in my room. My last boyfriend insisted on keeping his computer next to the bed. I never got a lick of good sleep while I was with him."

She felt Olivia shift against her, the smaller woman's chin digging into the soft flesh of her shoulder. It seemed to be instinctive, the need to turn the eyes toward something they would never see. "Boyfriend?"

"Bi," said Tory. "Some boyfriends, some girlfriends, one friend in high school who didn't like either gender for themselves, but liked girls enough to get with me." She paused before asking, "Is that a problem?" The question, as always, came with a vague wave of disappointment. She and Olivia weren't dating—sex and relationships did not always go hand-in-hand, nor did she believe they should—but she was having a nice time, and had been hoping to keep the option open to do it again. Sadly, way too many girls who liked girls (and boys who liked boys, although that wasn't a dynamic she'd ever been a part of) had issues with girls who liked both. She wasn't a slut or a fence-sitter, or any of the other terrible things she'd been called since she was sixteen and started figuring out her sexuality. She just was pickier about personalities than she was about genders.

Olivia was silent for a long moment. Long enough for Tory to start thinking about what it would take to extricate herself from the bed and make for the door. This was her cabin, but that didn't matter: she could always retreat to the lab until things had died down. Luis would be there, ready to put a comforting arm around her shoulders and remind her that she had terrible taste in women, but her taste in men was even worse, so it all balanced out in the end. She could get away from this. If she had to, she could get away from this.

269

"No," said Olivia finally. "It's not a problem. I just had to..." She stopped again. The silence felt lighter this time; it was hesitation to find the right word, and not hesitation to find the right rejection. Tory discovered that she could breathe again.

Finally Olivia said, "I don't normally sleep with somebody I'm not dating. I mean, I wanted to get to know you better, and cruise ships are where romantic assignations are supposed to happen, right?"

"Even when under siege by man-eating mermaids?" asked Tory, and instantly regretted it as Olivia stiffened beside her. Cheeks burning, she said, "I didn't mean..."

"I know," said Olivia. "But the man-eating mermaids are a stressor for both of us. That's why we didn't have this conversation before we did anything that couldn't be taken back. I don't mind if you like boys. Unless you want to ask one of them to join us. I'd mind that. I'd mind that a lot."

"I take it you don't like boys, then."

"Not really." Olivia hesitated. "It would be more about too many people, though. I don't always do well with too many people in a small space. Ray was...A big part of Ray's job was making sure no one crowded me. He was my bubble. I don't know how I'm going to do the conventions without him." A small sound escaped her, somewhere between a gasp and a sob, and she pressed her face against Tory's shoulder again.

Tory stroked her hair with one hand, thinking dismally about how it might not be a problem. This had been a moment stolen from the silence, a brief time to be human in the midst of coming chaos, but it had only been a moment. They were still miles from home, adrift on an uncaring sea, and the worst was yet to come. The worst was *always* yet to come.

"It'll be okay," she said, and it was a lie, but it was the *right* lie, and that made it okay. They lay there, tangled up and warm in the dark room, and neither of them said anything, and that was okay too. Sometimes silence was the only correct thing to say.

A light flashed from the floor. Tory craned her neck to see. "I think my phone is ringing," she said. "Let me up."

"Or you could ignore it and stay with me," said Olivia.

"So tempting." Tory kissed Olivia on the temple before rolling away, untangling herself from limbs and bedding at the same time.

The room had gotten colder, possibly as a consequence of contrast; up until very recently, they had been doing an admirable job of making their own heat. Now...

Had this been a mistake? And even if it had been, had it been a mistake she was going to make again? She hoped it would be. Even if there was no future for them off this ship, having this time, in this place, was worthwhile. Humanity was worthwhile.

The caller ID on her phone read "Luis." Tory frowned. Of everyone on the *Melusine*, he was the one who knew her best—better even than Jason—and the only one who'd been aware that she was running off with Olivia for a little time alone. For him to be calling, there had to be something important going on.

She swiped her thumb across the screen. "Hello?"

"Victoria, you need to get down to the wet lab, and you need to do it *now*." Luis's voice was vibrating with barely contained excitement. "We got one."

Tory frowned. "Got one what?"

"A mermaid. We got a mermaid. It came onto the ship—"

She gasped. Behind her, she heard Olivia sit up, suddenly alert. She didn't know whether it was a reporter's instinct or just the reaction of a naked woman hearing sounds of nearby alarm. It came down to the same thing, in the end.

"I'm *fine*," said Luis, identifying the source of her dismay. "It chased me, and I ran into the Abneys. They shot it. They shot it more than was strictly necessary, I guess, but it's dead, and we're about to do the necropsy. I thought you might want to be here."

"Where?"

"Wet lab, like I said. It's closed to all but essential personnel— which means Dr. Toth, Dr. Lennox, Dr. Wilson, a couple marine biologists from the research team, and a bunch of guys from Imagine. And the Abneys. They're not helping with the dissection. They're just standing around with their guns in their hands, making sure everyone remembers who killed the thing." He lowered his voice. "I convinced them to let you in, and Mr. Blackwell wants you to bring Olivia, but you need to get down here. They're going to lock the doors before the news gets out to the rest of the ship. The captain's making another announcement about staying out of the halls. That should distract people, but it won't get you in if you're slow."

"I'm on my way," said Tory, feeling around for her discarded clothes with her free hand. She hung up the phone, shoving it into the pocket of her jeans before stepping into them and yanking them on. "Olivia? Did you catch any of that?"

"Not really," said Olivia. "What's going on?"

"We have a dead mermaid. There's going to be a necropsy. I need to turn on the lights."

"My eyes are closed. What's a necropsy?"

"You know what an autopsy is?"

"Yes."

"It's like that, but for something that isn't human. Everything but us gets necropsied when it dies."

"Oh," said Olivia. Then: "You're going?"

"I am. Mr. Blackwell wants me to bring you, but I can say I didn't know where you were, if you'd rather not." Tory slapped the wall. The cabin lights flickered on, dim at first, rapidly brightening to standard levels. She snatched her bra off the floor. "I don't know how much of it will make sense to you, but—"

"I have a camera. I'm coming." Olivia began retrieving her own clothes. Tory paused to watch her. Not for long—they didn't have the time to waste—but long enough for her to take in the curve of Olivia's hip, the sinuous line of Olivia's back. The room had been dark when their clothes had come off. Some opportunities were not to be missed. Especially when there was a chance that they weren't going to be repeated.

"Fair," she said, beginning to move again. She fastened her bra and tugged her shirt on over her head. "How's your stomach?"

It was Olivia's turn to pause. She frowned at Tory. "What do you mean?"

"The first time I was present for a marine necropsy—a big sea lion—I nearly threw up in the thoracic cavity. The smell that came out of that thing was like nothing I'd ever encountered before. So how's your stomach?"

"Oh," said Olivia. "That's...Oh."

"Here." Tory grabbed a small jar off the edge of the bookshelf and lobbed it underhand to Olivia. "Put this under your nose."

"Muscle relaxant?"

"Menthol. It'll overwhelm your sinuses. You won't be able to

272

smell anything but mint for hours. It'll ruin your appetite, but that's better than puking on the specimen."

Olivia nodded, applying the gel to her upper lip and making a sour face before pulling her trousers on. "Where is it?"

"The wet lab. You know how to work that camera?"

"I used to do my own videography, when I was just getting started," said Olivia. She offered a quick, shy smile. "Ray came later. Imagine said I had talent, but they wanted me in front of the camera, not hiding behind it."

"Makes sense." Tory stepped into her shoes, checking to see that Olivia was fully clothed before moving toward the door. "Come on. They're going to start without us."

The ship was silent. Tory and Olivia hurried along the deck, neither of them able to shake the feeling that the quiet was somehow ominous: the calm before the storm. They knew the predators were coming, that at least two of them had reached the *Melusine*—at least two, because the one that had taken Ray would have had no reason to come back to the surface for hours, if not days. Predators didn't work like that.

There were more mermaids out there. And they were, without question, hungry.

The wet lab door was closed. Two people Tory vaguely recognized as being part of the too-pretty Imagine security team were standing there. Both were dressed in black, their hands resting lightly on their belts. She could almost have missed the Tasers, if she hadn't been looking for them.

"This lab is in use," said one of them.

"Dr. Toth is expecting us," said Tory.

The men exchanged a look before one of them nodded and opened the door. Voices drifted out, some raised in mild annoyance, others hushed, almost reverent. Tory offered a polite nod in return and slipped through, Olivia moving close in her wake.

The wet lab was designed for this, for dredging things out of the ocean and slicing them into pieces to see what made them work. Plastic sheeting covered the floor and most of the cutting surfaces. A stainless steel table sat at the center of the room, covered by more plastic sheets. And on top of those...

All thoughts of frivolous things like infection and invasion

273

slipped away as Tory stepped forward, jaw dropping open, eyes fixed on the mermaid. It should have been less impressive after seeing the live specimen in the hold, but somehow, it was *more* impressive in contrast. The mermaid in Mr. Blackwell's tank was a mystery, inscrutable, too valuable to kill, too alien to understand. This, though... this was a solvable mystery, something that could be taken apart and reduced to its component pieces.

Mermaid behavior required live subjects. Mermaid language required live subjects. But some questions—how did they mimic human voices? How did they make the transition from water to air? Were they fish or amphibians, or some third option, something stranger still?—could only be answered with a dead one.

The room seemed enormous in its emptiness. Dr. Lennox and Dr. Wilson were off to one side, both wearing plastic scrubs over their clothing, expressions of profound discomfort on their faces. The marine biologists Luis had mentioned were standing near Luis himself, along with...

"Jason." Tory barely recognized her own voice. "What are you doing here? You're a botanist."

"Thank you for the reminder, Victoria," said Jason, lips twisting in a thin smile. "As it happens, I'm here because we need to figure out what these things eat, and they seem likely to be omnivores. So I'm going to be looking at its digestive system. And the term is 'botanical plankton specialist.'"

"Good, you know each other." Dr. Toth turned away from the tray of surgical implements she'd been arranging. "Victoria, scrub and suit. I want you to assist me."

Tory blinked. "Me? But I'm not—"

"Pursuing a specific research goal? That's right. You can hand me tools without my needing to worry that you'll get distracted by a lung bladder. Get your scrubs on." Dr. Toth's attention switched to Olivia, her eyes softening slightly. "Miss Sanderson. You're welcome, of course, but I wasn't expecting you."

Olivia held up her borrowed camera. "I need to record this for Imagine."

"Imagine has things under control," said Mr. Blackwell. Olivia turned. He was sitting in a nearby chair, leg extended stiffly in front of him. If he was in pain, he was doing an admirable job of not showing it. "We have camera and makeup crews en route. I want you in front of the lens, not behind it."

Olivia hesitated, fingers tightening on her camera. Her discomfort and the desire to object were visible in her expression. Finally she nodded. "All right," she said. "I could use some foundation."

"As I've said, makeup crew." His eyes went from her to the mermaid, motionless and cold, waiting to have its secrets spilled. "We can wait for you to be ready. After all, what's the point in preserving something for posterity if we don't do it correctly?"

Olivia, who suspected that the point was getting out of the line of fire, said nothing. She just stood there, alone, and clutched her camera, and waited.

CHAPTER 23

Western Pacific Ocean, above the Mariana Trench: September 3, 2022

Daryl walked the upper deck, anxiety making his hands shake so badly that he feared dropping his borrowed pistol. He wanted to be indoors. No, that wasn't right. He wanted to be on land, miles away from the ocean, well out of the reach of any terrors from the deep that might be looking for hot meat to fill their bellies. Instead here he was, checking the servos that controlled the shield, assigned to wander in the open air while the security teams—the people who had signed *up* for this shit—were safe in the halls. It wasn't right. It wasn't fair. Who cared if the mermaids would have to climb past all those armed fools in their spotless uniforms, with their untried guns, before they got to him? He still should have had a guard. Or two. Or twenty. Not just him and Gregory, alone, exposed, and vulnerable.

"I hear they've got one of those *things* on board," he said. "They're going to dissect it. Take it apart like a salmon and see how it fits together."

"They're scientists," said Gregory. He was smoking, a hand-rolled cigarette that smelled of cloves and pungent marijuana. Tobacco was banned on board—something about tobacco mosaic disease and the plants the botanists were trying to culture in their hydroponic beds—but there was nothing in the rules forbidding pot. It was a loophole no one was in any hurry to close, especially not now.

276

Without the pot to soothe his nerves, he might never have stopped screaming. If it slowed his reaction time a bit, it would also take the edge off any pain that happened to come along—and if one of those watery horrors found them, there would be a lot of pain. "Taking things apart is what they do."

"But these things, they look like people, right? Don't you think they look like people? They've got faces and hands and ... and all the other bits."

"No legs, though. No feet. I think they're halfway to being people at best."

"Those marine biologists say dolphins are people. If humans are people, and dolphins are people, and mermaids are half-human and half-dolphin ..."

"Those marine biologists smoke more weed than I do. They'd probably tell you a glacier was a person, if you got them high enough."

"I'm just saying. If you take a human apart, the other humans will want revenge. That's what humans *do*. And we know dolphins will chase down orcas and sharks that eat their babies."

Gregory gave Daryl a sidelong look. "What are you trying to get at?"

Daryl took a deep breath, tilting his head until he was staring at the sky. Even with the ambient light from the ship, the stars out here were amazing, like beacons to guide the lost ships home. He could have looked at the sky back in California every night until he died, and never seen half that many stars.

"I'm just saying maybe before ... That Wilson girl went into their territory, and they took her. And one of them came up on the ship and took Ray, but we don't know that it was actually hunting, or even that it was trying to hurt him. They go from water to air without a problem. Maybe it was just trying to say hello. Now we've killed one of them. We've killed it. So maybe they're going to be looking for revenge."

Gregory stopped walking. It took Daryl a moment to realize. He stopped in turn, frowning as he lowered his gaze from the sky to the older engineer's face.

"What?" he asked.

"You really think those things are smart enough to understand revenge?" Gregory asked.

"I don't know," said Daryl. "If you'd asked me a week ago, I would've said mermaids weren't real, and that this whole damn trip was just PR. But now they're real, and they're killing people, and we don't know anything about them. They were smart enough to sink that submersible thing. What else can they do?"

Gregory didn't answer. They stood under a sky filled with a million stars, and the night had never seemed so vast, or so cold. Neither of them went near the rail. They were both sensible enough to be afraid of what they might see if they looked down at the unforgiving sea, which roiled and rolled and did not care that they were alive, or that they were small and far from home. The sea would continue as it always had, indifferent to the concerns of humanity.

Had they looked, they might not have seen anything. Daryl was inexperienced compared to Gregory, and more, he was letting his nerves get the better of him; he was seeing danger in every corner, and allowing it to blind him to the danger that was actually lurking. He would have seen the smooth sweep of the hull, the fruit of human labor and innovation, intended to protect them from the dangerous waters. He would have seen how high up he was, and how far the mermaids would need to climb, and felt this rendered him safe, somehow. Protected, sheltered, like a small fish choosing to believe the coral reef can offer genuine protection from the jaws of the eel, the arms of the octopus.

Gregory, who had sailed on vessels like this one in the past, might have fared a little better. He might have seen the scrapes along the bottom fifteen feet of the hull, the ones that hadn't been made by normal wear and tear. They didn't match anything he'd ever seen before. It was difficult for the modern mind to jump to "monsters" as the answer to what could have made those scratches on the side of the ship, those little nicks and rips in the metal. Monsters didn't make any sense.

But they had sailed off the edge of the map, into the waters the cartographers had marked with "Here be monsters" and a picture of something terrible and toothy—a warning to unwary sailors that this was, perhaps, not the best route to carry them home.

Daryl and Gregory remained on their high deck, in their seemingly safe place, and didn't notice the claw marks trailing from the waterline up the side of the ship. They didn't see the places where the rails dripped with sticky mucus, secreted from specialized glands, greasing the path of creatures that had evolved as far away as possible from the treetops and open plains of the cradle of humanity. They didn't *understand*.

Following the marks would have taken them to the water, and below; the nicks and scratches didn't stop where the sea began, but proliferated, becoming deeper, more common, more pronounced. There was no hesitation in the marks under the surface. There the creatures that had made them had not needed to contend with gravity, to fight for their grips against the constant motion of the sea. They could simply cling, claws hooking onto metal, and plan their next moves.

Below that, where the bulk of the *Melusine* created a patch of artificially calm water, was the photic zone—a seemingly false name now, with the sun down and the waters as dark as they had ever been. But light *could* pierce these depths when someone turned on one of the *Melusine*'s running lights, or when the scientists activated another of their clever little toys. Drones and autonomously propelled cameras moved through the dark beneath the ship, turning the water into a teeming web of motion.

The deepest any of them dove was fifteen feet below the hull. They were small machines; they needed tethers to keep them from being swept away by the current, and their operators needed a clear signal to continue issuing commands. Diving any deeper would have resulted in losing the connection, and possibly consigning expensive research equipment to the abyss.

So none of the cameras saw the forms lurking another fifteen feet down, hovering suspended, staying stable with sweeps of their webbed hands. The glitter of their hair would show up on the recordings, but it was faint, low, in an area known for the bioluminescence of its night things. There might be a few operators who would put together what that distant sparkling meant, who might realize they were being watched...but then again, there might not. It was so faint, after all. It was so delicate. And even with the evidence of their eyes and Heather's and Ray's deaths speaking to the truth of the matter, even with the captain putting the ship on alert, there were still people on the *Melusine* who didn't believe in mermaids. They were chasing myths, not monsters. The evidence of their eyes would be, not ignored, but certainly discounted, given less weight than the things they *knew*.

The things they knew were the things that were likely to get them killed.

In the dark below the hull, the front line of mermaids lingered. There were nineteen of them, eyes turned toward the outline of the boat, hair drifting in tangled, light-spangled clouds. The light it put off wasn't enough for human eyes to pick out fine details, but for the mermaids, whose pupils had expanded to their widest, hungriest state, it was more than sufficient. Their hands moved in constant conversation, all speaking and answering at the same time, never pausing, clawing their way toward consensus one signed disagreement at a time.

Half the mermaids advocated for immediate assault. They remembered other ships that had sailed through these waters, with their steep sides and their soft centers. They remembered the taste of man-flesh, even if they hadn't shared in the bounty already taken from the *Melusine*. It was sweeter than dolphin, more filling than squid; if this ship was half as full as others had been, it could feed the entire colony for as much as a month—even the eldest—and allow them to lay in stores against the next change in the waters.

The other half called for caution, for patience, for moving slowly in the pursuit of a cleaner kill. They, too, remembered the taste of man-flesh, but unlike their more eager cousins, they remembered harpoons, bullets, the reality of death at the hands of these strange air-breathing creatures. There were few things in these waters that could kill an adult mermaid. They were too fast, too deadly, and too clever. The two-legged things in their artificial floating reefs were born killers, and they would do what they were made for if they were given half a chance.

The argument raged, tucked safely away beneath the waves. When it was done, things would continue. When it was done, things would change.

"Scalpel."

Tory dropped the tool into Dr. Toth's palm, unable to tear her eyes from the mermaid's chest cavity. The bullets had ripped through several internal organs (including a lung; Tory thought

Dr. Toth might never stop glaring at the Abneys for that), but the beauty of the body was in its symmetry: for everything that had been destroyed, there was usually a parallel organ still intact, waiting to be taken out and studied.

"Thank you." Dr. Toth leaned forward, positioning herself within the butterfly span of the mermaid's ribcage, which had been snipped open and spread using a tool intended for spreading the ribs of dolphins. It was a bit too aggressive for the task: several of the thin, delicate ribs had been snapped in the process, breaking like kindling. Only the fact that the specimen was already damaged had made it possible to continue with the tools and facilities provided. Data loss on this scale was no longer a concern.

Pressing her scalpel against the membrane surrounding one of the upper organs in the mermaid's chest, Dr. Toth said conversationally, "The structure appears to mimic the pericardium, leading me to believe that fluid retention is an essential part of the creature's biology. Based on location in the body, I believe I am about to reveal the heart."

She had been narrating her every move for the cameras. Tory admired how smooth her voice was, and how careful she was to say "I think" and "I believe," rather than making definitive statements. She didn't *know* she was about to reveal the heart. She might be slicing into a ball of fat, or a nesting site for some symbiotic parasite. Everything about this creature was a mystery, and by never claiming anything for certain, Dr. Toth made sure she would never be caught in a lie.

The scalpel bit into the membrane, which opened to reveal the knotted muscle of the creature's heart. Dr. Toth continued, "The heart appears to have multiple chambers. Further study will need to wait until I have finished my initial assessment." She cut the heart free with quick strokes of her scalpel, lifting it out of the chest cavity and placing it in one of the waiting pans.

Blood gushed from the heart as it was set down. The fluid was thin and viscous, as much yellow as red. It was not mammalian blood. Nothing mammalian could have survived with that fluid running through its veins.

"The left side of the chest was severely damaged when the creature was killed; the tissues will be analyzed, but as there's no way to guarantee a lack of cross contamination, they won't be used in the formal results." Dr. Toth reached into the right side of the chest. "All the organs in the upper body are separated by what look to be unusually large, spacious membranes similar to the one around the heart. Hypothesis: the gas or fluid contained in these sacs allows the creature to balance its water retention, and hence weight, depending on where it hangs in the water. There may be an element of conscious control to the retention and release of water."

"That would also change the effects of pressure on the body," said Dr. Lennox, not quite interrupting, but sliding into the space between her words. Dr. Toth shot him a hard look. He didn't seem to notice. "These creatures are moving between incredibly different environments just by going from the Challenger Deep to the surface. Coming into the open air is almost a step too far. They should explode, unless they have a way to compensate for pressure changes."

"Why, because they have lungs?" Dr. Toth got her hands under the offending structure, lifting it out of the mermaid's chest cavity. "Please note that the lung in question is two-thirds the size I'd expect in a mammal of this size, and does not show the same complexity of form. Victoria?"

"Here," said Tory, sliding a tray under the mermaid's lung. Dr. Toth put it gently down.

"Take this to the secondary dissection table; we're going to get into it in a moment," said Dr. Toth.

"Yes, Doctor," said Tory, and retreated with the lung, watching the light strike rainbows off its smooth, grayish surface. It was a color like but unlike the connective tissue hidden beneath a salmon's scales. It smelled oily, astringent; if she'd been asked to identify the species on smell alone, she couldn't have done it. She supposed that was exactly right. Something this new shouldn't be too similar to something old.

Dr. Toth continued to work. "I have a secondary lung here," she said, a note of excitement in her voice. "The previous lung was more like our classic understanding of the organ. This is more like an air bladder. It's the sort of structure I'd expect to find in a snakehead or other fish capable of surviving out of the water." She eased the secondary lung free, holding it up.

It was small, dense, and almost pitch black. No blood dripped from the severed tubing that had connected it to the rest of the organs. Instead a brackish liquid trickled out, intensifying when she turned the organ in her hand. The liquid was accompanied by a strong fishy smell, like something decaying on the beach. Dr. Toth's smile grew.

"I understand now," she said beatifically, and set the secondary lung in one of the waiting trays before turning to Mr. Blackwell. "I know how they're doing it."

Theo raised an eyebrow. "How?" he asked.

"They don't just have a dual breathing system. We expected that. It made *sense*. Gills for underwater, lungs for above. Sure, that would make them evolutionarily unique and more than a little redundant, and it wouldn't explain the pressure problem, but it would enable them to exist."

"The pressure problem?" asked Olivia. She managed to make the question sound intelligent, despite the fact that it was what Bill Nye the Science Guy would have called a straight line: it was there purely to get the people who knew more than she did to perform for the cameras.

Dr. Toth turned to her, looking baffled. Like everyone else, except perhaps Tory, she'd forgotten about Olivia as soon as the woman had gone to have her makeup fixed. Olivia hadn't made any effort to reinsert herself into the conversation. People who knew what they were doing were working: she was just here to record it all for posterity and, when necessary, to make sure they verbalized their work.

"Oh," said Dr. Toth. "Yes. The pressure problem. Water has weight. So does air, but the weight of air is negligible compared to the weight of water. Because water is an immersive medium, most creatures that live in it don't notice it's there—they've adapted to the pressure. They can handle it. They can't all handle sudden changes, which is why deepwater fish have been known to explode when pulled to the surface by a fishing net. We know these mermaids live deep but surface to hunt. Not unknown—many species of squid do that, as do some types of shark—but rare enough to be worth remarking upon. I'd been wondering how they were able to accomplish the transition. It's harder on air breathers like us, you see. Our lungs are filled with gas. Gas doesn't do well with pressure changes. Whales and dolphins have incredibly powerful lungs. They can hold their breath for hours. That lets them dive at a measured pace, and come back up the same way. There's a reason young whales tend to stay closer to the surface."

"We know the mermaids don't behave like that," said Dr. Lennox. Dr. Toth shot him an irritated look, but didn't say anything. He was young, handsome, photogenic; he would play well on the camera, and she wanted this to come out. She wanted people to watch and *understand*.

They were going to die. She'd been sure of that since the moment she spread the mermaid's ribs and saw the puzzle-piece organs nestled inside, waiting to share their mysteries. Some of those mysteries had been self-solving, so obvious that every incision and examination just confirmed what she already knew. The secondary lung, for example. The conclusions were clear. There had never been any other way for this to end.

"The mermaids can't raise their young at the surface; unless they undergo a metamorphosis so profound that juveniles are literally unrecognizable, which is unlikely—it's metabolically inefficient—there's no way they could be nurturing their infants above the bathypelagic level without being seen. Further, we know they're true water breathers. They're not amphibians, or if they are—"

"And they are," said Dr. Toth calmly.

Dr. Lennox shot her a sidelong look and continued, "—if they are, they've somehow pulled off a redundant system that nothing else on Earth has achieved. They're air breathers *and* water breathers."

"Dr. Toth," said Olivia. "As the supervisory biologist on this necropsy, do you have a comment?"

"First, you are correct that I am a biologist: I have a degree from the University of Hawaii, and another from Columbia." Dr. Toth shot Dr. Lennox a look of barely veiled contempt. "Despite my focus on supposedly nonexistent creatures—one of which, I will note, is on my dissection table—I am fully competent, and can analyze my findings without the need for a dissenting voice."

"Are you saying you have a contradictory suggestion?" asked Dr. Lennox.

"The axolotl," said Dr. Toth. "They're amphibians. Native to Mexico—or they were, before they became extinct in the wild. Still popular in the pet trade, and since they're all captive bred at this point, I suppose that's for the best. At least it means there are still axolotls in the world. They were viewed as primitive for a long time, because even the adults retained their external gills. Frogs can't breathe underwater, you see. Tadpoles can, but once they transition into their adult forms, that capability is lost. They become air breathers, like mammals. Like all other adult amphibians. Except for the axolotl, which likes the water a lot, and doesn't care much for the land. The axolotl never becomes an air breather."

"It's an adult with attributes of its own juvenile form," said Dr. Lennox, smoothly retaking the reins of the conversation. "Scientists believe the axolotl was a more standard salamander once, before going back to the water."

"Wouldn't it have been easier for the axolotl to never leave the water in the first place?" Olivia somehow managed to make the question sound perky and even smart. Tory's heart ached for her. They were both back to work in the wake of Ray's death, but while he'd been a shadow on the wall for Tory, he'd been the world for Olivia.

For the first time, she realized how much she genuinely cared about Olivia's feelings. Maybe this wasn't just a shipboard fling after all.

Dr. Toth shook her head. "It would have been easier, yes, but evolution has never been about easy. Evolution takes risks. It puts things in new environments, and leaves most of them there to die when they don't work out. But some, if they're quick, or lucky, it allows to come back to where they started. We've always wondered why there weren't more saltwater amphibians. They existed once, in huge numbers, before multiple extinction events cast the seas into the shape they have today. Being an amphibian in the middle of the ocean might not seem to make much sense, but neither does being a dolphin, an otter, or any one of a number of forms that would be more suited to life on or near land, and which nature has chosen to cast utterly adrift." Dr. Toth's hand found the table where the mermaid had been laid out. Gently she put the scalpel down. Still gentle, she turned and brushed the mermaid's tangled hair back from the line of its scalp.

The motion dislodged some of the water trapped there. A small eyeless shrimp scuttled into view for a heartbeat before scuttling away again, vanishing into the hair.

"Air-breathing creatures have difficulty descending too deep because of the bends. Bubbles in the blood. Nitrogen poisoning. And the pressure, of course. You can never discount the pressure. Water-breathing creatures struggle making the transition between the abyssopelagic and photic zones. The absence of pressure is as fatal for them as the presence of pressure would be for us. It's a way of isolating one ecosystem from another. Never the twain shall meet. But these beauties...Ah."

She stroked the mermaid's hair again. It was a strangely tender gesture, until she picked up a bowl. With one quick, concussive motion, she lifted the mermaid's head, breaking the seal its hair had formed against the sheet. Water cascaded out, washing into the bowl, carrying dozens of eyeless shrimp in its wake. They weren't the only things to wind up in her artificial tide pool. Tiny crabs with shells like jewels tumbled into the water and scuttled to the edges of the tub, their claws raised in warning. Worms, segmented and delicate and no more than an inch long, curled in tight balls, apparently dying on contact with the light. One of the crabs grabbed a worm in its claws, retreating to the corner and stuffing it, segment by segment, into its waiting maw.

"Amphibians that learned to dive deeper and deeper, but never gave up the convenience of their adult forms. They kept their gills. They kept their lungs. They developed air bladders, to let them balance themselves in the water. And they developed secondary lungs, not to let them breathe better, but to filter the gas out of their blood. They use the secondary structures to purge themselves as they dive. That way, they don't get sick. They don't die. They can code switch faster than any other life form on the planet, and all because they were frogs who didn't like the estuary they started in."

Dr. Toth picked up her bowl, casting around until her eyes settled on Jason. "You," she said. "What's your name?"

"Uh," he said. "Jason Rothman, ma'am."

"The plankton specialist; good," she said, thrusting the bowl in his direction. He stepped forward to take it with shaking hands, staring in awe at the tiny creatures within. One of the crabs had a scrap of kelp in its claws, and was waving it like a terrible pom-pom. Dr. Toth ignored his expression as she turned back to the creature, saying, "I think you're going to find some new species in here. Go. Sort through the microscopic debris and make a bigger name for yourself. I have bigger fish to worry about."

"I believe the phrase is *to fry*," drawled Michi. The cameras switched their eyes to her. She was striking: photogenic, dangerous, with an accent that threw American audiences off their stride. People who'd never left their hometowns might expect a woman who looked like her to have an accent. They wouldn't expect it to be Australian. "Speaking of, remember, that's our kill. If we're slapping this prawn on the barbie, me and Jacques get first bite."

"It's your kill, and it would be more than happy to kill you," said Dr. Toth dryly. "We haven't done tissue analysis yet. For all we know, this creature is packed with heavy metals and novel toxins. Your first bite would be your last."

"But we'd be the first people in history to eat a mermaid, so maybe that wouldn't be such a terrible way to go," said Michi. Her tone was mild; her eyes were cold, and while she was speaking to Dr. Toth, her gaze never left the mermaid. Neither she nor Jacques had been pleased that their kill was going to be dissected—or that their contracts with Imagine meant they had no grounds to object.

"There are issues with the word *mermaid*, but we'll go into those in a moment." Dr. Toth settled the creature's head on the table, moving to the open wound of its chest cavity. She reached for her scalpel. "The location of the secondary lungs indicates a slow development cycle. The creatures probably start fully aquatic, and move closer to the surface in adolescence, as adult structures develop. This would account for their continuing awareness of the surface world, and the surface world's continuing awareness of them. Lungs grow, creature rises. Sailors see creature, creature eats sailors, everyone remains aware of one another. It's a novel hunting pattern. They got the whole damned sea, and it wasn't enough for them. They wanted everything above it. If there's anything that confirms their intelligence, it should be that. The only other creatures that push their habitat so hard are humans."

Mr. Blackwell frowned. Tory tensed. If there was any point at which the rest of them would be tossed out of the room in favor of Imagine's pet scientists, this was it. A gross biological study wasn't the same as unraveling the secrets of the deep, but it was a start. All the NDAs in the world couldn't cause them to unlearn something they'd learnt.

"You haven't explained the vocal mimicry," said Mr. Blackwell. "How are they copying our voices?"

"That's going to be in the larynx," said Dr. Toth. "I'm still trying to figure out—"

"Mimicry, please."

Dr. Toth paused. Looking at her, Tory couldn't help but think that if anyone else had tried to shift her area of inquiry, they would have been at risk of getting that scalpel jammed into their eye.

Finally Dr. Toth said, "All right. But I'm going to need someone to photograph everything in the central cavity as it is now, in case of tissue loss. These structures were never intended to be exposed to air. Victoria, get over here and help me steady the head."

That was all; with those words, Dr. Toth put down her scalpel and moved a foot to her left, palpating the skin of the creature's throat with her thumb and forefinger.

"The throat contains rigid structures which feel analogous to the structures found in mammalian throats. There are no known structures of this type in amphibians."

"So you're saying you're wrong, and it's not a giant frog after all?" asked Michi.

The look Dr. Toth shot her was pure irritation. Mr. Blackwell had the authority and history to contradict her. This Australian upstart in her khakis and her bloodlust did not.

"I never said it was a giant frog," she said. "It may not be an amphibian at all, according to modern definitions of the word. The trouble with nature is that nature doesn't care about us. The world made us, and it was done. Sink or swim, we're on our own. The thing people forget about survival of the fittest is that it doesn't *work*. You really think the giraffe was the fittest? Or the kakapo? Even our friend the axolotl has no business existing. Nature has made and rejected and lost and remade more biological diversity than currently exists. These creatures are amphibious as we understand the word, because we need to put things into the framework of what we know. I'm still making guesses. I'm sure at least one of them is going to be wrong enough to make me look pretty damn stupid when we understand these creatures better."

"You keep saying 'creatures,'" said Olivia. "Why not call them 'mermaids'?"

"As I said before, we're going to get into why that word is inaccurate in a moment. Mr. Blackwell would like to know how they're able to mimic human voices. That has to take priority, as he speaks for Imagine's interests on this voyage, and they're paying the bills." She tilted the creature's chin up. "Victoria, steady the head."

"Yes, Doctor," said Tory, moving into position. She was grateful to be out of the line of fire, even as she was sure it wouldn't last. Clamping her fingers around the curve of the creature's skull, she held it fast and watched Dr. Toth begin palpitating the gills.

Inaccurate. Why would the word *mermaid* be inaccurate? The creature was clearly the truth behind the myth. Even if there were similarly formed cousins in its family, things that resembled it as humanity resembled apes and chimpanzees, it was so much closer to the myth than anything else had ever been that there was no question. It had a hominoid upper body and a piscine lower body; it had clouds of flowing hair surrounding a face that was simultaneously alien and distressingly human. Nothing else could have been the source of the mermaid myth.

Tory paused, eyes going wide. Dr. Toth glanced up, catching the change in her expression, and nodded approvingly.

"Now you've got it," she said, voice pitched low. "I knew you were a clever one." More loudly, she said, "I'm going to open the throat. This will almost certainly sever some of the connections between the gills and the breathing structures; we're going to need another specimen to determine how those work."

"Maybe you should stop," said Dr. Lennox. "We can do a more thorough examination of the intact specimen, and then—"

"We still won't know how they achieve their mimicry." Dr. Toth looked to Mr. Blackwell. "What do you want me to do?"

"Proceed," said Mr. Blackwell. He silenced Dr. Lennox's objections with a raised hand and a mild, "I have absolute faith that this creature won't be the last one to land on a lab table before we're done here. No matter how intelligent they are, we're going to fight back if they attack us, and now that contact has been made, we can't retreat and leave them to be exploited by people with fewer scruples. We need to understand them."

It's hard to get less scrupulous than killing intelligent creatures and taking them apart just to understand how they work, thought Tory, and said nothing. This was Dr. Toth's show. Tory might have resented that once, when all she'd been thinking about was revenge on something as vast and implacable as the sea itself, but that had been a lot of miles ago, standing on solid ground. This was the middle of the sea. Things were different here.

Dr. Toth sliced into the throat. The skin opened like a seam. It was thicker than human skin, clinging to a thin layer of yellowish subcutaneous fat. The opening revealed the complex folds and creases of the larynx, the soft flaps of the vocal cords. Dr. Toth put the scalpel aside and slipped her fingers into the opening, moving smoothly. There was no hesitation on her part; she knew what she was looking for.

"Structurally, this is like nothing I've seen before," she said. "There are aspects that mirror the human throat, to a certain degree; they would certainly be able to replicate most of the sounds we make. But there are structures closer to the breathing apparatus of the octopus. Essentially, the creatures can mimic us because they have a sophisticated organ designed for that exact purpose nestled in their throats. Why? I don't know. Why not might be the better question, evolution being what it is."

She removed her hands from the throat, nodding to Tory to indicate that the younger woman could release the creature's head. Calmly, she moved back to the cavity of its abdomen, reaching inside and moving the liver out of the way.

"It's almost nice to have a specimen so damaged," she said conversationally. She knew the cameras were drinking in her every word; she didn't look at them, but she smiled as she spoke. "Normally, we'd be concerned about cross contamination. The bullets did so much damage that it's moot now. We can just work. It's a brute force form of biology, and it's a good reminder of where we came from. This may be the most sophisticated necropsy ever performed on one of these creatures. It's still close kin to every procedure performed in the belly of a whaling ship. We have better lighting. That's about it."

Dr. Toth lifted an object that looked something like a bladder. "It would be foolish to assume these creatures were live-bearers just because they superficially resemble primates. But it would be equally foolish to assume they wouldn't have some sort of system for storing eggs. This is a sperm sac. More importantly, if you look lower in the body, you'll find something that looks very familiar to anyone who knows anything about cephalopod anatomy."

There was a long pause before Jason asked, sounding scandalized, "Are you telling us this thing is a *male*?"

"I am," said Dr. Toth. Her voice was mild, her gaze steady; she knew what she was saying, and had already looked at it from all possible angles. She was confident of her conclusion. "A male of breeding age. We knew they weren't mammals. They don't have breasts; they have curved ribs, giving the illusion of an appealing form. This has always been about mimicry. They want to look attractive so we'll lower our guard. What better way to accomplish that than by looking sexually available? But they're not. They're not mammals; even if some of them are females, not all of them are, and they're not mermaids."

A sound broke the pause that followed her words. It took a moment for Tory to realize that Mr. Blackwell was laughing. Every head turned toward him.

He smiled without humor. "Two ships," he said. "Millions of dollars, hundreds of lives, and for what? We still haven't found the mermaids we were looking for."

"Perhaps not," said Dr. Toth. "But we've found sirens. They're real. And more, they've found us. What comes next...That's what's going to determine whether any of this was worth it."

"Do you think it was?" asked Olivia.

Dr. Toth turned to look at the smaller woman. She raised her eyes to the camera, looking into the lens for a long moment before she said, calmly, "No," and turned back to her necropsy.

"Dr. Toth, this is all fascinating, but what is it going to tell us about these things?" Michi stretched. She was like some large predatory cat, waiting for the opportunity to kill something. It was difficult not to watch her, not out of admiration, but out of a sense of self-preservation. "I can go get you another one, if you need a basis for comparison."

"Oh, you don't need to go get me another one; I'm sure they're on their way," said Dr. Toth. "We've killed one of their own."

"They've killed two of us," snapped Olivia, professional façade breaking for a moment.

Dr. Toth turned to look at her. Not at the camera; at her. There was sympathy in the older woman's eyes. It would have surprised many of her students. It didn't surprise her husband, who watched her from his seat as he had watched her from the decks of environmentalists' antiwhaling ships. He'd fallen in love with her because of that sympathy, which was as bottomless as the living sea.

"When someone kills an American citizen, we don't say, 'Oh well, we killed one of theirs last week; we're calling it even,'" she said. "We declare war. We sweep civilizations off the face of the globe. They won't care that they started it. They're only going to care who finishes it, and to be honest, I'm not sure it's going to be us."

She turned back to the body. "Scalpel," she said, and the necropsy went on.

ZONE FIVE: ABYSSOPELAGIC

I guess I just wanted my sister to be proud of me. That's what sisters want, right? They want to be good enough to be proud of.

—Victoria Stewart

I'm not a reporter. I'm a propaganda machine, and I've never written my own script.

—Olivia Sanderson

We know Imagine—acting under the auspices of failing CEO James Golden—has launched a follow-up to the doomed *Atargatis* mission. What we don't know is exactly why. However...

You may remember last year, when we managed to get on a whale-watching tour hosted by none other than Victoria "Tory" Stewart, younger sister of Anne Stewart, the Imagine "television personality" who died on the *Atargatis*. She was fun, savvy, and unwilling to discuss the Mariana mermaids... even though we knew she was working with cryptid enthusiast Luis Martines (whose parents have essentially been funding her research for the last few years). News flash, Victoria: we know you're looking for the little mermaid who can give you back your sister's voice. You're not going to find her.

Now the question becomes, can anyone find Tory? We went to inquire as to her feelings about the Imagine mission, only to discover that she'd been fired by the whale-watching business. She's no longer telling tourists what an orca looks like. What's more, both she and Luis are missing from the aquarium where they'd been conducting the bulk of their work. Add the absence of Dr. Jillian Toth from her teaching position, and, well...

Whatever Imagine is looking for out there, they appear to have collected the world's experts on mermaids to help them find it. Maybe we're about to find out what happened to the *Atargatis* after all.

> —From *Looking for Bigfoot: A Cryptozoological Journal*, by Alexander Townsend, originally posted 2022

I've spent my life looking for mermaids. And I've found them. Oh yes, I've found them. I've found them in the spaces between stories, in the breaks in the fossil record, and in the oral histories of a hundred civilizations. I don't think we forgot them on purpose. I think we did it because we had to. These were monsters we could neither fight nor flee. Our only choice, if we wanted to claim the seas and hence the world, was to learn to pretend that they weren't there.

We ignored them out of our daily existence. Only now, when airplanes have freed us from the seas, do we have the luxury of believing them back into being.

—Transcript from the lecture "Mermaids: Myth or Monster," given by Dr. Jillian Toth

CHAPTER 24

Western Pacific Ocean, above the Mariana Trench: September 3, 2022

The clock in the closed wet lab ticked toward three in the morning. The necropsy was done, the air smelling of fish and the deep. Dr. Jillian Toth stood silent and alone, eyes playing along the wreckage of the monster she'd pursued for most of her life.

Nothing would be wasted. Even now, technicians were sectioning and preserving the organs. They'd be coming soon to claim the rest of the body and strip it to nothing. The bones would be articulated, strung like a classroom skeleton, minus the ribs smashed by the Abneys' bullets. The flesh would be packed for later analysis.

(Jillian was sure Michi Abney was arguing with Theo, defending her right to at least a few fillets from the siren's tail. She respected the hunter's single-minded determination to taste her kill, even as she knew it was a terrible idea. It would be weeks before the siren could be fully analyzed. No meal, however unique, was worth dying over. But there were people in the world who thought nothing of preparing their own blowfish sushi, so she supposed if Michi died of this, at least she'd be in good company.)

Mermaids had become Jillian's obsession after her husband's injury left them marooned on the great island of North America. Theo had said, again and again, that he'd understand if she went back to sea; they'd been reaching a point where they'd need a terrestrial

297

home regardless of their health, because Lani needed to go to school with children her own age, needed to learn how to live in the world, not move alongside it, rendered alien by cultural illiteracy.

Maybe if they'd settled in Hawaii, as Jillian had proposed, she would have been...not well, but better. Better able to adapt. Better able to feel the roll of the sea beneath her feet, moving into her hips, keeping her spine in the alignment she was used to. But Theo hadn't wanted to be close to the water. Theo hadn't wanted to be reminded of what he'd lost. He'd been fine with the idea that she'd be out there, having adventures, touching the waves he was denied, as long as he didn't have to watch.

His injury hadn't shattered them. The healing that came after had. One day she had looked at her husband and realized everything about her life and career had become a shameful secret, something she had to hide when she was home, lest she break his heart all over again. She hadn't blamed him then and she didn't blame him now. He'd been through something terrible, and he'd found the strength to come out the other side, not stronger, but intact. "Intact" had been more than they could dream, once. Now...

Intact wasn't enough. Broken wasn't bad. She would have settled for serviceable, for a shape they both could live with, and that was exactly what she hadn't been allowed to have. By the time the *Atargatis* had happened, with its cargo of guilt and recrimination, their marriage had already been all but over.

"You were the lovely ladies of the sea," she informed the siren, looking at its alien face. There were things to be learned from the structure of its eyes, from the way its teeth slotted together, like a zipper meant to rip and rend, but those things were for other people, not for her. She would use their findings to establish a better understanding of everything else about the creatures, how they moved, how they hunted. The gross aspects of their physicality were already answering so many questions.

They used their voices for hunting more than for conversation; if they had a spoken language—Daniel and Tory seemed certain they did; Hallie was less sure—it was primitive, probably intended for use with children too young to have mastered signing. In hearing humans, at least, basic sign came before speech, with more complicated sign following verbalization. And if they metered their mimicry, picking and choosing the sounds they put out into the world, they would inevitably have found some way to use that mimicry to communicate.

It didn't really matter whether they had a language of their own. They stole language from every creature in the sea. If Jillian were asked, she would have said they had no spoken language, because they had too many teeth. The risk of injury was worth it if their stolen songs lured in dinner for the school; it wasn't a fair trade for a whispered phrase or a muttered complaint. What's more, the structures of the siren's larynx indicated that lips weren't used as extensively in its mimicry as they were in human speech.

The lights in their hair . . . Bioluminescence was common in deepsea organisms. Trying to decide which had come first—the lights or the enormous light-hungry eyes or the intricate sign language—was a fool's errand. They had all three. She might as well join the age-old argument of which had come first, mankind's brain or fleshy buttocks or flexible tongue. Nature made what nature wanted to make. Sometimes it came together perfectly. Other times it all fell apart.

"You were the perfect predator," she said softly. "You look like us, you sound like us . . . There must have been a time when you lived closer to shore. There's no other reason for you to be so good at playing pretend. If you'd stayed in shallow water, we might never have set sail. We would have been too afraid of the voices in the deep. So what drove you away? What kept you from coming back? What aren't you *telling* me?"

The siren didn't answer.

Dr. Jillian Toth, the world's foremost expert on creatures like this one, creatures that had been only myths and legends until a ship sailed above the Mariana Trench and sent footage home, stood looking at the body in front of her. She was missing something. She knew that she was missing something. And if she didn't figure out what it was soon, they were all going to pay for it. One way or another, someone always, always paid.

Jason carried the basin with the utmost care, trying to keep his hands from shaking. His heart was beating too fast, rendering him unsteady, and he wasn't watching where he was going. He knew that was dangerous; one trip and he'd be watching a whole new world of biological science run down the nearest drain. That didn't help. He still couldn't take his eyes off the things—the living, impossible things—teeming in his stolen tide pool, going about their business, unaware that everything had changed.

The crabs! They were unlike anything he'd ever seen. From the way they carried their elegantly curved claws tucked against their bodies, he half suspected them of being stomatopods that had undergone unchecked carcinization, becoming more and more crab-like. There were tiny pseudoshrimp, their tails banded in palest pink and transparent white, and if the crabs had evolved from mantis shrimp, he was reasonably sure these had as well, continuing to exist alongside their cousins, seeking cooperative niches in the same self-contained ecosystem.

Humans did not enjoy having head lice, had created tools and medicines to dispose of them, choosing to pretend that people were individual organisms, not merely the largest component of a colony composed of mites and bacteria and viruses. In the sea, cooperative symbiosis was much more common. He could picture infant mermaids—sirens, whatever Dr. Toth wanted to call them—cradled by their parents, scalps touching, until the tiny parasites transferred from one to the other.

(It was a very anthropomorphic idea of an underwater civilization, complete with nuclear families of sirens guiding one another through the depths. He knew that, even as he contemplated it at giddy length. There was so much here to discover, so much to learn and know, and they were all going to be superstars when they made it back to land, because they were going to be the ones who'd been *there* when it happened.)

There was also the chance—small as it was—that examining the creatures in the shallow basin would reveal some unsuspected metamorphosis. Dr. Toth thought the sirens were amphibians, or something so close to amphibians as to make no functional difference. Well, even the largest frog started life as a tadpole. Unless the sirens were like the paradoxical frog, which was larger as a juvenile than it was as an adult, there was every reason to suspect they might look completely different in infancy. They could be tadpoles, or sleek, squid-like creatures, darting through the deep.

Or they could be jeweled, segmented worms, cradled in the hair of their parents until they were mature enough to develop clutching hands and thrashing tails, and propel themselves out into the deep and generous sea.

He could be holding a basinful of baby mermaids.

He could be holding the goddamn *golden ticket*, and Dr. Toth had just *handed* it to him, like it didn't matter as much as her dead monster. He could raise his own sirens from larval form, raise them to respect him as their parent and keeper, and she'd be the one standing on the sidelines then, wouldn't she? Let Dr. Toth come to him, hat in hand and his moon-eyed ex-girlfriend at her side, begging for scraps of his research, and would he grant her requests? Would he be magnanimous?

Of course he would. Because her name would carry the weight of legend after this trip, when the sirenologist sailed across the world, looking for mermaids, and came back with irrefutable proof of their existence. She'd be involved, because her involvement would benefit him. Tory, on the other hand, could just watch as he unraveled the mysteries of the creatures that had taken her sister and consumed her every waking moment. That would be a fitting punishment for her transgressions.

Part of him knew he wasn't over her, and wouldn't be until he stopped thinking of "fitting punishments" for the crime of breaking up with him. The rest of him didn't care. She'd hurt him. He would never be immature enough to go looking for revenge, but if revenge happened to come his way...

The door to his advisor's lab was unlocked. Jason breathed a sigh of relief. Dr. Lyons didn't always feel like sharing space with his assistant; even though it was Jason's association with Tory that had tipped the balance on their being offered a place on the *Melusine*, Dr. Lyons still had a tendency to act as though Jason were some kind of scientific freeloader, looking for a tropical cruise more than he was looking for the truth.

(It didn't help that Jason had overstated his relationship with Tory, even going so far as to imply that they were still a couple, merely "taking a break." It had been expedient. He wasn't sorry to have done it. But he might have been better off finding another way, or at least one that came with fewer awkward questions about why his so-called girlfriend was avoiding him so assiduously.)

"Jason." Dr. Lyons pushed away from his microscope, hands already outstretched to take the precious basin away. "What took you so long? I was getting ready to send a search party." The words were jocular, but there was a warning in his tone, reminding Jason that all the work they did here—everything, from the analysis to the dissections to the preservation—was going to have someone else's name listed first. Nothing he did was going to get him ahead of the story.

Well. Maybe nothing. There were always options, if he was feeling clever. If he was feeling brave. "I had to wait for Dr. Toth to let me take the specimens," he said.

Dr. Lyons looked almost sorry about that, like he'd been hoping for the chance to blame Jason for the delay. He took the basin as he asked, "How many casualties?"

"Four worms died on contact with the light. Two more were eaten by the crab-like things. It seemed less aggressive than reflexive. The crab-like things and the shrimp-like things have been avoiding each other as much as possible. Someone passed me on the stairs and startled one of the crab-like things out of its corner. It was speared and shredded by one of the shrimp-like things." The tiny scrap of chitin and flesh had moved faster than Jason's eye could follow, and the bits of pseudocrab were already gone. The encounter, brief as it was, had him itching to get one of the pseudoshrimp under a microscope. If anything in the basin was a protoform of the sirens, it would be the shrimp.

"There was nothing you could have done to avoid the encounter?"

I could have installed a private stairway when the ship was under construction. Jason bit back his first response. He bit back three more before saying, "No, sir. There's only one available stairway, and I don't have the authority to reserve it for my own use."

"The lift—"

"Was being used by Mr. Blackwell. I'm not allowed to put my needs above those of the corporation, and you instructed me to take the stairs if it was that or spend unnecessary time waiting."

Dr. Lyons glowered before subsiding and saying, "You did well. I expected more fatalities." He turned his back on Jason, dismissing him as he walked to the counter.

Let him try to hog the glory. Jason wasn't going to be that easily disposed of. He followed his mentor, saying, "One of the crab-like creatures had some scraps of plant matter when they were put into the basin. If you find any of it, I'd like it for analysis. I want to determine whether it was harvested near the surface, or whether they have a type of kelp growing around the deep thermal vents." The material he'd seen had been green. Either it came from someplace where there was sunlight, or his theories about underwater photosynthesis were about to get a great deal of additional support.

"You can have what's left when I'm done, Jason. Patience is the watchword."

Patience was *never* the watchword in science. Patience came later. Patience came when they were back on land, milking the results of this journey in an unending effort to make the funding last. Patience came after the first hot rush of discovery.

Dr. Toth understood that. Dr. Toth had chosen knowledge over patience. Without her making that choice, their precious basin would have been empty; the creatures it now contained would have suffocated in the siren's hair.

The hair...Jason went still. There would be no more living specimens there, but it wasn't like Dr. Toth had gone through the siren's hair strand by strand. Any number of specimens could be trapped in the tangles, slowly drying out and losing essential data.

"I have some paperwork to finish," he said, trying to sound nonchalant. "I'll go take care of it now. I can bring back coffee in about an hour, if you don't mind."

"That sounds excellent," said Dr. Lyons, waving dismissively. His eyes stayed on the basin. Jason might as well have already been gone. "Remember, I take mine black."

"I will," said Jason, and turned and fled.

The trip back to the wet lab took less than half the time; he didn't have a basin to carry, no deep-sea wonders to coddle and protect. He mentally reviewed the equipment brought for the necropsy. There were tweezers. Tongs. Gloves, yes; gloves were necessary when dealing with unknown marine organisms. There was no telling how many toxins they carried on their claws and shells. Even the ones that looked harmless could—

"Oof!" exclaimed the woman he had just run into.

Jason staggered back, unsurprised to find that he had, on a ship with over a hundred passengers, collided with his ex-girlfriend. "Victoria," he said coldly.

Tory blinked, getting her feet back under herself. "Jason?" She looked past him, studying the empty deck. "Is something chasing you? I thought we weren't supposed to be out here alone."

"Important errands," he said. "If you're so nervous, why are *you* out here? As you say, we're not supposed to be alone."

"Luis and Olivia are in the lab. A security sweep just came through, so it should be safe for a few minutes. I'm getting coffee." She nodded over her shoulder toward the cafeteria. "No coffee there, in case you wondered. I have to go to the kitchen."

"I'm not looking for coffee," he said. "Olivia. That's the little blonde from Imagine, isn't it? The girl who stole your sister's job?"

"She's the same age we are, Jason. There's no way she could have *done* my sister's job until long after Anne was dead. Imagine wasn't going to retire their entire live-action news division just because they lost a few people."

Jason stared at Tory for a moment. Then he smirked. "You're screwing her."

"What?"

"You heard me. You're screwing her. The way you used to talk, Imagine *should* have shut down their entire news division. Imagine should never have been pretending to care about the news in the first place. Imagine should have done a lot of things, and none of them included hiring pretty little blonde things who look like that girl whose picture you used to keep on our bulletin board. What was her name? Susan? Shawna?"

"Shira," said Tory. "Leave her out of this."

"Shira," echoed Jason. "You know, Tory, I don't know many guys who'd put up with their girlfriend keeping a picture of her ex on the bulletin board behind her desk. You should have known I was a keeper just because of that."

"And see, I knew you were a loser because you kept telling me how awesome you were for not getting mad when I kept a picture of my *good friend* who I happened to have been in a romantic relationship with once in a place where I could see it." Tory scowled. "Shira and I broke up before I met you, remember? She's an archeologist.

She had shit to do that didn't involve hanging around Santa Cruz waiting for me to get it together and stop obsessing over mermaids."

"Looks like you were the smart one," said Jason. "The sea's out there, and the mermaids are out there, and you're going to have your face on every science site in the world. You can write your own ticket after this. And you're still screwing the blonde."

"It's none of your fucking business who I am or am not screwing. We broke up. You don't get to dictate who finds their way into my bed."

"Oh, like I ever did before."

Tory's eyes narrowed. "I never cheated on you, you self-righteous prick. Watch where you're going." She pushed past him and stalked away down the deck, off to whatever destination she'd been seeking when they'd collided.

Jason turned to watch her go. Tory was obsessive and perfectionist and sometimes preferred science to sex—not always at the most convenient of times, either; there had been nights when they'd been an hour into heavy petting, him straining against the front of his pants, her bra hanging off the bedpost, when her phone would ring and she'd go running, saying something about that asshole partner of hers and new results. Jason had occasionally wondered whether Luis had hacked her Fitbit, using it to decide when he needed to be a fucking cockblocker. But that wasn't why they'd broken up.

They'd broken up because she hadn't known how to play politics. Because she'd been more comfortable playing guide for those dead-end whale-watching tours and talking about the vengeance she was going to have someday than she'd been getting out and *doing* something. He'd played the politics. He'd found the ladder and started his upward climb, reasoning—accurately—that if he could hitch his wagon to the right star, he'd be able to reach a position where he could get things done. The fact that they'd wound up in the same place didn't matter. Luck was always a factor, and Tory had gotten lucky. There were a few other people on the *Melusine* who could say the same, people who'd been in the right place at the right time, who'd shown their faces in the right doorways for the wrong reasons. But most of them...most of them were like Jason. They had worked hard for what they had. They were going to keep working hard.

They were in the same place now. That wasn't going to last. Tory was going to have the opportunity to watch her ex-boyfriend make the future while she wound up standing in the past. He hoped her little slut could make it up to her. He sincerely doubted it.

Jason resumed walking, passing the cafeteria and heading for the closed doors to the wet lab. They weren't guarded. He scoffed. The greatest biological discovery of the century, and no one was making sure it didn't get up and walk away. He slipped inside.

"Hello, Jason." Dr. Toth was at the foot of the operating table, resting her hands to either side of the siren's tail, her eyes fixed on the open chest cavity. She looked like a woman who'd been trying to solve the mysteries of the universe without leaving her own head. "I wondered how long it would take you to come back."

"Ma'am," he said, coming to a halt. Dr. Toth was Mr. Blackwell's wife. They didn't advertise it—he wasn't even sure most of the crew knew, since it had been years since they'd been a couple in anything more than the legal sense—but there it was. If she wanted to ban him from the biological tests, she probably could. Best to tread lightly.

"Let me guess: you carried the specimens I gave you to Dr. Lyons, and he took them, because he's the real doctor and you're the graduate student. Young people always think they're hungrier than we are. You forget that you're omnivores, while we've become specialists. It's like a goat asking a koala why it doesn't want to share the eucalyptus." Dr. Toth turned to look at him. "He'll devour you if you let him. Strip you down to your bones and sap every bit of nutrition he can from your flesh, because you're what he used to be, and somewhere deep, he hates you for that. We all do."

"Dr. Toth?" Jason risked a step forward. "Are you feeling all right?"

"I feel fine, and why shouldn't I? I was right about everything. There's something I'm not seeing, but that will come with time. That sort of thing always comes with time." She shook her head. "But you, you're here to ask if you can comb the siren's hair, aren't you? You *were* intending to ask?"

"Of course," lied Jason.

"Good. Yes, you can comb its hair. Pretend to understand what the sailors saw, and pick out every scrap of information you can find. Just make sure you catalog things thoroughly. We'll need to be able to account for every scrap of material we were able to retrieve. You have"—she glanced at the clock on the wall—"ten minutes, maybe a little more, before Theo sends the retrieval team. This pretty thing is going to be sliced up and stored in a hundred jars, until we unpick every mystery it has to offer."

Jason took another step before hesitating. "I thought you'd be happier," he said.

"How's that?"

"I've read your books. I attended one of your lectures." With Tory on his arm, her breast pressed against his elbow as she listened to the woman on stage. She'd been so excited by hearing someone else talk about mermaids like they were real that she'd ridden him hard that night, her passion slamming them against the headboard until his head rang. "This is what you've been looking for. I thought you'd be happier."

"Ah." Dr. Toth looked back to the siren. "It was never about being right. It was never about gloating. It was about proving the existence of a deep-sea predator we kept forgetting about the second our backs were turned. It was about showing the world there was a *threat*. Well, I was right. The threat is real. Two people have died so far on this journey. They're putting safety protocols in place, but they're not going to be enough, and the captain says that we can't close the shutters until we're sure we're under attack, since they use so much power—which is a lie, by the way. Something is keeping them from closing, and he doesn't want to admit it. How many more people are going to die?"

She stepped away from the body.

"I need a drink," she said. "Do what you came here to do. When Theo's men come, you'll have to release the body, so I suggest you do it quickly."

Jason watched her make her way to the door and out onto the deck. Then, as if magnetically drawn, he started toward the body of the siren.

From a distance, it could be mistaken for a bad special effect; it was rubbery and strange, scaleless, limp. The open striations of its muscles and skeletal system were detailed enough to be those of an anatomical model, but those could be fabricated by clever artists with good reason to deceive. From a distance the world hadn't necessarily changed.

As he drew closer, it became more and more apparent that no, the world had changed; the world was never going to be the same. The most skilled makeup artist in the world couldn't have fabricated the delicate texture of the skin, the gleaming pallor of the exposed musculature, the yellow shine of the fat. It was too imperfect and hence perfect, crossing the line between artifice and reality without any hesitation.

Rigor had set in, drawing the siren's lips taut across the sharp-edged bones of its skull. It was hard to look at it like this and understand how the sailors could have mistaken it for a beautiful woman; it was a monster, an alien dweller in the deeps.

"You are ugly as hell," Jason informed the siren, and pulled on a pair of gloves.

He had always had an eye for detail: that was part of what had drawn him to the study of plankton and photosynthesis, both of which required a remarkable amount of patience and fine motor skills. As a child, he'd yearned for his grandmother's needlepoint kits, which were far more appealing than Legos or paint-by-numbers kits. He wanted the tiny nuances of needle and thread, the interplay of distance and attention, to know that missing even a single stitch would change the entire picture. His father had refused to let any son of his play with embroidery hoops, but Jason had found ways, sneaking to his grandmother's room and sitting next to her on the love seat, each of them with needle in hand, watching gardens grow beneath their hands.

He still did needlepoint to relax. Not those pointless "emBROdery kits" that the craft stores tried to force on him, claiming, even as his father had, that real men didn't embroider lilacs and roses; no, he did the *real* kits, the *hard* kits, the ones even battle-hardened grandmothers couldn't tackle without preparation and prayer. He'd won a few awards at the state fair. No first-place ribbons yet, but they would come. Give him time.

Carefully he separated each section of the hair, seeking the scalp and, once there, seeking the small forms that had been trapped when the water went rushing into the first basin. And what treasures he found! Not just pseudocrabs and pseudoshrimp, some still twitching feebly, their mouths bubbling with the frantic effort to breathe; he found more worms, anchored at the roots of the hair. They were motionless but huge compared to their cousins in Dr. Lyons's lab. He'd be able to achieve a full dissection.

He found clusters of fat orange eggs. They were affixed to the hair with a thick, gluey substance, and some of them popped as he coaxed them loose, but most came away intact. He found tiny barnacles rooted to the scalp itself. He even found white, eyeless fish that must have become tangled when the siren surfaced. A few were half-eaten. The pseudoshrimp, judging by the claw marks. It was an entire ecosystem, like every siren was an individual coral reef.

Jason hummed as he worked, unaware of his surroundings, focused entirely on the task at hand. He was going to make history. If he had to do it with a mermaid's head lice, that was fine by him. As long as they remembered his name, he'd be fine.

All they had to do was remember his name.

CHAPTER 25

Western Pacific Ocean, above the Mariana Trench: September 3, 2022

Theo."

Theodore Blackwell stood in front of the tank with the sort of rigid stiffness that spoke to recent application of his medicine, watching the captive siren explore the limits of its confinement. His hands were folded behind his back. He didn't turn.

"Yes, Jilli?"

"Where are your linguists?" Jillian crossed the room to stand next to him.

"Daniel went to get some things from his lab; Hallie is checking on her sister. She realized Holly might not know about the mermaid in the wet lab, and thought it best she hear it from someone who cared about her feelings." He frowned. "I'd been hoping to keep her here a little longer. She really has been immensely helpful."

"So you'd leave Holly to deal with everything that's happened alone? That's cold, Theo." Jillian's eyes sought the siren. "You shouldn't call them mermaids."

"The world will call them mermaids."

"Yes, but we're not the world, and you know better. The one I dissected was male. I suspect this one is, too."

"Why? Fish have low sexual dimorphism. This could easily be a female."

"Amphibians have more pronounced sexual dimorphism, and I'm missing something." She shook her head. "It's staring me right in the face, and I can't see it. I'm tired, and I think I'm a little bit in shock."

"You didn't think we'd find them?"

"We *didn't* find them. They found us. I always knew that would be the case. They don't have our technology, but they have the whole damned sea. If they didn't want to be seen, they weren't going to be. That's how they've stayed out of the science books: when they didn't want us getting in their business, they disappeared." Jillian paused before saying, "I knew we'd wind up sharing space. But somehow, I never translated that into my laying hands on one of them. Seeing how they worked, how they fit together...and now this. A live siren, right in front of my eyes."

"I told you I'd give you the moon one day. You only had to be patient with me."

Jillian sighed. "Have you spoken to Lani recently?"

"She called a little after midnight. I told her we were still taking readings, but that we were hopeful." Imagine's media stranglehold extended to even Theo: he could talk about things that were officially approved for public distribution. He couldn't be the source of any leaks. "She asked how we were getting along. I said it was like old times."

"Even though it's not."

"I don't know. You, and me, and some beautiful thing swimming around its tank, flipping its fins for us to admire. Seems exactly like old times."

Jillian gave him a sidelong look. His eyes were on the siren—on the prize he was taking back to his employers, for whatever reason. Because she knew him. She knew that even if he wanted to claim he was planning to release the thing, he wasn't going to. It was going to accompany the *Melusine* all the way back to shore, and from there...

From there, what would happen would happen. She'd be surprised if there was any word of a "mermaid" touring the aquariums of the world. This was the first, and it was going to disappear.

"From what I remember, in old times, we would have been the ones standing in front of this tank with hammers in our hands, getting ready to set the captive free."

Theo's expression, what she could see of it, hardened. "Some things have to change for the rest to stay the same."

"What are you going to do with it?"

"I'm going to do nothing with it. I have a job, and so do you."

"My job is to learn as much about these creatures as I can. Where this one is going is something I don't know, and that means I need to learn it."

Theo turned to face her. "I love you," he said. His tone was dispassionate: he could have been telling her about the weather. "I've always loved you. We could get divorced tomorrow, we could remain separated for a hundred years, and still I would love you. That doesn't mean I can put your curiosity above the needs of my employers. Please stop asking that of me."

"Oh, Theo." Jillian sighed, reaching out to touch his cheek. It was a glancing contact. He recoiled like he'd been struck. "That, right there, is why I don't trust you, and why I left. You wouldn't give me the ocean, and you wouldn't tell me the truth. I've been second in your life for years. I wasn't going to stand by and let you make me second in our marital bed."

She turned and walked away, leaving Theo alone with the creature she had been chasing for most of her adult life, and neither of them said a word.

'Where have you been?' Holly's fingers were a blur. She wasn't shouting—her hands were close and tight to her body, shutting her off, closing her down—but she was anxious enough that she couldn't seem to slow down.

Hallie, who'd been reading her sister's conversation for as long as she could remember, sighed and signed, 'I was doing my work. When I signed on for this trip, I said you should bring a second translator. I said I might not always be available.'

'Heather is *dead*. How can your work matter now?'

'My work matters more than ever, *because* Heather is dead. I have to make sure she didn't die for nothing.'

Holly stared at her, eyes going wider and wider, until it seemed like they would consume the lower half of her face. Her hands stilled, shaking before they sank into her lap. Stunned to silence, she continued to regard her sister until Hallie squirmed, casting her eyes downward, away from that accusing stare. Holly reached out and tapped Hallie's shoulder, signaling her to look up.

Hallie looked up.

'I don't understand how you can say that,' signed Holly. 'She was your sister. She was my sister. She was the world. Of course she died for nothing. There's no other way she could have died. If she'd been dying for something, the world would have realized it was a stupid thing, and given her back.'

'I'm sorry,' Hallie signed contritely. 'But she knew the risks. She knew what she was doing. She wanted to see the Challenger Deep.'

'Now her bones get to rest there. I don't think that's fair.'

Hallie sighed. 'No,' she agreed. 'It's not. I still have work to do. You have work to do. Don't you want revenge? Don't you want payback? We can have it. I'm going to figure out how these things communicate. I'm going to learn their language, and I'm going to tell them to go to hell. They don't get to kill our sister and live.'

'You aren't just fascinated by the science?'

'I have the chance to learn the first full nonhuman language. Of course I'm fascinated.' Hallie knew better than to lie to her sister. It would have been transparent. Her hands continued moving. 'You should be fascinated too. Their bodies are probably full of novel compounds. Things you've never seen before. But if you start testing their blood, looking at the water, maybe you can find something that will kill them. I want to kill them. We can do a better job of killing them if we understand them.'

Holly nodded, eyes filling with tears. 'I miss her,' she signed. 'I woke up and I opened my eyes and I thought it was a dream. I thought she would be here. She wasn't here. She isn't going to be here ever again. She's gone.'

'She is,' agreed Hallie. 'So let's make sure they pay for what they did. Are you with me?'

Holly nodded again, faster this time, some of the fire coming back into her eyes. 'Yes,' she signed, and there was nothing else to say.

Jason's basin was a treasure trove of wonders. A dozen new species at minimum—some of the specimens he assumed were related might actually be cousins rather than siblings, the finches of the deep blue sea. Pseudocrabs and pseudoshrimp, worms and fish and barnacles and other, stranger forms. One of the pseudocrabs was unlike the others, with twelve delicate, frond-like limbs that had curled inward when it died, making it resemble a mutated huntsman spider, still clutching desperately at its prey. They were scientifically priceless, every damn one of them, and they were *his*.

Tory considered him naive for letting Dr. Lyons set the course, but what Tory had never been able to comprehend was how much freedom it gave him, having a mentor who didn't need him and whom he didn't rely upon. Dr. Lyons was a grasping, greedy bastard who would seize everything he could get his hands on. Jason knew that. Lyons had never seized anything Jason didn't want him to have. In exchange for occasionally letting his grip on something weaken, Jason had a lab, a patron, and, best of all, the plausible deniability to keep his research moving forward. "Dr. Lyons needs it" was a phrase that could open considerably more doors than his own as yet untried name.

But this... this was going to change all that. Dr. Lyons had the living specimens. That didn't mean he would be able to *keep* them alive, or that he was going to learn the things he needed to know without killing them. By the time Dr. Lyons brought himself around to the idea of making sacrifices, Jason would be recording his own conclusions, writing them down and codifying them, analyzing his samples. He would be the first to get his answers. The time stamps on his research would prove that. He would also be the first to publish. Dr. Lyons, for all his considerable skills, had been depending on grad students and research assistants to handle his filing for too long. He'd never think to have his paper in the queue, waiting for the moment Imagine cleared research for transmission to the mainland.

Jason was going to get the scoop. Jason was going to *win*. And if winning required him to perform dissections in his cabin, behind a locked door, then that was what he was going to do. Whatever it took.

Carefully, he used a pair of tweezers to adjust one of the pseudoshrimp on his dissection board. This would have been easier with a microsurgical robot, one of the clever machines designed for operating on small animals and human arteries. Sadly, while there *was* a microsurgery suite on the ship, it was intended for medical use, and getting clearance would require explaining why he wanted it. Involving Lyons at this stage would have made everything else he'd done pointless. So it was the old-fashioned way for him, pins and cork-board and a scalpel in his hand. The *traditional* way.

He'd be able to spin that into an incredible story, when he was telling it to the news blogs. A scientist, a ship, a creature from the watery deeps, and none of this newfangled scientific equipment to make things easier on him. It would look rugged. It would look *authentic*.

It would look like another zero on the check he'd receive for his eventual memoirs. Anything worth doing was worth doing meticulously, from top to bottom.

The pseudoshrimp was three inches long. Its shell was curved enough that it refused to lie flat on the board until he spread its five-lobed tail and drove pins into the two largest segments, stretching the creature's hindquarters to their full length. He followed it up with a pin to the throat, effectively severing any internal structures. He had other specimens. If he had to dismantle five or more to get a full idea of their anatomy, then that was what he was going to do.

Jason paused in the act of reaching for the scalpel. Pulling back the pseudoshrimp's head seemed to have triggered some biological mechanism; a long spike, maybe an inch long—a third of the pseudoshrimp's body—protruded from a previously unseen sphincter at the base of the tail. He leaned closer, studying it. It was thin as a needle, with a wicked barb at its tip.

"Well, hello," he murmured, picking up his tweezers and using them to grasp the end of the spike. He tugged. It held fast. He was enough larger than the pseudoshrimp that he could have pulled the thing free, no question; any anatomical structures designed to hold it wouldn't stand a chance. The question was what the structure was meant to be in the first place. A stinger? That would make sense, given its location on the creature, but wouldn't fit with any known species of prawn.

The deep sea kept secrets. If the sirens were mimics playing at being humans, what was to stop the shrimp that combed their hair from being some form of spider, or ambulatory mollusk, or even something stranger? There was no reason to discount the idea of venom just because of what the thing looked like. If not a stinger, it could be an ovipositor, designed to deliver eggs into the body of an unwary prey creature, or some sort of biological anchor. Drive a spike into a siren's scalp, never get knocked loose.

Jason gave the spike another tug. It squirted a yellowish liquid with surprising force; it splattered all the way to the end of the corkboard. He let go and stepped back, surprised. His heel hit a wet spot on the floor, created when he'd been preparing a saltwater bath for his waiting specimens. His foot slipped and he flailed, arms pinwheeling to catch himself before he fell.

In his haste to lay out his specimens, Jason had lined up four of the pseudoshrimp, setting each on its own piece of corkboard. His hand hit the third in the row, slamming down on its abdomen. The impact caused the creature's stinger to burst forth, hard enough to puncture the thin blue plastic of his glove. Jason stopped flailing and lifted his hand, looking at the tiny, smashed creature now hanging from his thumb.

"Dammit," he muttered. He plucked the thing from his hand. The stinger remained, buried deep. "*Dammit,*" he repeated, and plucked the stinger loose. A bead of blood followed the removal, gleaming deep red against the glove.

"*Dammit,*" he said, for a third time. He dropped pseudoshrimp and stinger to the board before stripping off his glove, revealing the puncture at the base of his thumb. The stinger had gone in at an angle, creating a pocket in the skin that was rapidly refilling with blood. He squeezed it. More blood dribbled out.

"Dammit." This time, the word carried an air of desperation. He still didn't know whether the spike was a threat or some harmless quirk of anatomy. There were species of snake whose fangs carried venom long after their death. There were others whose fangs were harmless unless the snake chose to activate its venom glands. He could be fine. He could be dying. He had no way of knowing which it was.

Help. He needed help. Calling for someone to come here would just waste time. The medical bay was only one floor down, and the elevator opened directly in front of the doors. He could make it that far. He was certain of that.

The wound in his hand was still bleeding as he staggered out of the cabin, his heart racing at a tempo that could have been the result of poison or panic. That was the trouble with situations like this one.

It was so damned difficult to tell the difference between medical crisis and paranoia.

Had he taken a closer look at the blood, and realized it was trickling from the wound at a speed that implied an absolute absence of clotting factors, he might have realized that paranoia was not the issue here.

Inside Jason's body, red blood cells were beginning to break down, shredded by a toxin they had no idea how to fight. As they were destroyed, they clumped together, forming knots of tissue that bore no resemblance to healthy blood clots. His body struggled to form a functional immune response. Nerves went dead, refusing to transmit any sensation to the body around them. In their absence, Jason pressed onward, not realizing that only necrosis was saving him from agonizing pain.

His head spun. His lungs tightened. The whites of his eyes turned red as blood vessels burst, spreading broken blood through the sclera. He reached the elevator, and pressed the button with his blood-sticky hand, staring in dismay at the fingerprints he left behind. There was so *much* blood. How could there be so *much* blood from a little pinprick?

He looked at his hand. There was even more blood there, covering his fingers, washing along his palm all the way to his wrist. Something was very wrong.

The elevator dinged. The doors slid open, and Jason stepped inside, slumping against the wall. The elevator dinged again as the doors closed. He punched the button for the level of the medical bay and closed his eyes. Almost there. Almost to someone who could help him. It was just a little prick. There was no way this could be anything truly dangerous.

The world was going to remember his name. He was absolutely certain of that. All he had to do was get medical treatment and get back to work. That was...that was...

The red behind his eyelids turned black as his heart stuttered in his chest, unable to keep forcing the increasingly thin blood through his veins. He fell. He was dead before the elevator came to a stop, one deck down. All things considered, that may have been a mercy.

CHAPTER 26

**Western Pacific Ocean, above the Mariana Trench:
September 3, 2022**

Tory was at her desk, pulling apart the audio recordings of the last hour. The sirens were still down there, shouting across the void, their voices including so many "ordinary" sounds that she could only isolate them through their incongruity. She didn't believe an orca could have gotten under the ship without showing up on a single sonar reading, or that one of the RIBs had not only been launched, but somehow continued to run despite having been hauled easily forty yards below the surface.

"They must have a way of understanding one another, even when they're speaking in borrowed sounds," said Tory.

Luis, who had shared a lab with her for years, did the sensible thing: he ignored her, continuing his own work. Olivia, who hadn't been sharing a lab with either of them for more than a few hours—and technically wasn't sharing this lab; she just wanted a place to sit while she watched a playback of the necropsy—looked up from her laptop.

"Did you ever watch *Star Trek*?" she asked.

"Which one?" asked Tory.

"*Next Gen.*"

"Sure. Who didn't? The special effects are terrible, but it was the foundation for the modern series."

"What if their language *is* the borrowed sounds? I mean, what if they're talking in mermaid metaphors?"

Tory's hands went still as her head came up. She stared at the waveforms on her screen. "It's not the words, it's what they represent," she said, tone bordering on awe. "It's not the sound, it's where the sound was encountered. It's what the sound *does*."

"There you go," said Luis. "You put a quarter in her. Everything that happens now is on you. You understand that, right? This is your fault."

"What's my fault?" asked Olivia.

"Orcas. To us, orcas are intelligent animals in need of conservation, but once, they were viewed as dangerous killers. Why? Because the people encouraging that idea of them wanted people to be willing to stand by while they were killed and taken captive. Orcas represent one thing now, and something else then. What would they represent to the sirens? Food. They're prey. Dangerous prey. There aren't any orcas here, so when the sirens use their calls...what if they're talking about us? What happened with the Abneys?" Tory began opening files. "The RIBs...They didn't come for us while those were in use, but we split ourselves up to use them. We would have been easy to take."

"Why didn't they?" asked Luis.

"If they're as smart as we're starting to think they are, they left us alone because they were trying to get into position to take us all at once." Tory kept moving files. "We were ignoring the issue of cultural literacy. We didn't think they *had* culture. That was on us. All these sounds they've been collecting, all these things they've been shouting at one another—they're coordinating through shared experience. Listen."

She pressed a key. The distorted roar of engines came from her computer. The wailing songs of orcas sliced across the sound, high and bright and clear. She pressed the key again. The sound stopped.

"That was the exchange right before the siren came up the side of the ship and took your friend," she said, turning in her chair to look at Olivia. "They talked about a successful hunt. They talked about prey. They talked about prey that hunts via ambush. They're coordinating. Everything they steal, everything they share, it's another piece of the continuity they have with the rest of the school. The spoken component of the siren language isn't learned. It's *felt*."

319

"So how do we decode it?" asked Luis.

Tory shook her head. "I don't think we can. We can map out every logical connection, and some of the illogical ones, but we don't think like they do. There are going to be components we can't prepare ourselves for, because they're coming at them from such a radically different direction."

"Like the sirens wouldn't understand what I was doing if I started humming the *Star Trek* theme, but you'd know what I was doing," said Olivia.

"From context, yes. I would—"

"Miss Stewart?"

Tory stopped talking and turned toward the doorway. Olivia and Luis did the same, Luis calmly, Olivia with a sudden taut tension, like every bone in her body had been yanked into alignment at the same time. She was a student of human vocal inflections—had to be, to navigate the world she lived in—and this man's voice was filled with the echoes of nothing good. Nothing good at all.

We only had a few minutes, she thought, like a plea to an uncaring divinity. For a few minutes, they'd been safe, they'd been comfortable, they'd been distant enough from the reality of the deaths around them—even the deaths that had touched them all, that could never be forgotten or forgiven—that they'd been able to relax and be human again. To think, to plan, to care, to do those plain and human things that mattered more than anything else in the world. And now it was all resuming, the consequences of their actions and the dangers of their situation crashing down with a brutal, undeniable finality.

From here, it doesn't stop, she thought, and she wasn't wrong.

"I need you to come with me," said the man in the doorway. He was tall, broad shouldered, and too good-looking to be anything but one of Imagine's security staff. There was a pistol at his side. That was less reassuring than it could have been.

Tory, conditioned by years of exposure to obey the orders of uniformed people on ships, started to stand. Then she paused, frowning. "Why?"

"I'm afraid I'm not at liberty to divulge that information."

That was enough to put some steel into Luis's spine. He stood, faster than Tory had, and turned to offer his hand to Olivia. "Bring your camera," he muttered, through gritted teeth.

Olivia didn't say anything. She simply nodded, taking the offered hand and levering herself off the floor. The camera was a reassuring weight in her right hand. She never took her eyes off the man in the door. Unlike Tory, she recognized him, and she didn't trust him. She didn't trust any of Imagine's security forces. They weren't trained well enough. They knew more about their angles on camera than they did about how to use their weapons. It wasn't safe.

"In that case, I'm afraid I'm not at liberty to accompany you." Tory crossed her arms and looked witheringly at the stranger. "Please feel free to tell whoever sent you that I'll be happy to come see them as soon as they're happy to tell me why I'm wanted."

The man frowned. "Miss—"

"Brett, right?" Olivia stepped forward. "I knew I'd remember your name if I looked at you long enough. It's a gift. Also I made flash cards. Brett, Miss Stewart is a contractor in the employ of Imagine for the duration of this voyage, but is not subject to Imagine's authority unless she's working on a specifically sanctioned project goal or has been accused of malfeasance. Her audio analysis is approved but not funded by the corporation, and she's been with us since leaving the company of Dr. Jillian Toth. So unless you're here to accuse her of having terrible taste in music, this is where you tell us what you want or go away."

Brett's eyes narrowed. "Miss Stewart needs to come with me to be questioned in regards to the death of Jason Rothman. We understand that she was seen speaking to him on the deck shortly before he died, and we need to determine what, exactly, was said."

Tory went pale. Plastering her hands over her mouth, she gave a low moan before asking, "Jason's *dead*? But that's not possible. He can't be—I mean, he's not—I mean, what *happened*? He was *fine* when I saw him." She looked frantically toward Luis. "He was *fine*," she repeated.

"Who's Jason?" asked Olivia. "Did the sirens get him?"

"Had the creatures taken Mr. Rothman from the ship, we would not be here to question Miss Stewart," said Brett stiffly. "She'll need to come with me now."

"So will we," said Luis. "There are dangerous creatures in these waters. We're not leaving our friend alone."

Tory's hands were still clapped over her mouth. Tears overflowed her eyes, trickling down her cheeks. She didn't look like she remembered how to move, or what it was to want motion.

"Tory." Olivia touched her elbow. "You need to come on, okay? Mr. Blackwell can send more men to get you if you don't, and that's not going to go very well for you. For any of us. We know you didn't do anything to this Jason guy."

"He's my ex-boyfriend." Tory lowered her hands, looking bleakly at Olivia. "We were together for three years. We broke up at the start of the summer. He said...he said I had no ambition. I said he was wrong."

"He *was* wrong," said Olivia. "Come on. We need to go."

Brett scowled. "I don't recall inviting the two of you."

"I don't recall asking you for an invitation," said Luis. "Isn't this fun? We're having fun. Let's keep having fun. Let's not make things worse than they have to be."

Olivia tugged on Tory's arm, guiding her away from the desk, toward the doorway. Luis followed close behind.

Together the four of them walked down the deck. Tory pulled away from Olivia and Olivia let her, falling back a step to put herself level with Luis.

"What is going on?" she whispered.

"Jason's a jackass, but there's no way Tory killed him and got caught," said Luis. "If she were going to kill him, she'd have done it at school, and there wouldn't have been anything to link her to the murder. Whatever this is, it's amateur hour enough that there's no way she was involved."

Olivia blinked. "You know she didn't kill him because if she'd killed him, she wouldn't have gotten caught?"

"Pretty much."

"That's...Okay, you're right. That's oddly reassuring."

Luis grinned, the expression not touching the worry in his eyes. "I know, right? It's good to know your friends well enough to have faith in their limitations."

"But who was he?"

"Like Tory said: ex-boyfriend. Controlling asshole if you asked me, which, naturally, she never did, since it was none of my damn business. He had the future plotted out for both of them. Used to say her fixation on mermaids was going to be the death of her career,

322

and then he had the gall to show up on this boat, like he had some sort of a right to be here just because there was scientific discovery going on."

"He was a science hipster," said Olivia. "Everything was awful until enough other people liked it, and then he was there bragging about how he'd gotten in on the ground floor."

"That's a good description," said Luis. "I thought you didn't know him."

"I'm a geeky woman whose job involves looking cute on camera for a major genre media producer," she said. "I've seen his type before."

"And been quizzed by a few of them on the convention floor, I bet," said Luis. His eyes went to Tory's back. "She had every reason to mistrust him. I'd even believe it if someone said she'd slapped him and he was pressing assault charges. He always knew how to press her buttons. He'd do it just to get a rise out of her, since once she started yelling, he was obviously in the right. Didn't matter who started it. What mattered was all those people seeing him getting picked on by his crazy girlfriend."

"Sounds like a real prince."

"He was part of some fucked-up rebellion against the establishment, like dating an asshole would prove that she didn't care what people thought. She dumped him. Didn't stop him from going around telling people that *he'd* been the one to dump *her*, and didn't stop a lot of them from believing him."

"People are credulous," said Olivia. "If they weren't, I wouldn't have a job."

Luis chuckled darkly, and kept chuckling as it became obvious that they were heading back to the wet lab. The doors were still closed. Apparently, once the place had been turned into a makeshift surgical bay, there was no rush to reopen it for casual use. It made sense that they'd go there for an interrogation. With nothing to cut open, the lab was unlikely to be in high demand.

Brett opened the door. The reason for the wet lab's closure became even more obvious. The tables where the siren had been dissected were still in the middle of the room. They weren't empty: Jason's body was there. Tory's eyes went to his face, expecting to find it covered by a sheet. It was not. He was staring at the ceiling, eyes open, thin rivulets of blood running down his cheeks. She gave a short, sharp cry, clapping her hands over her mouth again.

"I told you she didn't do it," said a female voice. Tory turned. Dr. Toth was standing next to the captain, arms crossed. "The fact that they used to be romantically involved isn't relevant. Not in a situation like this one."

"It's usually the bitter ex," said the captain.

"Victoria isn't bitter. She's moved on, if I'm not mistaken. Jason, on the other hand, was working for a jealous man with a history of stealing breakthroughs from his students. You should be looking at Dr. Lyons. That is, if you must insist on looking at anyone at all." Dr. Toth unfolded her arms. "I don't think you should be."

"Dr. Toth?" whispered Tory.

"It's all right, Victoria. We're just waiting for the other participants in this little passion play to put in an appearance—and there they are, right on time." Dr. Toth looked past her to the open door. "Dr. Lyons, Mr. Blackwell, please, come in."

"What is the meaning of this?" demanded Dr. Lyons, before catching sight of Jason, motionless on the table. He gasped. "My student. He's—"

"Dead, yes. Theo, come here, would you?" Dr. Toth approached the body. She had looked more concerned—and more reverent—when dealing with the dead siren. It, at least, had been filled with mysteries. Jason was just one more dead human. If there was any novelty in him, it was that this time, they had a body. The sea hadn't claimed him the way it had claimed the others.

"It's amazing how quickly you code switch," said Mr. Blackwell.

"You're Mr. Blackwell when I'm being formal, and Theo when I want something," said Dr. Toth. "It's not that complicated."

"I didn't say it was complicated. I said it was amazing. What's going on?"

"Two engineers accompanied a security team to answer an alarm from the port elevator. Something was jamming the doors open. They expected to find a mechanical failure at best, another siren at worst—the people on this ship are seeing sirens every time they turn around. Can't imagine why." Her tone turned dry on her last words. "He was dead when they discovered him, lying in a pool of uncoagulated blood. They notified the captain, who promptly dispatched one of his security staffers to arrest Miss Stewart."

"Miss Stewart?" Mr. Blackwell turned, surprised, to face the woman who had been one of his first recruits. "Did you kill this man?"

"No," she said, and sniffled. "But we used to go out, and I guess Jason had told some people that, so maybe it seemed like I...Like when he died, it was because I..."

"Because you'd murdered him, yes," said Mr. Blackwell. "It's an easy, if simplistic, conclusion to jump to. As you say you didn't do it, we should move on."

Luis blinked. "Just like that?"

"Just like that." Mr. Blackwell chuckled at the stunned expressions around him. "Interesting fact: we're currently in what can only be regarded as 'international waters.' The *Melusine* was constructed in the United States, but her papers of incorporation are in three different countries, none of which have extradition treaties with the US. There were several reasons for that, primarily relating to taxation, but one of the side effects is that here, there is no greater governing body. I could kill you all, and while the American government might try to have me arrested, they'd have trouble convincing me to come back into their jurisdiction. Here, the word of Imagine is law, and I am the voice of the company. If you say you didn't kill this young man, I have no reason to doubt you."

"I don't believe he was murdered in the anthropocentric sense of the word," said Dr. Toth. "Is it murder when a hawk kills a mouse or an octopus eats a crab? Murder implies someone was killed, intentionally, by a member of their own species."

"What are you saying?" demanded Dr. Lyons. His face grew redder with every word, like the enormity of his loss was starting to sink in. It might not be a personal tragedy, but on a staffing level? Jason represented the whole of his research team. The voyage had been under way long enough that every other group was full; he'd be hard-pressed to find someone to rinse his beakers and stand by watching as he dissected his treasures from the deep. They would want a piece of the research pie if they helped him, and he wasn't that willing to share.

(On the positive side, Jason's death meant the boy wouldn't be using any of his notes, now would he? A whole world of research, already finished and ready to be used. It wasn't like Jason had a lot of close friends he would have confided in. It would be a *shame* to let all that hard work go to waste.)

"Look." Dr. Toth pulled on a rubber glove before turning Jason's palm toward the ceiling. There was a red, inflamed puncture in his skin, covered in watery blood and visibly swollen. The motion of Jason's wrist knocked something loose; another trickle of blood ran from the puncture, thinner than it should have been.

"He came in here to collect more samples," she said. "He extracted an assortment of small organisms from the creature's hair. Dr. Lyons, did he come to you?"

"No," said Dr. Lyons. He scowled. "Are you saying he was concealing research materials from me? Why, that ungrateful little—"

"Yes, I can't imagine why he'd be unwilling to share his findings," said Dr. Toth dryly. "It appears Mr. Rothman's blood has lost its clotting factors. He bled out. From this puncture, but also from his eyes, nose, and, judging by the dampness of his trousers, other orifices. There are venoms that could have done this, even among terrestrial species. I believe he cut himself on one of the specimens. We should find them before it happens again. All of them."

Dr. Lyons's eyes widened. "But—"

"This is a matter of ship security," said Dr. Toth. "You're not an organic chemist, Dr. Lyons. Surely you can see where getting this substance to the people who can do something with it will be more beneficial than leaving it locked in your lab."

"Do you think we can use it against the sirens?" asked Luis.

Dr. Toth looked at him. "That, or they're immune to it, and we need to know that. Something that's a minor annoyance to them might prove to be fatal to us."

"It's like the reverse of Wells's Martians," said Olivia. "It's us getting killed by the common cold."

"By fleas, more like, but yes." Dr. Toth looked to Tory, her expression softening slightly. "I'm sorry for your loss, and I'm sorry you had to see this."

"He was an asshole," said Tory, eyes on Jason. "But he was my friend once, and I didn't wish this on him. I wouldn't. No one would."

"Are you satisfied, Captain?" asked Mr. Blackwell.

The captain sputtered before nodding and saying, "I'll accept your ruling on this matter. We're almost prepared to lower the shutters. Recent events have our engineering crew slightly on edge, which is slowing their progress, but we're getting there."

"Recent events meaning 'killer mermaids eating people'?" asked Luis. "Yeah, I can see where some folks might find that unsettling. Probably best to offer two-for-one mojitos the next time we have an open bar. Maybe we'll get lucky, and alcohol will be fatal to the things. They'll eat a couple lightweights and decide to leave us alone."

"Not likely," said Dr. Toth. "Several recorded disappearances in these waters have involved private yachts of the sort that are either used for poaching or partying. I'm sure the sirens have encountered drunk humans before. They probably think we're even more delicious when we self-marinate."

The captain's lips twisted. "This is no laughing matter," he said.

"Do you see me laughing?" asked Luis. "Whistling past the graveyard is a time-honored tradition. Keeps us from screaming."

"Captain," said Mr. Blackwell. "That will be all."

For a moment, the captain looked like he was going to object. Then he nodded, shoulders going stiff, and walked toward the door. The security staffers trailed after him. Mr. Blackwell turned his attention on Dr. Lyons.

"You've lost your assistant, and it seems your lab is now home to some remarkably potent biological weapons," he said. "I suggest you collect them for me."

Dr. Lyons scowled. "You can't do that."

"Check your contract. All specimens derived from or relating to the unknown creature or creatures designated as 'mermaids' in the official mission description remain the property of Imagine, and can be reclaimed at any time. I don't own your findings, Dr. Lyons, but I own the things you're hoping to use to make them. If you want to make history, you'd best move fast."

"I'm working," snapped Dr. Lyons. "Jason was an assistant, nothing more. Losing him affects nothing. *Nothing*."

"Prove it," said Mr. Blackwell.

Dr. Lyons turned and fled.

It was interesting, noted Theodore Blackwell as he looked at the trio in front of him. Olivia was in the employ of Imagine, and had been poised to be the bane of Tory's existence. She hadn't needed to do anything; just being alive and in Anne's position would have been enough. But they were standing together, so close their shoulders almost touched, and the camera in Olivia's hands was consistently pointed at him when no one was speaking. It was like she was trying to keep a record that could be used to protect her friend, even if it meant acting against her employer.

Luis, on the other hand...he had always been expected to take Tory's side. He was her friend and lab partner, and those were two bonds that could take a great deal of strain before they snapped. The *Melusine* mission hadn't needed funding beyond what was provided by Imagine and its corporate partners; the Martines money was no good here. There had been people higher up in the chain who questioned Theo's decision to include a cryptozoologist among the approved scientists. What Theo had never been able to make them understand was that Luis, through his mere presence, would keep Tory calm and stable, and Tory, by sailing with the ship that answered the mystery of her sister's death, legitimized the whole thing. She was a PR coup given flesh, and she made it real.

He simply hadn't expected her to be real enough to start wooing his own people away from him.

"The sirens are aware of our presence," he said. "I've tripled security sweeps. Every dock has a full contingent of armed guards. Michi and Jacques Abney have joined the security teams, and they're carrying sufficient firepower to stop a charging rhino."

"You say that like it's something to be proud of," said Dr. Toth.

"No. I say that like it's reassuring, like it's something that will make our people more able to finish doing their jobs. We have sufficient proof of the creatures now. We have a body. We have fulfilled our basic mission objective."

"So we leave," said Tory. "We can...we can tell the navy, and they'll come back with bigger guns."

"They'd come back to drop a nuke into the Challenger Deep, and you know it," said Theo. He sounded tired more than anything else; this was not the first time he'd considered this. "They'd set the seas to boiling before they'd share them with a hostile sentient race, and when that made the weather even more unpredictable—when that killed the fish and destroyed the people living on the local islands— they'd say all of that had been unforeseen. Even though anyone with eyes could have seen it. No. We need to go back with as much data as possible. We need these creatures protected."

"Protected?" Tory stiffened. "Why would we want to protect them?"

"Because waging war on things that normally live a mile below the surface of the sea does no one any good, and could do us quite a lot of harm," said Dr. Toth, stepping in before Theo could open his mouth. "Because they represent something otherwise unknown to science, and studying them could tell us things about our planet that I never thought we'd have the opportunity to learn. But most of all, we protect them because it's our *job*. We don't just conserve the things we like, or the things we find adorable. We conserve everything. We take care of the planet. We've been doing a piss-poor job so far, but that doesn't mean we can't get better."

"That's all well and good and, oh yeah, *insane*, but what are we supposed to be doing *right now*?" asked Luis.

"All three of you have lost someone to the sirens," said Theo. "Some in a more abstract way than others, and yet. You're viewed as people with an active stake in things. Stay alert. Keep your eyes open. If you hear people speaking of mutiny, let me know."

"You want us to spy?" Olivia frowned. "That's not part of my job."

"That is exactly your job, Miss Sanderson."

"I think you're overlooking something," said Tory. "These are *scientists*. They're not going to want to leave while there's a chance that they could learn something. The problem isn't going to be people rising up to overthrow you in order to get out of here. The problem is going to be someone sabotaging the engines so they can finish their chemical analysis of the surface water."

"That, at least, isn't a concern," said Theo. "The *Melusine*'s engines are the best in the business. Nothing could be done to sabotage them."

"I don't think you're listening," said Tory.

"He never does," said Dr. Toth. "Please. Will you all just be careful, and let one of us know if you see anything out of the ordinary? And...stay alive. We know there's danger here, but we're working to minimize it. I don't want any more losses."

"Right." Tory's eyes went to Jason's face. It was still uncovered. That seemed obscene, somehow, and so much worse than he deserved. It wasn't fair, leaving him like that. She wanted to close his eyes. She wanted to cover his face. "Because there haven't been enough of those already."

"That's what I'm saying," said Dr. Toth. "It's time for us to finish and get out of here. This is their place, not ours, and the longer we linger, the worse things are going to become."

CHAPTER 27

Western Pacific Ocean, above the Mariana Trench: September 3, 2022

Night filled the sky with stars, rendering it distinguishable from the sea. Without those stars, the two bodies would have seemed to be one and the same, like the sirens could swim between them. All over the *Melusine*, lights blazed behind closed lab doors. The greatest scientific minds in the oceanic world had been handed physical proof of one of the sea's great mysteries, and they were going to take it apart, down to the smallest atoms.

Dr. Lyons bent over a dissection board, studying a pseudocrab he'd concealed from the men who cleared his lab, careful to avoid any contact with the creature's tissues. When he closed his eyes, even for an instant, he could see Jason's bloodied face, hanging there like a warning of the costs of hubris. He was not going to go out the same way.

Hallie and Daniel worked side by side, watched by the unblinking eyes of Mr. Blackwell's captive siren, and any guilt Hallie felt about leaving her sister again was washed away by the sheer passion of discovery. There was so much to learn. Hallie spoke to the siren with her voice and her hands, constantly expanding the scope of their shared vocabulary. Daniel's work was less flashy; he recorded everything, picking it apart for repeated themes, incorporating the notes he'd received from Dr. Toth after her conversations with Tory and Luis. They were close to answers. He knew it in his bones.

Holly sat alone in her lab—which she'd never shared with either of her sisters; no, their disciplines took them elsewhere. Her lab mates were a pair of scientists she didn't know, hearing women who spoke to each other constantly, but had never made the effort to learn to speak to her. She'd tried, at first, offering to teach them simple signs like the gift they were, using Hallie as a bridge between herself and their casual, cheerful ignorance. Here and now, she was grateful for their inability to communicate. She didn't want to talk to them. She didn't want to see the pity in their faces. It was a reminder of what she'd lost, what she was never going to have again, and it was like Heather died over and over when people looked at her like that. So she bent over her work, and she tried to focus, and she let the silence comfort her.

Michi Abney prowled the third deck at the head of a squad of Imagine's security dolts, rifle slung over her shoulder and finger hovering near the trigger. The hunt was finally under way. She'd been waiting for it since they'd left the dock, and now she was going to have it, every scrap of it, every *drop*. She'd shared the first kill with Jacques—which was, perhaps, the most romantic thing she could have imagined—and now she was going to fetch the first trophy. These mewling scientists were afraid of what was to come. She was overjoyed.

Two decks down, her husband's thoughts paralleled her own. They'd met, fallen in love, and married because of their shared love of the hunt; to most of the world, they were bloodthirsty freaks, too dangerous to be allowed in polite company, no matter how nicely they cleaned up, no matter how good they were at greasing the wheels of diplomacy. No one who took that much delight in killing belonged among normal people. But oh, how those normal people begged for what he and Michi could do when they felt their lives were in danger! How they screamed and pleaded. And bled, of course. Bleeding was par for the course when soft, pampered things like these scientists moved through the living world.

In her own lab, the door closed and barred against the rest of the ship, Dr. Toth watched the mass spectrometer return reading after reading explaining the chemical makeup of the samples she'd retrieved from Jason's room. If Dr. Lyons had been as smart as he believed himself to be, he would have gone there immediately upon leaving the wet lab; he would have cleaned out whatever Jason had found and pled ignorance when asked about it. No one would have known. But he'd been so interested in preserving what he saw as the important specimens—meaning the ones belonging to *him*—that he'd left three times as many sitting around for her to find.

It would be days before she understood the protein makeup of these toxins, weeks before she finished analyzing them to a degree that would allow her to make any sort of counter. Not that it seemed possible. In at least one case, the toxins acted on blood samples with a vicious swiftness that would make antitoxins virtually impossible to administer. She would need to inject the treatment at the same moment as the venom to have a chance of success.

If these were the natural parasites of the sirens, the toxins they secreted couldn't be fatal to the creatures. That meant there were answers in these protein strings, in these tiny, chitinous scraps of marine life. And she was going to find them, before they ran out of time to find anything.

All over the *Melusine*, the work continued. All over the *Melusine*, people looked for answers. Some of them were available to be found. Some of them were not. All of them were essential.

Tory looked up from her screen, covered once more with the curling sine patterns of recorded sound, and said, "We're not getting anywhere. I need more data. Luis?"

"I'm feeding you everything I have, but they're not talking," he said. "It's just water down there right now."

"Wait." Olivia looked up. "They left?"

"I don't think so, although I guess they could have gone back to the Challenger Deep," said Luis. "We haven't been able to get proper sonar going down there. Too many walls, too narrow of a space. They're just quiet. They've stopped talking."

Tory frowned. "We figured they switched to using other sounds when they were hunting. What does it mean when they're quiet?"

Olivia, for all that she was the nonscientist of the three, was the first to realize the implications of Luis's words. She jumped to her feet, camera clattering against the floor, and ran for the door. Tory and Luis gaped at her.

"What are you doing?" asked Luis.

"Cats," she said, flipping the deadbolt.

"That... isn't an answer," said Tory.

"Cats chitter when they see a bird," she said. "They make this little squeaky noise. People think it's adorable. I've used it in videos. Cats chitter, because they're excited, because they're about to start hunting. But when the hunt *begins*, they're silent. They don't make a sound. They come at their prey as quietly as they can, because a hunt only counts if there's a kill at the end."

Tory and Luis exchanged a horrified look.

It was a simple thing, after a life spent swimming through the crushing depths, to climb the side of a reef-that-should-not-be. It might rise out of the water, steep and hard sided, but it was only a reef, and reefs were made for ascending. From all sides the sirens came, their claws digging into the metal, their bodies draped against the steel, passage smoothed by the mucus secreted from their skins.

Some cut themselves on the holes made by their brethren. But every cut, every scrape, just encouraged the production of more mucus, covering the metal in a thicker and thicker layer of slime. By the time the third wave reached the ship, it was like grayish jelly, inches deep, shielding them completely. It did nothing to slow their ascent; they did not slip, did not slide, did not fall back into the water. They simply came, one after another, moving with steady relentlessness toward the rails.

For all that they seemed to move as a single body, an observer would have seen that the sirens were not cooperating with one another for any reason beyond biology. When one drifted too close to another, they were likely to be warded off with bared teeth and displayed claws. There was no actual fighting, but that may have been a matter of necessity more than anything else; by the time the first wave had reached the rail of the lowest deck, they still hadn't made a sound.

A dozen gripped the rails of the lowest deck, hauling themselves up and over, bodies striking the wood with a soft thudding sound. The rest moved toward the steel strip that concealed the ship's as-yet-undeployed shutters and continued upward, scaling the *Melusine* one level at a time.

On the lowest deck, a team of Imagine guards walked, Jacques Abney at the front. Like his wife, he carried a rifle. Unlike her, he had it in front of him, not seeming to care who he pointed it at. It was a loaded weapon, yes, but his fingers were far from the trigger, and he lacked Michi's ease in moving a rifle into position. The time he lost in disengaging the safety was more than balanced by the time he gained in having the gun already braced to fire. When they went into the veldt, he was the one who fired first, while she was usually the one who fired best. They balanced each other.

In a situation like this, where keeping them together would have been a misuse of limited available resources, he simply had to hope that whatever might come at them would come at a speed Michi could respond to, and in a line of fire that didn't require particular finesse on his part. It was a gamble. It was always a gamble. That was the beautiful thing about it. Here and now, on this ship, under this glorious and unending sky, he was fully alive. He knew his bride would be as well.

This might be the last real hunt for both of them. They had traveled the world, taking their prey from every environment, every ecosystem. They had bribed, bartered, and trespassed to line up the perfect shot, creating their own Noah's Ark of ghosts. Two by two, that was how they'd taken the animals; two by two, and all for the sport of it, the thrill of it, the God-given necessity of it. Mankind was designed for the hunt. People who forgot that might as well have been prey animals themselves. But all things came to an end. There was no thrill in a hunt repeated. Even Michi, with her whaler's background and her endless bloodlust, recognized that. They would shoot sirens in the defense of Imagine's mealy-mouthed scientists, and they would return home as legends, living off the spoils of their greatest job and hanging up their guns until something else came along to shock them out of retirement.

The guards with Jacques cast glances in his direction as they reassured themselves that the volatile French-Canadian was still on point. He unnerved them. They were doing their best. Imagine had paid to train them, and they wanted to do a good job. But...

Jacques Abney was a killer. In another life, another world, he would have been a serial murderer, carving bloody smiles into throats across Quebec. In that regard it was fortunate that he had

335

somehow found his way into big game hunting—and even then, boredom might have set in had he not found Michi, the only woman who could keep him distracted long enough to keep the razor blades out of his hands.

Uncomfortable as the guards patrolling with him were, they knew they would have been even less comfortable with *her*. He was a killer, brute force and bullets. She was something more subtle, more vicious, and hence much more terrifying.

Jacques stopped abruptly, signaling the rest of them to do the same. All motion ceased. He raised his chin, sniffing the air, eyes narrowing. Then, with an expression of deep and absolute pleasure, he smiled.

"Ah," he said. "I cannot say whether it is accident or tactics, but regardless, perhaps we are facing in the wrong direction, no?"

The men around him looked confused. Jacques sighed.

"Turn around," he said, and spun.

The three sirens that had been slithering their way along the deck stopped when the men turned. The men were equally still, even Jacques, all of them regarding the face of their enemy.

The sirens were arrayed in a rough V on the deck, one leading the pack by almost two feet. It was the largest of the three, arms thick with muscle and lips barely able to contain its teeth. It peeled back those lips, baring a forest of knives at the humans. Then it lunged, pulling itself hand over hand with a speed as alien as it was terrifying.

Jacques's gun spoke, loud and ringing over the water. The top half of the siren's head disappeared. He racked the next shell and fired again while the guards were shaking off their shock, blowing a hole through the shoulder of the next siren in line. It shrieked, loud and shrill and strangely honest: this was not a sound the creature had stolen from some other denizen of the deep. This was its voice, its true voice, for the first time.

The uninjured siren reacted instantly, grabbing its wounded fellow and hurling them both at the rail. They'd come over it to reach the ship, but they went under it now, the lead siren flattening itself in a way that spoke clearly to its amphibian origins, dragging the other with it. They fell to the waiting sea, vanishing without a splash before the first guard snapped out of his shock and ran to see where they'd gone.

The other guards fell into a defensive position, guns drawn, watching for a second wave. Jacques walked forward and knelt next to the siren he had killed, careful not to touch it. He might not think much of the scientists running this voyage—as if scientists knew the first thing about safety, when they spent their professional careers courting disaster like they were hoping to take it to a school dance? Giving scientists control of safety was like giving apes control of the banana supply—but he believed them when they said the creatures contained venoms that could kill a man. Scientists were very good at finding things that could kill a man. It was, along with the creation of more and better guns, the greatest benefit of science.

His shot had been clean from a killing perspective, if not from a trophy-taking perspective: the thing's head was effectively shattered, leaking blood and brain and other, less identifiable fluids out onto the deck. Tiny crustaceans fled the tangled mass of its hair, scuttling for safety. Most died before they traveled more than a foot, done in by the alien environment in which they found themselves marooned. He chuckled.

One of the guards looked at him sharply, face broadcasting fear and dismay. "Something funny?" he demanded.

"Look." Jacques pointed to one of the larger crabs. It was scuttling for the rail, moving slowly but still trying to survive. "These things, they're ships too. See? It brought us passengers, and now it is sunk, and they drown in open air." He laughed.

The guard shook his head. "Right," he said. Anything more might have come off as criticism, and he didn't want to anger the man. Instead he looked uneasily at the slime trail the sirens had left in their wake, and said, "I didn't even hear them come. How the hell can something without legs move so quietly?"

"I heard them." Jacques straightened, pulling the walkie-talkie from his belt and pressing the SEND button. "Michi, my dearest, are you there?"

A hiss of static before: "All's clear so far. I heard shots. What's your situation?"

"Three of the things came up the side. Shot two, killed one. The one I didn't have time to hit grabbed the wounded and went under the rail. Watch yourself. If there were three, there will be more."

"I'll let my boys know. They're uneasy enough as it stands.

Somebody's going to wind up getting shot." Michi chuckled low, making sure he understood she wouldn't mind, as long as the person catching a bullet wasn't *her*. "Honestly, I'm hoping we get a few nasties up here soon. It's boring, walking around with nothing to shoot."

"Have faith; you'll be swarmed soon enough." He clipped the walkie-talkie back to his belt and indicated the slime trail. "We go this way."

"Why?"

"Because mucus is an easing agent. It makes the path smoother. Things that slither—snakes, alligators, anything that likes to *crawl*— take the smoother path every time. It's not laziness. It's tactics. They stick to the path, they save energy for more important things."

"Important things like what?" asked one of the guards.

Someone screamed.

Jacques smiled, as if that had been answer enough, and stepped carefully over the puddle of slime before breaking into a run. The guards followed, letting him take the lead. They might not be slithering things, but they knew the wisdom of letting someone else blaze the trail. Those who came in first often died that way.

Jacques Abney would not have the privilege of dying first tonight. Even if Jason Rothman had not already claimed that dubious honor— even if his corpse hadn't lain, silent and staring, in the wet lab—there would have been someone ahead of him in line.

Everyone on the *Melusine* knew about the increased security, and knew it had started with the death of Heather Wilson. The captain had ordered them to stay together and in their labs. Unfortunately, orders have never changed human nature, and it was inevitable that some people would think the warnings were just hyperbole.

Michelle Lawrence and Andrea Hoffman had been assigned to share a lab with Holly Wilson. They were organic chemists, focused on finding the shifts in the pH balance of the water. Michelle had a minor in climatology, and was hoping to find keys to help her project long-term change to the ocean. Andrea was planning to go into pharmaceutical development, and was using the *Melusine* mission as the opportunity to test and sample water that was as close to untouched as anything left on the planet.

At first they'd enjoyed having a lab essentially to themselves.

Holly frequently took her computer to wherever her sisters had decided to congregate. When she was in the lab at all, she was silent, shut in her own little world. They wrote notes when they needed to ask her for something, and she used the text-to-speech function on her phone when she needed to talk to them. It was a pleasant sort of isolationism.

(Neither of them had ever stopped to ask themselves if she *wanted* to talk to them, whether the company of her peers might not matter as much to her as the company of her sisters. It had seemed like an easy answer, after all. She was deaf and they weren't. Even if they were all organic chemists, the fact that she couldn't hear meant they couldn't possibly have anything in common. Really, they were doing her a favor by not insisting on trying to spend time with her.)

Now one of her sisters was dead. They'd left a Post-it note on her monitor to express their regrets. She had crumpled it and thrown it on the floor, which seemed remarkably uncharitable. It wasn't *their* fault her sister had decided to drive a ball to the bottom of the sea and get killed. Her other sister, the translator, was sad and sulking somewhere on the ship, leaving Holly alone. Which meant Holly was in the lab. Constantly. She was this silent, almost sullen presence in the corner, running tests, making them feel like monsters for laughing, for trading jokes that had grown up over the course of the voyage, for *living*. They were alive. So was she! So why did she make them feel like it wasn't okay to act like it?

In the end, Holly's presence had been too much to take, and they had fled to Andrea's room, where there was a bed to sit on, and a bottle of brandy to spike their coffees with, and science to do. Always science to do.

"See, that's the problem with most of the people on this ship," slurred Andrea, pouring more brandy into Michelle's cup. She had a heavy hand with the pour; their coffee had been getting increasingly transparent. "They don't understand how to have *fun*. You think Einstein was a stick in the mud? Curie? Lovelace?"

"Her daddy was Lord Byron," giggled Michelle. "He knew how to party."

"And party we shall," said Andrea, with artificial gravity. Then she, too, broke down in giggles. "We *found* them."

"We did."

"We found the mermaids."

"We did!"

"They're real and we *found* them."

"We did, and we're gonna be famous." Michelle offered a sloppy salute with her cup. "We're gonna have any jobs we want, and all because we went on a cruise. Prolly the only one I'm gonna go on."

Andrea blinked at her owlishly. "Really? Why?"

"Because this is a hard act to follow, 's'why. Give me more brandy."

Andrea obliged.

Both women were so wrapped up in their two-person party that they hadn't been paying attention to the sounds outside the door, which was propped open in clear violation of the captain's orders. They had intended to let the night air in.

The night air hadn't come alone.

Something scraped the door frame. Michelle looked up, laughing, ready to welcome the newcomer. Then she froze, mouth rounding into a shocked O, every muscle in her body locking up. She couldn't move. She couldn't *breathe*.

The siren pulled itself forward a few more inches, looking at the two human women. They were so soft, so defenseless, with no weapons to speak of. They had soft coverings on their bodies, like kelp, but layered, loose and flowing. It might be skin or it might be ornamental. Either way, it looked unlikely to present much of a challenge.

"What?" asked Andrea. She followed Michelle's eyes to the door. Her cup slipped from her fingers, spraying coffee and brandy in all directions as it broke against the floor.

The siren flinched. Then it hissed, and lunged. Two more appeared behind it. Michelle remained frozen, apparently unable to process what was happening. Andrea had no such limitations. She stumbled backward, beginning to scream.

Michelle found her voice when the first siren reached her and closed its terrible teeth on her hand, slicing off three of her fingers and gulping them down like a child taking a bite of ice cream. Her eyes bulged. Her mouth worked. And then the screams began, high and keening and terrible.

The screams didn't last long. The siren's head snapped back, mouth opening to an impossible width before it snapped closed on her throat, ripping out larynx and vocal cords in a single convulsive thrust. Andrea continued to scream, until the two unoccupied sirens grabbed her and yanked her to the floor.

Their claws had not been blunted by the climb up the side of the *Melusine*. One ripped open her abdomen while the other slashed at her chest, spilling blood and fat and organs out onto the carpet, which turned a deep shade of red, verging on black. The two sirens buried their faces in the hole that had been her abdomen, gulping and rending, digging deeper and deeper into her flesh. Their hair hung lank around them, growing newly wet with blood. The siren feeding on Michelle continued to gnaw at her throat, slicing through cartilage and finally miring itself on bone.

"My God," breathed a voice. The sirens pulled themselves free and turned. The guards stood there, clustered together so closely they could barely raise their weapons. Jacques hung back, scanning the deck, watching the rail. This was only the beginning, he knew that, and those girls—those poor, unwary girls—were already lost. Better to leave a kill for the weaklings, to give them an idea of what was to come. He already had the shape of it. They still needed to be shown.

Gunfire started behind him, accompanied by the shouts of the guards. One of them howled, following the sound with a bellow of *"Oh God oh Jesus it's got my hand."*

The gunfire stopped. All sound stopped, except the sobbing of the injured guard. Jacques looked back. Three of the guards were apparently untouched. The fourth cradled his hand against his chest. The wound was concealed under his other hand, but the blood pumping forth made it clear that something catastrophic had happened.

The women were dead. Michelle had been opened like a present, her intestines spread across the floor in a terrible pinkish swirl, and her throat was a gaping ruin. Andrea's wounds were simultaneously more and less dramatic: pieces were missing from her arms, chest, and cheek, and everything was blood, but her internal organs were gone, not on display.

The wounded guard continued sobbing, blood flowing from between his fingers.

"Six so far," said Jacques, turning his eyes back to the deck. Let them think him callous. Where there were six, there would be more. "It begins."

341

"We need to get Skip to medical," said one of the guards. Jacques realized with distant surprise that none of these men had names to him; if he'd heard them, he'd forgotten them immediately. Their names didn't matter. They took no orders from him, heeded no commands. A shout of "Run" needed no name attached.

He mattered. Michi mattered. Every other body on this ship was simply bait, something to push in front of the sirens while he took a moment to reload.

"Medical is two decks up," he said. "Can your, ah, Skip, can he go unescorted?"

"What? No, man!" The guard sounded appalled by the suggestion. A pity. Jacques had been starting to hope these people might show a measure of self-preservation. "We have to take him there. He's bleeding bad."

"Yes, and this room smells of nothing but blood, ours and theirs," said Jacques. "It's chumming the waters. We need to continue patrolling this deck."

"You do that if you want, you heartless bastard," said the guard, wrapping an arm around the stunned Skip's waist, keeping him upright. "We're going to the medical bay."

Jacques stepped to the side, letting the guards go past. Amateurs all, hired for looks rather than skill. He could go with them, he supposed—but ah, they smelled so strongly of blood now. They'd be leaving a trail behind them as they walked. If the sirens were anything like the predators he knew, they would follow the smell, and the guards would learn the wisdom of leaving their wounded to fend for themselves.

He checked the chambers of his gun and started down the deck, moving away from the doomed men. There was much to do, and at last the hunt was on.

On the top deck, the mechanism that controlled the shutters strained and whined, attempting to engage. Again, it failed.

Daryl and Gregory exchanged a look.

"I'll call the captain," said Gregory. "You get back to work."

They were running out of time.

CHAPTER 28

Western Pacific Ocean, above the Mariana Trench: September 3, 2022

The *Melusine* had seven decks, with labs and living quarters on each one. Imagine had consolidated certain functions—one pool, one laundry room, one banquet hall—but had placed laundry chutes on each deck, recognizing that no one wanted to tote stained sheets down three flights of stairs. There were smaller café-style kitchens on decks one through three, and again on five and six, leaving only the top deck, with its open-air view and wide central space, without an eatery.

Jacques prowled the lowest deck alone, watching the floor and rails for traces of mucus. Many of the rooms he passed were occupied, doors shut and the lights that signaled the locks were in use switched on. He smirked. The *Melusine* had been designed for the comfort of her passengers as much as for the functionality of her mission, and the doors were effective sound baffles. Add the shape of the ship, and the normal properties of screams, and half these people wouldn't even have heard the slaughter. They were sitting ducks.

He considered the wisdom of stopping at the closed doors, hammering on them until they opened, and sending the occupants to the next deck. It wasn't safe there, of course, but it was a little farther from the water, and hence less likely to be the site of an all-out massacre. That wasn't his job. The men from Imagine should have been conducting the evacuation, if the captain saw fit to order one. Instead, the guards who were meant to be watching his back had gone to take care of their own.

Jacques kept walking.

He found what he'd been looking for midway around the ship's curve: a fresh slime trail, thick and gray and glistening in the star-light. "There you are, my pretty thing," he murmured, crouching. The smell was fishy and sharp, more acrid than he expected from something that lived at the bottom of the sea. It must have possessed some helpful properties, to make it a viable use of limited biological resources. Perhaps the scientists could take it apart, after the ship had been rendered safe again.

His walkie-talkie crackled. He plucked the clever little box from his belt as Michi's voice, distant and echoing, said, "Jacques, are you there?"

"Still patrolling, my love," he said, depressing the SEND button. "The men assigned to do it with me have gone away, but never let it be said that I would shirk my duties."

"I know," she said. "They came by heading for the nurse. They were getting blood everywhere. I don't like this."

"Have you made a kill yet?"

"Two of the damned things, by the prow. They're coming up the sides. They can scale sheer metal surfaces. Bit of a stunner, that."

He laughed, delighted. "You're always so droll when you're excited. What are you thinking? Shall I come up and you come down, and we meet in the middle? There's plenty to be done, and these people from Imagine, peh. They don't know how to hunt."

"They're listening, you know." Michi made no effort to hide her amusement. "My team didn't get hurt. That's a point in my favor."

"Ah, but I've killed more than you have, so the score is tied." He straightened. "I have a fresh trail here to follow. Will you be coming down?"

"No, and you won't be coming up. Not until a new team comes to join you. There are civilians on that level. They need to be protected."

"We're all civilians when there is no war," he said, and clipped the walkie-talkie back to his belt. Michi had long since grown accus-tomed to his need to have the last word, even found it endearing, in her way. She wouldn't call back unless it was to start a new discussion, to report a kill or ask about his status.

Following the trail of mucus, Jacques stalked farther down the deck.

"We *can't* just stay locked in here," said Tory, standing fast enough to knock her chair to the side. It rolled across the floor, coming to rest against the wall. "If they're coming, if they're actively attacking, we need to tell someone."

"So pick up the phone," said Olivia. "We're not going out there."

"Olivia—"

"*You didn't see them.*" Olivia's voice was low, tight, and fast; she was obviously struggling not to scream. "They're...they're so *fast*. You don't understand how fast they are. They shouldn't be able to be so fast when they're not in the water, but they are. The one that took Ray moved like it was flying. It wanted him, and so it took him. I can't. I can't do it. I can't stand there while it takes you too. I can't."

"It won't," said Tory. "But Liv, I have to. I have to see them. They took my sister. I can't hide."

"So you'll die?" asked Luis, sounding surprised. Both women turned to face him. "Sorry, Tory, but that's not rational. I can't let you charge out there unarmed and unprepared just because you want to see the deep-sea killing machine before it chews your face off. I'm with Olivia on this."

"What if they take the ship? This isn't a defensible location. This is a *lab*." She spread her arms. "No food, no water, no bathroom. We can't stay here forever."

"I have a bottle of Mountain Dew and some granola bars. That should get us through the night."

"Not good enough."

"Come up with a plan that does something beyond getting us all slaughtered, and I'll think about it." Luis folded his arms. "We're not going out there without a plan."

"I'll call the bridge," said Olivia. "Tell the captain they're coming. He can send some guards to pick us up. We can go where there are more people. People with guns."

"Because being locked in a room with Jacques Abney would make me feel better about the situation," said Tory sourly. "He shot

345

a Crimean tiger. He bribed seventeen government officials, and he shot a Crimean tiger. They're critically endangered. He did it because he wanted to."

"Well, I want to live," said Luis. "I don't care if the captain thinks we're safer in our labs. The captain also thinks a few security fire drills mean the same thing as being ready for a disaster, and look how far that's gotten us. Make the call."

Olivia nodded and lifted the receiver off the wall. The *Melusine*'s phone technology was outdated, necessarily so: cellphones didn't like to work in the middle of the ocean, miles away from any terrestrial relay towers. The satellite relays on the ship were dedicated to the wireless network. They could be used for Skype and other internet calling services, but they weren't as convenient as an ordinary phone, run off a limited network that only covered the ship itself.

Tory and Luis glared at each other, Olivia briefly forgotten.

"You knew we were coming out here so I could face them," she said.

"Face them, yes; fight them, no," he said. "They'll kill you. They won't even spit out your bones when they're done. You think I can let you do that to your parents? You think I can let you do that to *me*? I'm not going home without you, and I'm not getting eaten by a fucking fish. That means we're getting through this alive, and if I have to keep you locked in this lab to do it, that's what I'm going to do."

"We don't even know that there's anything *out* there," snapped Tory.

"Yes we do," said Olivia in a small voice. They turned. She was placing the phone back into the receiver, slowly, moving with a deliberateness that looked like reverence, until they realized how hard her hand was shaking.

Taking a deep breath, Olivia steadied herself and said, "There have been mer—I mean, sirens seen on three of the decks. There have been at least three deaths. They're getting the shutters ready to deploy, but it's going to take time. The captain said to stay put, and that they'll send guards to pick us up. That we'll be fine as long as we stay put."

"Why don't they close the shutters *now*?" asked Luis. "Bring those down and nothing can get in here. We can be safe."

"The sirens are already on board," said Olivia. "I guess maybe..."

maybe they don't want to trap them in here with us? Or maybe there's something mechanically wrong. I don't know."

"That's insane," said Luis. "Lowering the shutters should be the first response to danger. See a bird you don't like, lower the shutters. Big wave, lower the shutters. They should have kept them so highly attuned that they kept slamming down and cutting birds in half. Are you telling me we have *killer mermaids* murdering people, and that's not a good-enough reason to hurry up and finish their repairs? What do we even have the shutters for?"

"It probably keeps insurance rates low." Tory walked back to her desk, opening the bottom drawer and rummaging through it. She withdrew a tranquilizer pistol. Turning to her companions, she smiled. "They're not going to save us fast enough for my tastes. Who feels like taking a walk?"

"Tory, no," said Olivia.

"We have to do this," said Tory. "We can't cower here and wait for them to come. Do you understand that? They tore down doors on the *Atargatis*. I've seen the footage, and the damage. I've *studied* the damage. When they get hungry enough, they'll find a way inside. At least this way we stand a chance."

"A chance at what?" asked Luis. "Dying outside instead of dying inside?"

"If we can get to the kitchen, we can bar ourselves inside there," said Tory. "It's a bigger space, there's food and water and the staff bathroom. We can make it if we stay there. If we stay here, it's not a question of whether we die, just how."

"This is not good," said Luis. "This is a not-good idea. Let's not do this."

"I think we have to," said Olivia, stepping up next to Tory.

Luis made no attempt to hide his betrayal as he looked at her. "I thought you were on my side."

"I'm on the side where we live," said Olivia. "She has a gun—"

"It's a tranquilizer gun! It can't kill anything!"

"—and she's going to go out without us if she doesn't go out with us. There's safety in numbers." Olivia paused, wincing as she remembered Ray hitting her as he knocked her aside. "They can't kill us all that fast. The cafeteria is on this level. It isn't like it's far."

"This is a bad plan," said Luis.

"Maybe. But it's the best plan we have."

"Oh my God." He shook his head. "Can we at least have a few minutes to pack our laptops? Tory, you know we need to be able to keep an eye on things. You'll go crazy if you don't have your computer."

"Fine," said Tory. "Five minutes, and then we move. Got it?"

"Got it," he said, and moved toward his desk.

On the third deck, Michi and her guards—her boys, as she kept pseudo-affectionately calling them, subtly shifting their ideas of loyalty from the corporation onto her, where all loyalty belonged—walked, looking for traces of blood or slime. The nasty things were doing them a favor, leaving trails; if someone was paying attention, they'd never be taken by surprise. It was like fighting an invasion of giant slugs.

"How are the damn things making it all the way up here?" asked one of the guards, a nervous, broad-shouldered specimen named Carl.

Michi wasn't sure how Carl had been able to get a job like this one. It was proof that people didn't have standards anymore, really. In the two encounters they'd had so far, he'd only been able to draw his weapon once, and he hadn't been able to bring himself to fire. He'd just stood there, gaping, while the rest of them cut down the sirens and left them bleeding on the deck.

(It was a waste of trophies, the way they kept abandoning perfectly serviceable bodies. All of them had unsightly bullet holes, but the creatures were virtually identical; Michi had absolute confidence in her ability to take pieces from one creature and use them to patch the holes in a second. She could make a functional specimen from what she had available, if she was allowed to claim her fair share of the kill.)

"They can climb," she said, as calmly as she could. Losing her temper would do her no good, and might do her considerable harm. Jacques could rant and rave and people would view him as roguishly dangerous, possibly unbalanced, possibly just unpredictable. If she did the same things she'd be labeled as a crazy bitch and lose any respect she'd gained among these men. "Goannas do it, in Australia. Metal is no challenge for something with big enough claws if they're only looking to pull themselves up. Be more concerned about what those claws can do to flesh, and look alive."

Carl grimaced and nodded. At the start, they had been a team of seven; now they were a team of five. One of their men had been hauled over the rail by a siren that appeared from nowhere and knocked him off balance. Michi still wasn't sure where the thing had been lurking. That made her nervous. If the creatures had camouflage capabilities—which were not unheard-of in the ocean—they were in serious trouble.

Another guard had turned tail and run after they came across the first human body, a scientist, still in the white coat that some of them wore even in the middle of the ocean, his belly sliced open and his guts spilling out onto the ground. The guard had been overcome with horror and fled.

The screams had come shortly thereafter. His body had been nowhere to be seen when the rest of the team followed the sound to the place where he'd died, but there had been two more of the creatures there. Both had died in a hail of bullets.

The absence of bodies was beginning to make Michi nervous. The creatures killed, that much was certain; she had seen with her own eyes. She had watched the footage from the *Atargatis*. It was unclear, jumpy, but it was still evident that for every person the creatures consumed, three more were being taken over the rail. It was an unusual hunting pattern. It was not a unique one.

It spoke to something being fed somewhere beneath the surface. Unless the creatures spawned like salmon, feeding hundreds and thousands of young with the bodies they hauled over the side, whatever they were feeding was large, to have such a healthy appetite. Lionesses hunted like this, dragging prey back to their mates and cubs.

Just going by the number of creatures she'd seen, this was a swarm larger than any pride of lions she had ever seen, and all of them seemed bent on taking *something* with them when they went back into the water. It was unnerving. It was dangerous. She adjusted her grip on her rifle, trying not to let her anxiety show.

Michi Abney was aware that most people thought she and her husband were unbalanced, and more, that she was regarded as the saner of the pair; that people who would have screamed the heavens down if they'd felt judged were judging them and their choices every minute of the day. They were killers. They were monsters. They were throwbacks to a less enlightened era, and if they were tolerated in places like this one, it was because even throwbacks can be necessary; without them, the monsters at the door would become the monsters inside the house, and the fairy tale of conservation and tolerance would end, swallowed alive by something older and redder and wetter.

Knowing what people thought of her meant she could work to combat it, or at least leaven it. Jacques played to type, and she played against it. It kept the world guessing, and a world that was busy guessing wasn't running them out of town on a rail for the crime of doing as their natures bid them.

The men around her had come because they'd been ordered to do so, and they stayed because they were coming to trust her, a little bit at a time. With every order she gave that didn't get them killed, their confidence in her grew. If she could keep them in line long enough, continue to smile and flatter and exchange pleasantries for another few circuits around the ship, they would follow her into Hell itself. That was a good thing. With the way this night was unfolding, Hell itself wasn't far away.

They moved in a diamond formation, with Michi in the lead, rifle now held at the ready. Their footsteps were damnably loud on the wooden deck; it felt like there was an accompanying echo, signaling their presence to every terror the deeps had to offer. Michi tried to tread as lightly as she could, but it wasn't easy, not with slime coating the decks and four large men following at her heels, their own steps clumping and heavy. She would have tried to get away from them if not for the fact that there was safety in numbers. If she needed to, she could leave them and run, buying herself time to make an ignoble escape.

Nobility was for those who never stepped into the line of fire. Given the circumstances, she would gladly accept survival over anything of the sort.

The slime trails were getting thicker. The slime didn't dry quickly, but it did deflate, losing volume and shriveling in on itself. This trail was still plump and moist, freshly laid. It continued to the middle of the deck, where it stopped easily two feet from the rail.

"Where did it go?" asked one of the men.

Michi didn't have an answer. She looked around, trying to find some trace of the creature's passage. They couldn't *fly*. Whatever else the damned things were, they were still sea creatures, still unable to do much on the land other than pull themselves along, hand over hand, slithering toward their prey.

But they had incredible upper body strength. They could pull themselves up the side of a ship. Up...

Michi looked up, and then, before her eyes finished registering what they saw, she dove to the side, raising her rifle and firing twice. The siren wedged in the bend between the wall and the bottom of the next deck hissed, mouth gaping wide. Then it let go of the wall and fell, landing on one of the men who had been walking behind Michi in the formation.

He screamed. The siren bit down, burying its teeth in the soft flesh of his throat, cutting off the sound.

"Fire!" howled Michi.

It was an enclosed space. Ricochets were inevitable. Six bullets caught the siren's body, joining the bullets Michi had already put there. It howled, the sound bright and electric and horrible—and most of all, loud enough to drown out Michi's own scream, which was human and hence almost irrelevant. The siren went limp. The man under it thrashed once and was still.

Michi clapped a hand over her upper arm, swaying. "I don't feel well," she announced, and collapsed.

"I don't like the way this thing is looking at me," said Daniel, eyeing Mr. Blackwell's captive siren. It was hanging in front of the glass again. It tracked him with its eyes, watching him move around the room. "Why does it keep focusing on me?"

"Maybe it's female after all, and showing solidarity: it only wants to eat you." Hallie started another video playback, trying to mirror the way the creatures moved their hands. "You're taller than I am. It's a predator. It knows how to be careful. It probably assumes you're more likely to eat it than I am, so it wants to know where you are."

"That's great," said Daniel. "What wonders will it reveal next?"

"Unless it can break glass, probably nothing," said Hallie. There was a trick to the way the sirens moved their hands. They had long fingers, but only one extra knuckle, functionally speaking; their first two knuckles were held in place by the webbing, keeping them from moving much during normal use. She twisted her wrists to the sides, trying to mimic the finger placement from the video. She was so close...

There. A flick of the thumb, and the phrase closed. She didn't know what she was saying, but she was *saying* it. "I want to try something. Stand in front of the tank."

"Stand in front of the deep-sea horror that wants to eat me, you mean."

"Yes," she said serenely. "I mean exactly that."

Daniel glared at her. "I have a PhD."

"That's nice. So do I."

"I also have two master's degrees, and I've addressed the United Nations."

"I can run in four-inch heels. Are we done playing 'who has the bigger dick'? Because I have things to accomplish, and I need you to stand in front of the siren."

Daniel kept glaring as he moved into position in front of the tank. The siren swam over to hover in front of him. He shuddered.

"That is one ugly freak of nature," he said.

"I thought you were the biologist," said Hallie, moving next to him. "Aren't you supposed to find beauty in all living things?"

"I find beauty when it's there. There's no beauty here." Daniel knew he was wrong. Dr. Toth saw the beauty, and Dr. Toth was less of a romantic than most people took her for. If she said there was something to admire, she was telling the truth. But he couldn't get past the reality of those terrible teeth. The creature—mermaid, siren, whatever she wanted them to call it—was a predator from another world, and it would kill him if he gave it the chance. He knew that, and deep down, in the part of his soul that would never come out of the trees, he was afraid.

"These things killed my sister. I want to agree with you. But I can't, because I found the beauty. It's in their hands." Hallie held up her hands, wiggling her fingers in a beckoning wave until the siren looked at her, attracted by the motion. Before it could look away, she made a complicated gesture. It involved both hands, and while it lacked the fluidity of the siren's own gestures—the fingers that shaped it were too short, too bound to gravity—it was enough to make the creature go still.

Hallie repeated the gesture, more emphatically.

"What are you saying?" asked Daniel.

"I have no idea," she said. "But these things are mimics. They're used to the idea that intelligent creatures can steal words from one another. I've stolen something from it. Let's see what it does."

The siren's mouth closed as its gills flared, making its neck seem twice as thick, making its outline somehow less delicate. It raised its own hands and made a short, choppy gesture.

"We have no shared culture," Hallie said. "I can't spread my hands and expect it to know I mean I don't understand." She pressed one hand flat against her sternum instead, before making her name sign. When she was done, she touched her chest again.

"What did you say?"

"My name."

The siren hung motionless for a moment. Then, almost cautiously, it touched the glass in front of Hallie before echoing her name sign and touching the glass again.

It was all Hallie could do not to punch the air in triumph. Instead she smiled, lips closed in case the siren took showing her teeth as a sign of aggression. She touched her chest, repeated her name sign, touched her chest. Then, moving with deliberate care, she touched the glass.

The siren made a new sign before touching its chest.

"What did it say?" asked Daniel.

"Its name," said Hallie softly. "We're communicating. We're *communicating*. I got it. We can do this."

"Great," said Daniel, blissfully unaware of what was going on above them. "Maybe we can get out of here without anyone else dying."

CHAPTER 29

**Western Pacific Ocean, above the Mariana Trench:
September 3, 2022**

Michi was moaning when her boys carried her into the medical bay. The sound was low and constant, like an animal with its leg caught in a trap. She had resisted all efforts to bind the bullet wound; it was too high for an effective tourniquet, unless she wanted to risk losing the limb. Instead she was just bleeding out. Her eyes were closed, and she had stopped responding to questions halfway down the stairs.

The two doctors on duty looked up when the door banged open. The guards keeping watch over them drew their weapons, falling into a defensive posture. Michi would have been impressed, if she'd been able to open her eyes long enough to see them.

"Medic!" shouted the man holding her shoulders. Her head was lolling, and he was starting to worry about her breathing. "We need help here!"

"What happened?" demanded the senior doctor. She'd worked in a major city hospital before being hired by Imagine; she'd expected this trip to be a chance to relax, treating nothing worse than dehydration, sunburn, and the occasional case of norovirus. This—a woman with her shoulder bleeding so copiously that the entire left side of her body had turned black with blood—was a step beyond. "Put her down here."

"Here" was an open cot, with plastic sheets as morbid as they were practical. The men lowered Michi carefully onto it, getting a pillow under her head. She moaned again, but didn't otherwise react.

"Bullet to the shoulder," said the leader, turning to face the doctor. Michi's blood was smeared across his chest, making him difficult to look at directly. "We were fighting one of those damned sea monsters, and there was a ricochet."

"And you just let her bleed?" demanded the second doctor, sounding horrified. "What were you thinking?"

"We were doing what she told us," said the guard. "The bullet went through the thing before it went into Ms. Abney, and we don't know jack about their biology. Could be laden with all sorts of nasties. She asked us to let her bleed, in an effort to flush the wound, and we were close enough to here that it seemed like a reasonable thing to do."

The first doctor was already cutting Michi's clothes away from the bullet hole. She frowned at the sight of Michi's skin. It was streaked with blood—not quite red washed, but close enough so as to obscure its original color in places—but there seemed to be something wrong apart from that. "I need a sterile wipe," she snapped.

The second doctor went to get what she had asked for. The men who'd brought Michi arrayed themselves around the door, guarding it, their eyes never leaving the wounded, motionless woman. She had earned their loyalty. She would have been pleased, had she been even slightly aware of her surroundings.

"You said the bullet passed *through* the creature," said the first doctor, voice low and tight and urgent. "What do you mean, exactly? Where was it shot?"

"I didn't see, Doc," said the lead guard. "The bullets were flying all over the place. Why? What's wrong with her? Whatever it is, you can fix it, right?"

"You have a walkie-talkie, yes?"

"Yes," said the guard, and frowned. "Why?"

"I need you to find Dr. Jillian Toth." The doctor looked back to Michi. "You may also want to locate Mr. Abney. I think he's going to want to be here."

A war was being waged inside Michi's body. The battle was complicated; the siren had no venom to speak of, no toxins designed to take down its prey. That would have been more straightforward, and easier for the medical team to combat. No. The siren, being a deep-sea creature of unique and unstudied biology, had other surprises to deliver, and more subtle poisons to bring to bear.

Like the flamboyant cuttlefish, the siren was poisonous. Not venomous; poisonous. The flesh of the creature was relatively inert, but the mucus it secreted contained a complicated mix of anticoagulants and neurotoxins, designed to slow and sedate anything foolish enough to bite it. Whatever ate a siren would become prey to the rest of the school, unable to build up the speed to escape them.

In something the size of a sperm whale, with the attendant circulatory system, the amount of mucus that had entered Michi's body would have been negligible. It would have done some damage, sure, but nothing catastrophic. For someone Michi's size...

Her red blood cells were shredding. Her white blood cells attempted to rally, only to find themselves similarly destroyed, filling her veins with gunk. Her shoulder still bled, faster than it should have, her body pumping out plasma and antigens as quickly as it could. At the same time, synapses in her brain were starting to misfire, unable to contend with what was happening to them.

It was sheer bad luck that saw Jacques running into the room as the first seizure began.

"*Mon dieu!*" he cried, too shocked to remember his second language. He ran to his wife's side, knocking the doctor away as he grabbed for her hands. "Michi? *Michi!*"

She didn't open her eyes. The doctor tapped him on the shoulder and he turned, eyes wide and almost devoid of comprehension.

Dr. Vail had served in the army before going into private practice. She knew the eyes of a man on the verge of losing his senses. She shook her head, holding up the syringe she had been preparing. "You need to let me work," she said. "Your wife has been injected with an unknown toxin. If you do not let me work, she is going to die. Stand aside."

Jacques stared at her for a few more precious seconds. Then, shaking, he stepped to the side and let her in.

The race between medical science and natural poison was a swift one, and one that had been run over and over again since the dawn of mankind. Inside Michi, the siren toxins and the broad treatments Dr. Vail was able to prepare without more information hammered against one another, waging brute force attacks for ownership of her circulatory system. More blood cells shredded. Another seizure began, this one violent enough to bring her back off the cot, arching upward in an almost perfect half circle. Jacques shouted in French. One of the guards moved to restrain him before he could strike Dr. Vail, and he turned, punching the guard in the nose instead. The guard, who outweighed him by more than a hundred pounds, looked at him impassively before grabbing his hand and squeezing. Jacques howled, and the guard enveloped him in a tight hold.

The door opened. Dr. Toth stepped inside. She stopped for a moment, taking in the scene: the struggling Jacques, the harried Dr. Vail, the seizing Michi. The other guards stood around, watching helplessly.

Dr. Toth placed two fingers in her mouth and whistled. All motion stopped, save for Michi, who could no more stop seizing than she could heal her wounds through sheer force of will. Michi continued to thrash, more weakly now, her body no longer accurately interpreting the signals it was receiving from her oxygen-starved brain.

"Status report, *now*," said Dr. Toth. She pulled on her gloves as she walked toward Michi, snapping them tight before leaning forward and prying open Michi's left eye. It had rolled so far back that only the startlingly red sclera showed. Dr. Toth allowed Michi's eye to close again before Jacques could see. "Muscle relaxants and fluids, now. What have you given her so far?"

"Broad-spectrum antibiotic, injected intramuscularly, and a dose of pit viper antivenin, based on the anticoagulant properties of whatever she's got in her system."

"Good, good," said Dr. Toth. She pressed on Michi's shoulders. The other woman's back did not unbend. "I need that muscle relaxant. Be ready with a shot of epi. She may go into cardiac arrest at— Why the hell are you people standing around? *Move!*"

Dr. Vail moved. So did the other doctor, who had been standing near frozen since Dr. Toth's whistle. The medical drama sprang back to life, all three of them clustering around Michi, blocking her from view, fighting the age-old fight between medical science and trauma.

"My wife," said Jacques, clawing at the air. "Please. You must let me go. I must go to her. I must be with her. And *her*! Why is she commanding the doctors? She is no doctor! This is *her* fault!"

"You'll get in the way," said the guard who was holding on to him. "If you want her to live, you'll stay where you are."

Jacques went still. Finally, in a tight voice, he said, "You may put me down. I will not do anything to compromise my Michi's safety."

The guard looked at him dubiously. "You know I don't believe you, right?"

"Have I done anything—anything—on this voyage to make you think me a liar? *Non*. Put me down."

"Put him down, Paul," snapped one of the other guards. This one was taller, bulkier, with a larger Imagine-logo pin on his shirt. That alone denoted him as higher in the pecking order, which was opaque to anyone not actually involved in the chain of command. That was how Imagine wanted things. The more this could look like a normal scientific expedition, the better it would be for everyone. "Dr. Toth is managing things because she's the one with the best idea of the damn things' biology. She isn't doing open heart surgery. She's trying to figure out how to stop the fucking poison."

Someone outside screamed. The sound was shrill and terrified, and quickly cut off. This no longer seemed like a normal scientific expedition.

Paul put Jacques down. The smaller man took a step to the side, putting himself out of easy snatching distance. His eyes went to the crowd surrounding Michi, who was blocked almost entirely by the bodies around her; he could see the sole of one foot, jerking randomly as seizures continued to rack her body. They seemed less pronounced than they had been. He honestly couldn't tell whether that was a good thing, or whether it was a sign that she was running out of strength.

"Fight, Michi," he whispered. "Fight as you have fought everything since the day you were born. This is not the beast that kills you."

A heavy hand landed on his shoulder. He turned. The man who had ordered his release was standing there, looking at him with a mixture of steel and sympathy.

"We can't do anything here," he said. "Want to help me save some lives?"

"*Oui*," said Jacques, relieved beyond coherent thought. This, at least, was something he could do. The sirens were concrete enemies. They could be seen. They could be killed. "Only we had best hurry.

Michi will want to join the fight if it is still going when she awakes, and that would not be good for her."

The guard, who had gotten a good, clear look at Michi before she was blocked from view, said nothing. He simply nodded, and motioned for Jacques and the others to follow him as he walked toward the door. Jacques, blessedly, came without complaint.

Before exiting, the man turned to the medical team. "Lock the door," he said. "Anyone human will be able to let you know what they need."

Then he was gone.

Inside the medical bay, the battle for Michi's life continued.

Outside, the battle for everyone else raged on.

CHAPTER 30

The deck was abandoned. Thick trails of grayish slime marred the wood, some running up the walls, but there were no people, and more, there were no sirens. The *Melusine* might as well have been a ghost ship, drifting aimlessly forever.

Tory, her hands wrapped around the tranquilizer gun, frowned as she looked around, trying to find something, anything, to indicate that they weren't alone. "Shouldn't there be guards or something?" she demanded. "Where is everybody?"

"Locked in their labs like sensible people, probably," said Luis. He stepped daintily over a patch of slime. It would have been funny, if he hadn't looked so afraid. He held a small blowtorch, also taken from his tool kit. It was intended for underwater drone repairs, and it burned hot enough to vaporize flesh. It would do.

Olivia had no weapons. Olivia had her camera, watching everything through its screen. It was a way of distancing herself from the scene. Tory was almost envious. It would have been nice to have a little distance.

They inched their way along the deck, flinching from every sound. Danger could be lurking anywhere, and so the deep-down primitive portions of their minds had kicked into overdrive, seeing disaster in every shadow, hearing death in every scuffed foot or rasping breath. This was not their world anymore, if it ever had been in the first place.

They were halfway to the cafeteria when Tory stopped, staring at the wall. Luis and Olivia came to a halt behind her, both making sounds of confused protest.

"What is it?" asked Luis.

"Look." Tory pointed.

Luis and Olivia followed her finger, frowning. Luis continued to frown as Olivia gave a small gasp.

"The light is on," she said.

"The light is on," echoed Tory, and moved toward the lab assigned to Dr. Holly Wilson. She raised her hand to knock, stopped herself, and rang the doorbell. There was no sound, but she knew that inside a light would be flashing, telling Holly someone was outside.

"We can't wait here," said Luis. "Those things might come back."

"We can't *leave* her here," said Tory. "She'd never hear them coming." Unspoken was the fact that Holly wouldn't have heard the screams. She could lock herself in her lab and wait for rescue, but she deserved the choice to come with them.

"We need to go," said Luis.

Tory rang the bell again.

There was a pause, followed by a click. The lab door swung open, revealing Holly, looking at them bemusedly. She moved her hands. Tory shook her head.

"I'm sorry," she said. "We don't sign. Can you read my lips?"

Holly made a wobbling motion with one hand.

"Thank God," said Tory. "You need to come with us."

"Why?" asked Holly.

All three of the others jumped.

Her accent was odd, which made sense: she knew the mouth-shape of the word, but not what it sounded like. Still, it was clear enough that they could understand her.

"I didn't know you could talk," said Tory.

"Of course I can talk," said Holly. "But you can't understand me, so I had to learn to make sounds with my mouth. Why am I going with you?"

"The sirens are on the ship," said Tory. "They're killing people. You need to come with us."

There was a pause while Holly finished absorbing this. Lipreading wasn't the effortless party trick it looked like in the movies: it was a laborious process of mapping lip motions to possible phonemes, rejecting words that looked the same but made no sense in context. Sign was so much easier. With sign, what you said was what you meant, and not some complicated guessing game.

Finally she asked, "Can I grab my laptop?"

Tory nodded. "Just be quick."

Holly turned and ran across the lab, gathering the precious parts of her research, the things a backup couldn't replace. Maybe it was silly. Maybe it was frivolous. But she'd already lost one sister, and her second sister was somewhere on this ship, out of reach, out of range. She wasn't going to lose them both *and* her work at the same time. If that happened, she might as well give herself to the sirens. She'd have nothing left.

Tory, Olivia, and Luis formed a semicircle around the lab door, each holding their weapon—gun, torch, camera—in front of themselves, as if that small talisman would be enough to keep the entire world at bay. When Holly returned and tapped Tory on the shoulder, Tory jumped and squeaked. Olivia and Luis whipped around, and for one frozen moment, it looked like all four of them were going to scream.

The moment passed. Tory gave a nervous laugh.

"Okay," she said. "Okay, let's not do that again. Come on, let's move." She started walking again, once more taking point. Holly followed close behind, while Luis—as the only other person who had an actual weapon—brought up the rear.

They moved down the deck, only the soft thuds of their footsteps betraying their location. More of those terrible slime trails extended over the rails and up the walls. Holly stopped to study one more closely, but didn't touch it. It smelled faintly fishy, and glistened where the light touched it.

Tory frowned at Holly and waved, trying to get the other woman's attention.

"I need a sample," said Holly. She looked around, finally settling on Luis. "You have a test tube in that backpack?"

"No," he said, before digging a plastic baggie out of his pocket. A few crushed candy shells stuck to the inside. He held it out toward her. "Will this work?"

"Sure," she said, and took the baggie, turning it inside out. Candy shells littered the deck at her feet. Careful to avoid touching the mucus with her bare skin, she scraped a small amount off the wall and wrapped it in the plastic bag before tucking it in her pocket. She turned back to Tory and nodded, signaling her readiness to resume.

Their progress was slow but steady. They were almost to the cafeteria; soon they'd be in a position to close the doors and forget about the world outside, letting it become someone else's problem. Tory was relieved. She'd come here to find the things that killed her sister, and she'd done that. She'd come here to see them with her own two eyes, and she'd done that too. Before, locked in the lab, she'd felt like she was running away. But now, out in the open...

There were monsters in the night. They had sailed off the edge of the map, and there was a good chance they were going to die here. Anne wouldn't want her to die here. Anne would want her to make it home, to tell their parents what she'd learned, to introduce them to Olivia, to watch them fall in love with the idea that maybe she was finally going to fall in love. Anne would want her to *live*. And she couldn't do that if she got herself killed.

"Almost there," murmured Luis.

Olivia, watching the scene through her camera, screamed.

It was a short, sharp sound, cut off and swallowed almost as soon as it began, but it was enough. Tory fell back, her shoulders bumping into Holly and bringing her to a halt. Luis stepped forward, pressing in next to Olivia.

"You want to say something?" he asked, voice low and tight. "Because if you just saw a bug or something, I'm going to set your hair on fire."

She didn't say a word. She just raised one shaking hand and pointed at the place where the ceiling met the wall. Shadows pooled there, and Tory knew they shouldn't have been that thick, or that motionless; there were lights running the length of the hall, and even where the light didn't reach directly, refractions and ripples bounced off the water, making the darkness move. This darkness was perfectly still, like a cat preparing to pounce.

"Olivia..."

"It's watching us," whispered Olivia. She kept her eyes on her camera's view screen, where the balance between dark and light had conspired to make the siren visible. "It knows we're here, and it's watching us. If we keep walking…" Her voice trailed off. She didn't need to explain what would happen if they kept walking.

"Back up," said Tory, her eyes still on the unmoving shadow. She took another step back, nudging Holly, who did the same.

The shadow twitched.

"*Run!*" shouted Olivia, and Tory grabbed Holly's hand, and they ran.

For Holly Wilson, this entire day—this entire *voyage*—had been like a dream. She was accustomed to people ignoring her, thinking she was somehow less than they were because she couldn't hear them. She was accustomed to people talking to her translator even when she was standing *right there*. That was part of why she preferred to have Hallie translate for her. Hallie would remind people that Holly was the one with the chemistry degree, and things would continue the way they should have from the start.

But Hallie was off somewhere doing her own research, and much as Holly wanted to be okay with that, she couldn't. Not when she didn't have another translator on board, not when monsters were coming out of the sea and devouring everything in their path.

Not when Heather was dead. Dreamlike as everything else seemed, she had no illusions about Heather's death. Even in her worst nightmares, she'd never been able to conceive of a world where Heather was dead and she wasn't. Part of her didn't want this trip to ever end, because strange and horrific as it was, it wasn't *real*. Once they got back to land, things would be *real* again, and she would have to start figuring out how she was going to live in a world without Heather. She wasn't sure she could.

So she'd been trying to take refuge in her work. But her lab mates had gone and not come back, and now these semistrangers were hauling her around the ship, running from something she hadn't spotted and couldn't hear coming. Most of the time, she didn't feel like her deafness slowed her down. Here and now, she would have given almost anything to know that when her death showed up, she'd hear it coming.

Tory shouted, lips moving too fast for Holly to follow. The group changed directions, dragging Holly in their wake. Their destination came clear up ahead: the elevator, which was standing open, apparently waiting for them. The light was on inside, making it clear that nothing was lurking there. It was, however temporarily, safe.

The group ran for the elevator, and Tory hit the button to close the door. She turned to the others, once again speaking slowly and clearly as she said, "The captain should be in the control room. We can go there, find out when the shutters will be ready. Maybe we can help. Maybe this is the only deck that's been swarmed."

They all knew she was…not lying, not exactly, but being willfully optimistic, like optimism could change the reality of their situation. If the sirens had been on a single deck, the guards would have descended like the fist of God, sweeping them away, making things safe again. The shields would have come down. That was the truly troubling thing about what was going on. If this *wasn't* ship-wide, if this *wasn't* some sort of disaster, why were the shutters not down? Why were the sides of the ship still open, allowing anything that wanted to come up from the depths to come aboard?

Holly slumped against the wall, trying to take comfort in the feel of the metal vibrating against her shoulder blades. They *would* be safe, soon. They *would* be. They *had* to be. She could barely function without her twin, her friend, the other half of her now perpetually broken heart. She couldn't imagine what would happen to Hallie if she died too, and left her big sister alone.

(The thought that something could have happened to Hallie didn't cross her mind. Hallie was the big sister, the mountain that protected them from the ravages of the world. If Hallie had been in that submersible with Heather, Heather would have survived. If Hallie were here, she'd know exactly what to do. Hallie could be bossy and annoying and I-know-best in the way of big sisters and hearing people combined, but she was also a superhero, and superheroes always knew what to do.)

The others were talking again, too fast for her to follow. Luis gestured wildly, indicating the elevator doors; he was upset about what they were going to find when they disembarked. Tory was more restrained. She kept glancing at Olivia, taking the other woman's measure—worrying about her. That was interesting. Holly hadn't been aware they were a couple. Heather had been under the impression that Tory didn't care for Olivia, and had said so several times when they were alone in their cabin.

Guess you were wrong, she thought, and it burned that she'd never be able to tell her sister that to her face.

The elevator's shaking grew more pronounced, shuddering and stuttering. Holly stiffened. The car was still moving, and the change in its tempo hadn't been extreme enough for the other three to have noticed it; they were continuing to argue, Luis shouting, Tory replying too rapidly for Holly's eyes to follow, Olivia aiming her camera at the elevator doors like recording whatever happened next could somehow change it.

What I wouldn't give for one of those translation apps right now, thought Holly, and stepped away from the wall, touching Tory's arm. Tory stopped yelling and turned to face her, lips forming a silent but recognizable "What?"

"Something's wrong with the elevator," said Holly.

"What do you mean?" asked Tory, not entirely succeeding in hiding her panic.

"The car just jerked. Something's wrong."

Luis touched the wall. "She's right," he said. "We're slowing down."

"Aren't elevators supposed to slow down when they get where they're going?" asked Olivia.

"Not like this," said Luis. He was speeding up; whatever he said next was too fast for Holly, but it was enough to cause the other two women to look alarmed. Olivia took a step back, still focused on her camera, like she thought it was going to protect her.

Somehow, Holly doubted that.

Tory glanced up at the readout above the doors before hitting the button for the next floor. It was two decks shy of their destination, but it was substantially closer, and might mean getting off the malfunctioning elevator before it got fully stuck. Holly retreated into her corner, watching the others brace themselves, preparing for the doors to open. She didn't have a weapon. She didn't have a way of defending herself. She didn't even have the luxury of knowing what they were talking about.

You assholes should have learned to sign, she thought viciously, and then a hand slammed through the grate at the center of the elevator's roof, claws extended, snatching at the air. Everyone screamed, even Holly, who was startled into a wild, undulating yell.

The hand froze at the sound. The elevator stopped. The doors opened. Tory grabbed Olivia and ran out onto the deck. Luis paused, looking back at Holly, who was still backed into the corner, staring at the hand. Then he grabbed her by the wrist and dragged her after him, fleeing into the night.

"How did it know to get on top of the damn *elevator*?!" gasped Tory as she ran, hauling Olivia in her wake. There was more of that damned slime crisscrossing the deck, which they had come to recognize as a sign that the things had already gotten this far. The sirens were on the ship. The sirens were all *over* the ship; there was no escaping them. The best they could hope for was to lock themselves in a lab or cabin and pray the monsters outside didn't realize they were there.

(The door would not protect them; the door was not enough. The door was wood and riveted steel and it was *not enough*. Tory had known that even before they'd run past the first shattered door. The cabin beyond had been dark, but not dark enough; there was blood on the door, and blood mixed into the slime on the deck outside, and none of them were safe. Not here, not anywhere.)

"Where *are* they?" countered Luis. "They've got to be every-where on this damned ship. How have we only seen two?"

"They're inside." Olivia sounded almost serene. She was run-ning as fast as the rest of them, but there was no wobble or hitch in her voice; she might have been going for a lovely afternoon stroll. She didn't take her eyes off the camera. Whatever happened, she was going to leave a record. God help her, she was going to leave a record. "They went deeper. That's what predators do, when they're taking a reef. That's what the mermaids are doing here."

Tory didn't correct her. If she wanted to call the damned things mermaids, despite Dr. Toth's objections, she could go ahead. Olivia had earned the right as much as any of them.

"What do you mean, 'inside'?" demanded Luis.

"They're inside," said Olivia. She pointed down a corridor as they ran past it. "Go deep, get the young and the weak, the ones that wouldn't be on the outside of the reef. It means the quickest kills come first, and then they can move outward."

"Oh God," moaned Tory.

"There's a stairwell ahead," said Luis. "We need to get to the top of the ship."

Why that was so important didn't need to be discussed. The top of the ship meant finding the captain; it meant people with weapons, maybe even the Abneys, who were probably treating this whole thing as a grand adventure. It meant reaching the control room. Lowering the shutters with the sirens already on the ship might not do as much good as it would have if it had happened earlier, but at least this way they could keep the things from returning to the sea. They could sweep the *Melusine* one aisle at a time, shooting anything that moved, until they were free of aquatic attackers.

The captain had said not to panic, Imagine had everything in hand, but Imagine *didn't* have everything in hand. People had died. People had died before this—Heather and Ray and who knew how many others—but now it had passed some unspeakable threshold, becoming the sort of thing that should drive them back to shore, ceding the ocean to the sirens. They'd *have* to. They had enough, didn't they? No one could say mermaids weren't real after this. No one could say they were making things up. Imagine would be vindicated. Anne would be avenged. Everything would be all right.

But there was blood on the deck and the doors had been smashed by hands that weren't human, had never been human, *could* never have been human, and nothing was all right. Nothing was ever going to be all right again.

Luis reached the stairwell first. His legs were the longest, his arms had the most reach; it was inevitable that he be in the lead. Tory had enough time to think about how well suited he was for this headlong flight before the reality of the situation sank in, the fact that these sirens were ambush predators as much as anything else, taking their prey through subterfuge and guile.

She wanted to shout at him, to order him to stop, but the words stuck in her throat. He grabbed the door handle. He wrenched it open.

The siren hanging off the back of the door hissed, already launching itself at him.

Holly stepped forward and screamed again. It was an ear-piercing, horrifying sound, the primal shriek of someone who'd never heard another human being scream, had never learned how to scream the "right" way. She screamed in odd harmonics, in keys that should never have been combined. The siren froze, just like the one in the elevator.

Luis set its face on fire.

The blowtorch he'd grabbed before leaving the lab was small, but it burned hot. The siren screamed, the sound beginning as a pallid echo of Holly's shriek and morphing into something thinner and shriller and altogether alien. They were hearing what the sirens really sounded like, or at least what they sounded like while they were on fire. It was a terrible, earsplitting sound, and it rendered Holly's scream comprehensible by comparison.

The siren let go of the door to slap at the flames consuming its face, and fell, landing on the deck, where it writhed. Its "hair" was blazing now, a terrible torch that burned with a smoky, oily light.

"Up the stairs!" shouted Luis, continuing to aim his torch at the siren. "Go!"

Tory and Olivia ran, waving for Holly to follow them, which she did, and gladly. They all jumped over the writhing siren, careful to avoid its thrashing limbs and tail, scanning the stairwell as they moved. Nothing lurked there; the siren had been alone, for whatever reason. They seemed to be scattering around the ship. That was a good thing. That might keep them alive.

Luis turned to follow the women, and stopped as something locked around his ankle, claws piercing his flesh. He stopped and looked back. The siren had latched on, driving its talons through the fabric of his jeans. It was still writhing, still burning, but it had enough instinct remaining to hold him there.

He turned the torch on the soft flesh of its arm. It wailed, letting him go, falling back. He turned then, and ran, as fast as he could, toward the hope of safety. The stairwell door slammed behind him, leaving the burning siren alone on the deck.

CHAPTER 31

Western Pacific Ocean, above the Mariana Trench: September 3, 2022

Michi Abney died one hour and seven minutes after she'd been shot. It would have happened faster, if not for the medical team doing everything in their power to keep her alive. Her last breath was accompanied by a froth of bloody foam. Dr. Toth took a step backward. The other attending doctors did the same. All three of them stared at the body of the woman who had seemed so vital, so untouchable, verging on immortal.

"Call it," said Dr. Vail.

"Eleven twenty-two p.m.," said Dr. Odom. For the first time since the crisis had begun, he turned and looked at the medical bay. Drs. Vail and Toth did the same.

They weren't alone. Passengers had been arriving in a steady trickle for the last hour, coming in by ones and twos, some holding each other up, almost all of them pale and in shock. They sat on the folding chairs near the walls, on open cots, on the floor itself, anywhere that they would be safely out of the way and not need to fear being asked to leave. That seemed to be the greatest worry of everyone in the room: that they'd be asked to leave, to go out onto the ship and find some other safe haven, some other place to be.

There were four guards outside the door and two more inside, and Dr. Toth wasn't sure anything would have been enough to make these people feel safe. Maybe not ever again. If they made it back to shore alive, all of these witnesses to Michi's death were going to have nightmares for the rest of their days.

Good, she thought fiercely. Things like this, moments like this, were meant to be remembered. They were meant to be *felt*. Let these people feel what it was to truly sail to the ends of the earth. No one who went this far from shore came back unscathed. No one ever could.

Jillian walked to the sink and peeled off her gloves, red with Michi's blood, viscous with the yellowish fluid that had been pouring from the hunter's wounds. She dropped them into the basin with a soft thud. They didn't matter anymore. She was done with medicine on this ship.

Dr. Vail and Dr. Odom were trauma surgeons. They understood what it was to put a body back together. The only reason she had her EMT certification was her time on the old Greenpeace boats, when it had sometimes been necessary for her to perform emergency surgery on someone who'd gotten too close to a harpoon. She'd held men together with her bare hands and baling wire, and she wasn't sorry. But this...

This was not what she'd signed on for.

Returning to the table where Michi's body cooled, she picked up the samples taken over the course of the other woman's treatment, checking the seals on the test tubes and dishes before setting them systematically into her carryall. When she was done, she turned to Dr. Vail.

"I have everything I need," she said. "I'm going to return to my lab, and see if I can get a better idea of the structure of these toxins. If someone sees Dr. Wilson, please send her to me. She might be able to unlock the protein chains. Holly, please, not Hallie."

"You can't be thinking of going out there," said Dr. Odom. "Those things will eat you alive."

"I don't think so," she said. "Based on the reports we're getting from the refugees"—she waved a hand to indicate the scientists— "they're coming in waves. Haven't you noticed? They come wave after wave, and each one is larger than the one before. We're in the lull between right now. There may be a few stragglers on the ship, but for the most part, they're taking their catch to the bottom of the sea."

A gasp from somewhere behind her, a muffled sob. Dr. Odom glared. Jillian didn't care. Glaring wasn't going to change anything.

"I'll lock the door once I reach my lab," she said. "I'll notify Mr. Blackwell of my position. He won't blame you if I'm devoured. Any of you. He knows better than to expect anyone to keep me somewhere when I want to be somewhere else. Keep the doors closed. Keep the lights on. And pray. At this point that's the best you can do."

She turned and walked out before he could muster a response. That was good; that was what she'd been hoping for. It was always better if she could leave without a big argument, and sometimes saying the unthinkable would shut people down long enough for her to do that. The guards at the door looked at her with dismay but let her pass, presumably because they thought the guards outside would keep her from going any farther. The guards outside looked surprised by her appearance but let her keep going; after all, the guards inside had clearly known what she was going to do.

"No one wants to be the bad guy," she said, and walked on.

Trails of slime covered everything. Jillian looked up, noting the places where claws had dug divots into the corners. The sirens understood gravity well enough to use it as a weapon, then. That wasn't something they could practice often, living as deep as they did. Either they'd managed to sink more ships than anyone knew, or they had an excellent method of passing knowledge down through the generations.

"We forgot about you, but you never forgot about us," she said. "I suppose that gives you the advantage."

There was blood on the rails, great smears of it every few feet, marking the places where people had been dragged to their deaths. She looked at it impassively, noting how the slime varied in thickness and consistency, trying to find some rhyme or reason in the chaos. Hagfish didn't control the mucus their bodies created; it was an involuntary reaction to fear, to light, to existence in a cruel, uncaring ocean. Looking at the mess the sirens had made, she didn't think they had control over their slime either. They were intelligent creatures—there was no question of that—but that didn't make them monsters out of myth. They were flesh. They had limitations. They could be killed.

The trouble was, humans had been domesticated by their own

hand. Humans had given up violence as a way of life, and that was a good thing; that was the reason they had civilization and universities and scientific missions, rather than living in a great chasm in the earth, mirroring their aquatic cousins. But the sirens had never domesticated themselves. The sirens were still nature, red in tooth and claw, and while they might die, humans died so much more easily that it was almost comic.

Jillian kept walking.

For all her bravado in the medical bay, there was a difference between offering a theory and walking bodily into it. She hadn't felt like this since the first time she'd gone swimming in a sea rife with sharks, feeling their fins brush against her arms as they circled, knowing that at any moment she could be at the mercy of their gloriously efficient teeth. She *thought* the sirens had moved on. She *thought* she could make the short trip in safety. Thinking never changed the world. Research did, yes, and study, but that was action. Science was philosophy plus movement. Thought alone couldn't make the grade.

If she got eaten here, who was going to tell her daughter, and what would they say? Theo would candy-coat it, would say she'd been where she was supposed to be, doing what she was supposed to do, and had died a hero. If he didn't make it—if both of them died here—maybe no one would think to tell Lani at all. She'd read about it on the news sites. World-renowned, frequently mocked sirenologist dead at sea, along with her estranged corporate husband. Sorry, kiddo, you're an orphan now.

The thought quickened her pace, not quite goading her into a run. Running would attract the attention of anything that might still be on this side of the ship. Stay calm, keep her steps measured and easy, and she could—

The stairwell door opened. Jillian stumbled back, getting ready to run after all.

Victoria Stewart emerged, one arm around the waist of a weeping but uninjured Olivia Sanderson. Dr. Holly Wilson was behind them, her right hand moving in a constant litany of silent swear words. Luis Martines brought up the rear. Blood was spreading up the left leg of his jeans, and he was holding a small blowtorch.

Tory stopped when she saw Jillian, her eyes going wide. "Dr. Toth!" she said. "What are you doing out here? It's not *safe*!"

"No, it's not. I'm on my way to my lab. I have some blood samples for analysis." She turned her attention to Holly, raising her hands and signing clumsily, 'Come with me, you? I need help.'

'Of course,' signed Holly. Then: 'None of these people sign. They're assholes.'

'Assholes who are keeping you alive,' signed Jillian.

Holly laughed, a sound almost as unnerving as her screams. Olivia turned to stare at her.

"We need to get to cover," said Luis. He took a step, wincing as the loss of momentum translated into pain. "They're fucking everywhere. And why aren't the shields down?"

"Maybe because once the sirens reached the ship, lowering the shields would have trapped them inside with us, and we don't have that many guns," said Jillian. "Or maybe they ate the captain before he could hit the button. Or maybe because the fucking shutters have never actually *worked* worth a damn. I don't know. What I *do* know is that we shouldn't be standing around out here. I'm heading for my lab. Come on."

"Luis is hurt," said Tory. "He needs medical attention."

The images of Jason Rothman and Michi Abney flashed through Jillian's mind. She forced them down and said, "Trust me. You'd rather come to my lab. I can do first aid." And if those novel toxins had already entered his bloodstream, analyzing the samples she'd taken from Michi and contrasting them to the samples she had from the first siren might be their only chance at coming up with a functional treatment.

The group still looked unsure—all save Holly, who had pushed her way past the others to reach Jillian's side. It was a choice born of pure, ruthless practicality: Jillian spoke enough sign to let Holly make herself understood. Tory and the others were nice, but they couldn't understand her. Going with the person who knew her language was the only real choice she could make.

Olivia, who spent her life paying attention to what people weren't saying as much as to what they were, spoke first. "There's something you're not telling us," she said.

"The list of things I'm not telling you is longer than my arm," said Jillian. "Come with me now."

"All right," said Luis, and crossed the line to join Holly by her side. Olivia and Tory trailed after him, and the group started down the deck.

It was harder to move quietly in a group of this size. Every pair of feet increased the chances of attracting attention. Holly didn't know how to walk quietly; she didn't stomp, but she didn't set her feet down lightly either. That was a skill that required some awareness of what walking sounded like, and she didn't have it. Jillian ground her teeth and kept going, urging the others along with her, swallowing the desire to leave them. Holly was an organic chemist. The rest might have skills that were less immediately applicable, but there was strength in numbers, and under the circumstances, Jillian wanted any sliver of strength that she could get.

When they reached her lab, the light next to the door was on. Jillian stopped, motioning for the others to do the same.

"Someone's in there," she said, and signed 'Wait' with her free hand for Holly's benefit. She might not be able to give the woman full context, but she could at least keep her partially informed. She could at least *try*.

"Is there somewhere else we could go?" asked Tory, voice low.

Jillian shook her head.

"I was afraid you'd say that," said Luis, and strode forward, turning the handle before kicking the door open, bringing his blowtorch up and aiming it directly in front of him.

Theodore Blackwell, sitting in Jillian's desk chair, lifted his head and looked quizzically at Luis. "What are you planning to do with that?" he asked. "I am neither a marshmallow to roast nor a seam to solder. You might be better off with a brick, assuming you can find one. Blunt trauma is traditional for a reason."

"Theo," said Jillian, pushing past Luis. She made for the desk, leaving the others to follow or not, as they chose. They filed in behind her, Olivia pausing to close and lock the door behind them. "What are you doing here? My agreement with Imagine includes a *private* lab, which means you shouldn't be entering it willy-nilly."

"The ship is under attack; people are dying; the shutters are not ready for deployment; you are my wife," he said mildly. "I don't believe this can be considered 'willy-nilly.'"

"I'm not sure my contract includes exemptions for sea monster attack." She began emptying her carryall, putting her samples on the desk. One attempted to roll off; she caught it and placed it back with the others. "Don't you have work to do? Shouldn't you, at the very least, be with the captain, trying to figure out why he can't close the damn shields already? People are dying, as you so charmingly say, and I can't see where closing the doors and giving ourselves a shooting gallery could possibly make that any worse. Who knows? It might make a few things better. I think we're well overdue for something that gets *better*."

"The captain stopped responding to com calls an hour ago," said Theo. He didn't move from the chair where he had settled. "Two guard teams were sent to find out what was happening. Neither of them came back."

"That's encouraging," muttered Jillian. She began sorting her samples. "Where's the other Dr. Wilson, and your little protégé? Have they been eaten yet?"

"They were in my private lab, attempting to communicate with the creature, last I saw," said Theo wearily. He closed his eyes. "It's been some time. I haven't called down. I don't want to disrupt them."

"You mean you don't want to know if they're dead."

"Yes. That, too."

Tory frowned. "Hold on. What do you mean, 'communicate with the creature'? Do you still have the siren?"

"Of course he does," said Jillian, continuing to sort her samples. "He's planning to take the thing back to shore with us, see what he can find out when he has more time to work. See what Imagine can learn. They're not a scientific company, but I'm sure they can come up with *something* about a real, live siren that will benefit them. Barnum did pretty well for himself, after all."

"Did you stop to consider that maybe that's *why they're attacking*?!" Olivia's voice rose to a shrill squeak.

"Scientific advancement has always been a dangerous beast, needing to be grabbed and grappled before it could be fully understood," said Theo. "My superiors said, 'Get a mermaid,' and I've done my best to oblige. It's going to be a bit awkward if I don't survive the retrieval, but I suppose that's going to be someone else's problem."

Jillian's hands slowed, finally stopping as she turned to look at Theo for the first time since entering the room. He was reclining in the chair, legs extended. His uninjured leg was crossed over the other one; he often sat that way when he felt unwell, preventing any twitches or spasms from attracting unwanted attention.

He was pale. His skin looked clammy, and beads of sweat stood out on his temples, as if he had just been running. He couldn't possibly have been running. Even if he'd wanted to, his leg wouldn't have allowed it.

"Theo?" she said quietly.

"I'm all right," he said, opening his eyes and forcing a smile. "I really am. It's just that I've been away from my quarters for quite some time."

Comprehension dawned. "You don't have your medicine," she said. "How bad is the pain?"

"I'd consider an elective amputation at the moment, if I weren't sure it would make things worse. The creatures smell blood, and ours is different enough from theirs that they can follow it..." He paused, eyes locked on Luis's leg, like he'd just realized the other man was injured. "For the love of God, get that cleaned up, or we're all dead."

"We're aware," said Jillian. "Luis, come here and sit down." She gestured to the room's free chair as she moved to get the first aid kit from her desk.

"We may all be dead anyway," said Theo. "They're still on the ship, and it's not safe to assume they won't make another pass. They're *smart*. You understand that? They know what they're doing."

"Even predators who aren't this smart know how to double back for double the prey," said Tory. "Orcas, leopard seals, they all exhibit that behavior. You don't have to be a genius to know that something that runs will eventually come back."

"Maybe not, but these things *are* geniuses." There was an edge to Theo's voice that had never been there before, sharp and unforgiving and pained. Jillian gave him a worried look. He scowled. "Yes, it hurts. But as there's no way to get my medication without getting out of this chair, there's nothing I can do about it."

"Spoken like a man who's forgotten who he married," said Jillian mildly. "Luis, check my desk. Second drawer on the left. The chocolate drops, if you please."

Theo's eyebrows climbed toward his hairline. "You're not suggesting..."

"Cannabis is a highly effective painkiller, and I don't think you're in a position to be picky," said Jillian.

377

Luis stopped in the process of moving toward the desk, turning to stare at her in disbelief. "Are you telling me to get him high?" he asked.

"No. I'm asking you to reduce his pain. The chocolate drops are medicinal; the cannabis used in their manufacture has been bioengineered to reduce its THC content to negligible levels. Mr. Blackwell suffers from nerve damage incurred during the conclusion of his maritime career, and funny as I might find it to watch him grinding his teeth and denying how much pain he's in, we need him lucid if he's going to help us."

"Help us with what?" asked Olivia.

Jillian bared her teeth in the semblance of a smile. "Survival."

"I'll eat your damned candy," said Theo. "Just stop talking about it, and I'll eat anything you want."

"Promises, promises," said Jillian. "Please, Mr. Martines. The candy."

Olivia opened her mouth to ask what Jillian meant by "survival," and paused as the mass spectrometer beeped. She looked past the doctor to the lab bench, where Holly had been silently preparing samples and feeding them into the various machines for analysis. "Um," she said. "Should she be doing that?"

"Doing what?" Jillian turned. "Ah." Raising her hands, she signed, 'What do?'

'I'm preparing the samples for analysis,' signed Holly, picking up her dropper. She transferred two drops of Michi's blood to a vial, then slotted it into the centrifuge. Then she signed, 'You seemed busy.'

'They weren't labeled. Did you—'

'I know how to avoid cross contamination.'

'Okay.' Jillian turned back to the others. "Dr. Wilson is preparing our samples. Together, she and I should be able to determine what sort of toxins these creatures carry. Which reminds me: Mr. Martines, after you give the candy to my stubborn cretin of a husband, please sit down. I need to check your wound."

"Toxins?" asked Tory.

"How is she going to tell us what she learns?" asked Olivia.

"My ASL is poor in most areas, but excellent when it comes to science," said Jillian. "It seemed like a good place to specialize, given the people I was likely to be working with—and I did some review when I learned the Wilsons had signed on for this voyage. I have a great deal of respect for both Drs. Wilson, and their work in their respective fields."

"It would have been nice if the rest of us could have gotten a passenger list," said Luis. He handed the cellophane baggie of chocolate drops to Theo, who took it without comment.

"It would be nice if I had a pony, and yet here we are," said Jillian. She pointed to Luis. "Sit. Now. Roll up your trousers, and be grateful we're not asking you to take them off."

Luis sat, cheeks flushing, and hissed under his breath as he pulled up the blood-soaked leg of his jeans. Another gush of blood accompanied the action.

Tory couldn't watch her friend's pain. Instead she watched Jillian, and the way Dr. Toth watched the blood. She'd mentioned toxins; she had been unwilling to go back to the medical bay. The image of Jason rose unbidden in Tory's mind, and she shuddered, making no effort to minimize the motion. Something was going on. Something bigger and worse than just a swarm of sirens coming up from the deep and having their way with the ship.

"Dr. Toth, what aren't you telling us?" Tory asked.

"Too much," said Jillian again. "Help Dr. Wilson." With that, Tory was apparently dismissed, as the good doctor knelt in front of Luis.

He watched as she prodded the skin, only wincing a little, sucking air between his front teeth in sharp hisses. When she paused he forced a grin and asked, "How'm I looking, Doc? All good?"

"Not really," she replied. "You have four deep puncture wounds, and one that came distressingly close to compromising your Achilles tendon. You got off lucky, difficult as that may be to believe. The bleeding hasn't stopped, but given you've been on your feet this whole time, that's not as concerning as it might be. Does this hurt?"

She jabbed a finger into the deepest of the wounds, midway down his ankle. Luis yelped, trying to yank his foot away, only to be stopped as she closed her hand around it.

"I asked a question," she said.

"Holy fuck, yes, it hurt!" he shouted. "Is that what you wanted to hear?"

"Yes," she said, and removed an eyedropper from her pocket. "I'll give you the good news first: it looks like you might be okay."

"Uh, thanks," he said.

"Michi Abney is dead," she said calmly as if she were reading from a shopping list. While Luis gaped at her, she slid the eyedropper into the deepest of his wounds and sucked up about half an ounce of blood. He winced. Jillian ignored him. Voice still calm, she said, "This blood is contaminated; it's been exposed to air, it's experienced clotting, it's not a pure sample. That's what we need right now. The sirens are novel beings. They're not extraterrestrial—their biology is too similar to things we already know exist to be aliens or invaders. They're just another evolutionary path. They can eat us and not suffer for it. But that doesn't mean everything about them is as harmless to us as we are to them."

"I didn't understand half of that," said Luis.

"She's saying the mermaids—sorry, sirens—are toxic to us somehow," said Tory, with dawning horror. "But Jason stuck himself on one of their parasites."

"Yes, and those parasites don't kill their hosts, which means the sirens are resistant." Jillian straightened. "Oof. My knees don't belong to a young woman anymore."

Luis frowned. "Are you saying I'm going to die?"

"I'm saying you're probably *not* going to die; your blood is still clotting. Michi died partially because she bled out and partially because of the toxins in her bloodstream causing massive seizures, and you seem fine. Look at it this way, Mr. Martines: you've done science a great favor. Now we know these things don't have venom glands on their nails. Although you're probably going to need a *lot* of antibiotics, when everything is said and done."

She turned and walked back to the lab bench where Holly, head down, was preparing samples and loading them into machines with remarkable speed. Jillian touched her lightly on the shoulder and she lifted her head, a quizzical look on her face.

Jillian held up the dropper full of blood and indicated the centrifuge. Holly nodded and stepped to the side.

"This is nuts," said Tory. "This is insane. We can't just hole up in here and play with chemistry sets. We need to be closing the shutters. We need to be calling for help. Do we know if anyone called for help?"

"There are no ships larger than a private fishing vessel within two days of our location. In the best-case scenario, air support will take hours to reach us—and that's assuming I could call them. The internet has been out since the captain stopped answering calls. And before evacuation could take place, there would be other considerations, which might prove...problematic," said Theo wearily. He closed his eyes. "The cannabis is helping, but it will be a few minutes before I can assist further."

"I don't think we *have* a few minutes," argued Tory hotly. "We should be doing something. We should be moving. Where is the captain? We need to find out what's going on."

"On the top deck, preparing to deploy the shutters," said Theo.

"Well, then, we're done, because there's no way to get to the top deck," said Luis. "Not with those things in the elevators. We can't trust the stairs to be clear. The sirens are everywhere."

"What if we didn't take the stairs *or* the elevator?" asked Olivia.

Luis and Tory turned to look at her. Even Theo raised his eyebrows.

"What did you have in mind?" he asked.

Olivia took a deep breath. "Ray and I got to the ship early. I don't...I don't like new spaces that I don't know very well, and it was important that I be comfortable with the *Melusine* if I was going to do my job and interview the arriving scientists. We got an accommodation to allow us to board before anyone but the essential crew."

"You did nothing wrong, Miss Sanderson," said Theo. "I'm aware of your accommodations. I signed off on them. What did you find?"

"The ship was designed to be used for cruises and stuff after we finished using it for research, right? Well, um, there are tubes. For room service and dirty dishes and things like that. They open on every deck, but since they're not supposed to be used by passengers, only members of the crew, they only open if you have the code. I don't think the sirens could get in there, could they?"

"No," said Theo. "I don't believe they could. Unfortunately, without a member of the crew, I don't believe we can either."

"I can," said Olivia. "I can go to the top, and find out what's happening, and call back. I can do it."

"How?" asked Tory.

Olivia shrugged, looking briefly self-conscious. "Because I have the code."

Theo blinked before beginning to smile. "Well, then," he said. "Perhaps we can do something about our situation after all."

CHAPTER 32

**Western Pacific Ocean, above the Mariana Trench:
September 3, 2022**

The swimming pool served multiple functions. It was key to the *Melusine*'s water filtration; without the intake and expulsion of the surrounding sea, there was no way for water to be cleansed. It was a mobile sampling unit. Even as the water itself could be strained and sifted until all traces of salt were removed, small sampling tubes around the intake ports were constantly capturing and filing vials of water from the surrounding area. By the time they returned to shore, the plan was for most of the ballast to be made up of water samples, all ready to be taken ashore and analyzed.

Once the *Melusine* stopped above the Mariana Trench, the pool had been converted from recreation to research, scooping up samples of the local wildlife and holding them in what was effectively one of the largest tide pools ever made. It had become a slice of the living sea, brought inside for the amusement of the scientists on board. It had worked very, very well. Even as the screams had been starting elsewhere on the ship, people had still been walking to the water, sitting down, and trying to let the fish swimming there soothe them.

No one sat there now. Blood and mucus clotted the floor and dotted the ceiling. Bodies floated in the water, missing pieces, missing limbs. The sirens that had broken the screens and slithered through the intake had discovered the clever mechanisms designed to keep captive fish from escaping; they had been unable to slither out the way that they'd come in. Without the ability to take their prey back to the depths, they had been reduced to eating it, ripping off huge chunks and swallowing them whole.

Sirens lounged in the pool, chewing idly on their kills, prodding at the walls in their quest for a way out. Others explored the room, moving more slowly than their cousins on the upper decks. They had the luxury of curiosity, of *time*, and they were going to enjoy it.

One of them felt its way along the wall, fascinated by the different textures. It dug its claws into a strange black box, sliming the mechanism with mucus in the process. The keypad reader, unequipped to handle this sort of accidental biological assault, beeped once before it shorted out. The siren pulled back, hissing. Two more sirens slithered over to join it.

The wall swung open.

The room on the other side was reasonably sized, dimly lit, and dominated by a clear wall, looking in on one of their cousins hanging suspended in the water. The captive siren flared its fins at the sight of the others. The three of them pulled themselves rapidly into the room, silent now, looking around with wide, light-devouring eyes.

Daniel and Hallie had gone still as soon as the door swung open. They didn't know what else to do. Mr. Blackwell had been gone considerably longer than he'd said he was going to be, and no one was picking up, either in the command room or in Holly's lab. Hallie had been calling her sister every fifteen minutes, and had never been able to get through. They'd been expecting guards, or Mr. Blackwell, or refugees running from some terrible catastrophe. They'd been expecting *something*, although their curiosity had never been quite enough to make them open the soundproof door, betraying their presence to the world. They'd been waiting.

They hadn't been expecting three sirens, their arms and faces gummy with human blood, slithering into the room. There was nowhere for the two scientists to run, nowhere for them to hide; the sirens blocked the only exit. More, there were more sirens outside, some visible on the walls, others sliding into the waters of the viewing pool. None of them seemed to be interested in what the others had found. Hallie didn't know whether to be grateful for that or not. It was as easy to be killed by three as by thirty.

The sirens had seen them. The one in the lead bared its teeth in something that could have been either threat or warning. It didn't matter. They were dead either way.

Hallie fumbled in the dark beside her, stopping when her hand found Daniel's. He grabbed on and held tight, taking comfort from the small human contact even as she did. Together they backed up, stopping when their shoulders hit the glass wall of the tank. Neither of them had said a word. They didn't need to. They knew how this ended.

Holly, I'm sorry, thought Hallie. She wanted to close her eyes. She wanted to have some small sense of peace when the end came. She did no such thing. She watched the sirens slither closer, taking a deep breath and holding it. It was going to hurt. It was going to hurt, and it wasn't going to stop hurting until she died. All she could do was hope she faced her end with dignity, that she didn't try to break and run at the last moment. There was no way out. She might as well die with some sense of control.

The sirens were only a few feet away. Daniel squeezed her hand. She braced herself, waiting for the first lunge.

The sirens stopped.

She blinked.

They cocked their heads like they were distracted by something. The one in the lead leaned back on its pelvis enough to raise its hands, balancing there as it signed.

They must have incredible core strength, thought Hallie, and glanced over her shoulder to the captive siren. It was signing to the other three, hands moving in patterns she'd never seen before, patterns that had nothing to do with human ideas of sign. She glanced back to the sirens. They were answering.

This time, when Daniel squeezed her hand, Hallie squeezed back as hard as she could, hoping he understood what they were looking at. *Don't move don't talk don't do anything that could make them angry*, she thought. There was no way he could hear her, but oh, it helped to think it. It helped to feel like she was doing *something*.

The sirens kept signing. It was impossible to read their expressions, but something about them seemed perplexed, like they couldn't understand what was happening any more than she could. Finally, with a hiss like a deflating balloon, the lead siren turned around and slithered toward the door, with the other two close behind.

Heart in her throat, Hallie waited until they were safely out of the lab before running after them and slamming the door. She turned back to the room, slumping against the door frame, and sank slowly to the floor as her knees gave way.

Daniel was still standing in front of the tank, seemingly frozen. Behind him, their captive siren continued to sign. Hallie recognized a handful of words—her name, the sign the siren had given for its own name, and, oddly enough, the word *captive*, over and over again.

"Thank you," she whispered.

"The chutes aren't big," said Olivia. "Maybe three feet across at their widest points, usually narrower than that. There are doors on every deck."

"Can they be opened from the inside?" asked Theodore.

She nodded. "Ray and I tested it. We wanted to know, in case it ever mattered. They were more concerned with people not being able to get into places they shouldn't go than getting out of them if they were already there."

"Doesn't quite fit with being so concerned about appearances that they'd require a passcode to get inside," said Luis.

Olivia shrugged. "Safety and accessibility were handled by different teams. That's not unusual. A project this size, you're always going to have contradictions, because no one has the time to ask whether every little thing made sense."

"So I climb up to find the captain, and then what?" asked Luis. "He produces a squadron of trained marines with flamethrowers?"

"All the marines are already patrolling the ship, which means most of them are probably already dead, and you're not going," said Olivia. "I am."

Silence fell, broken by the soft whirr of Jillian's machines, which continued chugging away, turning samples into science, extracting results from ruin. Holly never stopped her work. She was tireless, maybe because science didn't care if she could hear it; she had a common language with the machines, and that could never be taken away.

Tory found her voice first. "What?" she said. "No. You're not… No."

"I am," said Olivia. "I'm smaller than you are. I have the narrowest shoulders. I work out every day. If you're going to dress like Emma Frost on national webcasts, you need to have the body for it. I know how to free-climb. I can make it up the shaft, and besides, I'm the nonscientist. If someone is going to find a better solution, it's not going to be me. This is the thing I can do."

"And when you die?" asked Tory. "What am I supposed to do then?"

"I fell in love for the first time at a convention," said Olivia. "Her name was Jennie, but everyone called her Otter, and she kissed like there was some sort of time limit on the idea of kissing. I met her on Friday; I fell into bed with her on Saturday; I missed two broadcasts because I was in bed with her all day Sunday. Um." Her cheeks flared red as she realized who was in the room. "Mr. Blackwell, I—"

"Don't worry about it," he said. "I think you've earned a little forgiveness. I'm not going to tell on you."

"Thank you," she whispered, before saying, "We had to check out Monday. I went to my room to pack my things, and when I came looking for her, she was gone. She didn't leave a note. I didn't know her number or her preferred online handle or even her last name. I never saw her again. I fell in love and got my heart broken on the same weekend, because conventions are this weird liminal space that isn't real and isn't false and doesn't count when the banners come down."

"Why are you telling me this?" asked Tory.

"Because this mission is like a big convention, or a reality show. It's a pressure cooker. They put us all in one space, and we can't get away, and everything happens so fast. It happens *so fast*." She smiled sadly at Tory. "If I don't come back, you'll keep going. That's what you'll do. I haven't been here long enough for you to do anything else. Eventually, maybe, I'll have been here long enough. If I come back, we can try for that. But right now, I'm the one who makes sense. So I'm the one who's going."

"She's right," said Jillian. "Mr. Martines is wounded. Theo can't climb, I won't fit, and in addition to her other advantages, Miss Sanderson is familiar with the space, which makes her chances of success higher than Miss Stewart's. Miss Sanderson is our best candidate."

"You didn't mention Holly," said Tory.

"Dr. Wilson is acting as my assistant. Even if I were a candidate, she wouldn't be. We need to understand what these creatures do when they bite or otherwise infect one of us, or we'll have no hope of saving anyone whose system is compromised. We're fighting a battle on multiple fronts, Miss Stewart, and while it would be nice to pretend it was fair, it simply isn't."

"How far to the nearest hatch?" asked Theo.

Silence fell again, lasting for only a few moments before Olivia said, "It should be about twenty feet from here. Inside the hall."

"Can you make it that far by yourself?"

Olivia paled. It was obvious, just from looking at her expression, that she hadn't considered that aspect of her plan. "I guess I have to," she said.

"No, you don't," said Tory. "Luis, give me your flamethrower."

"It's not a flamethrower," he protested, even as he was handing it to her. "It's a blowtorch, and not a very powerful one. It's hot, but it doesn't have much range."

"I don't care. Liv needs the tranq gun," said Tory. "I'll walk you to the hatch, Liv. From there you're on your own."

"How will you get back?" asked Olivia.

Tory offered a wry smile. "Blowtorch."

It was an imperfect solution. It was probably going to get one or both of them killed. There wasn't anything better.

"I don't think we should let you go," said Luis. "If Olivia can't make it to the hatch by herself, she's never going to make it to the top of the ship."

Olivia bristled, but it was Tory who spoke. "No one's letting me do anything," she said. "I'm going with her because it makes the most sense."

"God save me from the children," muttered Jillian. "We're done fighting. We're only doing it because some of you have managed to latch on to the delusional idea that we're safe in here just because this room has a door and a lock. We're not safe. We're not going to *be* safe until we finish getting the damn shutters deployed." Even then, they wouldn't be safe, not until they were miles from here, with their feet back on solid ground. That part didn't need to be said. That part was obvious to all of them.

"So we go?" asked Tory.

"You go," said Jillian. "Miss Sanderson?"

"I'm ready," said Olivia, as bravely as she could—and really, her voice was surprisingly steady. She stood up straight, squaring her shoulders, and even flashed the room a pale ghost of her usual camera-ready smile. "Let's do this."

Tory walked to the door, unlocking it and creaking it open a few inches, the blowtorch in her hand, ready to be shoved into the face of anything that might lunge at them out of the darkness. Nothing moved on the deck outside the lab. She opened the door farther, tense, waiting for the moment when all hell broke loose.

Hell seemed content to stay bound, at least for the moment. The deck was motionless. Tory eased herself out the door, motioning for Olivia to follow. Someone—Dr. Toth, probably; Luis and Mr. Blackwell couldn't walk, and Holly's hands were full—closed the door once Olivia was out. There was a click as the bolt slid home. Tory realized, with a sickening lurch, that they hadn't agreed on a secret knock or passcode; when she came back and tried to get inside, they might think she was a siren and leave her where she was.

That was something to worry about later. Right now she needed to get Olivia to her destination. She turned to the other woman, mouthing, "Which way?"

Olivia pointed. Tory nodded, and they started down the deck. Neither was in the lead; Tory had the weapon but Olivia had the information, and so they walked side by side, slow, careful, setting their feet down as gently as they could. Avoiding the slime was impossible. They had to pause several times, one of them providing a stable arm for the other while they walked, one by one, through the sticky trails. Getting back was going to be an adventure . . . and that, too, was something to worry about later.

Dimly, Tory realized that she was already starting to write herself off. The situation was too dire: there was too much blood. She wasn't going to survive. Maybe none of them were. No matter what happened, the *Melusine* couldn't be allowed to go the way of the *Atargatis*; she couldn't be lost with all hands and no clear narrative of events. The world had to know. Lowering the shutters would help with that. Even if every person on the ship wound up ripped to shreds, the sirens would be trapped. They hadn't shown any real inclination toward destruction for destruction's sake. The computers and lab samples and everything else would be intact when the rescue crews came. Too late to save the people, maybe, but not too late to save the science.

Not too late to save the science.

Olivia stopped at a rectangular depression in the ship's wall. It was recessed by roughly three inches, creating space for the small keypad that was set into the side. It was small and subtle and Tory had walked past it and others like it dozens of times without realizing anything was different.

"This is it," mouthed Olivia, pointing to the rectangle.

Tory nodded understanding, leaned in, and kissed her.

It was a brief, glancing kiss; anything deeper or more involved would have risked both their lives. That wasn't the goal. They might die here, but they weren't going to do it yet. Olivia's eyes widened in brief surprise before she leaned closer and kissed Tory back, putting as much as she dared into the gesture. It was a moment of peace stolen from the jaws of chaos, and it meant more than either of them could say.

They pulled back. The moment passed. Olivia offered a quick, half-shy smile before she turned to the keypad and punched in the code. There was a soft beep. A piece of wall, two feet by two feet, slid to the side, revealing the chute on the other side.

The ship's architects had anticipated the need for maintenance. Handgrips studded the wall, spaced like rungs, moving up and down through the clean white tunnel. There were no lights, Tory realized; once Olivia was in there, she would be moving through total darkness.

"It's okay," mouthed Olivia, and bent to climb inside. The keypad beeped again. The hatch slid shut, and Tory was alone.

Behind her, something hissed.

The inside of the tube was tight. It had been tight the first time she'd climbed inside, back when she and Ray were exploring the ship (don't think about Ray *don't think about Ray*, and it didn't matter how much she scolded herself, because she couldn't stop), but that had been a quick in-and-out. Open the hatch, climb in, get comfortable hanging suspended in the black, isolated space, push the hatch, climb out.

It hadn't been a prolonged isolation in absolute darkness. It hadn't been her, and just her, climbing through the body of the *Melusine*, putting one hand over the other, waiting for the sound of snarls to echo from above and tell her she'd been wrong, the space had been compromised after all.

Olivia Sanderson climbed through the dark, and waited for her death to find her.

She missed her camera. It had been a reassuring talisman against reality. As long as she was watching it through the camera, it wasn't real. But there was no way to carry a camera while she was climbing through the dark, and if she'd hung it around her neck, it would have knocked against the sides of the tube, echoing and attracting attention. The tranquilizer gun was bad enough, shoved into her waistband and rubbing against her skin.

She was moving through atrocities. She knew that. Outside her safe little tube there were monsters and murders and terrible things, and if she stopped to open any given hatch, she would be rolling the dice on her own survival. One thing they hadn't talked about back in the lab (which already felt so far away, like something out of a dream): when she reached the top, when she opened the hatch and slipped into the light, what was she going to find? It might be safety. It might be the captain and his men, holding the line against the monsters from below. Or it might be a slaughter. She could stick her head out and have it removed in the same terrible moment, her body falling to land on whatever laundry or debris had been allowed to build up in the belly of the ship.

There hadn't been any other way. There hadn't been any other choice. If she wanted a chance to save her friends—to save herself—she had to do this. Besides, it was nice to be the hero for a change. She was Mario, climbing through the pipes to save the Mushroom Kingdom, instead of Peach, getting kidnapped by monster turtles. She was April O'Neil, traveling through the sewers to rescue her beloved Ninja Turtles. She was...she was...

She was scared out of her mind. This wasn't what she'd signed up for. All she'd ever wanted was the chance to show the world who she was and what she could do, to make them understand that she was more than a collection of traits randomly generated by some cosmic lottery. She was a person. She could be a hero if she wanted to. She could save the world, she could change the world, she could *belong* in the world, and anyone who wanted to say she couldn't could learn to live with how wrong they were.

But she hadn't wanted to die. That had never been part of the plan. Do a couple of years with Imagine, build a fan base, build a brand, and then head out into the wider world, see if she couldn't get a job emceeing a reality show or playing host for a children's science program. Change the world by living in it, not by dying for it.

It was really a shame the way nothing ever seemed to want to go according to plan. Hand over hand, Olivia kept climbing, moving toward the inevitable future.

Tory turned.

The siren was a small one, as the specimens she'd seen went: it was about the size of a scrawny thirteen-year-old, holding itself rigidly up on its arms. It was hissing, but it looked as startled to see her as she was to see it. She could easily imagine the adults sending it to double-check an area they were reasonably sure had already been denuded of prey, getting the obnoxious kid out of the way.

(And that was a dangerously anthropomorphic way of looking at things, because this wasn't a child, innocent and trusting and looking for a friend. This wasn't a fairy tale come to life. This was a dangerous animal, intelligent or not, and it would kill her if she gave it half a chance. It was her job not to let it.)

It was too far away to be dissuaded by her blowtorch, assuming it would even realize what the odd, flickering light was. None of the sirens had shown any sign of understanding fire before it was *on* them, consuming their flesh and introducing them to a new flavor of suffering. She could have waved the torch at a lion or bear to scare it away. With the siren she was reduced to a tactic that had worked for humans since the dawn of recorded time: she turned, and she ran.

Hissing wildly, the siren pursued.

Tory ran as fast as her feet would carry her, watching for an open, undamaged door, for a hallway, for *anything* that might get her away from the monster rapidly closing the distance between them. She knew the ship hadn't rearranged itself to spite her, but it felt that way as yard after yard of deck unspooled without providing any answers.

She was so focused on where she was going that she wasn't paying attention to where she was putting her feet. Her heel came down, hard, on a deep patch of slime, and she found herself skidding suddenly out of control. She waved her arms frantically, trying to stop herself, but it was too late. She slammed into the rail, arms still flailing, and went over the side before she could get her momentum under control.

I'm going to die, she thought frantically, and tried to force her body into a proper diving stance, arms out, legs together, head bent at a protective angle. It was the only thing left that she could do.

She dropped along the length of the *Melusine*, hit the water, and was gone.

ZONE SIX: DEMERSAL

The truth is out there. And when we find it, I'm pretty sure we're going to want it to *stay* out there, while the rest of us go home to our beds.

—Luis Martines

The trouble with discovery is that it goes two ways. For you to find something, that thing must also find you.

—Victoria Stewart

Heather's gone and Hallie's God-knows-where, and for the first time in my life, I'm alone. I used to say I wanted this, when I was a kid and one or both of my sisters was getting more attention than I thought they deserved. I hated Heather for having my face and my hands and using them to do things I didn't approve of. It was like having my own personal Imp of the Perverse, constantly devoted to damaging my reputation. I got to know what I looked like with skinned knees and black eyes—and since neither of us could hear, and most hearing adults couldn't tell us apart, the only way I didn't get in trouble right alongside her was by staying so spotless that there was no possible way I could have done anything wrong. She rendered me sterile, clinical, all because I was looking for contrast.

Hallie, though…Hallie could hear. Hallie was the first and the eldest, and she was the one who'd had our parents' full attention, and I was so jealous of her that it burned. No one ever mistook me for her. Sometimes I wished they would.

And they're both gone, and I wish I could find my eight-year-old self and tell her to be careful what she wishes for, because the universe is listening, and someday, no matter how many times she changes her mind, she just might get it.

—From the diary of Dr. Holly Wilson,
September 2, 2022

Science is not a matter of belief. Science does not care whether you believe in it or not. Science will continue to do what science will do, free from morality, free from ethical concerns, and most of all, free from the petty worry that it will not be *believed*. Belief has shaped the history of human accomplishment—we believe we can, and so we do—but belief has never changed the natural world. The mountain does not vanish because we believe it should. The unicorn does not appear because we believe it will.

The mermaid does not care whether or not we believe in its existence. Somewhere far from here, the mermaid continues to do what it has always done: it continues to thrive. And it waits for us to realize that belief is, in the end, irrelevant.

—Transcript from the lecture "Mermaids: Myth or Monster," given by Dr. Jillian Toth

CHAPTER 33

Western Pacific Ocean, above the Mariana Trench: September 3, 2022

Momentum drove Tory at least ten feet down. The salt water stung her eyes, and she blinked rapidly, trying to acclimatize to her surroundings before she became too disoriented to remember which way was up. In a swimming pool, going limp and allowing herself to float to the surface might have worked, but the sea was not some tame backyard amusement, meant to coddle children as they learned the ways of the water. The sea was a jungle of currents and undertows, and the water *moved*. If she didn't fight to find her way back to the air, she never would.

The water around her was alive with glittering points of light, and it took all Tory's strength of will not to suck in a lungful of water. The sirens were here. They were swimming upward, toward the ship, and downward, into the depths, passing on all sides. Dozens of them, more than she had ever imagined. The lights in their hair allowed her to pick them out, creating dark outlines against the darker water.

They were, for the moment, ignoring her. She knew that wouldn't last. Still, as she got her bearings back and began kicking her way toward the surface, she kept her legs together, trying to draw as little attention to herself as possible.

Why aren't they grabbing me? She didn't dare thrash—thrashing would be a death sentence—and so she tried to focus on the science of her situation. The sirens were man-eaters. They'd been taking people off the side of the boat since they'd made contact. They had taken everyone from the *Atargatis*, and from uncounted smaller ships. So what made her so different? Why weren't they grabbing her and pulling her down?

A siren swam by, so close its fins brushed her arm. She glanced down automatically, and realized the water below her was brighter than the water above. The sirens were hauling their kills toward the greater light source. Maybe that was the explanation. The sirens on the way down had something to deliver, while the sirens on their way up weren't thinking in terms of prey being already in the water. They were smart, and maybe that was the problem. She'd seen humans ignore things they knew simply couldn't be where they were. Maybe sirens worked the same way.

Now she just had to get to the surface and find her way back onto the *Melusine* without attracting their attention, or going into hypothermic shock. She could feel the shakes beginning as the cold sank into her extremities, rendering them numb and sluggish. And her lungs were beginning to burn.

Every motion felt like a risk she couldn't afford to take, but if she didn't risk something, she was going to die. The sea would carry her body away, and no one would know what had happened to her. Olivia wouldn't know. Luis wouldn't know. Her parents, thousands of miles away and already and forever mourning their eldest daughter, wouldn't know.

Moving as quickly as she dared, Tory swam upward. She kept her legs together, pushing herself with fluttering kicks and pulling with great sweeps of her arms. It wasn't *exactly* like the graceful, natural movement of the sirens, but some of them were using their arms, either to change their direction or because they were carrying something. Kicking hard would have been an instant giveaway. This was the only way.

Foot by foot, she fought her way toward the surface, and the sirens paid her no mind, all of them so set on their own tasks that they dismissed her as someone else's problem. Intelligence, and its attendant blind spots, might be the thing that would save her.

If she could be saved. If she could find a way back onto the ship. If the sirens didn't see her. The world had been redefined by *if*, and she wasn't sure she was going to last long enough to change the conversation.

Lungs aching, feet cold, Tory swam, and prayed for a miracle.

"What the *fuck* just happened?" demanded Daniel. "Why didn't they eat us?"

"Our siren saved us," said Hallie. The siren was still floating behind the glass, keeping itself upright with tiny sweeps of its tail. It was watching her. She was sure of that. She couldn't read its facial expressions, and there was no reason those expressions would map to anything mammalian, much less anything human, but it was watching her. It *knew* her. She smiled, trying not to show her teeth, lest the siren take that as a threat and change its mind about protecting them. "I taught it my name, and when the other sirens came in here, it told them to go away. It saved us."

Daniel pushed away from the glass, turning to look at the siren. He frowned. "Why? We've got it locked in this big damn tank. There's no way we can let it out."

"And you wouldn't if we could, because you want to be part of the team that brings one of these creatures back alive." Hallie didn't try to keep the disgust from her voice. The siren was a person. It had saved them. Yes, its brethren were tearing through the ship like wasps through a beehive, but how much of that was a simple lack of comprehension? The sirens didn't know that they were killing *people*.

(*What about Heather?* whispered a small, terrible voice in the back of her mind. *Did they think her submersible was a shell? Did they think she was some kind of nautilus? They knew she was a person. They knew she'd made that thing. They don't spare us just because we're people.*)

She wasn't being a traitor to her sister by letting herself trust their siren. She wasn't betraying the human race by starting to see it as a person. She was doing what scientists always did. She was responding to the available data, and she was letting it tell her where to go.

'Thank you,' she signed to the siren—one of the handful of signs they'd been working on for the last few hours.

The siren hesitated. Then, with the deliberation of someone who was learning a foreign language, it signed back, 'You're welcome.'

Hallie smiled.

*   *   *

It wasn't just cramped and dark inside the tube: it was *hot*, almost dismayingly so. It was cold outside, but the ship's systems were still running, pumping warmth and comfort to all the occupied cabins. So many of them had been smashed into that the heater had to be working triple-time, struggling to keep up with the perceived demand. Sweat rolled down Olivia's cheeks and pooled in her armpits and under her breasts. Worse yet, her palms were getting slick. Sooner or later, she was going to—

Her hand failed to lock properly on the ladder, and she fell, plummeting easily ten feet before she managed to get her legs braced against the sides of the tube. Something inside her knee crunched, sending a bright bolt of pain racing through her leg. She whimpered, biting her tongue to keep the sound from turning into a scream. Screams would give her away. Even if the sirens couldn't get *in*, she was eventually going to need to get *out*. That would be so much easier if they weren't waiting for her.

Olivia let go of the ladder, leaning back with her shoulders against the wall and her legs keeping her from dropping any farther, and scrubbed her hands against her shirt until they were dry. Once she was sure she'd be able to hold on, she reached up, grabbed the ladder, and unlocked her legs.

Climbing was harder now. Every move made her knee ache more. She kept her lip pinned between her teeth and closed her eyes, trying to focus on the process of putting one hand over the next, pulling herself upward. At least she was heading for the top. Sure, that meant a longer climb, but it also meant she didn't have to pay attention to how far she'd already come. When she hit the top, she'd know. She wouldn't be able to go any farther, and she'd know.

The walls of the tunnel had been designed to muffle the sound of laundry being thrown down to the bottom, keeping passengers from asking what that strange noise was. They hadn't been intended to stop sound from coming in from outside. Screams came through from time to time, muffled by the walls, but still distinct enough to be undeniable. Olivia bit her lip harder, trying not to think about what was happening out there—and more, trying not to focus on the increasingly pressing thought that maybe Ray had been lucky. He'd died quick and early, without knowing how bad things were going to get for the rest of them.

Things were getting so bad.

Olivia kept climbing. The world had narrowed to that simple action, to putting one hand over the other. She didn't think she was bleeding. Her knee pulsed with every step; it was going to swell, it was going to need ice and a brace and elevation. She'd hurt her knees before, a natural consequence of having a job for which she sometimes had to wear high heels on the exhibit floor at large conventions. Of course, she might not get any of those things, not when the ship was swarming with sirens, when there were teeth and claws around every corner. She might not get any farther than the top of this tube.

That was farther than she'd expected to get when she left the lab. She hoped Tory was safely back with the others, shut in and safe and worrying about her. She hoped Tory wouldn't worry *too* much. Places like this, times like this, they were never meant to last. They were one frozen moment in a falling catastrophe, and their beauty was that they'd existed, even if it was only for a little while, even if they'd never been really real.

The air tasted like steel and disinfectant. Olivia breathed shallowly as she climbed, afraid that taking a deep breath would trigger a coughing fit and bring the sirens swarming. She just kept climbing, until her head hit something hard and knocked her back to a lower rung, where she clung, reeling, waiting for the shock of impact to fade.

Bit by bit, it did. She pulled herself up again, more cautiously this time, and felt around until she found the indented square in the tube wall. That was her exit; that was how she got out onto the upper deck, and brought herself to the captain. Or maybe that was how she delivered herself to the waiting sirens, gift wrapped and ready to devour.

She took a deep breath.

"My name is Olivia Nitsan Sanderson, and I'm reporting live from the deck of the *Melusine*, bringing you the latest scoop from Imagine," she whispered, and pushed on the hatch, opening it, revealing a dimly lit slice of deck. Mucus trails crisscrossed the visible wood. Some of them were tainted with red, and where it had mixed with the slime, it was still fresh and bright, making it impossible to tell how long it had been since the vein had been opened.

Getting into the tube had been easy; she had climbed in head-first, grabbing the ladder and pulling herself up. Getting out was trickier. If she went headfirst, she might dump herself onto the deck, and while Dr. Toth hadn't explicitly said so, she was pretty sure she'd regret it if she got a mouthful of mucus. But she couldn't go up any higher, and her knee protested every time she bent it.

In the end she ground her teeth against the pain, folding her legs as close to her chest as she could and extending them carefully out the opening, fighting to get her footing. There was enough slime that she still slipped before she could stabilize herself and ease her torso out, but she did, inch by inch, until she was standing on the deck, breathing in the cool night air, wishing she didn't feel so damn much *relief.*

This situation could end with her, and every other human being on the *Melusine*, dead and lost at sea, no bodies, no burials. But she was no longer in that damned tube, and she was breathing cool clean air that only smelled a little bit like human blood, and the relief came without her inviting it. The fact that it was inappropriate didn't seem to matter much, and maybe it shouldn't have. Maybe this was one of those situations where relief would come to anyone, not just to her.

She didn't think so, though.

She turned, intending to make her way toward the prow, and stopped as lights shone in her eyes, bright enough to be blinding. She put up her arm, trying to block them out.

"Who the hell are you?" demanded a male voice.

CHAPTER 34

Western Pacific Ocean, above the Mariana Trench: September 3, 2022

Silence filled the medical bay, broken by the steady drip-drip-drip of viscous yellow fluid coming from Michi's hand, dripping from her cot onto the floor. It was an almost hypnotic sound, getting mellower as it formed a puddle on the floor. Minutes ticked by, wasted, scattered like sunlight on the sea.

Dr. Vail shook herself out of her shock and asked, "Do we have a mop? I don't think the custodial staff will be coming."

Dr. Odom turned to stare at her. "What are you talking about?"

"I'm talking about mopping the floor before someone gets hurt," Dr. Vail snapped. "And for the love of God, cover her face. Give the woman a little dignity." She had never liked Michi—few people on the ship had, save for her husband, and the thought of what Jacques was going to do when he found out she was dead was *terrifying*—but that didn't mean she should be treated with anything less than the respect owed to all human dead.

When a person died, you covered their face. You told them they would be missed. You closed their eyes, if necessary. You lied to them. Perhaps all those things were superstitions, and perhaps she was flawed for believing in them, but... "As we're currently under siege by mermaids, I'd rather not do anything that might encourage ghosts to join the party," she snapped, and went off in search of a mop.

Dr. Odom watched her walk away before reaching up and closing Michi's eyes. Her flesh felt overly soft beneath his fingers, like it was decaying too fast. He suppressed a shiver.

Raising his head, he looked around the medical bay. There were a dozen people present, most watching him warily, while one helped Dr. Vail with the cleaning supplies. "Does anyone have a walkie-talkie?" he asked.

"I do," said one of the guards. "Do you want me to call for Jacques?"

"Yes," he said. "No. Maybe... Wait. Do you think we should call for him?"

"No, sir," said the guard. "I think we should find a way to triple lock the doors, and maybe set a few land mines to make sure he doesn't get in. He's going to lose it. I can't say I blame him. I'd lose it, if that were my wife. But he's going to lose it bad, and then we're all going to be in trouble."

"Define *trouble*."

"That's the problem: I can't. He's got no impulse control under the best of circumstances. Michi was the one who told him not to do things he shouldn't do, and he listened to her, because dealing with the rest of us was easier than having her mad at him. You take her out of the equation, and I genuinely have no idea what he'll do."

"This gets better and better." Dr. Odom removed his gloves and dropped them next to Michi before rubbing his forehead with one hand. "We have to tell him. His wife is dead. There's no way we can justify holding our tongues."

The skin of Michi's cheek sank inward and tore away, leaving gelatinous edges behind. Dr. Odom jumped back with a sharp sound of disgust.

"We may have a bigger problem," he said, eyes wide, face suddenly feeling too tight for his bones. "Vail! We need a biohazard bag. And more mops. As many mops as you can find. Bleach, and mops, and... and..."

There was a wet, sucking sound from Michi's chest. The dissolution was coming faster now. He thought of Jason, in his own body bag on the other side of the room, and wondered how much of the humanoid shape of the thing resulted from the fact that the skeleton was notoriously difficult to dissolve.

There was a knock at the door. Quick, almost polite, and very human. Dr. Odom's head snapped around, transferring his stare to the other side of the room. The guard who'd spoken before shifted his weight, clearly uncomfortable.

"What should I do?" he asked.

"Let the man in, and be prepared to restrain him," said Dr. Vail. She walked back with mop and bleach and bucket. "He's going to need you to do that. Can you do that?"

"As long as the little French fucker doesn't shoot me," said the guard.

"He might," said Dr. Vail calmly, and it was the truth, because Michi had died of novel toxins introduced to her body by friendly fire; she would have lived if she'd been scratched or bitten. Lots of people had been scratched or bitten. The sirens weren't venomous. It was introducing their blood to hers that had triggered this catastrophic collapse, first of her circulatory system, and now of her tissues. The clash between their proteins and hers had killed her, but without the bullet, that would never have happened.

The guard grunted before crossing to the door and easing it open.

"You may check for mermaids if you like, but there are none," said a calm, French-accented voice. "All of them are dead. Quite dead."

"Jacques." The guard opened the door the rest of the way, and Jacques Abney was revealed.

He was covered, head to toe, in gore. Some of it was human, kept fresh and red by a thick coating of siren slime. Some of it was more watery, thinner and darker, and recognizably inhuman in origin. None of it appeared to be his. He had gone into the night on a mission, and come back having fulfilled it.

The guard frowned. "Where are the others?"

"They were slower than I," said Jacques, stepping inside. "Your Davis was taken over the side before we knew what was occurring; I killed three of the creatures as they converged on the spot where he had been. Your Sandra I shot myself, after one of the things clamped its mouth over her face, and it was clear medicine would not save her. She did not survive, but they did not take her. The rest, I do not know. Where is my Michi?"

"Jacques, I want you to listen to me. The doctors did everything that they could." The guard moved to block Jacques from fully seeing the room. "No one here is at fault."

The door swung closed. Jacques frowned. "What do you mean?"

"Dammit, Jacques, you know what I mean."

"No. I do not. Because what you are saying, it sounds like you are saying my Michi is dead, and that is not possible. My Michi does not die. She is a killer, and killers do not die." Jacques stepped to the side. The guard did the same. Jacques scowled. "Let me pass."

"Not until you accept that the doctors did the best they could."

Drs. Vail and Odom exchanged a look. Normally they would have stepped in; normally they would have told the guard—what was his *name*? Too many people, too many problems, and there had never been time to circulate, to socialize, not when there was so much to be done keeping a ship full of scientists from dying of dehydration or heatstroke—this wasn't the way to deal with someone who was grieving, or about to be. But this was Jacques Abney. He'd been hired because he would not hesitate to pull the trigger if he saw something worth shooting, and there was a good chance he was going to see *them* as worth shooting once he accepted the situation.

Jacques tilted his head. Then, without flinching or changing his expression in any way, he brought up his knee and hit the larger man squarely in the testicles. There was a terrible crunching sound, like an eggcup being smashed, and the man went down, clutching his injured genitals.

"Men are weak," said Jacques dismissively. "Nothing which wants to survive should keep its genitals on the outside of its body. Where is my wife?"

The doctors stepped away from Michi's corpse. The gelatinous rot had continued to spread across her face. The shape of her skull was outlined in slime, a grinning death's head replacing what had been a beautiful woman.

"Ah," said Jacques. He walked forward, stopping just shy of the cot, hands fluttering in front of him like wounded birds. "Ah," he said again, and it was a sound of protest, not of understanding; it was the sort of sound a man who had just received a grievous wound might make, too small and soft to be anything but fatal.

"I'm sorry," said Dr. Vail.

His head snapped up. "*You* are sorry?" he asked. "Did you do this thing? Did you fail her, reach your hands into her chest and squeeze her heart until it ceased to beat, close her eyes because you were tired of their accusations? Is this on you?"

Dr. Vail lifted her chin and said, "Every death under my care is on me, Mr. Abney. That is what it means to be a doctor. But I did not shoot her. I did not introduce the toxins into her bloodstream. No one here is guilty of murder. I did the best I could."

"You say no one here is guilty of murder, but she was, my Michi," said Jacques. "She killed men who stood between her and what she wanted, as easily as she put knife to sturgeon, bullet to lion. She was a huntress, and she murdered a thousand times over to get what she desired. I murdered by her side. Would you truly look me in the eye and say there has been no murder here? Even when to say otherwise might save you?"

"There has been no murder here," said Dr. Vail.

"Ah." Jacques looked back to Michi. "What is wrong with her face?"

"The poison that killed her spread through her system before she died. It damaged her tissues. I'll be honest: we don't know why, or what effects it had on her body as a whole. It's going to take time and study before we know that." Time, study, and a goddamn CDC team. Michi was a novel biohazard now, and only the fact that the sirens were an even greater threat was keeping Dr. Vail from evacuating the medical bay. There was no point in running from the danger when the danger was everywhere.

"I see." Jacques studied Michi, lingering on the damage to her cheeks, the translucency of her forehead. "There was nothing you could have done."

"No."

"She was dead as soon as the bullet broke her skin."

"Yes."

"Who fired the gun?" Jacques turned away from Michi, prodding the fallen guard with his toe. "The team that accompanied my wife, who pulled the trigger on the bullet that took her life? Who killed her? Tell me, or I will start making guesses."

The guard groaned. Another guard stepped forward.

"Davis," he said. "I was there. I saw him pull the trigger."

"Ah," said Jacques, and sighed. "Taken. Too much mercy. Too

much mercy in the world." He prodded the fallen guard again. "I should shoot you for the crime of sharing a uniform with the man who killed my wife, but it would be to waste a bullet, and I have better things to kill. Stay out of my way."

He turned, then, and walked to the door, which he opened without checking for sirens. He stepped out onto the deck. The door closed behind him. The sound of gunfire began only a few seconds later, calm and methodical, one shot at a time.

"I think we should stay here," said Dr. Odom.

The guard on the floor groaned.

"My name is Olivia Sanderson," said Olivia, not lowering her arm. The flashlight was obscenely bright after the darkness of the tunnel and the perpetual twilight of the lower decks. "Please, we can't stay out here. We need to get to cover."

"How did you make it this far without getting eaten?" The second voice was also male, and slightly more familiar than the first. "They're everywhere lower down."

"I was in a tube. I have a tranquilizer gun." The words sounded senseless. Olivia resisted the urge to look over her shoulder, to confirm the tube was still there. "They didn't know I was there, because I was in a tube. I wasn't making any noise. Please, we can't stay out here." Maybe if she repeated herself often enough, they'd understand her urgency. She wasn't just talking to hear the soothing sound of her own voice; she had things to say, *important* things, and if they didn't listen, they were going to die. They were all going to die.

She was going to die, and she was never going to make it back to the lab to tell Tory and the others that she'd reached the top deck, that she'd done what she had set out to do. That wasn't acceptable. That couldn't be allowed.

"Why should we believe you?" The first voice again. If they would stop shining that light in her eyes, if they would let her see who she was talking to, she was sure she could get through to them. She could make them *understand*.

"Daryl, we saw her come out the hatch," said the second voice. It wasn't just familiar: it was calmer, more reasonable, like it was willing to accept that maybe, just maybe, the entire world wasn't out to get them. "She's human. Far as we know, these mermaids aren't shape-shifters."

"They could have people working for them. People on the inside." The first man's voice was flagging. He was starting to sound unsure.

Olivia knew how to deal with the unsure. "Why would anyone work for them?" she asked, voice as level as she could make it. "They've been eating everyone they could get their claws on, or taking them into the water. Nobody comes back once they hit the water. So no, I'm not working for them. No one's working for them. Please. I came up here to find the captain. He needs to tell us why the shutters aren't down but the internet is. Can you take me to the captain?"

"No," said the first man. The light was lowered. Olivia realized, with a start, that she was talking to the men who'd found her screaming after Ray died.

"He's gone," said the second man, before she could ask why not. "The damned mermaids got into the control room while we were working on the servos. Ate him, *and* the first mate, and two of the navigators. The place is a slaughterhouse."

"Why are you outside?" she asked, eyes going wide. "It's not safe."

"Turns out the mermaids don't like the taste of emergency flares," said the second man. "There were only six of them up here. They killed most everyone, but we were able to drive them down the sides of the ship."

There was nothing to stop the sirens from coming back up, nothing to prevent them from setting their claws to the steel sides of the *Melusine* and slithering back to the place where they'd been damaged and driven away. If they had been animals, maybe they would have written the top deck off as dangerous and left it alone. But they weren't. They were smart, they were intelligent, and intelligent things knew how to hold a grudge—knew how to get angry, and stay angry, and take revenge. They'd be back. They *had* to be back. Olivia shifted her weight from foot to foot, looking at the two men.

"Why aren't the shutters down?" she asked.

"The captain's dead," said Gregory. "We finished the repair, but we don't have the code. That died with him."

"Besides, we don't want to trap those things on board," said Daryl. "Leave the walls open and they'll leave."

"They're still *coming*," said Olivia, more heatedly than she intended. "They're coming up the sides of the ship, and they're not going to stop until they've killed us all. They didn't leave any survivors on the *Atargatis*, remember? They don't stop. They don't back down. They hunt until there's nothing left."

"Like it's better to trap them inside?"

"At least then there's a limited number of them!" Olivia shook her head. "We need to close the shutters. Where's the switch?"

Daryl and Gregory exchanged a look. Gregory said, "It's in the control room. But I told you, we don't have the code."

She smiled grimly. "Let me worry about that."

Luis had been staring at the door for the past ten minutes. "Tory should be back by now," he said.

"You've already said that," said Theo. "Repeatedly. I don't think it's going to make her come back any faster."

"I don't see you doing anything to make her come back."

"There are reasons for that," said Theo. "I still can't stand, for one. More importantly, I don't think anything can *make* her come back. We lack the resources to send a rescue party. We have no weapons, and no more bodies to spare. If you want to go after her, please, feel free, but understand that there will be no one to go after you. More, that you'll be leaving the rest of us defenseless."

"I wish you'd stay, Mr. Martines," said Jillian, not looking away from her laptop. She was typing rapidly, barely keeping up with the messages popping up from Holly, working at her own computer only a few feet away. The lack of internet wasn't a problem, thanks to a direct cable connection, and text was the perfect solution to their communication problems. "We're nowhere near an antitoxin, but we need to keep working."

"Because what we need, more than anything else right now, is to *understand* these things," spat Luis. "We need to be killing them, not comprehending them."

"Since when are those different things?" Jillian did look up this time, turning to frown at him, like a mother frowning at a willfully obtuse child. "Once we understand them, we'll be better prepared to destroy them."

"I thought they were your life's work."

"No, Mr. Martines. Proving they existed was my life's work. We know they exist now. One more mystery of the sea has been solved. I never said I wanted to protect or preserve them. Honestly, as long as I get a few to take apart at my leisure, I don't care if the navy wants to roll in here and nuke them all into the mythology they swam out of."

Luis stared at her. "That's not what you said before."

"I was talking to an audience before," she snapped.

Theo smirked. "People always did think of you as the conservationist in the family," he said.

"Most people don't know me very well," she said. "Mr. Martines, if you must go after Miss Stewart, I'll understand. I'll even walk you to the door, so that I can lock it behind you. But if she hasn't survived, neither will you."

Luis opened his mouth to reply, and stopped as the phone on the wall rang. "Who's calling?" he asked.

"Pick it up and find out," suggested Theo.

There didn't seem to be a way to refuse. Luis crossed to the phone cautiously, like he thought there was a chance the sirens might have figured out how to work the ship's communications system. But it could also be Tory. He lifted the receiver and brought it to his ear.

"Hello?"

CHAPTER 35

Western Pacific Ocean, above the Mariana Trench: September 3, 2022

The control room was as bad as Daryl and Gregory had said; maybe worse, since they hadn't said anything about the way the blood coated the fluorescent lights, distorting the lighting. Pools of deep shadow were scattered randomly through the room, making it hard to tell the blood and slime on the floor from the hardwood surrounding them.

There was a hand. A *human* hand, bitten off during the attack and left behind. There was a heavy ring on the third finger, and the stone at its center glimmered obscenely, as bright as if nothing had happened. It was wrong. All of this was wrong.

"This is Olivia Sanderson with Imagine Entertainment, coming to you live from the bridge of the *Melusine*," Olivia muttered, and forced herself into the room, heading for the ship's controls. Daryl and Gregory stayed by the door, watching for sirens, unwilling to go back into what must have seemed like a killing chute.

"Did the captain have time to activate the distress beacons before he died?" asked Olivia, looking at the controls. She had a video, somewhere, of herself giggling and preening for the camera, the captain's hat perched on her head, while he walked her through the ship's essential systems. It had been a filler piece, intended for release only if they ran out of more interesting footage to roll.

412

"I think so," said Daryl. "Check for a blue light."

Olivia scanned the controls, finally shaking her head. "Nothing."

"Then look for a glass slide over a black button."

"Black? Not red?"

"People push red buttons. It's best if no one is tempted to push the distress system controls to see what will happen."

The logic was sound enough. Olivia kept looking until she found the little glass slide with a bloody fingerprint in the middle. The captain hadn't activated the distress signal before he'd died, but he'd been reaching for it, intending to call for help. She reached for it, and then hesitated.

If she called for help, was she going to be leading more people to the slaughter? She had no way of knowing whether she'd be in a position to speak to anyone who wanted to come to their rescue, or whether they'd believe her if she did. "Under attack by mermaids" didn't sound reasonable even to her, and she was the one living through it.

In the end, did it matter? They needed help. Anyone who didn't believe in mermaids when they reached the *Melusine* would start believing shortly thereafter. She flicked the shield aside and pressed the button.

"All right," she said, turning back to the door. "How do I activate the shutters?"

"You need the code," said Gregory. "Neither of us has it."

"No," she said. "But this room has a phone." She picked up the receiver nested in the middle of the console, briefly grateful for the old-fashioned design of the ship's communication system. If the phone had been portable, it could have been lost with the captain. Then she paused.

Her cabin was located on the fifth deck. The number was 5-62: deck number and location on the ship. Dr. Toth's lab was on the third deck, and was two halls over from the position of her room. That would make the number...

She punched in 3-45. The phone began to ring. She took a deep breath, running and rerunning the math inside her head, trying to find a place where it broke down. There was no directory, and the ship's computer was covered in blood and slime. She wasn't sure she'd be able to pull up the information she needed if this didn't work.

"Hello?"

She gasped. "Luis! You're there!"

"Olivia?" He sounded bemused but not displeased. "Where are you? Is Tory with you?"

"What?" Her delight dimmed. "No. She should be back in the lab by now. Is she not in the lab?" *Of course she's not in the lab. He wouldn't be asking* me *if she was here if she was there.*

"No," he said, in unconscious echo of her thoughts. "She didn't come back. Where are you?"

"I'm in the control room. Everyone here is dead." That seemed like an impolitic way to say things, so she backtracked, amending, "The captain and first mate are dead. I found two of the crew. Daryl and Gregory. They're alive. They're watching the door while I call you." And they'd run at the slightest sign of trouble, because that was how they'd *stayed* alive as long as they had.

She couldn't even blame them for that. Survival was a human instinct, at the end of the day, and they had every right to hold on to their humanity, especially here, when it felt like the world was going to end.

"Is Mr. Blackwell there?" she asked, before she could follow her own thoughts down the rabbit hole of morbidity and distress. "The captain's dead. I need to lower the shields, but I can't do that without the security code."

"Yeah, he's here," said Luis. "Was Tory okay when you left her?"

"She was right behind me," said Olivia. "She said she was going back to you. She should have come back only a few minutes after she left."

"Well, she didn't."

Everything inside Olivia felt like it was being washed in gray. Of course Tory hadn't made it back to the lab. There was no way they could both have been lucky enough to make it to cover, no way they could both have rolled the dice and come up with a natural twenty. It was just her. Just her. She'd come onto the ship with Ray, and when she'd lost him she'd tumbled into Tory like an out-of-control satellite, and now she was being punished for daring to think she might not have to be alone. She was always going to wind up alone.

"Put Mr. Blackwell on the phone," she said, and her voice was dull and dead, and that was all she deserved.

There was a scuffle, followed by silence, followed—at long

last—by a new voice coming on the line, calm and urbane as always; she wasn't sure Mr. Blackwell *could* get upset with all the pot he had running through his system. "Miss Sanderson?" he said.

"I need the code to lower the shutters."

There was a pause. "Ah," he said finally. "The captain is dead, then, I assume?"

"Yes. So is the first mate, and everyone else who worked in the control room. I set off the distress signal—they didn't have a chance—but I don't want to stay in the open any longer than I have to, so please, what's the code for the shutters? I have two engineers here who say the repairs are done."

The shutters wouldn't save her. Or maybe they would, if she went back into the access tube and climbed down, back into the belly of the ship. She'd have to leave Daryl and Gregory behind. Neither one of them would fit in that safe, narrow space. If she moved quickly enough, they wouldn't even see the code she used, and she'd know they weren't going to jam the door open trying to follow her. She'd know she was safe.

What then? She couldn't hide in a hot, claustrophobic tube until rescue came. She'd pass out, lose her grip, and fall before anyone came along to save her. Maybe it was better to stay where she was and admit that sometimes, safety was for other people.

"Miss Sanderson, do you have a plan for what happens after you lower the shutters?"

She wanted to scream. Mr. Blackwell could afford to sound calm. Mr. Blackwell was in a room with a door that locked, with people who could defend him if the sirens came. They didn't have guns, but they had science, and they had tools. They had a *chance*. She had Daryl and Gregory, and she didn't know either of them well enough to know what was going to happen to her if things got bad. "No," she said. "I'm just going to lower them. That's what I came up here for."

"Miss Sanderson—"

"Do you think Victoria is dead?"

No reply.

"Because I think Victoria is dead. That means she died to get me here, so I could close the shields. If I don't do this now, she died for nothing, and everyone on this ship who's still alive is probably going to die with her. What's the code?"

He took a breath before beginning to recite, "Eight-alpha-bravo-ten—"

The code was twenty characters long: not the best choice for something that was supposed to be the answer to any major danger. Even if the captain had been keying it in when the sirens swarmed the control room, it was no surprise he hadn't been able to finish. She could see where some programmer, safely back on dry land, would have considered it a good idea; after all, closing the shutters would use a lot of power, both electrical and processing, and would grind many of the ship's systems to a halt. It would make it harder for rescue to be offered. The shields would have to be opened manually, deck by deck. No one wanted them to come down because someone hit the wrong button on the board.

Olivia typed the last character and hesitated. "You're sure?" she asked.

"I'm sure," he said. "Are you?"

"I'm sure," she said. "Now wish me luck." She hit the ENTER key.

All around her, systems whirred to life, clanking and clunking and beginning the rapid process of locking into place. She could hear Daryl and Gregory exclaiming from the doorway, and then whooping with delight as the shutters started coming down.

For you, Tory, she thought, and closed her eyes, and waited for the doors to close.

The *Melusine* had been designed to be as self-sustaining as possible. Her air and water filtration systems were top of the line; she could keep her passengers alive for weeks with no access to the outside. Her shutters were a key component of this feat of nautical engineering. They sealed the top deck from the rest of the ship, rendering the lower decks accessible only via keycard; nothing got in or out without authorization. The stairwell doors followed a similar lockdown process: someone on deck three could open the stairs to descend to deck two, but would find the door to the deck four stairs magnetically sealed. Anyone who chose to move around the ship would be inexorably driven lower, unless they did the intelligent thing and stayed where they were.

Already-dim decks became dark as the shutters slid into place, blocking out the moonlight. Sirens shrieked and fell from the sides of the ship as the metal plates of the shutters extended down and knocked them loose, sending them back into the blue.

More were knocked off the hull than were trapped on board. That was a small and almost useless consolation. The sirens that *had* been trapped were driven to an almost immediate frenzy as they realized they could neither escape nor carry their kills back to whatever was increasing the brightness of the waters around the ship. They tore along the halls, wailing, focusing their attacks on the few scientists and crewmen foolish enough to still be out in the open.

In the water next to the *Melusine*, Tory's head broke the surface. She gasped, a deep inhalation that devolved into a hacking cough. The sirens around her mimicked the sound, turning interested eyes her way. Sirens didn't cough—or if they did, they didn't do it with the force of an air breather's lungs. She clapped a hand over her mouth, trying to tread water with increasingly numb legs while also holding her breath.

There was a clang from above. Tory looked up, eyes going wide as she realized the shapes moving rapidly toward her were sirens, knocked off the side of the *Melusine* and plummeting toward the waves. She uncovered her mouth and dove, swimming as hard and as fast as she could to get away from the point of impact. Kicking might attract attention. Being landed on would *definitely* attract attention.

Her lungs were burning. She couldn't see. The sirens around her were visible as dark slices cut from darker water, lit from below by whatever was rising—more sirens, probably, or some sort of bioluminescent fish, moving in a great, panicky school. It didn't really matter. She was going to be dead long before they reached her.

The shutters are down, she thought. That was it; that was the ball game. With the shutters down, there was no chance anyone would come out on the deck and see her bobbing near the hull. She wasn't going to get saved. She was going to die down here.

Unless...

The swimming pool under the ship had channels connecting it to the open sea. There was a chance she wouldn't be able to fit through them; more, there was a chance she would fit just long enough to get herself well and truly stuck, consigning herself to a death by drowning that would only be discovered when they made it back to land. They'd have to identify her body by her dental records.

But they would *have* a body to identify. She would make it home to her parents. They wouldn't lose two daughters to the same stretch of open sea; she, at least, could be buried.

And there was a chance—however slim, however small—that she'd be able to navigate the dark, drowned tunnels and make her way back onto the ship itself. She could survive this, if she was quick and clever and very, very lucky.

Tory opened her eyes, orienting herself, and looked down into the abyss, where the rising light was getting brighter. She could see an outline there now, a shape sketched out of darkness and illuminated by a single biological lantern the size of an adult man. Her eyes widened against the stinging salt. Suddenly, finding a way back onto the ship wasn't just a matter of survival for her. It was a matter of survival for everyone. She *had* to find a way. She had to tell them what was coming.

She didn't have a choice. Everything in her life had been building to this moment. Lungs and throat aching, she drove herself toward the surface. She needed to prepare for the greatest dive of her life. If she failed...

If she failed, then all of this had been for absolutely nothing.

Jacques prowled the deck like a man possessed, hunting the creatures that had taken his Michi. How *dare* they. They'd had no right to kill her. She was more than they could ever be, in every regard; she was a goddess walking, and she was not *dead*. She was not *gone*. She could not be wiped so easily from the fabric of his life. She would be with him always. She was with him even now. If some of the people on this petty, puerile ship were too small-minded to see that, let that be on their heads.

Something reared out of a shadow. He fired without waiting to see whether it was siren or human. The head was in roughly the same place, when the damned things clung to the walls; if it was a member of the crew, they shouldn't have been jumping at him without declaring themselves.

(The thought that he might not have heard them if they *had* declared themselves was more academic than anything else. He'd been firing his guns in enclosed hallways and stairwells, without ear protection, since leaving the medical bay where his Michi—his

Michi, who was meant to be immortal, if any living woman could be—lay, rotting from within. Anyone yelling for his attention might go unheard, and whose fault was that? Really, he could not be bothered. Let them die. Let them all die. All that mattered was how many of the monsters he could take with him before he was taken down.)

Jacques Abney had been hired to accompany the *Melusine* into uncharted waters because he was a dangerous man. Like many dangerous men, he came with his own safeguard: Michi, who had always been the better of the two of them at handling the places where civilization insisted on rubbing up against the calm simplicity of their chosen lives. This had been the big job, the one that would take them from well off to wealthy, putting them in a position to buy their way onto every game reserve and hunting ground left in the world. Oh, they would have retired for a while, but a lion never puts aside his claws. One day, the job would have called them back. They could have painted the horizon in blood off the take from this one assignment, and the fact that their contracts had come with clause after clause after clause regarding the chance of accident or other misfortune had seemed almost pointless. There were always clauses. They were never true.

But this one had been. *This* clause had borne bitter fruit, and Michi had eaten, and now she was lying still as stone in a room full of soft fools who could only watch as she disappeared, one piece at a time.

They would pay. Somehow, they would all pay. But first the monsters would pay, because for monsters there was no point in waiting. The people would learn to be afraid. The people would dread his return, because they had the capacity for such things. The monsters...If he let them, they would forget what they had done. They would fail to appreciate the gravity of their trespass. He needed to show them.

Something moved in the dark ahead. He fired again. He kept walking.

The shields' coming down had been an inevitability, too late to do any real good, too late to save the dead, but still, the sort of thing he had known would have to happen eventually. It was the last thrash of the doomed and the dying, grabbing for anything that might keep them alive a little longer. He would have sneered at them if he'd possessed the energy. His Michi was gone. His Michi was gone, and he was so damned tired.

If Jacques had possessed the clarity of thought necessary to step back from the situation and truly look at what he was doing, he would have realized his mistake. He was cutting a straight swath through the ship, shooting everything that moved, stopping only when he needed to reload. He had already descended two decks, clearing the stairwells and the open rooms along the way. More than thirty sirens lay dead in his wake, felled by bullets to the head and throat. They might be monsters from the watery deeps, but not even monsters could survive that sort of damage.

He hadn't been checking the rooms to either side for sirens smart enough to hang back while their braver companions lunged for him. He hadn't been looking up, to find the dark shapes packed into corners and clinging to the ceilings. He hadn't been careful. That, in the end, was what turned his shortcomings from mistakes into tragedy. He hadn't been careful.

There was a soft, slithering sound. He turned, rifle raised. Then he froze, staring at the mass of sirens that had gathered behind him, following their schooling instincts one last time. They were going to die on this ship. There was no way out for them, any more than there was a way out for anyone else. But they weren't going down without a fight.

"Soon, Michi, soon," Jacques breathed, and began firing.

He was still firing when the first wave of sirens washed over him, bearing him down to the floor. His last shot passed through three sirens before ricocheting off the ceiling, finally coming to rest in the nearby wall. He did not scream. He didn't need to.

The thrashing mass of sirens writhed atop his body, their hands rending him into pieces. In the end, he was barely a mouthful for each of them. Those who had survived the encounter slithered on, lips bloody, bellies empty, looking for something more to kill.

CHAPTER 36

Western Pacific Ocean, above the Mariana Trench:
September 3, 2022

It worked," breathed Daryl, looking out the window at the deck. Moonlight washed it silver, glinting off the blood and slime. "It fucking *worked*."

"The shutters are down," said Olivia almost dreamily. She looked around the control room. The windows were intact. That was good. That might be enough. "Is there a mop? We need to get these pieces out of here, and I don't want to touch them."

"What are you going to do with them?" Daryl asked. "The doors locked when the shutters came down, and I don't want to attract attention."

Olivia shrugged. "We can push them over the side—don't look at me like that. The captain isn't coming back to get his hand. He's dead. Dead people don't need their bits." Dead people didn't need anything at all. It must have been very peaceful, being dead. They were free of all the complications that still waited for the living.

"And then what are you going to do?" asked Gregory, finally snapping out of his own quietly relieved amazement.

"Mop the floor, I guess, since I'll already have a mop. Clean as much of the mess off the controls as I can. The sirens have bad things in their bodies, toxins and stuff. They can hurt people. So I don't want to touch them if I don't have to." Olivia looked toward the

421

windshield. It was remarkably clear. Most of the slaughter had happened in the middle of the room, well away from the glass, and while there were a few arterial streaks, she could still see. "I need to stay here. I'd like it if you stayed here, too, so I wouldn't have to be alone, but I *need* to stay. So if you could find me a mop, I'd appreciate it."

"Now, hold on," said Gregory. "Why do you need to stay here? Those things will find you if you stay here."

"Those things will find *us* if we don't move soon," hissed Daryl.

"I don't think so," said Olivia. "I think they went lower, looking for things to eat, and then the shutters closed, and the ones in the water haven't had time to climb this far." But the ones in the water *would* climb back to the top, and when they did, that would be it, because there was nowhere to hide up here. The top deck was as close to featureless as possible, save for the control room; it had been designed that way, in case of storms. There was nothing that could be washed away.

Olivia would have welcomed a storm. It would have cleaned the wood, rinsed off the blood, and if it took them too, well, at least drowning would be a merciful death compared to what the sirens were offering. She wasn't ready to jump over the side and let the water have her, but she could see the appeal. Was it suicide when death was inevitable? Or was it just refusing to let someone else—some*thing* else—decide the way she ended?

"But they *will* find us," said Gregory.

"Yes," said Olivia. "It was the word *soon* I was objecting to. If you need to go, go. Just help me find a mop first. I want to be here if someone responds to our distress call. I want to be able to tell them what's going on. I can't save myself. I can still save this ship. I think that would be enough."

Gregory hesitated before saying, "I think I know where I can find a mop."

Olivia smiled.

Tory hadn't been free diving in years. It wasn't a hobby that appealed to her, and the dangers—the risks—far outweighed any joy she took in it. Still, she braced her hands against the hull of the ship, trying to avoid the places where the metal had been shredded by the sirens, and hyperventilated to overoxygenate her lungs. Finally she took a breath so deep that it ached, and dove, swimming toward the center of the ship.

She didn't dare look down. This was already going to be a tight deadline, and if she wasted time and oxygen gaping at a horror from below, she was going to die here, pinned against the bottom of the *Melusine* until the current came and took her away. Sometime in the last five minutes, between the cold in her limbs and the terror rising toward them, she had stopped fearing death. Now she only feared being swept away.

We should have known, she thought, as she pulled herself along the hull toward the intake ports for the pool. How big was the *Melusine*? The size of a floating football field, easily, and those ports were located almost dead center. Her air would be half-gone before she even started the complicated part of her journey. And *that* navigation would have to be performed in total darkness, because the light (the light, the light, *oh God the light*) wouldn't be able to follow her inside.

If there was any blessing to her current situation, it was that the light wouldn't be able to follow her inside.

All the sirens on the original *Atargatis* recording had been similar in size and build, showing no signs of sexual dimorphism. That wasn't so strange, for fish. Fish often demonstrated little to no sexual dimorphism. There were exceptions—the anglerfish among them—but so many looked alike across genders and age ranges that no one had flagged that as strange. Not even Dr. Toth, who should have caught the problem, if anyone was going to. Dr. Toth was the one who should have seen, should have said.

They weren't fish. They were amphibians, impossible oceanic amphibians, and their life cycles and transformations were the stuff of biological insanity, taking place so far below the surface of the sea that there was no convenient map to compare them to. Tory's fingers felt for purchase on the hull, pulling herself hand over hand faster than she could have made the swim. It also kept her from being as visibly "other." The sirens hadn't attacked her yet—and that didn't make any sense, that didn't make any *sense*, unless they were so blinded by the light from below that they no longer cared what was in the water with them. Which they might be. Many species of amphibian experienced mating frenzies.

The light from below belonged to something so much bigger

than the sirens that Tory's mind kept balking at the thought of it, trying to ignore the evidence of her eyes. She didn't want to have seen what she had seen. But she couldn't let that stop her. She needed to warn the others. They needed to turn on the lights.

The port was large enough to scoop up sharks and sunfish. It had to be large enough for a human body. But the ship was huge and the port was small in comparison, and if she missed it, she was going to have to make it to the other side and start all over again. The ache in her lungs was shifting from "overfull" to "running low on air," and she knew that this was her best, if not only, shot. She needed to do this.

Middle of the ship, she thought, and adjusted her position. Her fumbling fingers met a sudden lack of resistance as they slid up and into a trench cut into the hull. She closed her eyes and reached in with both hands, pulling herself up, easing herself out of the open sea and into the machinery of the saltwater scoop.

The shields are down, she thought. It was such a science fiction phrase that it made her want to giggle—although that might have been the early stages of hypoxia speaking. Normally when a ship's shields were down, that meant it was vulnerable to attack by sneering villains with lasers that somehow made a sound in the vacuum of space. Now it meant the *Melusine* was supposed to be protected from all attackers, shut off from the world outside. What did that mean for the water intake system? Had it closed off, somewhere deep inside the mechanism? Was she pulling herself, even now, toward her inevitable watery grave?

(And so what if she was? She had known this was a risk when she dove, when she swam for the center of the ship. Staying in the open water would have been a guaranteed death, with no chance to warn anyone of what was coming. At least this way, she would die *doing* something.)

(There was no way for Tory to know how closely her thoughts paralleled Olivia's, a ship and a lifetime away. If she had known, she might have taken some comfort in the fact. Or she might have cried, adding her tears to the sea around her, because neither of them was walking away clean. Neither of them had ever stood a chance.)

The water intake port had been designed to funnel sea creatures into the pool, without leaving enough room for them to turn around or make their way back out. Tory pulled her legs in, and discovered there was no way for her to go back. Forward was the only option. She pressed onward, pushing against the walls, pulling herself across every obstacle and through every thin plastic sphincter, until she felt like she was crawling through the digestive tract of some unspeakable beast. Her lungs burned with increasing urgency, and thin trails of bubbles escaped from her lips every time she moved. She closed her eyes, choosing inner darkness over the dark that was being forced upon her.

At least she couldn't see the light from below anymore, or the terrible shape of the thing that bore it. At least she was spared that much.

The space beyond her eyelids began growing brighter. At first she thought it was a function of her oxygen-starved brain thrashing around, looking for something to focus on. Then she realized that it was steady, lighting up a degree at a time. She opened her eyes. Artificial light welcomed her. The pool. She could see the pool. A single sheet of clear plastic remained between her and salvation. She reached for it, trying to haul it upward.

It wouldn't budge. It was locked, and she was trapped, and this was where she was going to die.

"The shutters are down," reported Daniel, looking at his monitor. "No more of those things are going to be able to get onto the ship."

"Now if we only had a way to get the ones already here to go *away*," said Hallie. She shot a glance at their captive siren, floating almost serenely in the tank, and added, "No offense," pairing the words with the sign for *sorry*.

"It can't understand you," said Daniel.

"It doesn't matter. It saved us. I'm going to show it as much respect as I can." She paused to shoot him a venomous look. "Real respect would let it go." He scoffed. "I'd like to hear you say that to Mr. Blackwell."

The phone rang. Both of them turned to look at it in mute dismay before Hallie picked it up, brought it to her ear, and said, "Hello?"

"Ah, Dr. Wilson." The voice was Mr. Blackwell's; the tone belonged to someone who had run hard and finally collapsed. "I trust you and Dr. Lennox are both well?"

"The sirens came in through the pool," she said. "We're in the lab with the doors locked." She wanted to tell them how their captive had saved them, but she couldn't figure out where to begin. It was already starting to feel like something out of a dream—or, more accurately, a nightmare.

"Excellent," he said. "I have your sister with me. She's fine. She's working with Dr. Toth on unsnarling the biology of these creatures. We may have a serviceable treatment for the toxic shock their tissues induce in humans, soon enough."

"That's wonderful," said Hallie. Privately she was more concerned about the shock of teeth and claws and tearing flesh, but as long as the door remained shut, she didn't have to worry about that as much. "Sir, the shutters are down. Does that mean the captain has signaled for rescue?"

"It means Miss Sanderson has signaled for rescue. The captain is dead, I'm afraid. Stay where you are. Continue your work. I'll call if we need anything, but for the time being, the best thing you can do is hold your ground." The line went dead.

Hallie lowered the phone before turning to Daniel and saying, "My sister's alive."

"Great," he said. "Let's hope the rest of us can stay that way."

Mopping the floor had been a quick, messy affair, but it had yielded several treasures, including the captain's keycard, apparently ripped from his neck during the fight that killed him. Olivia had plucked it from the slime and wiped it dry on the hem of her shirt, ignoring the damage she was doing to the fabric. When she was sure she'd cleaned the card as much as she could, she slung it around her neck and turned to Daryl and Gregory, trying to look braver than she felt.

They looked at her like her bravery was sincere, like she knew what she was doing. Maybe that was the secret of bravery. Maybe it was always a matter of puffing out your chest and lifting up your chin and looking like everything was going to be okay. She was an actress, not a fighter. Here and now, the one was the same as the other.

"If you want to run, you should run now," she said. "If you want to stay, I'll be grateful, but gratitude isn't going to protect you. I can even walk you to the nearest stairwell and let you into the ship."

Gregory looked to the keycard dangling around her neck and then up at her face, studying her before he nodded. "If it's all the same to you, I'll be staying here," he said. "A lot of these systems need two people if they're going to work properly."

"I'm not going anywhere *alone*," said Daryl, sounding disgusted, and that was that; they were all staying.

Olivia walked back to the controls. "Let's see if I can get this up and running," she said, and swiped the captain's card through the reader on the security system. The system beeped and began powering back up, lights activating one by one, followed by the flickering, rolling monitors. Some of them were dark, and others glitched steadily, making the pictures virtually impossible to understand.

Others showed scenes out of horror movies. Bodies, ripped open and left in the middle of walkways; sprays of blood painting walls in red. Sirens slithering through the corridors, their flat, expressionless faces seeming to look directly into the cameras. There were survivors—not many, most locked in cabins or hiding in corridors, makeshift weapons clutched tight—and every one she found made her heart leap a little. They represented hope. If help came fast enough, all these people might still make it home. They'd lost more than half the crew, and more than two-thirds of the scientists, but that left plenty of people to tell the story of the *Melusine*. Unlike the *Atargatis*, it wasn't going to be a ghost ship.

The camera for the bottom deck came on, showing sirens collapsed on the floor or curled into tight balls at the bottom of the pool. Olivia frowned, glancing from that to the other cameras still showing active sirens. They were moving more slowly than they had been when they'd started the attack, she was sure of it. She didn't know as much about their anatomy as some of the scientists probably did by now, but the way the sirens were moving made her think of people who were suffering from oxygen deprivation.

Maybe there were more reasons for their lightning-fast strikes when the fight had just been getting under way than the need to surprise their prey. Maybe they could only stay in the open air for so long before they started to suffer for it. The idea was cheering enough to make her feel warm and faintly giddy. They could just... wait the sirens out, and the air itself would punish them for daring

427

to come to the surface. With the shields down, the sirens couldn't even get back into the water. The ones in the pool were probably doing a little better than the others, but not too much, because that water wasn't deep enough, and they were all clustered in the deep end, struggling to inhale.

Something was moving at the far end of the pool. Olivia squinted at the image. "How do I make this zoom?" she asked.

"Like this." Gregory leaned over her, typing something on the keyboard. The camera shifted, zooming in on the panel that was keeping more water, and more sirens, from washing into the pool. It must have come down with the shutters.

The movement was two pale shapes, like starfish, pressed against the glass. Olivia squinted. Not starfish; hands. Not siren hands either; human hands. *Human* hands.

She *knew* those hands.

Olivia gasped, recoiling from the screen. "That's Tory," she said, through the hand that was clamped over her mouth, blurring and blocking her words. "She's in the pool. How do we get that wall up?"

"What?" Gregory leaned closer. "Oh, dear God. Olivia, we can't— it's connected to the shutter, but it's not the same system. Someone needs to lift it from the outside."

Tory's hands were still slapping against plastic. They were weakening. They weren't going to keep thrashing much longer.

"How do we contact the pool level? There are—there are *doors* there. There might be *people* there."

"Here." Daryl grabbed a microphone, pulling it toward her. "We can reach any deck from here, for announcements."

"Call it." Olivia grabbed the microphone and began shouting into it. "Hello! Hello! This is Olivia Sanderson, calling from the control room! If there is anyone on the lower deck, I need you to proceed immediately to the shallow end of the viewing pool and raise the glass shield on the entrance port. We have a crew member trapped behind the glass shield, and she is going to drown if you don't do something. Please proceed immediately to the shallow end of the viewing pool and raise the glass shield—"

She kept talking, repeating the same information over and over again, while Gregory and Daryl stood anxiously behind her, waiting for a response.

She couldn't be sure that anyone was listening.

There was nothing else that she could do.

"—on the entrance port. We have a crew member trapped behind the glass shield, and she is going to drown—"

Olivia's voice poured into the sealed lab from a speaker above the door. Hallie and Daniel both stared at it, aghast.

"She's not *serious*, is she?" asked Daniel. "She doesn't honestly expect us to go out there?"

"She must have a working camera," said Hallie. "There's no other way she could know someone was trapped in the pool. She wouldn't be telling us to go out if there was any danger."

"How do you know? If it was one of your sisters, you'd lie to have a chance at saving her!"

"You're right; I would." Hallie started for the door.

"Wait! Where are you going?"

"I'd lie to have a chance at saving my sister, and if I don't go out there right now, this person is going to drown. You think I can sit here while they die? You're wrong." Hallie glared. "Stay here with the siren. It'll keep you safe."

Hallie ran for the door and wrenched it open. Daniel watched but didn't move to stop her. Instead he backed up, and kept backing up until his shoulders hit the glass wall separating him from the siren. He stopped there, shivering, and when Hallie slipped out of the room, he didn't try to call her back. He just stayed where he was, Olivia's voice ringing from the speakers.

"Please proceed," said the siren, in a passable imitation of Olivia's voice.

"No," he whispered.

Hallie slipped out of the lab. The sirens seemed to have disappeared, at first glance; then she looked down and realized they had retreated into the deep end of the pool, where they were curling over and around each other like eels. The water around them seemed thick, almost clotted. The slime rolling off their bodies was thickening, forming a protective film between them and the rest of the world. Hallie hesitated, almost retreating.

The sirens slithered sluggishly around one another, staying in their ball. One waved a clawed hand in her direction, but made no move to separate from the cluster. Something was wrong with them.

"Okay," she whispered. "Okay." She couldn't bring herself to run, but she had the strength to hurry to the shallow end of the pool, where the plastic shield (not glass; it looked like glass, but it wasn't, glass broke too easily) had come down to stop anything larger than a trickle of water from sliding into the ship. There, as Olivia had said, were the hands, human hands, still beating weakly against the final barrier between their owner and the safety of the air. She thought she recognized the face behind the hands, but the water was dark, and she couldn't be sure.

Bracing herself against the shock, Hallie jumped into the shallow end of the pool, cold racing up her legs to her waist, encompassing enough to hurt. The sirens at the pool's other end moved sluggishly again, starting to take an interest. She glanced anxiously back at them before bending to dig her fingers into the slot at the base of the shield, pulling upward.

Nothing human could have budged the exterior shutters. They were too powerful, designed to cut the entire ship off from the world. The shields on the pool intake, however, had been installed after the fact, as part of a different set of systems. They were never meant to stand up to direct force. So Hallie pulled, while behind the shield Tory thrashed, trying to escape, and the plastic moved. Just a little at first, and then with more speed, until the obstacle was out of the way and Tory was spilling through the opening into the pool.

She was still thrashing, but weakly. Hallie bent and lifted her head and torso out of the water, hoisting the smaller woman up and onto the side of the pool. Tory lay in a mixture of siren slime and water, choking and coughing, seeming to spit out more water than her lungs could possibly have held without drowning her.

"Look out!" The warning was Daniel's. Hallie didn't turn to look behind her; she just grabbed the rim of the pool and hoisted as hard as she could, shoving herself out of the water and onto the floor next to Tory.

The siren that had been coming up behind her swiped at the water where she had been, submerged mouth open in a soundless hiss. Hallie stared at it, panting, before gathering Tory in her arms and hauling her back into the small lab.

Tory kept coughing, but she was starting to breathe more regularly by the time the door was shut and locked once more. She leaned against the wall, spitting water and sucking in great, painful-sounding breaths. Finally she raised her head, looking blearily at Hallie and Daniel, and said, "We were wrong. We were so wrong.

"I know why everyone on the *Atargatis* died."

CHAPTER 37

**Western Pacific Ocean, above the Mariana Trench:
September 3, 2022**

The phone rang. Daniel moved to answer it while Hallie remained next to Tory, holding her up.

"Yes?"

"Is she all right?" The voice was Olivia's. She sounded slightly flat, like she didn't know how to feel, and had opted for not feeling anything at all.

"She's fine," he said. "Suffering hypoxia. I think she was seeing things down there. But she's fine."

"Good. Good." Olivia exhaled. When she continued, her voice sounded almost human again. "I'm glad."

"Are you in the control room?"

"Yes, I'm—"

He didn't hear what she said next. Tory, moving with a speed he would have thought impossible when Hallie had hauled her into the room, slammed into him as she snatched the phone out of his hand.

"Olivia?" There was an edge of hysteria in her voice. "Are you in the control room?"

"Tory! Um, yes. Daniel just asked me tha—"

"I need you to turn on *all the lights*. Do it now. Every single light this fucking ship has, turn it on *right now*. Light us up like the Fourth of July. Do you understand?"

"No," said Olivia. "But I'll do it. Hang on." There was a thump as she put the receiver down, followed by the distant sound of conversation and switches being flipped, one after the other.

The lab was sealed off from the rest of the ship: there was no way to know what effect all that switch flipping was having. Tory closed her eyes, trying to shut out the memory of impossible light rising from the depths, of the *thing* she had seen outlined in its own eldritch glow.

Let there be light, she thought. *If nothing else, let there be light. Let there be hope.*

Let there be a chance.

"Tory?" Hallie looked at her nervously. "Are you all right?"

"I know why the *Atargatis* couldn't fight the sirens off and I know why Heather lost control," she said again, not opening her eyes. "They're fast and there were so many of them, but they're small, and the *Atargatis* had weapons. There should have been survivors. There should have been bodies. There wasn't anything, because *she* came, and the males were willing to do anything to feed her."

"What—"

"They call her. They tempt her with as much food as they can gather, and when there's enough, when it's worth her while to move, she comes to the surface. She comes to feed. But only when it's worth her while, and I'm betting—I'm praying—only at night. She's not as quick as the males. She wouldn't come to the surface at all if she didn't have to. I don't think she likes the light. Not when it's bright. Not when it's not hers."

There was always the chance the terrible thing she'd seen rising from the darkness would view the lit-up *Melusine* as competition, something to fight. If that was the case, Tory might have just condemned them all. But if she didn't, if the light scared her away...

"She who?" demanded Daniel.

"The female." Tory finally opened her eyes, turning to look at the siren in its tank. "They're like anglerfish. The female is hundreds of times larger than the males, and she's so hungry. She could eat the world. She can't leave the water, but she can drive the males into a frenzy, and she can slam into a ship this size and throw everyone off their feet. She'll make everyone easy pickings for her boys." One more assault added to the ongoing massacre. One assault too many.

"And it's *here*?" Hallie sounded less horrified than resigned.

"She's right below us," said Tory. Maybe Anne's bones were there too, cradled in the belly of the beast, a finned, living graveyard moving through the ocean like a promise of destruction.

"Tory?" Olivia's voice, back in her ear. "I turned them on. Are you okay?"

Tory took in a shaky breath, letting out a brief burst of laughter that dissolved into a cough. "I hope I am," she said. "I hope we are." She leaned against the wall, eyes still closed. "How're you?"

Olivia's laughter was even shakier than her own. "Oh, you know," she said. "Never going to eat sushi again."

Tory laughed, and Olivia laughed, and the lights of the *Melusine* blazed into the sea, bright as daylight, chasing the monsters away.

CHAPTER 38

Western Pacific Ocean: September 5, 2022

Help arrived two days later, just after dawn, in the form of the USS *Datlow*, a naval ship that had been patrolling nearby waters when the *Melusine* began broadcasting her distress call. They were horrified to find the ship sitting silent in the water, shields covered in slime and strange puncture marks. They were even more horrified when they boarded and discovered the nightmare waiting for them in the halls.

Blood and bodies and slime and most of all, the sirens themselves, dead or dying, huddled in corners, struggling to breathe through gills that had long since dried out, leaving them with no chance of survival. The human survivors crept out of hiding at the sound of boots stomping down the decks, terrified, traumatized scientists clutching their research and greeting their saviors with haunted eyes.

Dr. Toth was the only one to smile when her lab door swung open to reveal the sailors who had come to save her. "What took you so long?" she asked, as behind her Holly continued to work and Luis began, helplessly, to laugh.

"Who is in command here?" asked the man at the head of their formation.

"Mermaids ate the captain, so I guess he is," said Luis, hooking a thumb at Mr. Blackwell. "Better let him sober up before you try to

435

question him. He's pretty stoned. His wife sort of lied to him about the drugs she was using to make his leg feel better."

"Gentlemen," said Theo, and smiled.

In the control room, Olivia ceded the controls while Daryl and Gregory laughed in confusion and delight at their own survival.

In the medical bay, Drs. Vail and Odom reviewed the list of injuries with their rescuers, demanding the medical supplies they'd run out of, which they still needed to save lives.

In the pool room, Hallie closed the door to Mr. Blackwell's private lab, knowing without being told that if she wanted the siren that had saved them to survive, she needed to hide it. Together she and Daniel supported Tory on their shoulders, and the three of them walked toward the stairs, heading out of the darkness and into the light.

Below the *Melusine*, deep and descending deeper, the matriarch swam. She had been close to a healthy feeding when the brightness had come, searing her sensitive eyes, turning her away. She had eaten a full dozen of the males in her anger, and would eat a dozen more before she could be soothed. They knew her anger for the terror that it was. They teemed around her in a great cloud, throwing human bodies into her path for her terrible jaws to claim, darting away before she could inhale and take them as well.

Her biology was not so novel as to be unique in the ocean, although her size was; she had outlived and outlasted most of the creatures on her scale, thanks in no small part to the efforts of her helpers, the small, swift males, which brought her food when she could not rise to take it for herself. She and her kind had endured for millions of years. They would endure for millions more.

They had, after all, nothing but time.

EPILOGUE

Kahului, Hawaii: September 15, 2022

I see. Thank you."

Jim Alway set the phone gently back into its cradle before turning to face his team. They were watching him with guarded eyes, hopeful and wary in equal measure. His smile, when it came, did nothing to lessen their wariness.

"The *Melusine* will be docking in six hours for repair and refueling," he said. "The package is being delivered. Get ready."

The team—oceanographers, cetologists, zookeepers, security guards—scattered as Alway turned his eyes back toward the window that dominated his office wall, providing him with a panoramic view of the ocean around them. From the sea humanity had come; to the sea humanity would always return. In the meantime, men like him would always find a way to profit from what the water offered. Let the conservationists and the bleeding hearts take his whales. His mermaid was being delivered.

At long last, all things were going to be dragged out of the darkness of the deeps, and out into the living light of day.

Two hundred miles offshore, in a small cabin surrounded by damaged steel and the survivors of a voyage that had been damned from the beginning, two women lay tangled in one another's arms, adrift in a sea of tangled sheets. The ship's whistle blew, signaling their proximity to shore. Neither of them woke. Each, in her own way, was far away: Olivia running forever through a ship of ghosts, trying to save what had already been lost, and Tory swimming through the frigid water, lured on, ever on, by the dancing, impossible light of the lovely ladies of the sea.

ACKNOWLEDGMENTS

No book is written in a vacuum: as always I must thank the people who helped me to make this one the best it could be.

My usual Machete Squad was on hand with helpful suggestions and even more helpful demands: Brooke Abbey, Michelle Dockrey, Alexis Nast, Torrey Stenmark, Amanda Weinstein, and the rest of this strange motley crew kept me honest and kept me eager to see what was around the next bend, which is vital when putting together a puzzle as large and complex as this one. Lauren Panepinto's covers are a delight beyond measure, and knowing that I would get one when I was finished meant that I never lost sight of the prize. And all the aquarium employees who were willing to talk about mermaids with me, well…I'm so sorry.

Rebecca Williams was a new addition to our review process for this book, and she provided essential, story-changing information. My biggest thanks are for her.

During the writing of this book, I accomplished a life goal I had been moving toward for several years, relocating from Northern California (which is on fire again as I write this) to the Pacific North-west (which is decidedly *not* on fire). The actual move took place while I was on a book tour, and my mother, Micki McGuire, and my dear friend Kate Secor were rock stars of the cause. Mom handled most of the move all by herself, while Kate made sure my cats were safely taken care of. They are both amazing.

(The cats are fine. Alice sulked for all of five minutes once we

439

got her to the new house, while Thomas was clingy and shy for a few weeks, but has calmed down completely. I know I don't usually provide cat statuses here. In this specific case, it seemed like a good idea.)

Because the move was so big, and so all-consuming, I want to also thank Sarah Kuhn, Amber Benson, Randall Mulholland, Charlaine Harris, Amanda Weinstein, Michael Ellis, Merav Hoffman, Jon Lennox, Terry Kearney, Nikki Purvis, and Caroline Ratajski, as well as my entire Overwatch team, for their patience and tolerance over this past stretch of time. I can see the light at the end of the tunnel, and I'm reasonably sure it's not a giant bioluminescent predator.

My soundtrack for this book consisted of a great deal of Cake Bake Betty and the Counting Crows, as well as the full musical version of *Hadestown*. All errors are mine, and I am reasonably pleased with them.

Watch out for the water. You never know what might be down there.